THE SERPENT'S CROWN

The Serpent's Crown

HANA SAMEK NORTON

Guidono Press ❀ Brooklyn

The Serpent's Crown

Cover Image: Jean-Joseph Benjamin Constant, *The Empress Theodora*, 1887, Museo Nacional de Bellas Artes, Argentina

ISBN: 978-1-944453-00-8
eISBN: 978-1-944453-01-5

Cuidono Press
Brooklyn NY
www.cuidono.com

To my husband, for living with me
and my ever-growing . . . library

Characters
1204-1210 AD

Parthenay, Poitou

Juliana de Charnais, Viscountess of Tillières, Lady of Parthenay
Rannulf de Brissard, her guard captain
Joscelyn de Cantigny, Névelon, Peter de Blaye, her guards
Father Urias, her confessor
Guérin de Lasalle, Jean Armand de Lusignan, Lord of Parthenay, her husband
Eleanor of Parthenay, their daughter
Pontia, Eleanor's nurse
Beraud, their steward

Geoffrey de Lusignan, Brother Geoffrey of the Order of Solomon's Temple, his brother
Brother Reginald, Geoffrey's brother-companion of the Order
Armand de Lusignan, Count of Rancon, Geoffrey's and Guérin's father

Abbot Arnold, of Saint Maixent
Brother Isidore, of Saint Maixent
Abbess Mathilde, of Fontevraud Abbey
Sister Domenica, Mistress of Novices

*Geoffrey de Lusignan, Lord of Lusignan
*Ralph de Lusignan, Count of Eu, his nephew
*Hugh the Lusignan, Count of La Marche, his nephew

* Denotes historical characters

The kingdoms of Cyprus and Jerusalem

*Guy de Lusignan, Lord of Cyprus and King of Jerusalem by right of his wife Sybilla (deceased)
*Sybilla, Countess of Jaffa and Ascalon, Queen of Jerusalem, his wife and half sister to Isabella d'Anjou (deceased)

*Isabella d'Anjou, Queen of Jerusalem and Cyprus, half sister to Sybilla
*Maria de Montferrat (*La Marquise*), heiress to Jerusalem, her daughter by Conrad de Montferrat
    *John de Brienne, Maria's husband
*Philip d'Ibelín, half brother to Isabella
*John d'Ibelín, Lord of Beirut, half brother to Isabella
    *Helvis, his wife
*Maria Komnene, Dowager Queen of Jerusalem, their mother
    *Balian d'Ibelín, her husband (deceased)
Beroniki, Queen Isabella's waiting woman

*Aimary de Lusignan, King of Jerusalem and Cyprus, Queen Isabella's husband
*Almaric, *Melisande, *Sybilla, their young children
    Madelena, the children's nurse
    Xene, her sister and the children's nurse

*Eschiva (Civa) d'Ibelín, Aimary's first wife (deceased)
*Alix, *John, *Guy, their young children
*Hugh, their son
    *Alice de Champagne, Hugh de Lusignan's wife
*Heloise, their daughter
*Burgundia, their daughter
    *Walter de Montbéliard, her husband
    *Odo de Dampierre, Walter's nephew

Niketas, *Sekretikos* of King Aimary
Rhoxsane, Lady of Kolossi
    Ionia and Eulogia, Rhoxsane's daughters
Athene, nurse to Lady Juliana
Morphia, nurse to Juliana
Leontios, Morphia's husband (deceased)
Sister Vigilantia, Abbess of Saint Mary's of Tyre
*Fulk d'Yvers, baron of Cyprus and Jerusalem
*Renaud Barlais, baron of Cyprus and Jerusalem
*Phillip de Plessis, Grand Master of the Order of Solomon's Temple

Servants and others in the kingdoms of Cyprus and Jerusalem

Father Silbo, Hugh's tutor and confessor
Djalali, leopard keeper
Wink, his assistant
Darius, steward of Kolossi
Harion, serjean of Kolossi
Persephone, housekeeper at Famagusta
Martianus, a mariner

It sometimes happens, that exploits, however known and splendidly achieved, come, by length of time, to be less known to fame, or even forgotten among posterity.

Itinerarium Peregrinorum et Gesta Regis Ricardi
c. 1200 AD

Prologue

The kingdom of Jerusalem
Summer in the year of the Incarnate Word 1204

The ambush came just as they left the last *wadi:* eight men in black robes, swords drawn.

Billowing dust whipped up by forge-hot wind had obscured their charge so that they tore through the king's surprised escort before the first warning shout went up. They toppled two of King Aimary's mounted men-at-arms from their saddles, and aimed at the man in the cloak of blue silk embroidered with heavy silver thread.

The others in the small royal cavalcade ought to have rallied around their lord. They did not. They threw themselves at the attackers, leaving the king of Cyprus and Jerusalem to fend for himself. The dust choked and blinded the contestants, and in the confusion the attackers wasted several precious moments before they grasped that they faced a unified front–by which time three of them had bled out their lives into the soil. As suddenly as the dust storm had appeared, it vanished along with the remaining attackers.

Wearing a *serjean's* hauberk under a plain cloak, the man who led the rout halted his horse, forestalling the pursuit. "Let them go, Barlais."

The man in the royal blue cloak rode up, worry in his voice. "Are you all right, Sire?"

Aimary de Lusignan leaned forward and with the hem of the man's costly cloak wiped the blood from his sword. He sheathed it, and took off his helmet and coif. "Quite." He spat out a mouthful of grit. "Thank you for impersonating me, Barlais. That wretched thing is finally useful. It was a wedding gift from my mother-in-law. The old Medusa complains that I never wear it. I don't want to hear about it ever again." He waved to his companions, his graying blond hair bristling with sweat; his eyes, the color of blue chalcedony, blazed with exhilaration. "No word to anyone, understood?"

The men, this time surrounding their king, all nodded.

Renaud Barlais reached for the water skin and handed it to his lord, not bothering to stifle a chuckle. Maria Komnene, the dowager queen of Jerusalem, could make any man, king or not, tear out his hair. He privately wondered if the Komnene woman was the reason why the widowed Aimary de Lusignan had at first refused the crown of their beleaguered kingdom, since it came with marriage to Maria's daughter.

No one could fault the luscious Lady Isabella for the three husbands who had already occupied her bed, if only chastely in one case. But to acquire Maria Komnene for a mother-in-law was surely a penance. Seven years and three children later, the marriage Aimary de Lusignan only reluctantly agreed to had been a harmonious one, though the Holy City still remained in the Musulmans' hands, and Maria Komnene still carried on her schemes. These imperial women were born intriguers, and age did not hinder them. On the contrary. Ah, women.

Barlais caught the water skin Aimary threw him while Aimary wheeled his horse to ride back to the dead attackers. Their erstwhile victims who had tumbled readily from their saddles in order to lure the attackers into overconfidence dusted themselves off and went to catch the horses. Aimary dismounted and toed over one of the bodies.

Renaud Barlais dismounted as well. "Why would the *bedu* attack you, my lord? You pay them to spy for you."

Aimary tore away the cloth concealing the man's face. The features did not belong to a man of the desert. "They didn't and I do. These are *poulains*." He poked at the purse on the man's belt. The coins poured into the sand. He tossed one of them to Barlais. "Bought and already paid."

Barlais brushed away the sand grains. The silver bore a crude mint mark. He whistled. "The Ibelíns? I don't understand. We've tried to befriend the younger cubs. Why would they attack you again?"

"New cubs come with new jealousies and ambitions." Aimary gestured to his men to search the other bodies. "Keep the coins and the horses. I have no use for blood money. Not even Ibelín."

Practiced at battlefield looting, the men divided the contents of the purses between them and remounted to resume their journey. Several of them came from families who had served the Lusignans in *terre-sainte* through the fortunes and misfortunes of that family for thirty years and more. This latest effort to kill their liege lord had not surprised them, nor their lord's ability to outwit his enemies. Again.

They knew that for now *Fortuna* had smiled on Aimary de Lusignan, perhaps to recompense him for the disasters that had befallen his late brother who wore the kingdom's crown matrimonial before him. One would expect that after Guy de Lusignan presided over the Christians' disastrous defeat at Hattín—and the loss of most of the kingdom—the great lords of this land would not offer the throne, along with Queen Isabella, to another Lusignan. Yet they did. This thwarted ambush demonstrated why, in the end, the notoriously fractious barons of *outre-mer*, or at least most of them, had settled his brother's crumpled crown on Aimary de Lusignan's head.

Barlais nudged his horse to Aimary's and lowered his voice. Not that it mattered much. Now that the danger had passed, the men no doubt pondered the very same question he was about to ask. "My lord, you know that these attacks will not cease and one day—"

Aimary de Lusignan got back in the saddle. "One has to die sometime, Barlais."

"Yes, my lord. We're not concerned about your Jerusalem throne. It's your Cypriot crown, Sire. You were married to an Ibelín. Lady Eschiva was an estimable woman, but—"

Aimary looked away, his voice harsh, perhaps from the dust. "She was a proud, sharp-tongued shrew. She died to spite me."

"Yes, my lord." Barlais knew from his own experience that marriages contracted at the temporary convenience of both parties could become ones of passion as well as affection. Despite Aimary's tone, Barlais did not abandon the subject. "But she was an Ibelín, and if anything should happen to you, they will make a claim for Hugh's guardianship or regency. I say–"

"Renaud–"

"–you could choose your daughter to inherit Cyprus instead of your son. But since Burgundia is a woman, her husband would rule in her name, and your barons don't care for de Montbéliard." Barlais skimmed the issue of Aimary's son-in-law as tactfully as he could. "So your heir would be Hugh, and Cyprus would have to be ruled by a regent until the boy reaches his majority–"

"Renaud–"

"–and that's six years hence. Sire, you must find someone to keep the Ibelíns from Nikosia. Someone that also knows the lay of this land, if you know what I mean. Someone like . . . like you, sir. You have family in Poitou. You've called on them before. Surely you can send for one of your kin to–"

"Barlais!"

His hand on his sword hilt, Renaud reined in hard and stood up in the stirrups, alert to new danger. Aimary de Lusignan's hand clamped on his arm. "You are worse than an old nursemaid, Barlais. Stop your worries. I already did."

"You did?" Barlais breathed a sigh of relief and sank back into the saddle. "Who? What sort of a man is he?"

Aimary laughed and nudged his horse on. "Someone to your standards, I assure you."

"Good. Very good." Barlais took his time to contemplate that answer. "Sir," he decided to ask anyway, "will he bring his wife?" He wished it not so. Back home, wives could complicate things when, in a flood of tears, they clung to their husbands to prevent them from leaving, or worse yet, from leaving without them.

"Not likely. She's a new mother by now."

Barlais nodded. Good news indeed. This land, so blessed to be the Savior's cradle, did not bless young wives, nor their children in the cradles, with long lives.

They rode the rest of the way to Acre in silence.

In the nameless *wadi* behind them, a carpet of black flies frantically feasted on crusting puddles of blood before the ferocious *khamseen* returned and buried the blood in sand.

PART I

PARTHENAY

There is no saint without a past, no sinner without a future.

Saint Augustine

CHAPTER 1

The fortress of Parthenay, Poitou
Autumn 1204

A woman's life commences with her marriage. *But what does a marriage make?*

The young woman at the gate to the small yard behind the church of Saint-Jacques wore a damp cloak, muddy shoes, and an anxious smile. She held her hands folded at her middle in the monastic fashion, fingers fiddling with a gold band around one of them. "Father Urias?"

Father Urias hitched up his *casaque* and sat on the milking stool. "Come in, come in, Lady Juliana. You brought us a sliver of sun today. Don't worry about Blanche."

Despite the assurance, Juliana de Charnais circled the mud puddles to give Blanche a wide berth. The goat acknowledged the respect she had been accorded with a loud *meeah,* and buried her nose in a pile of willow branches.

Urias spread an apron over his knees. "Do you mind holding the bucket, Lady Juliana? She likes to kick it just when we are about to finish."

Juliana shook back the hood and untied her cloak. Eight generations of de Charnais no doubt turned over in their graves at the latest of their line helping a parish priest outwit a goat. She did not wish to think about how she had outwitted Parthenay's guards. Her heart still hammered from the climb to this house of God but even more from her clandestine departure from the fortress. She knew—she had been told—that there are five means of gaining a well-guarded citadel.

This citadel rose from the crest of a granite scarp which the Thouet wisely skirted in a sharp bend, offering its wide, deep waters as a barrier to foes before they could reach the killing flats on the opposite bank. Past those, would-be attackers encountered the sheer rock face of the lofty crag upon which the lords of Parthenay had erected a ring of ascending walls that reached to the very heights of the promontory; on the landward side, a wide and steep fosse protected the fort.

The lower wall surrounded a sizeable town that crept up the cliff's flank to the fortress itself. If the defenders destroyed the four river bridges across the Thouet and raised the citadel's drawbridges, the attackers would have to ford, swim, or span the stream with their own devices while under fire from the ramparts. If the attackers came from the north, along the pilgrims' route, as they more likely would, they would also have to contend with the oak and iron-shod portcullis of Saint Jacques's gate. Its two enormous guard towers, beaked and crenellated, challenged the outside world like the prows of battle galleys.

Pilgrims to Saint Jacques de Campostelle and other peaceful arrivals could gain entry by crossing the bridge and passing through the same gate and past the watchful guards. The pilgrims choosing to follow the verdant valley of the Thouet from Angers to Thouars would pass through Parthenay on the way to Saint Maixent and rejoin further south the principal pilgrim route from Tours. Along this road, Parthenay offered safety and rest in its hostels, hospices, inns, churches, and chapels.

To gain entry to the fortress, a traveler would reach the top of the street where the granite gate towers, Saint Jacques's twins, greeted him. There, the barrel-vaulted entry between them could be barred by lowering its portcullis. If unwelcome arrivals tried to breach it, they would be crushed by stones dropped from the opening in the floor of the guard room above the entry, while archers would rain deadly missiles through the arrow loops of the two towers until the bodies of the attackers became another defensive wall.

Parthenay's fortress, it was said, was impregnable.

But while the lords of Parthenay had ensured that enemies

could not easily gain ingress to their fortress, they had not expended equal effort on preventing one's egress from it.

One could walk out of the postern gate, but that would attract the attention of the men who guarded it. One could lower oneself down the cliff face, but that would have required a long enough rope and the means of hiding it from one's chamber women. The simpler way was to walk out under the citadel's portcullis wearing a maidservant's cloak and hood pulled close against the chill of the drizzling rain as well as against being readily recognized. One could then join the weavers, a straggle of pilgrims, wool merchants, traders and servants, pass several loitering men-at-arms and the occasional herdsmen with their bovines, all clambering up and down the *rue de Vau*, cross the drawbridge over the Thouet, and climb the opposite hillside of the valley.

There one would enter the narrow, terraced lanes and goat paths, and zigzag past the wattled garden plots of the residents in that part of Parthenay's neighborhood where several churches and hospices offered rest to the sick and exhausted pilgrims– and to those who wished to confess their mortal sins. *What does a marriage make?*

"Lady Juliana? Do you mind?"

"Yes, yes, of course." Juliana folded the cloak over the fence and, gathering her skirts between her knees, took up a position on a stool by Blanche's opposite side to grip the bucket's rim. "Of course, Father. Gladly so."

With a mouthful of fast disappearing leaves, Blanche gave her a look of displeasure so comical that Juliana momentarily forgot herself and almost stuck out her tongue back at the goat. Good thing she did not because Father Urias glanced at her over Blanche's rump. "And how fares Lady Eleanor today?"

In fact, Urias had noticed the mischief in the lady Juliana. Did her husband have the occasion to see the bright side of her or had she kept it and her worries hidden from him the way she hid her very red hair under her veil and matronly wimple?

From what Urias knew about the wife of the new lord of Parthenay, the lady Juliana required encouragement to converse freely with the residence of the *seigneurie*, including himself.

Urias did not blame her. Years spent treading the cloisters of Fontevraud Abbey hardly prepared a young woman to be pitched headlong in matrimony into the family of the notorious lords of Lusignan—and to the scion of one of its more unruly branches.

After all, the man still called himself Guérin de Lasalle, a name by which he and his *routa* of godless mercenaries had become infamously known during the recent troubles between kings John of England and Philip of the Franks up there in Normandy. No wonder Urias had yet to hear my lord Lasalle's confession; in fact, Urias doubted that he would hear it any time soon. That man displayed a blatant aversion to conventions spiritual and secular. The sainted Apostle Paul was right. Evil company corrupts good habits.

On the other hand, since their arrival at Parthenay, the lady Juliana had beaten a well-worn path to Saint Jacques. Perhaps worries about her husband's soul had brought her again this morning.

"My daughter is well, thank you. I pray for her every day. And for everyone at Parthenay, of course. She is a little fussy and noisy, actually," Juliana amended, not wishing to lie to the priest. At several months of age, the lady Eleanor already displayed a singular personality.

Father Urias nodded in sympathy. Even for a first time mother, Lady Juliana had an uncommon attachment to the infant. As for the young woman's true feelings about that husband of hers . . .

"You've come to confess again, have you?" Urias encouraged his visitor while a stream of frothing milk began to fill the bucket.

The venue for her most weighty confession yet took Juliana aback. Here in Father Urias's yard where chickens scratched and Blanche ruled? "No . . . yes . . . here? I—"

"Where better to tend to one's flock, my child? We are all God's creatures and live and breathe under His skies. All that you say is to His ears and mine only. And Blanche's, of course. But if you prefer to wait in the chapel, I will be there as soon as we're done here."

"Oh, no, thank you, Father." Juliana reproached herself. One ought not to inconvenience people, especially Father Urias who had been so kind to her. "I don't want Blanche to tip your bucket. And thank you for hearing my other confessions, but I did not tell you then . . ." *What does a marriage make?* "I don't know where to begin, how to explain. It's been such a burden to me, Father."

Perhaps shame at the prospect of disclosing her husband's infidelities tormented the lady? Urias knew that a man's fair hair and heavenly blue eyes usually quickened women's hearts, but this Lusignan sprung from the other side of that family. Nonetheless, Urias observed that whenever in their lord's vicinity, plenty of the servant women resorted to sighs deep enough to display an attractively heaving bosom and to curtsies with skirt hems held high enough for a sight of a well-turned calf. Parthenay's women were renowned for their comeliness, yet Urias was surprised to hear from their gossip and confessions that the master had thus far disappointed them.

After forty years of tending his two-legged flock, Father Urias's own youthful devotion to chastising the strays had mellowed considerably. In the case of this young woman, Urias suspected that becoming a mother had caused her to suffer from an overwrought sensibility. Not an unusual condition in young wives, especially if their first babe came about without the mother's full volition. Rumors had it that such was the case in this marriage. "It's like yanking a milk tooth, my child. Just say what the trouble is."

"I am living in mortal sin."

Urias gave Blanche's teat one last squeeze, wiped his hands on the apron and patted the goat's hide. "I will take the bucket. Now there is a good girl. Too much fussing sours your milk, my dear. You run along now."

Blanche flicked her ears and trotted off to rejoin her two half-grown kids. Deprived of the barrier, Juliana stood up, her face flushed.

Father Urias sighed. Better to put the young woman's mind at ease. "Marriage is a blessed union. Yours is made more so by the daughter you've brought into the world. And to encourage virtue and the detestation of vices in another is a virtue in itself. Your marriage is as our Lord had ordained it for –"

The young woman gripped his hand so hard that she startled him. "But my marriage is not—"

"Juliana."

Neither one of them noticed the riders, but they both knew the low, commanding voice. The young woman let go of Urias's hand as if it were an ordeal iron. She whirled about, her face scarlet, and sank into a curtsy required of a wife by the formality of public occasions. "My lord."

His fist to his hip, the lord of Parthenay pressed his mount on until the courser's shoulder sprung open the gate. Urias noted that Guérin de Lasalle eschewed sartorial splendor, a perverse habit from his *routier* days. His two men remained outside the precinct.

"Father." The lady's husband inclined his head to acknowledge Urias's presence. He was still young, but life had already left its marks. His eyes, resembling forest moss only by their color, rested on his wife. "There you are. You'd better go back. It will rain again." He looked about. "Where is Rosamond? And your women?"

Juliana reached for her cloak and secured it at her throat. She could feel her heart lodged there. "The blacksmith was shoeing her so I walked. By myself."

Urias heard in the young woman's voice someone resolved to claim her right to walk about as she pleased without attendants, yet aware that she had been wrong to do so. Her declaration drew from her husband a smile that carved lines at the corners his eyes. "Through all this mud? We do have other horses, you know. Your feet must be wet. Come here."

He kicked his foot out of the stirrup and reached for his wife who smiled at him with visible relief and climbed without difficulty behind his saddle. Once there, she locked her arms around her husband's waist. Squeezing shut her eyes, she pressed her cheek against his well-worn horseman's cloak as if aware that she held, at least for the moment, the uncapturable.

The rider pushed his horse toward Urias. The priest kept his place. The man's gaze, this time of unconcealed threat, fixed on him. Each of his words came precisely placed. "Do me the kindness, Father, not to receive my wife again unless she comes properly escorted. Perhaps you ought to assure her that not every broken kitchen bowl merits a confession."

The request, or rather the order, told Urias that whatever my lord Lasalle chose to call himself, he was not to be underestimated by his friends or enemies. Of the former he had a few, of the latter surely many, and clearly did not care if he made more. He knew that Urias could rally the Church against him, but that Urias would do it only if it came down to the lady Juliana's personal safely.

Urias neither acknowledged nor countered the challenge. Reins tight and mindful of the horse's burden, the lord of Parthenay carefully backed his mount through the gate. Urias watched the courser carry the lord and his lady down the slippery incline and cross the bridge to the fortress. The two men followed them at a distance.

Urias went to secure the gate; the latch was broken. He sighed and tied it with his apron's string. From the way Guérin de Lasalle looked at his wife, Urias knew that her personal safety was not at stake. And whatever troubled the lady Juliana about her marriage, it appeared that when it came to her marriage bed, she had not given herself entirely to the ecstasy of self-denial. Few of that man's women would. They were, after all, Eve's daughters.

Blanche nudged at his hand. Urias scratched the goat's forehead. One could also conclude that this lord of Parthenay was a man in love with his wife. Hardly a surprise there. Men like him sometimes thought they could find redemption in the wives they married—pious, young, virtuous, unstained by life. As for the girl's true feelings about her husband . . . Now what mortal sin could so trouble a pious young wife that her husband would not want her to reveal it to a confessor? Urias crossed himself. The Lord's four-legged creatures were so much easier to understand.

CHAPTER 2

Saint Jean d'Acre, capital of the kingdom of Jerusalem

I am informed," Maria Komnene, the dowager queen of Jerusalem, announced with gleeful anticipation, "that the king is in danger from another assassin."

"Is he?" John d'Ibelín, her eldest son, shrugged. He eyed the women attending her. The pretty one smiled at him for which she received a swift swipe of his mother's flywhisk. John ignored his mother's displeasure. He could always find the woman later. The obvious fact that Aimary de Lusignan had not yet fallen by an assassination was the only remarkable part in his mother's news. "I rode from Beirut for this?"

"Yes. And do try to keep your mind on the present, John." Maria Komnene flicked the whisk to dismiss her women who had arranged her robes in the style befitting the great-niece of the Greek Emperor and the widow of a Latin king. The tresses of her long, fair hair that had once belonged to a Rus slave presented an odd contrast to the *kohl* outlining her eyes in the fashion of the imperial court. She had left that court almost forty years ago, a bewildered thirteen-year-old, to become the second wife of the Frankish king of Jerusalem. Since then, in this much contested corner of the world, she had mastered the art of ruling its halls of mosaics and marble. Nor did she let her children forget that through her they had descended from an ancient line of emperors and queens.

"Aimary survived the other attempts," John said. No need to add, proof or not, that everyone anticipated the Ibelíns or their associates to be the conspirators. Despite past and more recent marriage-bed alliances between the Ibelín and Lusignan families, their relationship continued to range from covert to overt hostility.

The rubies of his mother's rings flashed at him. "*Aisiodoxos.*

He certainly won't survive this one." She handed him a folded piece of parchment. The seal was broken. "I wish you to know the name of his assassin."

John clasped his hands behind his back. "Why do you do this? You know I can't read."

The paint on his mother's cheeks cracked. "And after all the tutors I gave you? How do you ever manage?"

"My wife can read."

With a sigh of disappointed motherhood, Maria Komnene returned the parchment to a small coffer of ivory and locked it. "Helvis can read but she can't give you an heir. What use is one without the other in a wife?"

John pressed his nails into his palms. "Shouldn't you tell Isabella that she's about to lose another husband to an assassin?"

The long-suffering tone vanished. "Don't change the subject. Isabella wouldn't know what to do even if I told her."

"My sister always does as told. Especially when told by you, Mother."

Maria had learned a long time ago that Latin barbarians lacked the subtlety of her people. "Isabella is your half sister. She is the queen of Jerusalem by right of her father, and she's the queen of Cyprus by right of her marriage to Aimary. I made sure she became both. You are the lord of Beirut. Beirut! I gained nothing by my marriage to your father. He may be dead, but I will not allow my children by him to be slighted just because some of them remove themselves into the wilderness and cling to ill-blessed marriages to the Helvises of this world."

John kept his gaze on the floor's mosaic. As much as he disliked admitting it, his mother spoke the truth. It did not please her either that he took more stock in the blood on his father's side, murky in origins though it might have been. In fact, he had not ridden to Acre just because his mother had called him, but because he had not seen Isabella and her children for some time. He loved Isabella dearly, but he did wonder why God would grant some men progeny that not only lived but thrived, while to others . . . *Was he being punished for marrying Helvis?* "Then will you warn Aimary?"

"And why in Heavens would I warn one of those vipers?"

John laughed. Similar words described his parents, but his mother never saw herself as others did. "Because he's our in-law?"

The flywhisk landed on a tardy insect. "Precisely. Not blood. Besides, Aimary knows. And he's worried enough this time to send a messenger to Poitou. Don't you want to know why?"

John scraped up his patience. "Why?"

"Aimary wants one of their own to come to Nikosia to be ready to assume regency for Hugh. You do remember your own nephew? Aimary ought to be calling you!"

The regency of the kingdom of Cyprus.

And there it was. His mother had sent for him to further one of her schemes and, as usual, an ambitious one. "There are rules to the Cypriot succession, Mother. The High Court may choose Burgundia over Hugh."

"Must you be so legalistic? Just like your father. The High Court won't support Burgundia. Her husband hasn't been here long enough for the sun to peel him. I can't think why Aimary gave her to Walter of the Montbéliards. Who's he to merit a king's daughter? It's not like Aimary ran out of choices."

His mother was being disingenuous. Considering the scant number of Latin barons in *outre-mer*, betrothals, marriages, annulments, abandonments, and repudiations had mired everyone in alliances as much adulterous as incestuous. You could not spit without hitting a half brother, sister, or cousin by blood or marriage. When politically expedient, the Church handed out dispensations or ordered couples to separate while declaring children born of such unions legitimate. Besides, Aimary had a good reason to hand his eldest daughter, unceremoniously repudiated by her first husband back in Toulouse, to Walter de Montbéliard.

John picked up a silver goblet and held it out to his mother. He had married Helvis because they were not related closely enough to upset the Holy Father—how could he have known that they would not be blessed by children who lived beyond their first breath? Moreover, by that marriage, he had hoped to avoid the internecine rivalry that periodically tore apart the *terre-sainte* and he had managed to do so. Until now.

John d'Ibelín, regent of the kingdom of Cyprus.

His mother poured his cup brimful of wine. "Did you hear me? Rules are what we make of them." Her tone became one of a fellow conspirator. "Walter is not your rival. That Lusignan will be. The Court will support him. He's been in these parts before. He survived Hattín."

"An older man then. He may not survive this journey."

Maria decided to exploit the uncertainty in her son's voice. "About as old as you are."

Knowing well that his mother was gaining on him, John's irritation grew. "How do you know all of this?"

"That's what spies are for, my dear. Unfortunately, Aimary found mine. He had him killed. Of course I have others."

"Of course." John took a deep swallow of the wine–rich, sweet, head-beguiling, from Cyprus's own soil. "You'll find another. What else do you know of this man?"

"He calls himself Guérin de Lasalle. He has been at odds with his family for some time and has not used his true name or rank–Jean Armand de Lusignan."

"Why not?"

"Ask him when he comes."

"He may not be willing to come."

"Oh, he will. The Lusignans have a way of collaring their own. He has a brother here with the Temple."

"Does this Lasalle not have lands and family to keep him in Poitou?"

"Hardly such. His brother relinquished to him the lordship of Parthenay." His mother's nose twitched. "They raise cows there. The last duchess of Aquitaine made him marry an orphaned girl. A pious, plain, and stupid sort, I heard."

The wine began to pound in his temples. "The duchess?"

"Don't be silly, John. The girl. This call to Nikosia is just the opportunity for a man like Lasalle to rid himself of a vapid wife and seek here one a rank or two higher. Like the Lusignans and de Montbéliard have done. What man worth his salt would not?"

That jab struck deeper than her others. Why did the woman who bore him plague him so? Was it because he was Balian d'Ibelín's son? His mother's second marriage represented a monstrous disparagement to her–from the throne of Jerusalem to the wife of a hardscrabble lord of the land. After the disaster at Hattín, his father had saved Jerusalem's population from Saladín, yet gained little from it save the thanks of the refugees. Worse yet, the beneficiaries of the Hattín debacle that nearly wrecked the kingdom turned out to be those who had caused it in the first place–the Lusignans. And Aimary de Lusignan in particular.

John d'Ibelín, regent of the kingdom of Cyprus.

His mother was right. He owed nothing to them. Very well, let the man come. And if this interloper happened to lose his life on these shores, he was certain that back in Poitou his pious, plain, and stupid bride would not remain washed in tears for the rest of her life. John slammed the empty goblet down on the marble table top with the sound of steel meeting stone. Surely one had to yield to the other.

"Tell me then," John d'Ibelín, the lord of Beirut, said. "Who's to be Aimary's assassin?"

His mother smiled. "You."

CHAPTER 3

The fortress of Parthenay, Poitou

Juliana, when will you stop fretting?"

Juliana shivered. *The duchess gave me to a man she knew to be pledged to another.* "I am not."

Almost five years passed since the duchess had manacled them in holy matrimony, but only months had passed since their marriage resulted in Eleanor. Still, sometimes their marriage felt to her as recent as their arrival at Parthenay, only weeks ago. It was the more distant past that troubled her–hounded her–to this very place, to this very bed. The Church taught that betrothal was as binding as marriage. True, Guérin de Lasalle was pledged to another when still a child, but for the Church to release him, he would have to reveal his betrothed's name. That he would not ever do because, after the vicissitude of years and Fortune, many believed that to the now grown young woman properly belonged her uncle John's English crown.

And now King John held the ill-fated young woman in his custody. The revelation that Eleanor of Brittany, the granddaughter of Aliènor of Aquitaine, was already bound to a husband who could claim John's crown by right of his wife would mean Eleanor's death. The Bretons and others were certain that fate had already befallen her brother Arthur who possessed more of a claim to the English throne than John did.

How could she confess it all to Father Urias? King John had spies in Poitou, everyone knew it. To expiate her own unwitting complicity, she had named their daughter after the Pearl of Brittany, not after the great queen-duchess. Aliènor knew of Lasalle's previous pledge, that's why she had arranged their marriage, all to protect John's crown from a rival claimant married to a Lusignan. How cruel of the duchess, and how clever. Because of it, Eleanor of Parthenay was born into a union the Church considered adulterous. That fact could not be erased, only kept concealed.

"Liar. Come here." He rolled on his back and drew her to him, his lips on her shoulder, easing along her neck to her earlobe. "Are you cold?"

"N-no. It tickles." *The Church taught that betrothal was as binding as a marriage.* Juliana tried to calm her racing heart. *I lie here in sin with a man everyone takes to be my husband.* Lasalle would not bring up Father Urias, but he knew what her confession would have been; *I am an adulteress and our daughter is . . .*

Perhaps it was all her fault. She had imperiled her soul the moment she consented to their marriage because of her selfish longing to be free of a novice's veil. Worse yet, at times in the course of an ordinary day and nights such as this she forgot her unwitting complicity. And then she fretted about it even more. But what had she known about the world? She only knew what the books she had surreptitiously borrowed from Fontevraud's cupboards told her. *What does a marriage make?*

"Good. Now pay attention to your husband's instructions."

How could she when she could also hear that haughty, ironic voice, *her* voice, warning her: *Love can destroy . . .*

"Juliana, will you–"

No, she must not let the past impose, she must let it yield to the present the way the lamp's subsiding flame yielded to the darkness. She must allow that other flame, still so strange to her, to rise up within her until the flesh that surrounded it yielded to another's. Could a spiritual marriage be composed of such sharp delights? Could the communion of disembodied souls surpass it? How could it? *Oh Mary.*

"Now that was better." Breathless, he kissed her and shifted his weight to pull her to his shoulder. He said it as if congratulating himself on an accomplishment he was not entirely certain of. He drew the covers up to her chin. "Wasn't it?"

"Yes." The lamp flame had gone and only the embers remained in the brazier.

"Tell me what troubles you."

"You are away so much, I hardly ever see you." That much was the truth. She did feel marooned among these people. She found them clannish, churlish, and suspicious of her. They took to their new master from the moment he rode through Saint Jacques's gate. They took to young Eleanor as well, despite her surely being the world's most annoying infant. But Juliana could see the disappointment in their eyes when they saw her, a foreigner, plain and reticent, and one who had given their lord only a daughter.

He punched the pillow. "You know I'd rather cull hogs than flatter their flat . . . footed daughters and drink their atrocious wine. I could hang one of my *routiers* for it, but not my vassals. Yet."

The exaggerated wistfulness in those words horrified her and almost made her laugh at the same time. Guérin de Lasalle was unused to being the master of anything but a band of mercenaries and, temporarily, of the occasional fortress they took. In her anxious moments, she wished all of that could be escaped as well.

Unfortunately, since their arrival at Parthenay, compelling reasons kept him in the saddle days at a time, days he spent inspecting the fortresses held by his vassals, and attending the gatherings of the neighboring castellans. Rumors had recently spread that John of England had recovered from the shock of losing Normandy to Philip Augustus of the Franks and planned to land at La Rochelle with his hired army, then head north to reclaim his duchy.

Considering the fraught relationship between the Plantagenets and the perennially rebellious lords of Lusignan, everyone knew that if John of England came to Poitou, he would take his revenge on any Lusignan ally as well as on that entire clan–particularly the current lord of Parthenay. Those circumstances certainly contributed to Parthenay's coldness toward her. She was French, King Philip was her liege lord, and they suspected her loyalty.

"Do you think he'll come here?"

"Armand? Not unless you invited him."

The name jolted her. His first thought was not about the threat from King John, but from Armand de Lusignan, the count of Rancon, her peccant father-in-law. A force to be reckoned with even in that family, Armand de Lusignan had one son left to carry on his line; the other had rejected his patrimony to serve Our Lady in the Holy Land. For this son and namesake, the count had long harbored plans more ambitious than a marriage to Juliana de Charnais, an unimpressive heiress to an unimpressive Norman viscounty.

Juliana did not want to contemplate that perilous subject. "No. John."

"He will. He's too stubborn to learn from his mistakes in Normandy. He'll repeat them in Poitou."

"Do you think that our mistakes follow us through our lives?" She wanted to know the answer, she truly did.

Lasalle moved to his side, dislodging her, his arm heavy around her ribs. "Hmmm. Only if we marry them."

He nipped lightly at the back of her neck which made her catch her breath, and he laughed and buried his head against her nape and dropped into a sleep as sound as a rock.

Juliana remained still, listening to the rain tap on the shutters. Did he mean it to apply to himself or to her? Was their marriage truly a mistake? The duchess had chosen for her a man with more secrets than a confessor, a man born to a family famed for trouble and treachery. Or was Father Urias right and she should cease her worries if only for Eleanor's sake? Few knew about the blot on their marriage—the duchess was dead; her father-in-law was no doubt in Paris, betraying his liege lord to King Philip; Lasalle's estranged brother had left for the even more distant Holy Land. Parthenay was her home now. Hers and Eleanor's—and his.

But would he ever let her fully share his world the way he now wanted to share her bed? And what if not? Not ever. Many husbands and wives led parallel lives, coming together for the sake of progeny, needing no other private concourse. He knew Eleanor would be the only issue of his flesh that she would give him. The midwife had told her that when, after days of fever, she held Eleanor in her arms.

Any other man would have repudiated such a wife. He did not mind, on the contrary. He had his own private reasons, all to spite his own father. His relationship to his brother was not replete with fraternal love either. And yet, when she was with him like this . . .

Juliana listened to the rain, but heard *her* voice, brittle from age and bitter experience. *Love can destroy if you are subject to it . . . and one day love, like passion, simply vanishes.*

CHAPTER 4

The port of Limassol, kingdom of Cyprus

The *Falconus* wallowed at anchor under an azure sky, its piebald banner of the Order still secured to the mast, but no one would mistake this trim, oared galley for a merchantman of the Pisans or Venetians. In six weeks, five, God willing, this galley would find its final destination in La Rochelle, almost a thousand leagues distant from its moorings. From there, the rider would deliver an urgent message to a family he had abjured long ago for another one. But ties of blood were not easily sundered, not even in this distant land.

"Sir? Did you hear me? When they found Leontios he had nothing on him. His rings, too, disappeared. Who do you think killed him? The servants said he must have tripped on his way from the privy. Sir? Are you listening?"

"Attentively." Brother Geoffrey de Lusignan acknowledged Brother Reginald's unsentimental report. They stood at the end of the quay, far enough from the stores and custom houses not to be overheard. *Who indeed had killed Leontios? And why?* "At least whoever broke his neck had the decency to wait," he said. "You'd do well to see who's outside after you buckle up."

Brother Reginald tightened his belt under his sergeant's mantle. "We Poitevins are harder to trip up than these Griffons. The galley men are loyal to the Banner. If they tell you that I fell overboard, it will be by accident."

Geoffrey appreciated Brother Reginald's assurance, but he knew that the threat to Reginald's life was real. Brother Reginald used to be his vassal before he too had joined the Order, and they maintained their personal ties despite the Order's rules against them. But then, if in its interest, the Order allowed its rules to be bent and it had done it to serve Aimary de Lusignan.

Aimary had chosen Leontios as a decoy after the little Greek with a proclivity to cheat customers at Nikosia's market had wended himself and his wife into the royal chambers. Fortunately, Aimary was wily enough to smell an Ibelín spy, and used it to his advantage. The last document Leontios stole was intended to divert attention from the genuine message and messenger heading to Poitou. *But why kill Leontios for it?*

While his superior remained in his own thoughts, Brother Reginald watched a barge with its load of wine barrels negotiate the sea waves. "But why burden your family, sir? You too are the king's kin and I still say that no one would oppose the Order's candidate for Hugh's regent."

"You forget that we don't quicken the warmest memories on this island. These people will tolerate a Lusignan, but not one pledged to the Order as well. Not if he acts openly."

Reginald conceded that truth. A dozen years ago, under the Order's brief ownership and iron-fisted rule of the island, the Griffons had revolted and the Order retaliated in its customary and decisive manner. Even today, when the Order's knights rode through the streets, mothers rushed their children away at the sight of their badges, and from behind shuttered windows baleful glances followed them.

Lightened of its load, the barge steered away from the galley. Geoffrey knew why Aimary had called on him, discreetly, of course. He was not only Aimary's kinsman, but a member of an Order that had long supported the Lusignans in *outre-mer,* despite their occasional failings. For that reason, the Grand Master had appointed him commander of the small garrison at Gastria, an unexalted position in the Order's hierarchy, but of immeasurable importance to it on this island. For the Latins clinging to the sliver of the Holy Land's coastline, Cyprus occupied a strategic position, and the Order regarded its stable and competent rule as a prerequisite for maintaining a bulwark against the Musulmans' ambitions to regain the entire *terre-sainte*. For now, the Temple and the other military Orders preferred a Lusignan on the throne of Jerusalem, and even more firmly on the throne of Cyprus.

Reginald turned over in his palm the silver coin Brother Geoffrey had given him. He had faced many a challenge, but this mission proved most unusual. "Sir? How adept is your brother at handling these sorts of things?"

Reginald noticed that Brother Geoffrey smiled as if the question evoked a comfortless memory. "My brother is adept at handling all manner of havoc and whores, one from training, the other inclination."

Reginald decided not to ask whether Brother Geoffrey meant it as a condemnation or a compliment. "Do you truly think that he'll come?" he therefore said, his doubt not entirely eased.

"He'll come. But remember what I told you and go first to Lusignan."

Reginald returned the coin to his belt pouch. "Yes, sir."

Since no more needed to be said, Geoffrey nodded toward the *Falconus.* "God's speed, safe journey, and safe return with aid."

He gave Brother Reginald a brief blessing and watched him climb into the last ferry. He did not stay to see the oarsmen lower the blades into the water. He walked to the landing and mounted up. He wanted to make as much progress toward Nikosia as he could before nightfall in order to inform the king that the messenger with his urgent message had departed from these shores.

Geoffrey was certain that the message would bring back to this land a man Aimary could not only trust, but one who possessed the wits, cunning, and courage to impress on everyone that the newly consecrated crown of Cyprus belonged to the Lusignans of Poitou, and that it would continue to do so. Geoffrey was certain of it because he knew he had a way to compel his wayward younger brother to accept the blood that tied them, and the ineluctable duty that came with it.

CHAPTER 5

The fortress of Parthenay, Poitou

Beraud, the steward, dragged the shepherd boy by his dirty ear across the bailey. Years of being paid to kill in the service of others had taught Guérin de Lasalle not to trust shepherd boys with garbled messages, but then Beraud handed him a coin the boy had brought with him—a white *besant.* He easily made out the newly struck lettering: AIMERICUS DE LIZINIACO, Rex CIPRI.

Bloody hell.

He told Beraud not to breathe a word to the lady Juliana, ordered a horse saddled, and with the boy as his guide, set out into the forest. Not far from Parthenay's walls, the rider waited for him. Lasalle reached behind the saddle and dropped the boy to the ground. When the boy disappeared into the trees, the man rode up. He was middle-aged and sun-browned. The hilt of his riding sword poked from under his cloak.

"My lord de Lusignan." The man bowed slightly. "I am Brother Reginald."

Lasalle hesitated, noting that Brother Reginald pretended not to notice the hesitation. He nodded and turned his horse along the forest path. Better to hear this one in private before deciding what to do about Brother Reginald.

So far that's gone well, Reginald told himself. The lord of Parthenay could not deny his lineage. This Lusignan resembled a younger version of Brother Geoffrey, except for the color of his eyes and that scar across his throat. Nasty business Hattín must have been, but not much other visible damage. As for the invisible . . . The Lusignans were not an ill-formed lot, despite the rumored taint in their blood–or perhaps because of it. "I regret that our meeting has to be like this, my lord, but my master gave me strict orders."

Lasalle kept his courser alongside Reginald's. "What does Geoffrey want now?"

Reginald noted the frigid tone. "They are not just his orders, my lord de Lusignan."

"If you call me that one more time, I'll break your neck."

"I was told it would be most likely my jaw," Reginald said without animosity. Brother Geoffrey had warned him that addressing the lord of Parthenay by the wrong title could provoke an unpleasant reaction. Since Reginald could not avoid it either way, he decided to use the name in whose cause he came.

Lasalle did not like to think of himself as Jean Armand de Lusignan. However, in these parts and with his new rank he could no longer deny it even though he had spent the better part of his life at it. Not that there were many good parts–except for a mistress or two, and now the girl who was his current wife. The latter thought did not quell his temper. On the contrary. "I said, what does Geoffrey want?"

Reginald told him.

Three sentences into his recitation, Lasalle experienced the sensation of a noose sliding around his neck. "Then Geoffrey also knows that John intends to tear apart these lands as soon as he scrapes up enough scutage to hire new mercenaries. How does my brother propose that I divide myself to serve both Lusignan causes?"

"My lord Geoffrey told me to tell you that if the king manages to waste Parthenay, the Order will see to it that it is restored. That matter will be settled in Nikosia when you take up your obligations."

Lasalle reined in his horse, blocking Reginald's path. "You tell Geoffrey that my only obligations are to my wife, my daughter, and to this place."

Brother Reginald hastily pulled up. He wished he did not have to resort to the next move, but Brother Geoffrey had told him that it might be necessary, so Reginald had memorized his words.

"And which wife is that, my lord? The lady Juliana is a woman of modesty and more than ordinary virtue. What if a word of your irregular marriage reached the archbishop and he sent someone to make enquiries? Having your daughter declared a bastard would probably not wear on you, but would it not break her mother's heart? Some women love their husbands immoderately, but others have been known to love their children more than their sires. Especially women of virtue and–"

Although Brother Geoffrey had warned him, Reginald was not prepared for the fury of the attack which sent his horse to his knees. His attacker's courser also dropped to his haunches from the impact of their collision, prompted by well-set spurs. Lasalle was on him, and they were grappling, trapped between the frightened, struggling animals.

Reginald recovered in time to deflect the poniard that bore down on his middle with the cross piece of his sword hilt. In the end, the blade failed to deliver a fatal wound only because his horse sprang to his feet, throwing his attacker into the bracken. Before Lasalle could get free of them, Reginald was on his feet, his sword in hand.

Gasping for breath, Reginald flung back his cloak and aimed the sword's tip at the base of the lord of Parthenay's throat. "I am just a humble bearer of the message, my lord. Killing me won't change it."

Ignoring the blade, his assailant got to his feet without hurry and, bare-handed, shoved the blade aside and brushed away the crushed fronds. The man's reaction surprised and confused Reginald until Guérin de Lasalle took a step toward him, poniard in hand. He flipped it, catching it without his narrowed eyes leaving Reginald's, a tight, slanted smile on his lips. "No messenger, no message."

Reginald blinked. *Adept at havoc and. . . .* Good Lord. Brother Geoffrey had not mentioned that his younger brother might actually dispose of him. The look in those eyes told Reginald that it was more than a possibility. And while he could not hurt a hair on Jean Armand de Lusignan's head, the man obviously did not scruple to kill him. In these woods, no one would find his body to give it a Christian burial.

Reginald stepped back and drove his sword's tip into the ground. He knelt and crossed himself before the hilt's cruciform. "Then I am ready."

Instead of approaching him, Lasalle gave Reginald's attire a searching look. "Are you heading to Lusignan or from it?"

Go to Lusignan first. Now Reginald understood Brother Geoffrey's instruction to make himself known at the seat of these lords before he headed to Parthenay. He gave a silent thanks to the saints that he had followed it. "From it. In a few days the others will come to Parthenay for a council. It may be wiser . . . it may be easier to have Lady Juliana visit the sisters at Fontevraud with the little one."

Reginald tried to breathe evenly while Lasalle considered him. At last, the man shoved the poniard behind his waist belt. Nearby, their horses plucked at the grass. Reginald watched Lasalle lead them back. "Get up," he told him.

Reginald complied, still not entirely certain that he would not be buried among the bracken.

Lasalle handed him his horse's reins, mounted up himself, and threw the *besant* at his feet. "Keep away from Parthenay until then. And don't ever mention my wife."

This time Reginald bowed. "As you wish, sir."

Trotting past him, Lasalle gave him a look that could have slain him. Reginald crossed himself and pried loose his sword.

That was as close a call as he ever had. *Et bien.* It would appear that the rest of the lords of Lusignan would have to persuade this one to take up his family's cause in the *terre-sainte.*

"What are you thinking, Juliana?"

They stood atop Parthenay's ramparts. Having returned from his latest errand, Lasalle had wheedled her from the nursery in front of her giggling women by the deployment of flamboyant *courtoisie* and blatant male self-assurance, all of which he knew would make her flushed and flustered. "What? Oh, it's not what I expected."

Arching high one black brow, Lasalle drew back to scrutinize her face. "I see. Parthenay or our marriage?"

He imitated the inflection of skepticism she put on whenever she suspected him of trying to get one past her, and Juliana smiled at him for it, but her mind was elsewhere. *I am a sponsa superducta. I am a superfluous wife.* "Parthenay, of course. It's much larger than I ever imagined."

That, at least, was the truth. Below them curved Parthenay's walls, punctuated at intervals by seven drum towers. Over the years, weavers had settled on the river plain outside the town wall where they built a maze of wooden houses and workshops, and grew woad, weld, and madder to dye their cloth. In the Weavers' Quarter, the thud of treadles seemed never to cease.

To sell their wares, the weavers set up shops on the ground floors of the houses lining both sides of the street that climbed sharply from Saint Jacques's gate to the citadel. Along the same street, cheek-by-jowl with houses of prosperous merchants and burghers and in the side lanes, pilgrims' inns and hostels offered shelter and food of varied qualities and at various prices. At times, everyone had to share the street with spotted cattle driven to the markets conducted in the protective shadow of the citadel's walls.

Beyond them and beyond the Thouet rolled a green expanse of forest broken here and there by strips of fields and pastures, by hamlets and villages that clustered around white churches dotted by fortified manors and stout towers. At first glance, a prosperous and well-husbanded barony.

A barony that owed its existence and prosperity to Mélusine, a half-serpent creature, the purported ancestress of the lords of Lusignan, the creator and guardian of all they possessed in Poitou and elsewhere. Juliana did not want to think about what others said about Lady Mélusine's progeny.

She wrinkled her nose. Despite the frequent rains that came in from the sea, the place smelled of bovines. She found herself pinned against the wall so fast she yipped in surprise. He held her there. "Get used to it, woman." His voice went to its seductive rasp. "You seem to be becoming used to your other duties."

He kissed her, carefully and slowly, wanting to put her at ease with him as much as with this place. He knew that she was not telling him the truth, but did not want to reveal that he saw through her evasions. For all his experience of women, he was only just learning how to be a husband to the former Sister Eustace–and how to be Jean Armand de Lusignan, *Sieur* of Parthenay and numerous fiefs.

"Besides," he said, releasing her, "we tax everything with hide and horns. You saw Beraud's account books." He paused. "You didn't want to spend the night at Fontevraud when we passed by. Don't you want to visit it? Abbess Mathilde would like to see Eleanor."

"No!" Juliana did not know why she said that. No, that was a lie. Flushed, she pretended to assess the damage to her wimple. She did not want to return to the place where the queen-duchess arranged their marriage, one as unwilling as the other. In the bailey below, the product of that union screamed at the top of her lungs while her wet nurse tried to hush her and her other nurses clustered around, attempting to distract the infant. The heiress to Parthenay demanded to be noticed whenever awake which, fortunately, was not for protracted periods.

With a grin, Lasalle leaned against the tower wall. Arms folded, he watched his wife fret over her fustian. "I swear that I am not returning you there. With Eleanor's howling, the sisters wouldn't hear the bells."

The noise below would not cease. "It's not that," Juliana straightened her wimple, trying to hide her smile. "I . . . I'd better go before everyone in Poitou turns deaf."

Lasalle watched his wife make her escape, her hem carefully tucked up. When she reached the landing, she would drop it properly around her ankles, smooth her skirts, and set her wimple again before she faced those in the bailey. Sister Eustace would always remain a part of Juliana de Charnais, although she no longer tucked her chin when speaking to him, nor hid her hands in her sleeves.

He wished though that he could persuade her to give up wearing those conventual nightshifts. Knowing the former Sister Eustace, he expected that it would take not only patience, which he was learning to have, but also time. And that he had not.

CHAPTER 6

The rains passed, at least for a time.

Leaving Eleanor asleep in her crib and watched over by her wet nurse, Juliana ventured outside. Lasalle had ridden out again, telling her not to expect him back for a few days. She missed him. Moreover, she sensed that he had kept something from her. She sensed it when they had lain together last night. Why could he not confide in her? In truth, she had not confided to him her true worries either, had she? But how could she when nothing could be changed, save by her abandoning him, forever?

Oh, enough. She must not allow her worries about the past, about how to be his wife, Eleanor's mother, and a mistress of this place overwhelm her. Parthenay was her home. And Eleanor's. Here she must find some useful occupation besides her preoccupations . . .

Juliana looked about the bailey. Now there was a sight. A black-robed friar stood next to his mule, his habit and cloak muddy, being accosted by the steward. When Juliana approached, Beraud briefly bowed his head to her. "This is Brother Isidore from Saint Maixent."

Beraud said it with the tone of someone annoyed either at her or Saint Maixent. Or both. The abbey stood on the borders between Lusignan and Parthenay, a long day's ride away, and from what Juliana had seen in Beraud's account books, the dues, rights, and privileges of the three intertwined hopelessly. A small crowd of the citadel's residents began to gather. Juliana curtsied to the friar. "We are honored by your presence, Brother Isidore."

The Benedictine did not seem impressed. "My lord abbot would be honored more, Lady Juliana, if you ordered your steward to fulfill Parthenay's promise to our abbey."

To Juliana's surprise, the crowd hummed in displeasure. The steward opened his mouth, but Juliana gestured him to silence. "What promise?"

"The payment of a deer hide for the repair of our books." Brother Isidore raised his voice, not for Juliana's ears but for the crowd's. The sound from that quarter became louder.

Juliana ignored it to ask Beraud, "I am certain it's a misunderstanding, is it not?"

Beraud turned red. "No. No hide is due this year. Saint Maixent didn't pay Parthenay for protecting the abbey's pilgrims."

That was not a proper reply to give to one's mistress, but Juliana ignored it, for Brother Isidore's sake.

Brother Isidore folded his hands. "The road dues were too high."

"Rubbish. They are what they always were." Beraud moved a step closer to the monk. "The charter of Lord Ebbo says so. They have been so for a hundred and fifty years."

The onlookers voiced their support. Obviously, Parthenay and Saint Maixent had not seen eye to eye for some time.

"Not so in the abbey's charter," Brother Isidore insisted.

"Then a miracle changed the letters." Beraud invoked the crowd's support with an imitation of a monk scraping parchment. Jeering laughter broke from the crowd.

The friar crossed himself. "A false and blasphemous accusation. Saint Maixent would never alter an agreement. If our claim is not resolved, we will appeal to the archbishop."

This exchange did not promise to become more cordial, and turning the dispute over to Lasalle would surely not contribute to settling it amicably either. Perhaps if she repaired the relationship between the barony and the abbey, these people would embrace her as much as she wanted to embrace them. Ignoring the steward's glower and the grumbling around her, Juliana smiled at Brother Isidore. "Perhaps if Saint Maixent's charter is examined, the dispute can be resolved. Would that be agreeable?"

Finding an ally in Parthenay's lady, Brother Isidore assumed an expression of conciliation. "If the deer hide is paid."

"Parthenay will not pay a mole's skin!" Beraud gestured his final dismissal with the shouts of support from the others.

Juliana stepped forward. "But I will."

The crowd deflated into silence. Beraud gave her the look of someone who had had his authority crushed in front of inferiors and Juliana experienced the withering sensation of being the author of it. Beraud had exercised conscientiously the powers of his position in the interest of his absent masters for years without anyone's interference. But her words could not be retracted.

"Agreed," Brother Isidore smiled victoriously at Beraud.

"*And* I will examine Saint Maixent's charter." Juliana tossed in quickly to assure Parthenay that she minded its rights. The sound of surprise and disbelief came from the crowd. Oh Mary, these people did not know that she could read. Beraud did, but he would not reveal to his inferiors that his lady could read as well as he did. And write letters even better.

Brother Isidore did not seem surprised. "Very well, Lady Juliana. Tomorrow. With the deer hide."

And with that, Brother Isidore climbed on his mule and trotted out of Parthenay, leaving its novice lady standing there, holding the proverbial bag.

Saint Maixent Abbey

"Two deer hides, Lady Juliana? How did you manage to sneak them past Beraud?"

Abbot Arnold indicated a chair in the abbey's library to her. In the corner, an old brother poked about in a trunk of parchments. Juliana tried to ignore the rest of the carefully sorted volumes, even though her fingers itched to touch each one. As much as she loathed to leave Eleanor to her nurses, she had taken one of her waiting women and an escort of four men to ride to Saint Maixent. The men tended to the horses, and the woman had a list of remedies to buy from the infirmarian.

Juliana wished she had young Joscelyn de Cantigny and Rannulf de Brissard and the others of her usual guard to accompany her, but Lasalle had sent them to the four corners of the barony. Instead, a knight called Peter de Blaye offered to lead her escort the moment Brother Isidore climbed on his mule. She missed him. Lasalle. She missed him when she went to sleep, she missed him when she awoke, she missed his weight on her, his hands on her, his mouth on . . . no, that was not a thought to be indulged in this holy place. "I thought a second deer hide would assure Saint Maixent that if Parthenay is in error, it was a sincere mistake."

Abbot Arnold chuckled. He wore his habit like a man who used to don a hauberk in his younger days. "Brother Isidore considers it his duty to guard our rights. I suppose there is a competition between him and Beraud."

"You mean Parthenay doesn't owe a payment?"

"Not until next year. But we will offer our prayers for Parthenay in the meantime."

Juliana sat. She had been had by Saint Maixent's monks. Perhaps she could reclaim something from this situation. "Thank you. And the road dues?"

"Ah, the road dues." The abbot nodded to the librarian. Muttering to himself, the aged brother unrolled a piece of vellum tied with a new string and handed it to Juliana. The vellum was old, but the lettering stood out. Juliana peered closer at it. There did not appear to be any alterations in the amount owed to Parthenay but then in a trained hand, rubbing with a deer antler could hide signs of it.

"Abbess Mathilde said you have a steady hand with the pen, Lady Juliana."

Juliana started at the abbot's words. She did not realize that she was examining the vellum with the attention of someone determined to find it a forgery. And how did the abbot find out about her years at Fontevraud? "I thought that perhaps someone could have altered it before your abbacy. But I can't see any evidence," she conceded. "However," she added, "the hand looks to be of a more recent style."

Arnold smiled and took the scroll from her. "Ah. Well spotted. This is not Lord Ebbo's original charter. That one disappeared, and my predecessors replaced it. To perpetuate the rivalry between Parthenay and Saint Maixent, I imagine. Poitevin quarrels are devised to be long and ferocious."

Juliana stood up. This peacemaking had not turned out the way she thought it would. Abbot Arnold had an agenda that set off those little alarm bells in her middle telling her that she headed toward a disaster. "I see. I was brought here under false pretenses."

"Ah, falsity. Another of those Poitevin talents. The children of men are deceitful, are they not? We must discuss the nature of deceit next time you visit, Lady Juliana. For your generosity, allow me to show you our chapel with a crypt that might interest you."

Something told her not to venture into underground passages or crypts. Fortunately, she had her men with her. Juliana nodded.

❦

The well-adorned church announced the wealth of the abbey and the piety of its patrons. Juliana inhaled deeply the incense that had seeped into the very stones. Carved into the rock a couple of centuries ago, the entrance to the crypt opened in front of the altar. Arnold handed her a candle and lighting his, led the way down the steps. Juliana crossed herself and followed him.

The small chamber accommodated only two sarcophagi set side by side with the features of their occupants carved into the lids. One of them was a woman, the other, a man. Juliana looked at the abbot in surprise. The abbot nodded in encouragement. Drawn to the woman's effigy, Juliana approached it.

The artisan who had rendered her likeness was a skilled one. The straight nose, the shape of the eyelids, the slightly smiling lips and high cheekbones, and the drape of her gown spoke of a foreigner. Her hands were not clasped in prayer, as one would expect. When Juliana came closer, she saw the woman's stone fingers held in her husband's. There the two lay, touching for eternity.

"Who was she?" Juliana whispered as if her voice could disturb the dead.

The abbot raised his candle. "Saracina. The seventh Hugh de Lusignan brought her from Cordoba where he went to defend our Holy Faith. He made her his wife even though her faith was suspect. They had six sons, and their children and their children's children became staunch defenders of our Holy Mother."

"But . . . but she was buried in consecrated ground."

"Next to her husband, as he wished it. During his life, he also refused to part with her. Some doubt that the Church ever blessed their marriage."

A wave of cold sweat washed over her. Juliana turned on her heel and took the steps to the chapel, the abbot behind her.

"Fascinating. I thought that their ancestress was the enchanting Mélusine. Her husband discovered her to be a half-serpent that took her true form whenever she slipped into her Saturday bath." She wanted to ask whether Hugh the Seventh already had a Christian wife tucked away somewhere.

"A useful fable to dazzle the credulous, don't you agree? Saracina's and Hugh's descendants managed to beat and browbeat lesser men. They devastated the country for years. Once in power, they kept it by shrewd marriage alliances. Did you know that to claim Parthenay, Lord Ebbo killed his own brother?"

Wanting to avoid the subject of the history of the lords of Lusignan and Parthenay, Juliana said bluntly, "So better a fable than such an ancestry?"

"The common people around here believe that Mélusine still dwells in a secret spring somewhere in Parthenay. They believe she still brings the blessing of the ancient spirits that inhabited this land before our True Faith triumphed over them."

Juliana noticed that the abbot had not answered her question. She had encountered that tactic before. "Do they? And while at it, didn't she also snap her fingers to conjure all their fiefs and vassals?"

Arnold ignored her tone. "They say that she told her husband to ask the count of Poitou to grant him a piece of land only large enough for a deer hide to cover."

"I see." Juliana did not bother to hide her skepticism. "Then she surely must have been a sorceress. Parthenay is larger than a deer hide. So is Lusignan."

"They say that she cut the hide as thin as a thread and with it staked her husband's lands."

Annoyed, Juliana faced him. "You seem to admire a monster that in her human guise used trickery and lies. By concealing her true nature, she betrayed her husband's trust."

Abbot Arnold pinched the candle wick. The spiral of smoke obscured his face. "Mélusine did not betray him. He betrayed her when he broke his pledge not to question their marriage. Despite her own ancestry, she gave him her love, trust, and all of his earthly possessions, yet he doubted her devotion."

Juliana's annoyance grew. She should never have come to this place. She ought to take back those deer hides, too. "I see. I suppose the next time her husband learned to seek a wife whose nature and appearance were true."

"He did not. He lived out his life in anguish for having condemned his wife to remain in her serpentine form. Only to her children did she appear in her human flesh. During storms you can hear her cry for her husband and her children." The abbot shrugged. "Anyway, that's what these people believe."

Why would Arnold bring up such unpleasant tales of marriages, betrayals, and secrets just when she had tried to convince herself to let the past be buried? "So it appears. But shouldn't these people be instructed in more Christian beliefs, Abbot?"

"What is more Christian than love, Lady Juliana?"

Juliana opened her mouth before she formed an answer and was spared the trouble of finding it by the Vesper bell.

Abbot Arnold raised his hand as if he regretted not hearing her reply. "You must excuse me. Brother Bartholomew will show you and your woman to your lodging."

That night, Juliana could not sleep and not only because of the rain and the wind that tore branches from the trees and kept the men up to deal with the frightened horses. Huddled under the covers next to her maid who slept soundly, Juliana's mind raced along with her heart. In the wind, she could hear the wail of a forsaken woman who had lost her husband and her children because of a broken pledge of trust.

CHAPTER 7

At dawn's break, wracked with anxiety about Eleanor, Juliana hurried de Blaye back to Parthenay even though wind-blown trees obstructed the paths and mud made travel difficult. Urging her mare on, she obsessed about the abbot's words and relief came only when Parthenay's keep appeared through the trees. After that came the town's walls, the bridge and gate, the inner bailey–filled with men and their horse grooms, but without the usual contingent of hounds and servants. This was not a hunting party. This was a gathering more martial than for a boar chase, and about to depart.

Juliana noticed among them a bearded middle-aged man in a black cloak, but not all arrivals were strangers to her. Dear Lord. That was Count Geoffrey, the senior and current lord of Lusignan and the former count of Jaffa and his nephews–Ralph de Lusignan, the count of Eu; and of course Ralph's brother Hugh, appropriately called *Le Brun*, the count of La Marche, the third man Lasalle was talking to. They turned to her as one. And in the features of the foursome, she could see the legacy of a Saracen woman, generations removed.

They must have all gathered at Lusignan in the preceding days and, anticipating her absence, ridden the short distance to Parthenay.

The count of Eu moved first, not allowing himself to be surprised by her sudden appearance the way the others were. He took her hand and bowed to her. "Lady Juliana. How pleasant to see you again. Your daughter is a pretty little thing, just like her mother. Oh, that's Brother Reginald," Ralph de Lusignan waved his hand. "We must not keep you after such a long ride on a holy mission."

Ralph passed her to the count of La Marche who winked at her before relinquishing her to their uncle. During the proceeding, her waiting woman and de Blaye's men disappeared along with the man Ralph called Brother Reginald. Count Geoffrey greeted her without the jollity of his nephews and with an air of sympathy Juliana did not think the occasion quite warranted. "A belated welcome to Poitou and Parthenay, Lady Juliana, but it is a sincere one. May you and Eleanor find your home among us."

And with that, three of the Lusignans mounted up and trotted out of the bailey. The fourth one stayed. Ignoring him, Juliana picked up her skirts and crossed the bailey with the stride of Sister Domenica when she spotted a novice with a wrinkle in her wimple.

Lasalle reached out to her. "Juliana, we have to—"

She brushed past him. "I have to see to Eleanor."

He caught her by the arm, his voice more hoarse than usual. "Don't you give me that sanctimonious simper."

The words halted her more surely than the hold. Something dreadful was unfolding in this land of the descendants of the deceitful Mélusine. "You . . . you sent Brother Isidore here to lure me from Parthenay and keep me listening to Abbot Arnold's prattle while they came here. Why?"

He let go of her arm. "Because your presence would add nothing."

Juliana ignored the tone, now more pacific. It did not pacify her. "Oh, truly? Do you think me blind? Brother Reginald belongs to the Temple. Didn't your brother join it? To atone for your pedigree, no doubt. He can't be far behind. Where is he?"

For a fraction of a moment, he had the look of a man spat at. Mortified, Juliana opened her mouth to repair the sting of her heedlessness, but the stable boy had tiptoed nearer with a saddled courser. Lasalle took the reins and swung into the saddle. "Cyprus."

She waited for him the whole night. He did not come to her. She stared at the bed canopy, wishing she could retract her words, wishing she had not used who he was against him, wishing she had guarded her tongue, wishing she could breach this wall between them that the presence of those men had conjured up as if by the snap of Mélusine's fingers. *Cyprus.*

She had heard of Cyprus. It was an island, and one with not an entirely wholesome reputation. Its new royal crown sat on the head of Aimary de Lusignan, Count Geoffrey's brother. Her father-in-law wanted King John's crown to be sitting instead on a Lusignan head as well—a presumption that did not turn out as preposterous as one would think.

Juliana wanted very much to search out Father Urias and confess to him her thoughtlessness, but she feared that would only aggravate the touchy relations between the good Father and Lasalle—and herself. Instead, she spent the day in the nursery in the company of Pontia, Eleanor's wet nurse. The young weaver woman had buried her own newborn daughter, and she had taken to Eleanor with a possessiveness that had at first made Juliana jealous, but then Eleanor had become their common bond.

While Pontia dozed in her chair, Juliana sat by the window, holding swaddled Eleanor to her. From the bailey below, she could hear the men's replies to Lasalle's orders. Did he think of all of these events as just another campaign, with supplies to gather, men to recruit, a strategy to devise? His *routiers* were gone now, perhaps serving King Philip, perhaps King John. Did he miss them, did he wish to be with them instead?

Juliana sighed. Some things had to be faced. She had to apologize to him. She kissed Eleanor's forehead and laid her back in the cradle. In the hall, she dismissed the servants and waited for him. *Dear Lord, let this be just one of those Lusignan plots against John of England.*

Instead of Lasalle, Brother Reginald walked into the hall. He bowed slightly when he saw her and was about to retreat, but Juliana called out, "I know your vows forbid it, sir, but I would ask you why the Order would concern itself with this family."

Brother Reginald averted his eyes with a tolerant smile of someone in full sympathy with the husband of an errant wife. "The Order is not concerned with your family, Lady Juliana."

"But it is with my husband. Why?"

"That's for your husband to tell you."

Before Juliana could tackle that evasion, Lasalle stepped into the hall and Brother Reginald took advantage of the open door. Lasalle's expression told Juliana that he guessed the nature of their conversation. Juliana slipped her hands into her sleeves and curtsied with sincere submission. "I...I wait to be instructed, my lord."

Lasalle looked her up and down. "I doubt it. More vice versa, I'd say. And don't call me my lord when we are alone. It makes me feel like I should genuflect for it."

She felt relief, such relief that she had to stop herself from rushing to him. First, she had to make amends for her impulsive, inexcusable outburst. "I am so sorry, I truly am. Please, Guérin, tell me what is happening. I . . . I *will* find out, you know."

He went to the table where Beraud had left a strong box and rummaged through it. "I know. I am leaving for Cyprus."

The words struck her in the heart. She clung onto the table's edge. "Holy Mary, no. No. You can't. Why–?"

"Because Aimary's crown is at stake."

A Lusignan crown. *A serpent's crown.* Even across the distant seas, that family's cursed ambitions roared into her life. Their life. "But why must it be you? There are others. Hugh and Ralph and–"

"They have their lands to mind. They are all in John's path."

"So is Parthenay!"

"Their lands are more vulnerable. This fortress won't be taken easily, and it will slow John down long enough to defend them."

The irrefutability of it nearly choked her. "So all of this," Juliana waved her arms around her, "this is to be sacrificed?"

"It's just a pile of rocks."

She gulped, with fear and helplessness.

"Listen," he said, "Parthenay is now Eleanor's. I'm leaving Brissard here and your guards. If Brissard decides it's no longer safe, they'll take you and Eleanor to Fontevraud. Don't try to return to Normandy. The abbey is the closest and safest refuge. And if John takes Parthenay, Beraud knows how to rebuild it. Reginald has orders for the Temple to pay out my contract to you."

She had been handed a *fait accompli*. How could this be happening when they only had begun their lives together? She would not surrender. "But why must you be the one to protect that crown?"

He crumpled up a fistful of documents and dropped them into the hearth's flames, and then he looked at her, a direct, implacable look. "Because I am a Lusignan."

Juliana looked around the garden. A couple of days had passed. With all the rain, the flower beds resembled a wilderness. She took the shears to the trespassers, but did not feel any better. Surely this latest turn of events must be her punishment for wanting so much to be part of the world, not cloistered from it.

"Disciplining weeds, Sister?"

Juliana jumped and dropped her shears. Arms folded, Lasalle leaned on the gate post, only this time he did not laugh at her reaction to his intrusion into her sanctuary. His very black hair curled here and there, revealing a glimpse of a silver loop of an earring. The scar across his throat was there as well, half hidden by the edge of his gambeson. And there was that green glare of his eyes that had seen more of the world than hers ever would. He came toward her.

She stood there. "I didn't think it would be like this."

"Parthenay or our marriage?"

She did not answer. She could not answer because she threw herself into his arms and he held her while she cried into his gambeson a storm of tears that surpassed the cloudbursts over Parthenay. "I am so sorry. Don't go. Please don't go. I hate this place. These people hate me. We can't survive here without you."

"I won't."

She raised her head to see his expression–a crooked smile. He wiped her tears with his fingertips and she clung to him harder, her cheek against his heart. *Set me as a seal upon your heart . . . a seal upon your arm, for love is strong as death . . .* "You won't?"

His arms around her, he shook his head. "No. But only if you promise to be civil to Brother Reginald at supper."

"Truly?" She raised her chin to him, and for a moment she thought that he would kiss her.

He did not. "On my word of honor, Lady Juliana."

She pretended she had expected nothing more and chocked back a laugh that sprang up between her sobs. "But what about Aimary and the others?"

"They can fight their own battles."

He had rejected them. He did not belong to them. He belonged to her. She must not think about the stain on their marriage, she must not, not now, not ever. She rose up on her tiptoes, and he returned her kiss with an uncurbed passion that she still found so alien and unsettling.

"My lord de Lusin . . . Lasalle."

Juliana broke away at the sound of Beraud's voice. Beraud stood there, made uncomfortable either by the sight of them or by his address of his master. "I am sorry, my lord. Brother Reginald wishes to know if–"

"Tell him to pack his bags. He's leaving tomorrow. And early." Lasalle cut him short and Beraud scurried away, mumbling apologies.

That made her laugh again. She rubbed her palm along his jaw. "Thank you, oh thank you. I promise I will never ask anything else of you . . . you need to shave, you know."

This time he laughed. "I know. Tomorrow. Don't say a word to Reginald and try not to look too pleased." He gave her a quick kiss and left her standing there with her balmed heart.

She was civil to Brother Reginald by avoiding him and excused herself to see to Eleanor as soon as she could. Pontia smiled toward the cradle where Eleanor slept with the contented expression of all satisfied infants. Juliana nodded to Pontia to go for her own supper and knelt by the cradle, watching her daughter.

Their daughter. Lasalle had acknowledged his progeny without much demonstration. He would not leave them now, praise be. But did he love his daughter as much as she did or did Eleanor only remind him of the familiar ties he had sought all his life to avoid? Perhaps he knew that God could call infants to Him as unexpectedly as He had granted them. Juliana crossed herself. No, she must not think such thoughts. She could not bear it if anything happened to Eleanor. She could barely think of losing him to his family. "Holy Mary–"

"Look at her. She looks like a milk-fed piglet. She'll need a bigger cradle." Avoiding the creaking floorboards, he surprised her once again. He kept his voice low. "You can come out. Brother Reginald went to Saint Paul's."

She wanted to ask him about his decision, about their daughter, about Mélusine and Saracina. She wanted to ask him a thousand questions, but he pulled her to her feet and led her to their chamber, and shut the door behind them on the subject and on the rest of the world.

❦

She woke up with the light high on the shutters. She must have overslept and her maid had not come to wake her. The place next to her was empty. He must have told the girl to leave her sleep. My lord Lasalle knew how to sneak from a woman's bed. Only lately it was hers. Light-headed, Juliana smiled to herself and stretched cautiously. It felt good last night, even better than the other times. Perhaps she could persuade him to spend fewer days away from Parthenay.

Only she could not just ask him, could she? She had promised that she would not. He would be sure to point out her dilemma.

The thought made her giggle so she got up and dressed herself before calling her maid. The girl came on the third call. Perhaps one of the stable boys had kept her. The girl's tardiness could not spoil Juliana's cheer. "Go and tell my lord Lasalle that I wish to speak to him."

The maid curtsied. "He rode out before sunrise with that Brother Reginald, my lady."

Her heart froze. Juliana dropped the wimple, pushed away the startled maid, and ran. In the bailey, Beraud argued with Peter de Blaye, their voices loud. Hers topped theirs. "Where is he?" The servants paused from their tasks to stare at her. "Where is he?"

Beraud threw an accusing look at de Blaye. Eyes downcast, de Blaye stroked his tabard. "Where his duty takes him, Lady."

"Duty? Look at me. He said . . . he said he would not leave. He promised me. . . ."

Lasalle had lied to her.

Juliana turned on her heel to rush back . . . back where? Helplessness paralyzed her. Oh God, how could he? How could they? She hated them. *Lusignans.* Born of a deceitful serpent-woman. No, she could not allow such thoughts. Because of Eleanor. Her daughter. His daughter. He had abandoned them for his own kind. She hated him. She hated all of *them.*

Several servants drew nearer—the blacksmith, the stable master, the armorer, her serving women, and others from the kitchens and the forge fires. "You!" She lashed out at them. "You knew. You knew he would leave. You lied to me, all of you. God curse—"

The wail of a babe drowned her words.

"My lady!" Pontia stood among the laundry maids, her face white with shock, swaddled Eleanor pressed to her breast. The servants shrunk back, crossing themselves.

Juliana clasped her hands over her mouth. Oh dear Lord, what had she done? She took a step and reached out for Eleanor, only blackness enveloped her before she reached her.

Eleanor's crying woke her. Juliana sat upright. She was in her chamber, in her own bed. She had fainted and they brought her to her bed. Her own empty bed. Pontia paced the floor, trying to hush the babe, but Eleanor would not let up.

Dear Lord, what was she to do now? If only she knew what route he had taken, she could follow him, bring him back. Surely she could bring him back. Had he chosen the same route by which Brother Reginald reached this place? Before heading to English shores, the Order's galleys anchored at La Rochelle. From there a hard ride would have brought the Temple brother to Lusignan and Parthenay.

No, it could not be. Lasalle did not care for the seas, he had told her that. She did not care for the seas either. He must have decided to travel over land. But which route would he take? Without the encumbrance of men and equipment, he and Reginald would have traveled a considerable distance, relying on the Temple's resources along the way.

Exhausted, Eleanor finally slept against Pontia's bosom. Juliana dragged herself from the bed. Tears of pity in her eyes, Pontia handed Eleanor to her. Juliana held the babe to her heart, the small head with its reddish fuzz of hair, the pink mouth pursed with each soft breath, her eyelashes flat against her wet cheeks.

Eleanor of Parthenay was the most beautiful child in the world. Her father could leave her, but her mother never would, not for more than a moment. And Jean Armand de Lusignan knew it.

And one day love, like passion, simply vanishes.

CHAPTER 8

Juliana sat in the arbor, her hand on the silver cross around her neck, a snippet of Eleanor's hair hidden inside it. Eleanor slept swaddled in the basket by Juliana's feet. Juliana watched the gardener's helpers weed the flower beds. Autumn would come and then winter in this place with no friends. These people would tolerate her, but always consider her a stranger their lord had brought into their midst, one who had wished them ill. She was alone in this world. No, blessed Mary. She had Eleanor, she was Viscountess of Tillières and there in Normandy she had her own people.

"My lady? The men are here to see you."

Juliana dropped the crucifix into her bodice and picked up Eleanor to follow the servant. *Please Lord, let it be a reply to her message to Joscelyn de Cantigny.*

It was more than that. Young de Cantigny rode into the bailey with a full complement of her guard. De Cantigny and the others dismounted. The young man bowed to her with the manner of one assuming command. "Lady Juliana. How do you wish us to serve you?"

The rest of the young men came nearer, regarding Eleanor with cautious curiosity. Eleanor of Parthenay looked back at them with an expression of deep contemplation, uncertain whether or not she should break into a howl for her new audience. She decided against it.

Young men generally did not know what to do when confronted with babes and other fragile things, and their discomfort nearly made Juliana laugh. Their presence, however, raised her spirits for the first time in days. She gave Joscelyn her hand and smiled at the others. "I regret that such service will take you from Poitou."

The young men did not look at all regretful. On the contrary. "Will it? Where are we going, my lady?" the young knight Névelon stepped forward.

"To Normandy. Eleanor and I are returning to Tillières."

"Not without me. You shavelings couldn't find your boots, let alone your way." Another rider broke into the gathering; Rannulf de Brissard, Lasalle's man from his *routier* days and her guard's captain. Worried that he would prevent her from leaving Parthenay, Juliana had not called on him. No surprise to her, the old soldier had somehow found out about her plan. Obviously, with his lord gone, Brissard did not care to remain among these people either.

"Well then," Juliana said as if she had expected Brissard's appearance, "let's leave as soon as Sir Rannulf thinks wise."

Brissard dismounted and gave her a short bow. "The day after tomorrow, at daybreak, if you find it suitable, my lady."

Juliana held Eleanor to her, fighting tears of gratitude. "We find it most suitable, don't we, Eleanor?" Her eyes growing as large as an owlet's, Eleanor sneezed. Juliana laughed and raised her daughter high. "Yes, we do. Blessed Mother, we are going home."

They came within a couple of leagues of Fontevraud Abbey, where she had spent five years of her life, where she had encountered the queen-duchess in her declining years, still powerful enough to shape the lives of others. Only the Lord thwarted the queen's plans for their lives. Juliana did not wish to stay at the abbey even for the night. She did not want to have to tell Abbess Mathilde why she had left her husband's lands to return to her own without him. *A woman's life begins with her marriage. But what does a marriage make? Trust, duty, honor, passion, love–loyalty?*

In her case, none of it. Surely the Lord meant to spare her further distress by separating them. Surely so. Juliana looked back at their cavalcade. The first cart carried Pontia and Eleanor, the others their supplies. They could camp in the open or in the next village. King Philip's men were not about any more, and even if they were, he was her liege. She had nothing to fear from them.

They crossed a creek and climbed a low rise, the carts' wheels sinking into the rain-softened ground. Juliana let her mare have the reins and Rosamond surged toward the top of the rise. "My lady, wait." Rannulf de Brissard shouted after her, but the mare had already reached the crest.

From the shrubbery crowding into the path a rider emerged, barring her way. Ears flat, Rosamond shied, but it was the voice that nearly caused Juliana to lose her seat. "My dearest daughter, do be careful. You could break your neck."

Astride a black courser's silver saddle, Armand de Lusignan, the count of Rancon, materialized from the thicket like a malevolent spirit.

Juliana took it all in with Rosamond snorting and dancing under her. In the blink of an eye, her men surrounded them. Her father-in-law raised his hand, his voice conveying undisguised sarcasm. "*Pax vobiscum.* Leash your pups, Juliana, or I will leash them for you."

At his gesture, mailed horsemen emerged from the hawthorn and brambles—two dozen of them. Yelling at his men to retreat, Rannulf de Brissard grabbed Rosamond's headstall and turned the mare around.

"Brissard!" Armand de Lusignan's voice cut through the mayhem. "Don't meddle when I wish a word with my daughter. Tell him, girl."

Shock, fear, and confusion engulfed Juliana. Never had she imagined encountering her father-in-law in these parts. She thought him to be in Normandy, negotiating with King Philip for estates Armand used to hold of King John. Neither the counts of Eu and La Marche nor Count Geoffrey de Lusignan had mentioned the count of Rancon, but why would they? Their experience with their mercurial kinsman was not one of unmitigated joy. Armand de Lusignan sowed a whirlwind wherever he trod. Did he know that Lasalle had gone? *What did he want of her?*

"It's all right, Sir Rannulf. I will speak with the count." Juliana tried to keep panic out of her voice, to pretend that all could be settled by a reasoned exchange. "Will you please hold Rosamond? She is still frightened."

Brissard hesitated, regarding Armand de Lusignan with distrust, yet uneasy about stepping into the middle of a family affair—and a Lusignan one at that. Juliana gathered up her skirts and slid from the saddle. This situation Brissard could not resolve for her.

Her father-in-law dismounted as well and offered her his arm. Juliana ignored it. With a smile reserved for ill-mannered children, he clasped his hands behind his back and indicated the path ahead. "Let us speak privately, shall we? I always believed you to be a woman of staggering common sense, my dear. You approach complexity as if it were merely an untidy simplicity. Nevertheless, let me whittle it down for you."

Trying not to look at Pontia's and Eleanor's cart, Juliana followed him. *Did he know about Lasalle*? "I have no interest in your affairs, sir, nor in Parthenay's. I am returning to Tillières."

"But of course you are. My son traded you for the island of Aphrodite, my dear."

Cyprus, the island of Aphrodite.

Juliana stopped dead in her tracks. He knew. It did not surprise her any more than his taunts did. "He is fulfilling his obligation to his family. Is that not what you've always wanted him to do?"

Her father-in-law walked on. "Yes. And now you resent it as well as he always did, don't you."

It was a statement and not a question, and Juliana, forced to follow him, answered in the same vein. "I do, but you resent it as well, don't you."

Armand de Lusignan paused, then slowly turned and retraced his steps back to her. "I will tell you what I resent, girl. I resent your so-called marriage to my son. As long as he's propping up a Lusignan crown somewhere it mitigates my resentment. In Nikosia, he may stumble upon the daughter of the Greek emperor's fifth cousin. In that part of the world, alliances from the wrong side of the blanket and trice removed can become important. With the help of poison or a strangulation or two."

The alarm bells in her middle grew louder with his each approaching step until Armand de Lusignan stood before her, his hands behind his back, a smile of contempt settling on the haughty, handsome features. "Have you noticed that Guérin escaped your passionate embrace the moment his saintly brother whistled? This time, my dear, I will not allow you and your silly principles to meddle in our family. You are a pigeon among peregrines, Sister Eustace."

Eleanor.

Her hand reached for the dagger at her belt. He anticipated it and seized her wrist, inserting himself between her and her men. The resonant voice dropped into a soft note of menace. "Go ahead and raise fuss, girl, and I'll kill your men, beginning with that old fool Brissard."

Fear, sickening fear almost made Juliana drop to her knees, but the pain of his grip kept her from it.

"Juliana. Juliana!" Her father-in-law's voice breached the roar in her head. "Listen to me. You will go on to Fontevraud and there you will hand her to me. Do you understand? She is my granddaughter and too important to be left to your fancies of loyalty and honor."

A desire to scream as shrilly as Mélusine's own shriek came over her—except that it would have doomed her men.

"Smile, Juliana. You know you don't have the stomach to have them die for you. Eleanor will be raised as is befitting my heiress. Of course her nurse will come with her. What's the girl's name? Ah, Pontia. Eleanor will want for nothing that is in my power to give her, and as you know, that is considerable."

She found her voice, broken though it was. "You can never give her what I can."

"And what, pray tell, is that?"

"Love. You can't give her my love."

Armand de Lusignan laughed. "Don't be a peasant. She won't even remember you."

Her heart would burst, surely it would burst and leave her dead on the ground. Only it did not. Instead, a strange calm descended on her. She could not save Eleanor and her men. She had to bide her time. She had to think. She had to think like one of *them.*

Juliana steadied herself against Armand de Lusignan's forearm. He let her go. Hands shaking, she set her wimple and shook out her skirts, her every move watched by the eyes of a hunting bird. *You are a pigeon among peregrines.*

She curtsied just so slightly. "I see. It seems I don't have any choice."

Her father-in-law arched a black brow at her. Juliana suppressed a shiver at the gesture which made her see another man with very green eyes, a man who had left her at the mercy of this one. "Are you surrendering, Juliana?"

"Surrender is not a defeat."

Armand de Lusignan sniffed. "Good girl. You are learning. You are also thinking about how to get her back, aren't you? Let me assure you that the hounds of Hell could not prevail against me."

He had seen through her, but Juliana did not care. She did not expect anything less of that man. She found her voice. "I wasn't thinking of hounds."

A flicker of uncertainty passed over Armand de Lusignan's features, but the imperious tone remained. "We will continue to Fontevraud, and there you will hand over Eleanor and her nurse to me. My chatelaine and her women are waiting to take charge of them. Shall we?"

Juliana almost crossed herself, but caught herself in time. No reason to reveal her distress to her men. Head held high, she walked back to them. Confused, tense, and uncertain of what to do, they waited for her. She did not want to leave the slightest doubt that everything was as it should be, so she gave them her broadest smile. "We are fortunate to have the count's company. There are some brigands about. We are not far from the abbey. Sir Rannulf, lead the way. I will ride with Pontia."

Without waiting for Brissard's consent, Juliana climbed into the cart knowing that Armand de Lusignan watched her, whether with triumph or contempt she did not know, and did not care. She did sense Rannulf de Brissard's and her men's relief at being released from the possibility of a confrontation with the count of Rancon.

Brissard shouted at her guard to strike out, and her knights ordered themselves into a single line with Brissard leading the way. Her cart came next with the count's men and the rest of their company. Juliana did not see where Armand de Lusignan took up his position because she tore at the cart's curtains, shutting out the sight of him.

Cowering at the rear with Eleanor pressed to her, a panicked Pontia greeted her. "What is happening, my lady? I thought they were robbers about to murder us." Seeing Juliana's expression, Pontia burst into tears. "Oh, Blessed Mother, they are going to murder us!"

Juliana hugged the girl. "Hush, hush, now. They are not." She fought to keep her voice steady, trying not to burst into tears as well. "You love Eleanor, don't you, Pontia? You love her like she were your own?"

"Oh, you know I do, my lady. Why do you ask?"

"Because you will have to be Eleanor's mother, because you will have to protect her as much as you can, but don't ever, ever let her forget that she has a true mother. Do you swear to Our Lady you will?"

CHAPTER 9

Fontevraud Abbey, Poitou

It is possible to lose one's child without lowering her into a grave.

And it is something far worse than the finality of death because her mother is charged with the inescapable duty of recovering her. But how? *How?*

Juliana kept her composure long enough to convince Brissard and the others of her guard that she wished to remain at the abbey instead of travelling to Tillières, and told them to return to their homes. She would send for them, she promised, when she wished to resume her journey. Then, after Eleanor and Pontia departed with the count of Rancon, Juliana stumbled nearly senseless into the arms of the gate mistress.

Although Abbess Mathilde had granted Juliana admission to the abbey and allowed her lodging in the guest quarters, the abbess neither called on her nor asked Juliana to present herself, deepening her desolation. She hardly slept, dismissing the lay sisters who brought her food from the abbey's kitchens, feverishly planning one strategy after another to reclaim Eleanor—by siege, storm, surprise, subterfuge, suborning . . . surrender. No, not ever. Never would she surrender, not to *them*.

Unfortunately, the bare fact remained that she could not rely on anyone to intercede for her. She had no kin to champion her cause. Considering their own circumstances, her Lusignan in-laws would regard her domestic predicament with embarrassment. The count of Rancon enjoyed a status no one could challenge. She had only herself, and so each of her plans dissolved with the morning's mists.

Why didn't the abbess call her? Juliana wandered around the abbey's gardens, littering the pathways with leaves she tore from the tree branches. She had avoided the church where, she was told, the queen-duchess slept in a plain sarcophagus while new ones were being fashioned for her, her second husband, and for their Richard, her favorite son. After their strife-ridden lives, the queen-duchess had decreed that after her death they be joined at the abbey, and Abbess Mathilde had carried out her wishes.

Just as Juliana became nearly mad with worry, she encountered the abbess examining the potager in the company of the mistress of novices. At seeing her former challenging charge, Sister Domenica allowed herself a smirk of pleasure. Juliana did not care. She threw herself at the abbess's feet like a desperate penitent. No, not *like* a desperate penitent. She *was* desperate. And a penitent. Undisturbed, the abbess addressed Sister Domenica over Juliana's prostration. "It seems, Sister, that Lady Juliana brought us from the world some distressing news. We'd better make certain the doors are locked." And to Juliana, "Do get up, Daughter. Your gown will stain."

When the novice mistress glided away, Juliana obeyed. The abbess indicated Juliana's trail of destruction. "Do you object to our gardening, Lady Juliana?"

"No, Reverend Mother, I am so sorry, Reverend Mother, I did not think . . ."

With a nod, the abbess invited Juliana to walk with her. "It appears you do much thinking these days, Lady Juliana. It also appears that after you left us, you did not find the answers to your questions that made you so disquieted here."

Juliana slipped her hands inside her sleeves and tucked her chin. "No, Reverend Mother. I left here to serve the purposes of others. Sometimes I wish I had never . . . must we always serve the purposes of others, Reverend Mother?"

Abbess Mathilde took the path toward the cloisters. "We all serve His purpose. We all have our path in life."

"Yes, Reverend Mother, but could He not give me a little hint where mine might lead?"

Abbess Matilda smiled. "Always the impatient Sister Eustace, always the questioning Sister Scholastica. It seems your journey has only begun. Where it leads He will reveal as you travel along it."

Juliana thought that she had already traveled a thousand leagues from this place, if not in distance, then in understanding. Or so she thought. "But Reverend Mother—"

"Do you wish to reclaim your daughter?"

The question did not surprise Juliana. Despite being cloistered, the abbess kept a keen interest in the affairs of the world. "Oh, Reverend Mother, I would give my heart's blood for her."

The abbess paused. "But there is no need, is there?"

"Isn't it my punishment for leaving you? For wanting to be in the world? What penance can I do, Reverend Mother?"

"Since Brother Egremont left us, the library has been in a frightful state."

"But Reverend Mother—"

"When you were with us, you were seeking the world in our books. What have you learned of it?"

"It's full of lies and deceit!" Juliana caught herself. Such an outburst in this place that eschewed the rages of the world amounted to a sacrilege. "I am sorry. The books, they are not the world."

"Indeed they are not. Still, you may find your answers in the places where you first sought them."

So much for an answer to her predicament. Juliana knelt and kissed the abbess's ring. "Yes, Reverend Mother. Thank you, Reverend Mother."

Abbess Matilda made the sign of the cross over Juliana's brow. "We will keep you and your daughter in our prayers."

The library did not seem like a refuge anymore. The absence of Brother Egremont, the ancient librarian, reminded her of all she had lost—her innocence, her certainties, her daughter. She lost the man everyone thought to be her husband, too, but she did not wish to think about *him.* She had the abbess's orders and therefore each day after Prime she returned to the library to tackle the disordered volumes. She would have used the seclusion to cry, but that would have stained the vellum. Juliana therefore sniffled and swallowed her tears, and after a while the routine began to calm her thoughts.

One morning, a volume badly damaged by age and use came under her hand. Annoyed that someone would treat a book like that, Juliana opened it. Her gaze fell on the letters, lovingly drawn by a hand long since turned to dust. *The world is like a book and those who do not travel read only a page.*

Saint Augustine.

Among the neat rows of her volumes, Juliana dropped to her knees, pressed her cross to her lips, and burst into tears. *She would not.* She would not leave Eleanor. Not ever.

After a few more days of sleepless torment, Juliana asked to see Abbess Mathilde. She found her in the company of a sister in a cloak and robes suited for the road rather than the choir.

"Ah, Lady Juliana. I was about to call you," Mathilde said. "This is Sister Vigilantia. She came to us from Fécamp."

Juliana curtsied. She did not want to stare at the woman, but the nun returned her gaze directly. Her eyes were brown and round, her nose long and narrow, her skin darker than someone secluded. Juliana could not judge Sister Vigilantia's age which made her impression of the woman disorienting. There was a certain strength, perhaps the result of some long-endured affliction, in that gaze and the composed expression. Juliana smiled at the nun; the smile was not reciprocated.

"Will you excuse us, Sister? Lady Juliana wishes to enquire about Our Lord's intentions," the abbess dismissed the nun.

"Oh, no, Reverend Mother," Juliana protested. She did not think it wise to enquire about Saint Augustine's advice either. "I only came to ask if you could provide me with an escort to Normandy. I am certain that's where the count took my daughter."

"I see. Did you then decide how to recover her?"

"Yes. I will keep vigil at his gate until he returns Eleanor to me, no matter how long it takes. If I go alone, he can't harm my men."

"And do you plan to cover yourself with sackcloth and sit in ashes as well?"

Juliana nodded eagerly. "Why, yes. Do you think that would compel him to release Eleanor faster?"

"Would it not more likely cause the count to declare you mad and lock you up with the sisters at the farthest abbey? After offering them an unheard of sum to succor you for the rest of your natural life, of course."

Juliana swallowed. Mathilde had judged Armand de Lusignan perfectly. So much for her plan. "But Mother, then how can I make the count give her up?"

The abbess smiled. "You already know it."

The world is like a book. . . . She did not have to ask what the abbess implied, but that did not lessen Juliana's shock. "I can't! How can I leave Eleanor, too? I have to be near her. I am all she has–and Pontia."

"Do you think that the slightest harm can come to your child without God's will whether you are a day distant from her or a year?"

God was testing her, surely He was, but she heard Mathilda's words. "Sister Vigilantia is leaving tomorrow to become the abbess of Saint Mary's of Tyre. In Nikosia. The season for sea travel is almost over. Another ship may not sail for six or seven months."

Juliana stood there, her heart galloping. *Nikosia. The capital of the kingdom of Cyprus.* The abbess said it as if describing a stroll through the cloisters. "I don't understand, Reverend Mother.

What does He want of me? After I left you, so many terrible secrets from other people's lives came into mine."

"Have they?" Mathilde turned her gaze to the crucifix on the chapter wall. "Is it not true that He shall bring every work into judgment, with every secret thing, whether it be good or whether it be evil?"

That was not what Juliana wanted to hear, but how could one argue with His words? From her swirling confusion a single thought came. *Six or seven months.* And every moment she hesitated left Eleanor in the hands of Armand de Lusignan.

Gathering her skirts to her, Juliana knelt before the abbess. "Reverend Mother, I will pledge a year of Tillières's revenues to the abbey for your permission to travel with Sister Vigilantia to Cyprus."

Cyprus, the island of Aphrodite.

PART II

Níkosía

Near [Limassol] are the vineyards of Engaddi, concerning which see the Songs of Songs . . . 'my beloved is unto me as a cluster of Cyprus in the vineyards of Engaddi.'

Wilbrand, Count of Oldenburg
1211 AD

CHAPTER 10

Nikosia, the kingdom of Cyprus

Aimary de Lusignan wore well his nearly three score years. His once golden hair, which on his late brother's head had so beguiled the previous queen of Jerusalem, bore streaks of gray where the sun had not bleached it. Sun had also blanched Aimary's eyes and burned his skin the color of copper. He was a man who lived his life in the saddle, tall and sinewy as if molded from strips of ox hide, with gestures of one used to command.

From the servant Aimary took two goblets and handed one to Lasalle. They stood on a small balcony of the former Greek governor's residence which looked over the island's capital. Aimary waited for the mute to close the door behind him. "You'd better be careful. That's how Isabella lost her third husband." Aimary saluted Lasalle with his own cup. "Henri de Champagne fell out of the window in Acre. Just like that. That's how I got Isabella. In these parts, the way to a crown always seems to pass between a woman's knees. We Lusignans ought to give praise to low sills and high windows, eh?"

Lasalle took the cup. The grapes of Cyprus yielded a potent wine. And since he had arrived on the island, he had had an overwhelming urge to get gloriously drunk. Or to find a woman. Or both. Right after he killed Geoffrey, his perfidious brother. At least that was one thing they shared. Perfidy. And a sire. Unfortunately, Geoffrey had sailed to Acre at the request of the Order.

Aimary was too good a judge of men not to notice the muscle along the stubbled jaw of his nephew, however removed. Ignoring it, he said, "I've lost men when Count Baldwin offered them land and loot in Constantinople. Granted, Guy did the same to recruit men for this island. But I will not have my vassals here hold fiefs and fortresses of each other. I made the *archontes* hand to me half their lands in exchange for confirming the rest to them. I say keep all in your fist and open it only when necessary." Aimary clenched his fist, his eyes full of fire, and then he laughed. "Hardly news to you, no?"

Lasalle kept at his wine. The fall of Constantinople to the Franks and the Venetians drew away fighting men from Cyprus and the Holy Land, more to the detriment of the latter. "The men will slink back. The Greeks lost the city, not their entire empire."

Aimary nodded, his face solemn. "That they will. But you can wager that I am not handing this island back to the Griffons. A few summers ago a man claiming to be the husband to Isaak's daughter had the gall to bring her here and demand that I give up the throne to him by right of his wife. I sent both of them packing. Still, she does have a claim, I suppose. So, here we are," he added with the sigh of a man who had been in many places.

Lasalle had been in many places as well, Nikosia being merely the latest. Planted on a fertile plain under the range of the Kyrenia mountains, the ancient town straddled a small, reddish-colored stream that ran violently during storms. Some said that the town's name came from the white poplars that lined the banks, others that it came from the White Goddess, worshipped by the pagans.

Its gardens and orchards made Nikosia a pleasant if not well-fortified place. To the delight of their current occupants, many houses whose former owners had fled before the wrath of Richard of England boasted enough gilt, marble, and mosaics to rival the palaces of Damascus. The silver and gold in the cupolaed churches and white-walled monasteries hidden in the mountains' fastness offered up the promises of Heaven.

Aware of the vulnerable wealth around him as much as his vulnerable throne, Aimary de Lusignan had ordered the construction of a defensible palace-fortress on top of ruins of similar endeavors of past centuries; the first one constructed, some said, at the time of the great Constantine. The grand, single nave of the church of Saint Sophia, built for the new Latin archbishop, rose from the rubble of the site's previous spiritual tenants. In its crypt already resided the body of Guy de Lusignan, the island's previous lord, recently brought there from the Order's small chapel on the order of his brother.

For the past days, Lasalle had listened to Aimary's accounts which added the details of the challenges the House of Lusignan faced in *outre-mer*. Despite Aimary's plentiful progeny, in Cyprus it all boiled down to two facts: a ten-year-old heir to this crown, and good evidence that certain relatives on his late mother's side intended Hugh to inherit it sooner rather than later.

During that time, Lasalle had the unpleasant sensation that these domestic matters were only a part of a complex mosaic of Aimary's plans for him, a mosaic into which Aimary had yet to set the most essential pieces.

Aimary clasped his shoulder. "I asked your brother how he would persuade you to return here. Considering Hattín, it must have been pretty tempting, eh? At least my truce with Al-Adil bought us time. Six years, if no one breaks it."

The recently concluded treaty between Saladín's brother and Aimary de Lusignan by his authority as the king of Jerusalem resulted from the weakness of the Christian kingdom and the dissention among the Musulmans' after Saladín's death. Thanks to that dissension, Aimary had led successful raids on the towns along the Nile delta and seized the Egyptian fleet headed for Syria. However, the treaty benefited both sides–if no one broke it.

"Geoffrey was persuasive," Lasalle said.

"Ha. Nothing like family to know one's tender spots, no?"

"No."

Aimary decided not to query that reply. Still, better not leave any illusions concerning why he had accepted Brother Geoffrey's offer to summon his younger brother. Hardly a novel idea since Aimary had brought his own younger brother to this land. That turned out to be a stupendous success and a bloody disaster. This time, Aimary made sure that history would not repeat itself. "Then know that the cause here is high enough. My succession is not secured."

Lasalle tried to sound patient. "You have a son and a married daughter to inherit your crown. If the *Haute Cour* chooses Hugh, his mother's kin will hold his guardianship. The regency will belong to the nearest relative on his father's side."

Aimary poked his finger into the middle of Lasalle's chest. "So you know the customs here. Then know that half the Court doesn't trust the other, and I don't trust the lot of them."

"Make the lot turn on each other. You don't need me." Lasalle thought it the obvious answer to that problem.

"Ha! That's why Geoffrey vouched for you."

Lasalle did not take that as a compliment. Aimary had not risen to his position by timidity, naiveté, or soft-heartedness, and did not need his advice about how to deal with unruly vassals, having come from a family of such.

The king refilled his cup. "The power resides in the regency. Burgundia is not our late duchess, and her marriage . . . well. But I have a way to keep both sides from Hugh's crown."

Lasalle drank the cup dry. *This better be a good one.* "How?"

"You know that in Poitou if a fief comes to a minor heir, a senior relative on the sword side can be chosen to succeed instead. When the time comes, the succession reverts. Or not. Junior stays safe, the fortresses defended, estates preserved, a guardianship avoided. What do you say to that?"

That loud thump was Lasalle's heart. "We are not in Poitou. The High Court would not consent."

"This may not be Poitou but we are Poitevins. Appreciate my position. I am facing rivals who'd prop up Hugh's crown for their own benefit. You have neither aim nor ambition to wear one. Geoffrey said that you are tied to a girl devoted to virtue. An unfortunate trait in a wife of us Lusignans. Here a man can find a more amenable one." Aimary's gesture swept the scene before them. "Here is where you truly belong. You know it. That's why you agreed to come, isn't it?"

Lasalle ground his molars. No, that was not why he had come, but Aimary's dynastic dilemma did not need to be compounded by his domestic one.

"Well then," Aimary continued, taking his silence as a sign

of the persuasiveness of the arguments, "I'll give you your own place and men. One of Isaak's supporters used to own it. I can't keep their lines straight. I barely keep up with our own." Aimary laughed, a brief, hard laugh. "There is a woman. Her name is Rhoxsane. Take her, if you want her, but for God's sake, don't marry her. All her husbands die suddenly. I can't fault her. Yet. Ah, here's Niketas. What did you call that place?"

Having entered the chamber as silently as a nun, the *sekretikos* to the king of Cyprus bowed. "Kolossi, Sire."

A man of maturity, Niketas had the shape of an olive jar, widest in the middle. A luxuriant beard made up for a deficit of hair under a black cap. His long gown was equally black, as were his eyes, lively and all-seeing, giving him the appearance of a clever, overfed raven. Ten hennaed toenails peeking between the straps of his sandals somewhat contradicted his officiousness.

Niketas bowed to Lasalle as well. "My lord."

Lasalle duly acknowledged the *sekretikos's* presence. A survivor from the court of the self-declared emperor Isaak Dukas, whom *Coeur de Lion* had dislodged from this isle thirteen years ago, Niketas and his spies now served the new ruler. The *sekretikos* knew more about the inner workings of Cyprus and *terre-sainte* than anyone alive—except for the dowager queen of Jerusalem. Aimary de Lusignan obviously considered Niketas's services worth a few eccentricities.

"Ah," Aimary added, "Rhoxsane has a couple of daughters. I sent them to the sisters at Saint Mary's before they picked up their mother's habits. Maybe one of them would suit you."

Fighting a rising tide of temper, Lasalle said, "I have a wife." He had almost decided to tell Aimary that in the eyes of the Church he had two, but concluded that Aimary would only congratulate him. As Lasalle anticipated, Aimary waved his hand.

"Bah. I said hardly an obstacle here to another, is it Niketas?" He slapped Lasalle's back. "Niketas will send you masons and carpenters, your own men, a steward, and servants. Go to Kolossi and see to the place, then come back to Nikosia. I'll present you to the *Haute Cour*. I'll tell them that you are now *Sieur de Colos*." Aimary pronounced the title with a Poitevin flourish. "Guérin de Colos. Ha. Now come and meet my heir. You'll see what I mean. And you, Niketas."

Hugh de Lusignan, the heir to the kingdom of Cyprus sat on a stool, a bowl on his knees, a piece of almond cake in one hand and in the other a palmful of dates. He alternated between the two, nibbling with the sort of concentration that ought to have been reserved for his tutor.

Neither the finer points of Roland's demise at Roncesvalles expounded by the eager young priest nor the books piled on the knee-high table could compete with the tempting delicacies. When they entered, the boy gave Lasalle a disinterested glance and reached for another tidbit. Seeing his father, Hugh's pudgy hand paused mid-air.

The king snatched the bowl from his son's knees and flung it against the wall where it shattered into a shower of shards. "Get up, you fat little runt," he roared at his offspring and at the equally startled priest. "Didn't I order he was not to stuff his gullet? He can't mount a horse without someone hoisting him. When I was your age," Aimary reversed his aim at the boy, "I could run down a deer. Do you know what the Musulmans call you? *Khinzir.* The Pig. Stand up!"

Hugh did, his chin quivering, his mouth puckered. He dropped the dates, stood up, and wiped his hands on his overshirt.

"See?" Aimary turned to Lasalle, "They say I have a hog for an heir."

Lasalle picked up a couple of dates. "They do not, my lord," he said.

"What?" Surprised by being contradicted from those quarters, Aimary braced his fists to his hips.

Lasalle examined the date very carefully before subjecting it to his molars. "They said *khinzira.* A sow. They may be referring to Mistress Morphia, Leontios's widow. I heard that she smuggled a ham under her apron from the kitchens, claiming she was with child. Or so they said. Isn't that true, *Sekretikos*?"

Niketas cast a glance at the man whom the king had elevated into his confidence. Ah, so this Frank had a talent for subtlety. No, not a Frank; a Poitevin. So much the worse. Niketas suspected it the first time he laid his eyes on my lord Lasalle. A kinsman of the king Guérin de Lasalle might have been, but Niketas did not intend to be supplanted in position or power. Only one question remained–will they be allies or rivals? Niketas spread his arms in regret. "It is true, *basileus*, I have heard it myself."

Encountering two unexpected opponents, Aimary opened his mouth, then waved his hand. "Bah. Hogs, hams. Get back to your books, boy, and no supper. Did you hear me, Father?"

"Yes, my lord. No, my lord," the young priest stammered, rushing to gather up the books.

Aimary thrust his finger at Hugh. "Now get to your studies." And with that, he stomped out of the room.

Niketas expected that my lord Lasalle would follow the king, but with a wink at Hugh, the man spat out the date pit halfway across the room. Hugh blinked in surprise and shuffled his feet in a young boy's effort to conceal injured pride, but his eyes had brightened, and when the new lord of Kolossi gave him a bow, Hugh beamed.

They caught up with the sovereign of Cyprus who had not noticed their tardiness because he was still carrying on loudly about his offspring's failings, peppered with uncomplimentary comments about the High Court and the sundry vassals who composed it. "My heir. Hugh likes the sound of kitchen kettles better than the kettledrums. He'll make his chancellor whoever plies him with Damascus dates or *kandiq!*"

Niketas lowered his voice for the man next to him. "Why did you say that about Morphia, my lord? You know it's not true."

Guérin de Lasalle dropped a sticky date into Niketas's palm. "Why then did you agree?" he said, and followed the sound of the king's fulminations.

Niketas licked his fingers and smiled to himself. *Very good, my lord. We are rivals then.*

CHAPTER 11

Aboard the dromond Regina

Besides the king, there are four officers in the kingdoms of Cyprus and Jerusalem. The seneschal, the marshal, the constable, and the chamberlain." Juliana tried to mask her resentment of Sister Vigilantia's question by her flat answers. After days in Sister Vigilantia's astringent company, Juliana doubted that she succeeded.

Each day since they had left Marseille, Sister Vigilantia had taken it upon herself to instruct her in the labyrinthine affairs of the *Levante*, as one of the Venetian mariners called it, the place where the sun rose. More concerned about reaching the actual place than its celestial location, Juliana and the other travelers aboard the *Regina* thought of it as *outre-mer*.

While they were reaching it, thus far with God's good will, Juliana could not tell whether Sister Vigilantia intended to teach her or torment her for her own amusement. From such questions, the latter seemed more likely.

Juliana felt once again like a novice examined by Sister Domenica rather than a traveller on the deck of a pilgrims' ship in the company of Sister Vigilantia and a boy called Wink.

The urchin became appended to their party at the behest of the abbot of Fécamp. The brothers had caught the boy pilfering the abbey's dovecotes, and the abbot decided that the young culprit be best kept out of trouble by sending him along with Sister Vigilantia's escort. The boy hardly spoke a word, but he carried out orders with the devotion of a dog saved from drowning. The abbot and Abbess Mathilde paid the cost of their passage, and the sisters offered up daily prayers for their safe arrival.

Sister Vigilantia's next question broke Juliana's thoughts. "*Paroikoi?*"

"Serfs."

Alas, unlike Sister Vigilantia, Sister Domenica had no knowledge of Greek nor did she have such a minute knowledge of things which, rendered in Sister Vigilantia's accented pronunciation, struck Juliana as alarmingly secular.

"*Archontes*?"

"The Greek lords of Cyprus when King Richard gained it."

A pause in Sister Vigilantia's questions followed. Juliana wondered if she ought to elaborate. Her head already ached from this morning's lesson.

The *Regina* carried a full complement of souls brave or foolish enough to chance the early storms of the autumn seas. At embarkation, the entire crew and the passengers had joined the two priests traveling to the Holy Land in a rousing chorus of *Veni Creator Spiritu,* which ended when the lurching of the *Regina* sent the new choristers to the railing in a mass exercise of retching.

Fortunately, by the end of a few days some of the travelers, and Juliana thankfully counted herself among them, overcame the dreadful bouts of sea sickness. Strangely enough, neither Sister Vigilantia nor Wink suffered from it.

During daylight hours, the passengers spent their time on deck, retiring only at night to the dank and dismal bowels of the ship where they had strapped their trunks to the planking. Since they left Marseille, three passengers had died. Hardly grief-stricken, the others quickly took up their allotted portions of space outlined in chalk.

The travelers' trunks were large enough not only to store their possessions and prop up their mattresses, but if need be, to serve as their owners' coffin. Juliana noticed Sister Vigilantia's trunk was smaller than the others, an indication to Juliana that Sister Vigilantia did not intend to die at sea, a thoroughly impious presumption, Juliana thought, but did not voice.

Wink fought a young boy's boredom by exploring the ship. When he became a nuisance to some short-tempered traveler, Juliana sent him to look after a cage of chickens, a part of their provisions. After all, he had an affinity for feathered creatures.

"Who are the *poulains*?"

"Christians born in the Holy Land."

Sister Vigilantia's needle paused over her stitches. Juliana took a deep breath. "I meant all those who accept the authority of our Holy Father."

Sister Vigilantia's lips pursed in either disapproval or disagreement, or both. "*Audi partem alteram, domina.*"

"Yes, Sister," Juliana said, humbly this time. One could not escape Saint Augustine, not even aboard the *Regina*.

Yet she had to admit that Saint Augustine was right. As much as she dreaded sea travel, the weeks on the *Regina* had already revealed to her a world she had never imagined. The farther east they traveled, the stronger the rays of the sun became. The very air shimmered as if alive.

When not immersed in worries about Eleanor or in Sister Vigilantia's lessons, Juliana marveled at the power of the Lord's hand propelling the *Regina* through the slate-green waves, past rocky shores of distant islands, their sun-gold flanks rising from the waters. At other times, as frightening as the sound of the wind and the groan of the hull became, when the sea again quieted and those white-crested swells carried them along, Juliana stood on deck and looked toward the horizon in wonder. Those were the briefest of moments, but she felt completely and utterly free.

Fortunately, the *Regina* did not venture far onto the open sea and every few days she anchored to take on water and food. Juliana gladly set her feet on *terra firma* where she found herself in a veritable Babel of tongues amidst people of all hues, strange clothes and customs, selling odd fruits and fares with sharp and sour and sweet smells, some so pungent they made her eyes water. She would have wished to linger if only such victualizings had not delayed their arrival at her destination, an arrival for which she daily and fervently prayed.

"Dragoman?"

"A translator."

Sister Vigilantia nodded and resumed her stitching. Juliana breathed a sigh of relief. She glanced about her. A merchant from Champagne unashamedly consoled a woman who had lost her husband only a few days ago. Juliana frowned. She heard it said that women who boarded ships for the Holy Land as pilgrims left them as whores if they reached those shores.

She had taken umbrage at that sentiment when announced loudly by a debased sailor in Marseille's harbor for which the man received several sound blows from the shipmaster. That might have been true for some women aboard the *Regina*, Juliana conceded, but she would sooner become the queen of Cyprus than a whore on this ship, or anywhere else. Furthermore, despite her cloak, wimple, and gown displaying the utmost severity, she was not truly a pilgrim, was she?

"What is Queen Isabella's parentage?"

"Her father was King Almaric of Jerusalem by his wife . . . his second wife, Maria Komnene."

"And the queen's kin on her mother's side?"

"Her half brother, John d'Ibelín, the lord of Beirut, by the dowager's second marriage to . . . to . . ."

"Balian d'Ibelín. Do pay closer attention, Lady Juliana. And the others?"

Juliana bit her lip and frantically tried to recall the names of the other Ibelíns. Surely there were others. There were always others. The lineages of *outre-mer* presented to her an impenetrable maze of shockingly close and at the same time easily loosened marital ties. The thought occurred to her that her own marital conundrum appeared rather . . . mundane. She crossed herself at the thought. "I – I can't remember."

Sister Vigilantia tossed her a disapproving glance. "Shouldn't you be familiar with rivals of your husband's family, Lady Juliana?"

Perhaps Sister Vigilantia was right. In fact, the Lusignans' rivals ought to become her friends. Juliana swallowed that answer.

"Can you at least remember how Lord Aimary came to the Jerusalem throne? It too concerns your husband's family."

Juliana squared her shoulders. To redeem herself, she intended to recite the entire *lignage* of the Holy Land going back to the de Bouillon brothers, and even to include all of the scandalous gossip that sloshed around the deck. "Lord Aimary gained it by right of his second wife, Queen Isabella. She inherited her crown from Queen Sybilla, her half sister, who had been the wife of Aimary's younger brother, Lord Guy de Lusignan. Lord Aimary had arranged for his brother's marriage to Queen Sybilla. I heard it was because Lord Aimary became the lover of Sybilla's mother–"

"The lords of Lusignan are skilled at plotting marriages that bring them ever higher, don't you agree, Lady Juliana?"

Juliana regretted the interruption and she had not expected a gibe at her own marriage. Thus far, Sister Vigilantia had not evinced the slightest interest in hearing from Juliana's own lips the reasons for her presence on board the *Regina.* "I am told it's all the lady Mélusine's fault."

The nun smiled slightly. "How did King Aimary acquire his Cypriot crown?"

Sister Vigilantia obviously did not wish to pursue the subject of the Lusignans' ancestress. Very well, perhaps next time. "From the Staufen Emperor. Lord Aimary became his vassal when he inherited the island from his brother Guy, who bought it from King Richard, who had defeated there an *archonte* usurper called Isaak Dukas who–"

"What are the courts of Cyprus?"

Juliana wished Sister Vigilantia would not interrupt her just when she was about to recount another scandalous episode from that part of the world. "The High Court represents all lords temporal and has jurisdiction over all Franks."

"And?"

"And the ecclesiastical court has jurisdiction over matters of heresy, matrimony, and testaments of true Christians," Juliana added stubbornly. Sister Vigilantia looked up from her work. Blood came to Juliana's cheeks, but she did not amend her words.

What use was it to her to learn the intertwined lines of the rulers of *terre-sainte* and Cyprus, the names of their chamberlains and members of chanceries, and words in strange languages? She did not need a dragoman to tell Guérin de Lasalle that his own father had their daughter in his clutches. What Lasalle ought to do with that information seemed to her blazingly obvious. And after that . . . she did not dare to think, but perhaps it was good to know that an ecclesiastical court resided in Cyprus. Before it, she surely would not need a dragoman.

"Delfines, delfines!" Someone shouted and Juliana gladly leapt up with the others to rush to the railing. From the depths of the seas, half a dozen sleek grey forms breached the waters to race alongside the ship before departing on other adventures.

"They are called delfines after the oracle of Delphi," Sister Vigilantia had calmed the passengers when they first sighted these astounding creatures. One of the mariners told Juliana that the delfines' appearance announced storms, and the coxswain would try to find a sheltered bay to drop anchor. At other times, the wind would rise quickly, sending the sailors scurrying, and the passengers to below the deck and to their prayers.

Several times they sighted other ships and the cry of 'corsairs, corsairs, man the stations!' terrified the passengers with the prospect of Saracen slavery. At those times, Juliana prayed along with the others, but with a fierce determination that whatever happened, neither corsairs nor slavery would prevent her from completing her quest and reclaiming Eleanor.

Once a Venetian galley under Saint Mark's banner glided into view, followed by a court of lesser vessels riding low in the water. Prayers of thanksgiving went up at the sighting of Christian ships–not that renegade Christians were above seizing their brethren and selling them to whoever paid. The merchant from Champagne loudly announced that the galley and the other ships carried in their holds the treasures of Constantinople and marvelous relics to be properly housed in the churches of Venice and elsewhere. When Juliana excitedly shared the passengers' joy at their rescue with Sister Vigilantia, the woman looked at her with an arching of her eyebrow. "Rescued from what?"

Juliana bit her tongue. She truly did not know the answer. She did, however, have the distinct feeling that Sister Vigilantia did not care a whit for the current occupant of the thrones of Jerusalem and Cyprus, whether by right of his wife or not.

CHAPTER 12

Kolossi, Cyprus

Crossed by the Kouris river, his fief spread among carob and olive trees. Every crack in the sun-baked soil breathed the scent of thyme. Cattle gathered around a small pool where the water wheel creaked. A couple of boys herding their flock toward the watering place chased the sheep out of the way of their cavalcade.

They rode through a village of two dozen squat, mud brick houses, their occupants coming out cautiously. They regarded the riders with the usual obsequiousness of serfs, but Lasalle knew that the *paroikoi* were not happy with their Frankish masters.

The tower that emerged above the trees formed part of a manor whose defenses had fallen into disrepair. The walls missed any number of stones, the roof timbers of the stables and storage sheds sagged under the weight of the remaining tiling. Lasalle dismounted. *The lord of Colos*. Aimary must be laughing at him.

From the shade of the buildings servants approached. The more energetic guard dogs charged ahead of them, panicking the horses and the pack mules. Lasalle turned to the *bailli* Niketas had given him, a Syrian called Darius. Darius spoke Greek, very good French, and the Saracens' tongue. "Tell them to tie them up or I'll kill those damn dogs." To Harion, his new *serjean*, he said, "Have the men search this place from top to bottom. Be careful, I don't want them brained by those tiles. And find the cook and tell him we're staying for supper."

The men sprung to their tasks.

"You," Lasalle crooked his finger at Darius. "Come with me. Let's not keep the lady waiting."

From the brightness of the bailey, the manor's dark interior disoriented him until his eyes became used to it. He looked about. Three stories high, storage in the base floor, water cisterns half full. Winter rains should fill them. The hall in the middle, the chambers above. At the bottom of the stairs to the upper chambers, he said to Darius, "Find the accounts for this place, if there be any. Clean out the casements, store the supplies, new padlocks and keys."

The late husbands of Rhoxsane of Kolossi might have shirked their duty to safeguard the southern reaches of the island, but they had not spared attention to the interior of their residence—probably at the insistence of its lady. On the second landing, he faced the doors to three chambers. On one, a painted pair of mythical beasts devoured each other. Or mated. Perhaps both. He could not tell since the gold paint had faded where hundreds of palms had pressed to enter.

Lasalle was about to place his hand in the very same place when a slight sound behind him made him spin around, poniard drawn.

"That is my chamber. But you are welcome to share it, Lord de Lusignan."

Her smile was inviting, promise-full. A long time ago, he had been greeted by a smile like that, and the *kohl*-smudged eyes, and a voice as soft. An embroidered veil crowned her, pinned to her braided hair from which it fell along the curves of her body. Her gown was worthy of Constantine's court and, as far as he could tell, the flesh underneath all the paint, perfume, and powders well preserved. In previous circumstances, he might have taken up the offer. In the current one, it merely stoked his temper.

He let his poniard's edge glide along a jaw line surely close to two score years. No surprise that news of his arrival had travelled to this place ahead of him. The question remained who had sent it to Rhoxsane of Kolossi so speedily? "Wasn't it also shared by your two, or was it three, husbands?"

The lady of Kolossi languidly caressed her cheek against the steel's edge, the tip of her tongue sliding between her full, blood-red lips. She smiled. "Is that an accusation? The queen is wed to her fourth husband."

Rhoxsane kept her smile while the man's eyes took time to strip the layers of cloth and cosmetics from her. When he was done, he migrated the tip of the poniard to the softness under her chin and pressed it there. "Is that an accusation?" he said, a soft rasp in his voice.

She had expected Aimary de Lusignan to hand Kolossi—and her—to the next uncouth simpleton eager to display his ignorance and bravura. They were all anxious to marry her for their claim to this place, and to her. This man was not like the others—he did not care for either. What did a man like that care about? What, or who, was his weakness? All men had one. Or two. "Of course not, my lord."

The man shoved the poniard behind his waist belt. "I'll tell that to the king. Since he granted Kolossi to me, your steward and your servants will answer to Darius. You may keep your chamber, but you may find it a little noisy. The carpenters and masons are arriving in a few days."

She was being dismissed. No man had dismissed her like that. How dare he. He would come to regret it, this latest lord of her Kolossi, inflicted upon her by Aimary de Lusignan. She had taken care of the others and no one could prove a thing. The thought kept a smile on her lips and composure in her voice. "And who shall I answer to, my lord?"

The Lusignan turned his back to her. "If you think to counter Darius's orders, to me."

Choosing capitulation and conciliation, Rhoxsane curtsied. "My lord."

After all, this was their first meeting. The rebuilding of the fortifications would take the rest of the autumn and winter. She had time. Besides, she expected the arrival of another visitor. Someone who could make this one's ownership of Kolossi very short indeed—and King Aimary's possession of the crown of Cyprus just as short.

CHAPTER 13

The port of Limassol, Cyprus

The *Regina* dropped her anchor to the thanksgiving of the passengers.

Juliana barely noticed the straw-colored walls of the town crammed by the seashore since as soon as the transport barges surrounded the ship, pandemonium broke out among the passengers with a rush for their trunks and trundles, mattresses, wares, and wives.

In the rush, Juliana became separated from Sister Vigilantia. She rescued Wink from being swept into one of the boats only by snagging him by his tabard, and seeing to it that they ended up in the same ferry. Thus they arrived at the customs house while the other ferries brought the baggage to the quay. Once on solid ground, it took all of her effort not to waddle as if still on the *Regina's* deck, an effort which the other passengers also exerted with various degrees of success, much to the amusement of the natives.

Juliana did not care. She ought to have searched for Sister Vigilantia, but since they had only one place to disembark, that could wait. With Wink in tow, she elbowed her way through the crowd. She had to find Lasalle and would do so by the most direct means. "Do you know the lord of Parthenay? In Poitou he calls himself . . . he may be known here as Jean Armand de Lusignan, but he may not use those titles. Guérin de Lasalle? I am the viscountess of Tillières."

The customs clerk looked her over several times. Juliana did not care for his manners. For weeks she had been on the wretched ship, ever worried about Eleanor, forced to bank her anger at Lasalle, to defer to Sister Vigilantia's opinions, and to subject herself to her instructions. And now this man dared to cast aspersions on her appearance? She allowed him one more ogle. "Do you know him or not?"

"Where are your servants, Lady, if that's who you are?"

The question struck her as impudent as the man's examination of her. What business was it of these people to question how she travelled? Juliana caught Wink in time to prevent him from wandering off again. "This is my companion."

The man gave a huff of laughter. "A boy? Do you intend to sell him or yourself?"

Good Lord. They dared to accuse her of being a . . . a *Cyprian.* She had heard enough about this island's reputation for sundry immorality. The island of Aphrodite indeed.

Her hand struck the man–and hard.

The man jumped back, nursing his cheek. Shocked by her own audacity and the instant recognition that she had debased herself in front of all these people, Juliana stepped back as well, flushed with embarrassment. The squabble of voices around them hushed. A few of the onlookers laughed, but the man began shouting something and in the blink of an eye, she faced a wall of very unfriendly faces.

Another man bedecked in badges of his authority sailed toward them, the tip of his silver-headed staff clicking on the ground. Juliana prepared herself to battle her next opponent, but yielded to Sister Vigilantia who emerged from the crowd and into the man's path.

Vigilantia raised her voice to pose a single question, in Greek, which made the man blink in surprise. Juliana watched their exchanges with sudden regret that she had not taken Sister Vigilantia's lessons more to heart. None of that mattered now. She had to find Lasalle and make him return to Poitou.

"Your husband, Lady Juliana, is not far from this place. This man offered to arrange an escort for you and the boy. Unless you wish to rest and wait until tomorrow." Sister Vigilantia said, a current of agitation in her voice.

Juliana did not care to ask the cause of it. After all her travails, she had not expected to reach her goal so quickly. "Oh, praise be. No, I wish to travel on, but . . ." After so many days in the company of Sister Vigilantia, Juliana found their pending separation alarming. And how far was 'not far'? Forgetting herself again, she gripped the woman's hand. "Please, do come with us, Sister. I would feel so much better knowing that you are not left here on the wharf."

Taken momentarily aback, Vigilantia immediately censored her surprise and disengaged her hand with conspicuous care. To Juliana's relief, she nodded. "Then we ought not tarry."

Once again Juliana did not know what to make of the enigmatic nun who had travelled such a distance to be abbess of Saint Mary's of Tyre in Nikosia. It did not matter. The mules waited.

Kolossi

The rolling deck of a ship gave way to swaying panniers on mules' backs.

Riding on her own ahead of Juliana, Sister Vigilantia surveyed the countryside about her with keen interest, her usually inexpressive features softened. Perhaps a sign of her happiness at returning to a familiar place, Juliana concluded. And what a place this was.

Stonecutters, masons, carpenters, and laborers sawed, hammered, carted, hauled, and hoisted timbers and blocks of limestone in the courtyard of a fortified manor, rendering it more so. Their arrival brought the activity to a halt. One of the men yelled something, and the others reluctantly resumed their work. The man came to their lead muleteer and after a few words, to Juliana. Before he bowed to her, he looked her over with curiosity but without the contempt with which she had been treated at Limassol. "I am Darius, my lord's steward, Lady. The master went to Nikosia, but the mistress is here. Do you wish to speak to her?"

The mistress. Juliana's heart sank. It ought not have, but it did. Juliana would have told the man that she did not wish to speak to *the mistress,* but before she could answer, Sister Vigilantia spoke up for her, eagerness and even greater agitation in her voice. "Yes, yes. Let her come out."

The request surprised Juliana. It surprised Darius as well, she could see. Casting a glance at Juliana, he bowed to Sister Vigilantia. "I shall tell her, *Adelphie.*"

Juliana did not expect Sister Vigilantia's demand, but since she had asked the nun to accompany them, she could hardly object to it. In fact, her presence seemed to have entirely escaped Sister Vigilantia.

The nun's gaze roamed over the place as if it were more than familiar to her, her hands twisting the cross at her bosom. Glad to be ignored by Sister Vigilantia for the first time since they boarded the *Regina,* Juliana's mind skipped from one unpleasant thought to another. *The mistress.* What did Armand de Lusignan say? . . . *he may stumble upon the daughter of the former Greek emperor's fifth* . . .

The manor's gate opened for a woman in a green gown embroidered along the sleeves and hem with a riot of strange creatures. Two maids assisted their mistress through the debris in the bailey. A graying man Juliana presumed to be her household steward followed them. Juliana noted the woman's high forehead that sloped in perfect line with the bridge of her nose, her red-tinted lips, her eyes made deeper and larger by her cosmetics. From under a pearl-encrusted *casque*, her black hair fell loosely under her veil. *The mistress.*

As the woman approached nearer, Sister Vigilantia made a sound between a sob and a cry, of victory or pain, Juliana could not tell. Her confusion deepened when Sister Vigilantia urged her mule toward the mistress to the astonishment of the gawking men. Equally surprised to be so confronted, the woman halted, her mouth opened slightly, but before she could utter a word, a single one came from Sister Vigilantia.

"*Prodotis!*"

The mistress's features stiffened as if the word were a curse. Her maids gasped, their hands flying to their lips, her steward, taken aback for a moment, stepped forward to defend his mistress with a tone of outrage.

"*Sopa!*" his mistress silenced him.

The violence of it took Juliana by surprise, but not Sister Vigilantia. She sat back, her expression one of triumph and undiluted scorn. The steward, equally stunned by his mistress's response, looked at Juliana as if to ascertain whether or not she understood what had transpired. Since she did not, Juliana did not know what expression to assume which only added to her feeling of foolishness and helplessness. Oh dear, she needed a dragoman after all.

Instead of further engaging the woman, Sister Vigilantia pulled her mule around and rode past Juliana to the path whence they came. "We shall not be staying at this place tonight. We shall return to Limassol," she announced, her eyes those of a woman who found an enemy camped in her own abode, an enemy against whom she had successfully sortied.

Confused, Juliana crossed herself. The sun began to sink toward the horizon. Just beyond the bailey, the white dome of a small church stood out above the trees. Crushing exhaustion descended on her. She thought that today she had finally reached her goal. Moreover, she could not shake the sensation of stumbling into someone else's troubles. No, it could not be. She had one mission and nothing would distract her from it. But first she had to rest, to fill her groaning stomach, to gather her thoughts.

Juliana kicked her own mule to intercept Vigilantia's. "Look, Sister, there is a chapel. Surely we can spend the night in that safe haven. We must offer thanksgiving for our safe arrival." She turned to Darius who followed them, wringing his hands, caught between two masters, "Perhaps we could buy our supper from the village? Surely we can't be denied rest in that sanctuary?"

Darius stole a backward glance, but the mistress and her maids had already retreated behind the gate. "No, indeed not, Lady. If that's what you wish. I will see to it that you have food and bedding. Your men can sleep in the stables with the others. I will post guard so that you are not disturbed."

Juliana nearly burst into tears of gratitude. "Oh, thank you. Can we, Sister? Please, let us rest here. I don't think I can ride all the way back to Limassol."

Juliana thought that her plea would be denied, but after a brief hesitation Sister Vigilantia nodded, the feverish look in her eyes dimming. Equally relieved by the decision, Darius took hold of their mules to lead them.

When they reached the door of the chapel, Juliana tried to keep herself from falling out of her seat from exhaustion and emotions this unexpected detour had stirred. *The mistress* . . . "To what saint is this church dedicated?"

Darius helped her from the pannier. "*Ayios Eustathios.*"

Saint Eustace.

Thus the former Sister Eustace spent her first night in a foreign land not in the arms of a man everyone assumed to be her husband, but sheltered instead under a dazzlingly blue dome from which the face of *Pantokrator*, the All-Ruling Sovereign, looked down on her with His dark, all-seeing eyes, not unlike those of Sister Vigilantia.

CHAPTER 14

Nikosia

Back in the mule's pannier at sunrise and on the road to Nikosia, Juliana tried to pay attention to the land around her to silence the thoughts of the past day's events scurrying in her head.

After their prayers and a supper of olive pies and sweet wine that immediately cast her into a stupor, she had fallen asleep with Wink curled up at her feet. Just before her eyelids dropped for the last time, she glimpsed Sister Vigilantia prostrated before the altar, fervently whispering words Juliana did not understand. Or perhaps she had only dreamed it.

Now even the world around her appeared to be part of a strange dream. It was a world older than the ages, claimed, conquered, seized, and settled through endless centuries, surrounded by the seas and limitless skies, littered with tumbled ruins of pagan temples, smitten for their impiety. The arid, rock-strewn land by the seacoast farther inland puckered into blue-gray ridges of mountains. Their small caravan soon joined others heading to Nikosia on foot, donkeys, and in mule panniers.

Juliana noticed that not many leagues passed without the white dome of a church or a wayside chapel welcoming them. Members of their growing company paused at some of them to ask for favor, protection, or to give thanks. So the island of Aphrodite had a pious population, despite its reputation. After all, was not Barnabas born on this island and did not he and Paul convert the island pagan ruler?

They spent another night in a monastery's hostelry, a restless, sleepless night for Juliana, and a prayer-filled one for Sister Vigilantia.

Juliana's worries that Sister Vigilantia would abandon her the moment they reached Nikosia faded when Vigilantia accompanied her to the very gate of a walled palace-fort which, like all the other buildings, presented a windowless façade to the world.

They rode to it in a noisy stream of humans and beasts. One could tell travelers, pilgrims, merchants, burghers, clerks, or particular tradesmen by the shape and cut of their rich or humble cloth. Among them, the ubiquitous beggars jostled with servants, porters, and men-at-arms guarding maids and their mistresses carried through the crowd in wicker chairs and painted palanquins. Jongleurs and musicians outdid each other with their songs and antics. Tooth pullers plied their trade under awnings, charm-sellers extolled the efficacy of their goods, the snake charmers' repulsive reptiles drew a fascinated audience. The noise and smells from the stalls of cooks, bakers, butchers, coopers, potters, weavers, and makers of swords, knives, tents, sails, and ropes assaulted Juliana's senses. From the farmsteads and villages trotted humble donkeys all but invisible under burdens of wood and fodder or piled high with cages of birds or their poultry cousins. Sheep driven to market periodically blocked the passage to the annoyance of everyone although more often than not, the men hefted a sheep or a goat across their shoulders.

Like the crowds in the harbors, these people represented all colors of Creation. Most of the women appeared in public decently dressed and some even veiled, others vulgar in gaudy gowns displaying too much flesh, painted eyelids and cheeks, gesturing shamelessly even from the steps of a church to lure the passersby. A church!

She was prepared to change her mind about these people once again when at the mention of her name and that of the Lord of Parthenay, one of the gate guards trotted away and returned shortly with a girthy, bearded man.

Juliana tried not to stare at his splendid pair of sandals–and their wearer's painted toenails. After a few words from Sister Vigilantia, in Greek, the man's jaw dropped. He scratched his head under his cap, like a man unsure what to do with an unwanted gift. That gift, Juliana surmised, was herself.

"Yes, yes." The man impatiently interrupted Sister Vigilantia. "If you would follow me, Lady," he said to Juliana in accented French, "I will take you to your husband."

Dubious of this man's promise, Juliana gave him her severest frown. "I will not follow you, sir, unless I am accompanied by Sister Vigilantia."

The man's brows jumped up. Juliana did not care. Since her arrival on this island, these people had treated her as if she were a harlot, invisible, or a nuisance.

"I cannot. This is Niketas, the king's *sekretikos.*" Sister Vigilantia demurred, and when Juliana protested, Vigilantia raised her hand. "Our guides are paid to return to Limassol. Should you be in need, ask Saint Mary's for aid."

And with that, accompanied by the men of their escort, Sister Vigilantia departed for her own destination. Juliana felt stranded. Wink jumped from his mule and went to her rescue, offering his hand for her to dismount.

Juliana climbed down and smoothed her gown with deliberate care. As long as Niketas took her to Lasalle, she need not bother with the odd little man. She handed the reins to the remaining muleteer. "Thank you, Wink. Well done. Shall we?"

Niketas measured her from her shoes to her wimple. Juliana

raised her chin. Did this Niketas person think that he could intimidate her? The man's girth suddenly shook with suppressed laughter. "This way, if I may be allowed, Lady Juliana."

Her hand on Wink's shoulder, her heart in her mouth, Juliana followed him. They crossed interior courtyards with plangent fountains, flower beds and flower pots where the scents of laurel, lemons, roses and myrtle, the flowers of Aphrodite, lingered. They continued across marble floors, through colonnades. Juliana refused to gawk at the splendors around her because she did not want to appear a simpleton to these people.

Wink saw no need to pretend. He craned his neck at walls with eye-dazzling scenes–garlands, forests of fabulous trees full of birds in life-like plumage, others depicting seas boiling with strange fish and monsters. He tripped over his feet when forced to step on mosaics that seemed to come alive underfoot.

Niketas stopped halfway down the corridor and pointed to the chamber at the end of it. "Please excuse me, Lady Juliana. You will find your husband there."

"Thank you," Juliana said without much gratitude and took hold of Wink.

For Eleanor.

The chamber's latticed windows overlooked a ridge of grey-green mountains, one of its peaks the oddly-shaped *Pentadaktylos*, as Sister Vigilantia called it. The sound of angry male voices rising to the high, painted vaulting made Juliana halt at the threshold.

A dozen men surrounded a table with layers of documents and charters weighed down by clusters of seals. The men looked like the lords of this place. Some Franks, the others by their appearance and the cut and cloth of their tabards, gambesons, and cloaks those Sister Vigilantia called *poulains*–men born and raised in these lands.

Whatever their ancestry, they displayed power, prestige–and pride. And in that moment, riled tempers. Two of the men argued with each other more vehemently than the others.

"We say if you don't know who to suspect, you suspect everyone," one man declared over the forceful arguments of his opponent.

The man spat at his feet. "Bah! You Poitevins. You suspect each other even when there's nothing to suspect."

The insulted man reached for his sword. The others rushed to restrain him. The gathering dissolved into heckling accusations and equally heated disclaimers edging closer to violence with each shout.

Separated by his friends from his opponent, the man backed away . . . and noticed her standing there.

"We have a guest, my lords. Welcome, Lady."

Their quarrel instantly forgotten, the rest of the men faced her as well. From their amazed expressions, Juliana could tell that they did not know what to make of a young woman, much less one not from these parts, in a pilgrim's cloak, a wrinkled wimple, a young boy by her side. Juliana instinctively placed her hand on Wink's shoulder. The boy drew himself up to lend prominence to his mistress's dignity.

It was then that the one man who had ignored the commotion around him and remained leaning over the table with his fists planted wide on the parchments, looked up. He jerked upright.

"*Saint Vierge.* What . . . what are you . . . ? Eleanor. Where's Eleanor?"

"Armand took her."

And there it was: three simple words, and a voyage of a thousand leagues across an ocean of tears.

They waited until the others left the chamber with their tempers cooled and curiosity keen. The men filed past her and Juliana withstood their examination of her, her own emotions fraying with their every speculative scrutiny. In her inattention, Wink had wandered away, and she could not gather herself fast enough to prevent him. She had expected . . . what did she expect of the man who remained in the chamber?

Did she expect him to drop to his knee with a plea for forgiveness or to gather her in his arms and kiss her until her neck cricked and her toes tingled? He did neither. He did not even approach her. He stood there instead, wanting her to take measure of him.

She did. The strangeness of him came not only from the new gambeson in black *cendal* brocaded with silver thread, but from his composure, the composure of someone surrounded by those he did not trust. Had she noticed it because she knew him so well or so little? What else did the others see? Someone who would not stand out among the native-born either by the color of his hair or complexion, only perhaps by the color of his eyes, as tall as some but not others. For all that, his bearing would have told his rank even had he still dressed like a common *routier.*

"How did he . . . I left men to guard you and Eleanor." His voice strained with the effort at self control.

"I . . . I surrendered her. Armand would have killed them."

"What?"

"I–"

Lasalle's fist landed on a pedestal that held a vase of some antiquity. The vase toppled, shattering on the floor. "That's what they pledged! To die for their liege."

"But . . . but surrender is not a defeat."

He took a step toward her, his voice low and deceptively calm, echoing his father's so unmistakably that she shuddered. "You stupid . . . You gave up before you've even fought. You could have won. For Christ's sake, you're my wife. My wife. Will you ever understand what that means?"

Of all the possible reunions Juliana had imagined, such a one she had not. An overpowering urge to strike him seized her, strike him the way she struck that impudent man in Limassol. No, she would not lower herself to that again. "Oh, yes, I have learned well what that means." She curtsied with scornful disdain. "My lord."

A look flashed across his face, the same look he once gave to a *routier* who made the mistake of questioning him. The man did not know that the only question on his master's part was whether he should flog or hang him for it.

He took a step toward her. Juliana's feet grew into the marble under them. He stood so close that her neck cricked to look up at him, into his eyes, narrow and hard and ferine. "Now say it as if you mean it, Juliana."

Blood surged to her head. Here, in private, he demanded her surrender when none of it mattered but to him. She curtsied deeply and carefully in her ship-dank gown with the bitterest of thorough submissions. "My lord."

And one day, passion and love simply vanish. She picked up her skirts, what was left of her dignity, and turned on her heel. She had nothing and no one to seek on this island anymore. But for Saint Mary's and Wink, she had no one to aid her here either.

CHAPTER 15

Juliana walked out of the chamber trembling and so dizzy that she became instantly disoriented. She leaned against a pillar to collect herself. Something had changed about him. This place had changed him. No, perhaps it only brought back who he truly was.

She could not think of that now. She had to find Wink.

Except that finding Wink in this maze of a place proved to be difficult. She could hardly ask the servants if they had seen an urchin boy poking about their corridors. Besides, they probably would not understand her.

After a spurt of fruitless searching, Juliana lowered herself onto a marble slab of a bench in defeat, exhaustion replacing her previous burst of resolve. Oh Lord, she had abandoned Eleanor for this? And worse yet, what if she were wrong? Should she have let them fight for her, for Eleanor?

No, she must not cry. She must not despair. She must think about the one person who depended on her here now. Next time she would hang a goat bell on that boy. No, that was not Wink, the man approaching her.

The man's graying fair hair gave him a leonine appearance at odds with the wreath of fish strung through their gills in his hand, his *cotte* stained with their blood and smeared with their scales.

He had that solid handsomeness which years grant to certain men and hardly ever to women. Juliana smoothed her skirts and straightened her veil. He had to be one of the king's senior household knights, supplementing his supper with a fresh catch. The man tilted his head, examining her.

"Lady, have you lost your way?"

Such a simple question and in French, thankfully. After her prior encounter, Juliana nearly laughed with relief. "Yes, I have lost my way."

"Have you now." The man slowly drew nearer to sit at the end of the bench. He dropped the fish between his feet and rubbed his hands on his knees. "Breams. I get half a dozen for a penny," he said as if to share a secret. "A fishwife from Kyrenia saves me the best ones. Her husband doesn't know. I have to sneak them past the guards. So you've lost your way. I've lost my way many times. I usually find it again. Or I think I do."

After her encounter with Lasalle, this man's soothing manner eased Juliana's agitation. "So did I."

"Ah." The man nodded thoughtfully. "Then we have something in common. Tell me how you came to be lost. Maybe we can help each other."

She should have kept her own counsel, but what harm could it do to confide in a stranger? And so she told him about coming to the island in search of her husband, for her daughter's sake. A daughter he had abandoned to save a teetering Lusignan crown. *A serpent's crown.* The man would not fully understand, but he did listen, encouraging her with nods of sympathy.

"A teetering crown, you say. So the king lured your husband here to prop it up, did he? What do you think the king ought to do?" he asked when Juliana's recital drifted into an awkward silence.

"I don't know. It's his crown, isn't it?" She hesitated, afraid to ask the question the encounter with Lasalle had wedged into her conscience. "Should I have let them fight? They could have all died. Do you think I was wrong?"

"Your husband's men knew their duty to protect you and all that is his. Can you not forgive him for trusting you to let them do so?"

That did not sound like a criticism of Lasalle. "But they could have died."

"It's difficult to trust to chance, isn't it? But what is life without it?"

Juliana did not want to hear that answer. No, this man could not understand a woman's view either and she knew why. Men like him wanted to fight. Not as their duty, but because it was in their very marrow.

"What do you intend to do? Do you have a place for the night?" The man said when she offered no reply.

"Sister Vigilantia offered me refuge at Saint Mary's, bless her. She came to be the abbess there. She is not very . . . kindly, but I was not a very good student when she tried to teach me Greek words," Juliana acknowledged. "Like *poulains* and *paroikoi* . . . and *prodotis*." She did not know why she said that so she stammered, "But I forgot already what the last one meant." She was lying about that, good Lord, and to a man who had been kind to her.

The man's eyebrow went askew. "Hmm. An abbess, you say. And she speaks Greek, does she?"

Obviously, the man did not understand Greek either. Juliana wanted to tell him about Sister Vigilantia, but from across the courtyard half a dozen servants appeared with that man Niketas behind them. As soon as he saw them, her knight picked up his fish and stood. "Ay. No rest for the wicked. I must leave you, Lady Juliana, but fear not. A way will be found."

Juliana watched him head away the servants and even hand over his fish to them. She smiled to herself. This time his resourcefulness had caused him to neglect his guard duty and now he had to give up his catch for it. She did not have the time to thank him either for his kindness, and she did not even know his name. And she still had not found Wink.

Where could that boy be? Forcing her legs to carry her, Juliana resumed her search among marble columns so thick she could not span them, down corridors that led to others, through terraces and gardens. Servants going about their duties passed her, but none of them asked her whether she had lost her way.

She followed a passage leading to a courtyard enclosed on one side by forged bars. As soon as she entered it, the smell of blood, raw flesh, and animal musk assaulted her nose. Out of the corner of her eye she caught something moving and what sounded like a deep, sinister purr. The sound of it stopped her dead.

From behind a potted shrub emerged a beast the shape of a cat the size of which she had never seen, black-spotted over a light rusty coat. The tip of its tail as long as its lithe body curved elegantly. Around its neck the animal wore a jeweled collar. The beast moved with graceful leisure on saucer-sized paws. At the sight of her, the irises of its oval, green-gold eyes widened but the animal passed by her with feline disdain. Another such beast followed it. Over the lean-muscled hump of its shoulders, the cat's companion gave her an equally disinterested glance.

Juliana would have crossed herself but she dared not move. This is how Christian martyrs must have felt before being thrown to such beasts.

A man's low voice, not unlike the cats' rasp, came from not far behind her. "They won't hurt you. They are kept hungry only when Aimary hunts with them."

A flare of resurrected fury set her teeth on edge. She refused to turn around. Had he followed her or had he chanced upon her? She would keep to the essentials of the situation. "I see."

"They are leopards. There is a third one somewhere."

He had not followed her for the purposes of explaining to her the king's hunting habits, as if she cared for Aimary de Lusignan or any others of that breed. She already knew that she had to be careful around the half-tamed things that inhabited this land.

There was the third leopard. A man as black as night held it by its collar. The man wore finer livery than the ordinary servants, his eyes and teeth shone white in his face, a collar similar to the cats' hung loosely around his neck. The Ethiopian held the cat with both hands to keep the animal from breaking away. Juliana took a step back. The man laughed. "Zoë only play. She no eat you, Lady. You no sheep."

"I will take that as a compliment," Juliana said, retreating nevertheless.

The leopard keeper laughed again, allowing himself to be pulled along. "You too skinny for her. You eat!"

When the keeper and the beast disappeared after the others, Juliana had no choice but to confront her human menace. She did not care to look into eyes so similar in colors to the cats', and she did not have to, thanks to Lasalle's hand on Wink's nape. Having been in such a predicament before, Wink did not look all that distressed. Under his arm, he clutched to him a bundle wrapped in a greasy cloth.

Lasalle dragged Wink on his tiptoes to her. "Is he yours? He was stealing from the kitchens. He said it was for you."

Juliana did not like the inquisitorial tone and she did not intend to spend a moment longer in that man's presence, let alone grant him any courtesy. She pried Wink and his kitchen loot from his captor. "Yes, he's mine."

Lasalle noticed her lack of matrimonial submission but this time did not demand it. "How in Hell's blazes did you end up here?"

It was a question from an owner whose sheep had blundered into the company of wolves, or in this case, leopards. Her hand firmly on Wink's arm, Juliana shepherded her own stray away. "I was searching for my way."

"And where do you think you are going?"

"To the sisters at Saint Mary's."

"What? Wait." That came with an indrawn breath of extreme annoyance.

Juliana did not care. "I will not. I don't intend to wander around at night in a place packed to the rafters with drunkenness and lechery."

"The king's orders take precedence over your desire to avoid drunkenness and lechery. Unless indulged in by us, I imagine. You are to stay put."

He was being his awful self, just to get her goat. She would not give him the satisfaction. Not ever. She quickened her steps. "The king can hardly order me to stay put. He knows nothing of me."

"He does now. You've confessed to his minnows."

CHAPTER 16

No matter how objectionable, a king's order cannot be easily countermanded.

In the current case, two recipients of such an order shared the same sentiment about it, albeit for different reasons. Since neither one of them could do anything about it, they shared that in common, too. That, their invalid marriage, and the daughter engendered from it.

After being ushered into the king's presence and formally introduced, Juliana wished she had not bared her soul to a man with minnows. She wished that she had paid more attention to Sister Vigilantia's lessons, she wished she had never left Eleanor, she wished she had let Rannulf de Brissard challenge Armand de Lusignan's men, she wished she had never . . .

"It appears my teetering crown doesn't need propping up as much as your marriage does, sir. You are to devote yourself to your wife. And you, Lady Juliana, ought to devote yourself to your husband. I'd say he has not received much female devotion lately." Aimary de Lusignan said with a great deal of relish and a hint of impatience. He dipped his hands in a bowl held out for him by a servant and wiped them with a napkin handed by another. "Ah, here they come."

On a platter and dressed in lemons and parsley, the minnows made their formal appearance. Aimary de Lusignan rubbed his hands. "Ah, my breams. I would invite you to share, but I've waited for these, and I intend to have every one. Now go and celebrate your reunion."

"I am not leaving Nikosia." Since he had his back to her, Juliana could not see Lasalle's expression but she could tell gritted teeth.

Juliana did not say a thing, being occupied by her embarrassment. The table's platters occupied Wink. Juliana prayed silently for the royal silver's safety.

Aimary de Lusignan extracted the fish bones with expertise. "I am not sending you anywhere. Niketas has your chamber prepared. Lady Juliana, it would give me great pleasure, when you have recovered from your travels, to hear about Poitou. Lately I seem to miss that place. I last laid my eyes on it thirty years ago. I am getting old."

Juliana curtsied. "Yes, Sire."

"And it would please me if among us you'd call me uncle."

"Yes, Sire."

Aimary de Lusignan laughed. "You're not what I imagined, Lady Juliana. Not what I imagined at all."

Juliana did not know what to make of that comment. The twitch along Lasalle's jaw spoke loudly. A servant made his silent appearance at the door. Juliana curtsied to Aimary who waved her away with a final grin. Without a grin, Lasalle bowed to the king and indicated that she should lead. Juliana swung her skirts past him. "Come along, Wink."

Wink gave his mistress's husband a distrustful look and sprung to his place at her heels. A heavy hand yanked him back. Hunching his shoulders against a blow that did not come, Wink hugged his kitchen loot and took up the rear.

The servant led them through the corridors to a hefty chamber door. The two guards there opened it for them. Wink was about to follow his mistress but that man slammed the door in his face. Wink backed away to the laughter of the guards. Used to being laughed at, Wink pricked up his ears for the voices behind the door. He heard the voice of Lady Juliana protesting his ban. He could not hear her husband's answers, but hers came loud enough.

"He stays with me. I will not have him . . . Wink's my . . . what are you doing?"

Wink waited but no more sound came. Shoulders hunched, he curled himself on the floor next to an alcove with the image of a strange creature in it. These people had churches, so it probably was not the Devil. Still, he crossed himself. Husbands had rights to their wives. Maybe Saint Anne would not let the lady be too badly treated.

Lasalle dropped her to her feet, ending her useless struggle. Burning with humiliation and determined not to show it, Juliana tidied her skirts thoroughly before she looked about.

A tub of pink marble filled with steaming water and large enough for delfines to frolic in took up a part of a chamber. Painted columns held up its ceiling and delicate mosaics on the walls transformed the room into the interior of a polished jewel. Next to the tub waited three young women swathed in white gauzes, their hair dripping attractively against their shoulders, a trained smile on their lips. One girl held an iridescent beaker of soap or oil, the other bath linen, the third an armful of gowns.

From behind the columns appeared more maids, giggling and laughing. Several of them surrounded Lasalle to push him backward through the door whence he had carried her. Before the others swamped Juliana, she noted that he had retreated without objection. Before she could regain her bearing, they attacked her, untying, unwrapping, and unwinding her out of her cloak, gown, and wimple.

Chirping louder than a flock of stable sparrows, the maids' voices indicated dismay at the state of her hands, her nails, her tangled hair and peeling skin. A heifer at Parthenay's market would not receive as thorough an appraisal. When they reached for her shift's laces, Juliana tried to swat away their hands. "No. Don't. Please."

She would not allow these strangers to see her naked. She was quite capable of taking a bath by herself. The young women did not heed her objections, pointing to the tub and chattering as if to explain to her the entire idea of bathing. "No. Thank you. No. Please don't. I–"

A sea of Greek syllabics drowned her protestations. Her shift ripped under the onslaught of eager hands. Oh! Juliana tried to hold on to what modesty her shift offered. What would Sister Vigilantia say to make them stop?

"*Sopa!*"

Hands flew from her person to lips rounded in shock, then a few giggles spurted here and there, but the maids backed away, curtseying.

"That ought to teach the domestics not to trifle with the viscountess of Tillières." Lasalle stood at the opened door, barefooted, no longer in what he wore in the council chambers, but in a white robe down to his ankles topped by a lose black garment edged with red embroidery. The silver loop of his earring glinted through his hair. He was a deposed Byzantine prince and a Saracen, all wrapped into one, and she hated him for it.

The maids bobbed in a curtsey with that annoying sound silly young women make in the presence of certain men. Instead of acknowledging them, Lasalle sent the entire flock from the bath chamber. Juliana snatched up her gown and held it to her. "What did I say?"

"You told them to be silent, and not politely. After you pummeling the customs clerk, the gossip ought to be deafening."

Now he had accused her of disgracing herself–and him. "I didn't pummel him. And I only wanted them to stop."

"And they did. You'll have to take your own bath. When you are done, call for the women."

"Wait. Where is Wink?"

"Safe with Djalali."

"And who's that?"

"The leopard keeper."

Forgetting her precarious attire, Juliana took a step toward him. "I wish Wink back. And my trunk. My other gown is in it and . . . and other things."

He said, as if talking to an imbecile, "Niketas ordered your trunk brought here. The mules returned to Limassol. You've heard Aimary. You and I are to stay put."

"I will not. I don't trust anyone here."

"Good. I trust only two people on this island."

"And who would that be? Niketas?"

"Lord, no. Djalali."

"I see." She knew who the other one would be. *The mistress.* "And Aimary, I suppose."

"What an idea, Lady Juliana."

That surprised her enough to say, "Why not?"

"He's a Lusignan."

Enough of an explanation, surely. "I see. Who else here would you trust?"

"You."

Many wives would find that disclosure flattering. Unfortunately, to be trusted is to bear another's expectations. Having borne Guérin de Lasalle a daughter he had abandoned the moment his family whistled, Juliana did not think she owed him anything anymore. Considering his latest treatment of her, that sounded like sarcasm, too. "I see," she therefore said.

Lasalle noted the number of those 'I sees.' Juliana de Charnais had exchanged her suppositions for suspicion and although she would most adamantly deny it, she was turning into a Poitevin.

That did not bode well for his plan, concocted between the time she appeared at the door of the council chamber and the time Aimary de Lusignan told him, grimacing with some sympathy, about her confession to him. By then his temper had cooled enough to regret what he had said to her. He did not expect her to understand how she had frightened him and hoped that he had pulled back in time from the irrevocable.

"You must be very tired," he said. "The women will bring you food and whatever else you need."

"They won't understand me."

"You'll have a nurse who does."

"Oh, what's her name?"

"Morphia."

And that was my lord Lasalle's last word to her, delivered conclusively with the loud click of the hefty door's lock.

The nights spent on the *Regina* had made her a light sleeper. Lying still, Juliana opened her eyes just so. Several silver lamps, burnished and pierced, cast a muted glow over the chamber. She was alone in a grand Venetian bed with enough trimmings to sail a galley, but not alone in the room.

He had folded himself into the window's alcove, his knees drawn up, his face averted to the range of the *Pentadaktylos* emerging from the dusk. Juliana held her breath to watch him. He wore what he had in the council chamber, his outstretched arm resting on his knee, his hair, longer than she remembered, curled here and there.

Sensing her awake, he turned his head toward her. Now she saw the shadows under his eyes, the angle of his cheekbone. She did not know how long he had been there or what to make of his presence just as she did not know what to make of his trusting her. She would not trust him, not ever.

"It's past Lauds."

Juliana sat up. Islands of low, dainty tables inlaid with mother-of-pearl, cushioned seats and more pillows, mattresses and bolsters of fabrics the color of peacock feathers surrounded her. Carpets spilled over floors of mosaics so fine that the designs appeared painted. Fresh blossoms in vases found their imitation rendered on walls in colored marble, vivid pigments, and semi-precious stones–lapis lazuli, jasper, jacinth, and amber glittered in the oil flame.

The unfettered opulence of her surroundings only dismayed her. She had not noticed any of it last night since fatigue overtook her the moment she climbed out of the tub. She had fallen asleep without calling her new maid. What was her name?

Thankfully, she had fallen asleep in her shift from her sea trunk Niketas had sent to her, just as Lasalle said. At least he did not lie about that. "So it is. Whose chambers are these?"

"The queen's. Yours. Ours."

Juliana noted the amendment. "Won't Isabella mind sharing them?"

She thought he smiled. "No. Isabella never comes to Cyprus. She spends her time in Acre with the children. Aimary comes to Cyprus because of Hugh. He wants him to learn how to rule this place."

"I see," Juliana said without the slightest interest in the education of boy princes. She cleared away the pillows. Where had she left her shoes? "How do I secure passage for Wink and myself to Marseille without Aimary finding out about it?"

Lasalle sat up. "Marseille?"

Juliana ignored the incredulous tone. "That way he can't blame you. I will ask Sister Vigilantia to lend me the money."

Lasalle swung himself to the floor. "The storms are coming. There won't be any ships leaving these harbors for Marseille until spring."

She rooted about and found her shoes. "There has to be a ship to Constantinople or Venice or Genoa. From there we will travel overland or by another ship to Marseille. Messengers and merchants must take those routes without waiting for pilgrim ships."

He said very patiently, "Pirates will take any ship the storms miss. Those men know the risks."

"So do I. I am not afraid of pirates."

Lasalle rose from the alcove, his tone one of strained patience. "They carried away Aimary's first wife from Famagusta. He had to ransom her. If the queen of this island can be carried away, what makes you think you have special protection? Constantinople is looted and half abandoned. With that hair, you'll be sold from one master to another until you are too worn to turn millstones."

She sat on the nearest mound of cushions and tied her shoes as decisively as her determination. "You can't frighten me, my lord. Never again will I abandon Eleanor."

He sat on the edge of one of the short-legged tables. The table's height gave him the appearance of a schoolboy who had outgrown his place. Before she could prevent it, he took hold of her hand and held it, eyes downcast. "Listen. I promise that I will return with you on the first galley. But if you try to leave now, you'll be locked in these apartments until then."

Juliana twisted herself free. "You promised and you left us."

He looked up, no hint of compromise in his eyes or his voice. "This is not meant to be a punishment, Juliana. You don't know what you have done. This world plays by its own rules, and your presence here makes matters very difficult for a number of people."

Difficult? How dare he. He was not a mother, he could never understand what drove her across the seas. And how dare he call her stupid and ignorant after the calamity that he had brought on her and Eleanor. Juliana stood up. "That seems to be my lot in life. But I will not abandon Eleanor just because her father did!"

He lunged. She flung herself backward to get out of his reach and ended up sprawled among the pillows with his fist on her shift at her throat, his knee between hers, all done in one move by a man used to using force.

She had seen those specks of imperfection in the irises of his eyes, and knew what had followed. This time Guérin de Lasalle could not frighten her. She had Eleanor.

She raised herself on her elbows to meet those eyes, her voice so calm she surprised herself. "Go ahead. You play for your Lusignan crown. A serpent's crown."

He did not let her go, not at once, but then he went back on his heels and said, equally calmly, "Do you truly think that I wanted to leave you?"

Juliana picked herself up with a semblance of decorum. The morning light filled the chamber. Ignoring the fabrics and exquisite patterns of the gowns someone had laid out for her, she tripped her way to her trunk and opened it.

Someone had searched it. They had not folded her gown properly. Her other gown. They had searched it on Lasalle's orders. "Only you know why you did, my lord. Please call my maid. What is her name? I don't want to mispronounce it. No wonder Aimary didn't tell me what *prodotis* means."

"What?" He was on his feet as well.

"*Prodotis*. It sounded like it. I suppose it's not polite either."

His hand on her shoulder twisted her to face him. "Who said it?"

"Sister Vigilantia. That's what she called your mistress."

The gaze became narrower, the tone exasperated. "What mistress?"

She turned her back on him. "The one at Kolossi. We were not introduced. She seems to be a woman of means."

"What the–? Rhoxsane? She is not my mistress. Besides, she's a poisoner."

An odd defense against an accusation of adultery, surely, but then Guérin de Lasalle always took a pragmatic view of his mistresses. Juliana shook out her gown; not one to compete with the ones laid out for her, but at least it was her own. She wriggled herself into it. She could ask him to help her lace it, but a maid would accomplish it without the possible implication of intimacy. *Morphia.* The woman's name was Morphia. "Is she? Well, then, what does *prodotis* mean?"

He hesitated and then he told her.

CHAPTER 17

She's beautiful for such a deadly creature, isn't she? Some females are like that." Inside the opened cage, Aimary de Lusignan rubbed the leopard's ear.

A puddle of blood and a mangled sheep's head with the rack of spine still attached was all that remained from the leopards' supper. Pressing her head into his hand, the cat answered with a deep purr. The boy Wink squatted outside the cage listening intently to Djalali's whispered explanations of the cat's every twitch.

Her two companions lounged against the side of their cage, grooming their lethal claws. Lasalle knew what it felt like to be caught in claws–only they belonged to the man petting the leopardess. Aimary grinned up at him. "The reunion not all that reuniting, eh? There is always Rhoxsane. What do you say?"

"*Prodotis.*"

Aimary's grin went away. He brushed the cat's hair from his surcoat and nodded for Djalali to secure the cage. "Are you referring to me or the lady?"

"I don't know."

"Ah," Aimary sighed with a hint of guilt, "I suppose I ought to have told you, but I didn't know until your wife mentioned a nun who spoke Greek and called Rhoxsane a traitor." He chuckled. "Where is your charming lady?"

"She intended to return to Poitou by way of Constantinople. I don't think I frightened her enough with the prospect of pirates, so I locked her in the apartments."

Aimary waved his hand. "*Neh.* Let her out. Niketas said she doesn't have the money to hire a mule to Kyrenia."

Lasalle kept his temper with the greatest effort. "She will if she goes to Saint Mary's and gets it."

Aimary rubbed his chin. "Hmm. Would she now? Very well, let's have a chat with our good Sister."

Having miraculously escaped Saladín's seizure of Jerusalem, the valiant sisters of the Benedictine Abbey of Our Lady of Tyre found refuge on the island of Cyprus. There they resumed their devotions and their work caring for female pilgrims, although in the recent years far fewer of them needed care in the abbey's infirmary and hostel. As a result, Saint Mary's had settled itself quietly and comfortably among the gardens and mansions of Nikosia's current residents.

The arrival of the king with only one companion resulted in the excited patter of feet, the rustle of robes, and doors opened and latched. Without requiring the visitors to surrender their swords, the agitated gate mistress led them directly to the chapter house.

Ducking through the door behind Aimary, Lasalle crossed himself. He had not fared well in encounters with abbesses, novices, and nuns, and he did not expect that his luck would change in Cyprus.

He did not expect this nun to be old, and she was not. Her eyes, dark and luminous, looked directly at the visitors. She had expected them sooner or later. Abbess Vigilantia addressed Aimary without acknowledging Lasalle's existence. "You honor us by your presence, Your Grace."

Aimary opened his arms in a pretense of a familial embrace.

"There you are, Eirene. I knew it was you. What a surprise to find you back on this island. And as a nun. Are you certain of your current profession? And may I present my nephew somewhat removed you're so diligently ignoring? You two have something in common. His name is Jean Armand de Lusignan, but he prefers to be called Guérin de Lasalle." He turned to Lasalle. "This lady is Eirene Dukas, but she prefers to be called Vigilantia now. She's Isaak's daughter and would be the queen of this island if I didn't already own it. Wouldn't you, Eirene?"

Few things surprised Lasalle, but he would count this as one of them. Despite the introduction, the abbess did not deign to acknowledge him, but Aimary's gesture had dented her composure. "I said that I would return."

With a sigh of disappointment, Aimary hitched up his sword belt and took a seat in the sisters' wall stall. "So you did. What happened to your fool of a husband?"

"He died."

"Ha!" Aimary struck his fist against his knee. "And you became a nun? Why?"

Vigilantia's hand went to the crucifix on her bosom. "I will not be the means for men's ambitions. I am under the protection of the Church. I wish to live out what days remain to me where I was born."

Aimary would have none of it. "I do wish I could believe you, but you couldn't resist calling that Kolossi woman a traitor, could you? What do you think you were doing? The whole country will be buzzing with it."

"I said that I will not be the means for men's ambition."

Aimary gave the woman careful scrutiny. "As long as you don't have ambitions of your own."

"I am an emperor's daughter."

The king broke into a hoot of laughter. "Lady, you are the daughter of a renegade, despised by his own people."

The nun's eyes flashed. "And by what right but the sword are you king here, my lord de Lusignan?"

Aimary stood up, fists to his hips. "By the sword and by the decree of the Staufen Emperor. We came to this land to drive out the Musulmans while your ancestors bribed them with tribute. Besides," he shrugged, "we bought this place from King Richard. We paid good money for it. Now. My nephew has a favor to ask of you."

The woman gave Lasalle the look of an empress contemplating a horse groom, waiting for him to speak up, so he did. "I wish Saint Mary not to lend passage money to Juliana de Charnais should she come seeking aid."

"And why should Saint Mary turn away a young woman in dire need of aid?" Vigilantia responded with more than a hint of hostility.

Lasalle tried not to respond in kind. "She is not in dire need of aid. She is my wife."

"Precisely."

Aimary's hand landed on Lasalle's shoulder before he could take a step toward the nun. "Now, now, let us not quarrel. We're after all in the same boat, aren't we? If a word gets out that you are back on this island, who knows what these gullible Griffons might do. Another rebellion would be a bad thing. It would be a shame to force my hand. It would be an even greater shame if my successor did not hold to the same policy, wouldn't it."

Abbess Vigilantia smiled, but not confidently. "Hugh is young and easily led. I am informed he favors his mother's kin."

Aimary leaned forward, his conciliatory mood gone. "I wouldn't cast my lot with the Ibelíns just because you bear us a grudge, Eirene. You don't know for certain that Hugh will succeed me, do you? I suggest that you live up to your current name. Now. Grant him his request."

The two opponents sized up each other. Lasalle held his tongue, waiting. Vigilantia nodded to him, contempt replacing hostility. "Your wish is granted, my lord. But remember. A traitor will always be a traitor. One will be forced to deal with such sooner or later."

Aimary answered for him. "Let me worry about Rhoxsane. You have here sureties for her good manners. So, that's settled. As for the other problem, what do we do about it?"

Abbess Vigilantia curtsied with exaggerated submission. "You mistake my intentions, Your Grace. I have no desire to see my home troubled. Saint Mary will pray for your reign to be a long one."

"I can almost believe you, Reverend Mother," His Grace said to that one.

CHAPTER 18

A ship lost in a storm . . . delfines with the ghostly faces of children rising toward the surface, the shrill wail of Mélusine issuing from their gaping mouths. . . .

Juliana bolted up. Such vivid dreams. She reached for her cross and pressed it to her lips. *Eleanor, Eleanor.* Another day of separation faced her. From the cot by the door came a muffled sound. Juliana pulled the covers over her head and buried herself deeper in the grand bed to escape Morphia's sighs and sobs.

Her new nurse came with a row of tight curls that propped up a staggeringly structured wimple, a pair of hedgehog's round eyes, and a perpetually flushed face. When vertical, Morphia moved across the floors like a wheeled siege tower, thanks to the layers of her skirts. After introducing herself, in French, and becoming overcome with gratitude at being chosen to be Lady Juliana's nurse, Morphia burst into tears when Juliana enquired, for conversation's sake, after the health of Morphia's husband.

"Murdered, foully murdered, like the saint that he was. We must be careful, my lady, and lock our door every night. I don't trust the guards, sots that they are. Leontios was a saint, a saint I tell you, my lady."

Juliana apologized profusely, and the first time she had listened, politely and attentively, to Morphia's panegyric to her husband. She even inquired as to who "they" might be, but tender emotions again overcame Morphia. Days later, when Leontios's name inadvertently came up again, for the fourth time, and again rendered Morphia inconsolable, Juliana settled her among the cushions and leaving a ewer full of wine to restore her, fled the chamber to wander about the gardens.

Lasalle had informed her that the queen's chambers no longer needed to serve as her prison because he had made certain that her appeal to the sisters of Saint Mary's would not be granted. Juliana reminded him that her prison did not consist of the queen's apartments, but of the island on which they stood, and from which he had deprived her of an exit. They parted on no better terms.

At least she had made the acquaintance of Father Silbo, a young, talkative priest who tutored Prince Hugh, and heard her confession. Father Silbo brought her books. What joy those were—but his first duty was to teach Hugh, although Father Silbo took it far more to heart than his pupil, he confided to her with a sigh.

To cheer her, some days after morning prayers, Morphia invited Juliana to visit the wives of the Franks and *poulains* residing in Nikosia.

The women lived in various degrees of splendor surrounded by flocks of servants and children, and their native cooks offered tables of splendid fare. The unaccustomed dishes intimidated Juliana as much as they dazzled her palette but she sampled them all, to the delight of her hostesses.

She tackled tangy goat cheeses; all manner of fish swimming in sauces; grilled flesh of goats, lambs and all kinds of birds; stews composed with the ubiquitous olives; succulent meats wrapped in grape leaves and seasoned with thyme and rosemary; lentils ground into paste with mint and nuts; flat, warm bread to be dipped in olive oil rather than spread with butter; bowls of figs, raisins, and apricots; almond and sesame pastries coated in date paste or soaked in honey; and strong wines flavored with juice of pomegranates.

Only when a nurse brought out the latest gurgling, blubbering, smiling or screaming infant for Juliana to admire, could she barely keep herself from bursting into tears. The women clucked in sympathy when she told them of her separation from her own daughter, and assured her that she would soon have another to hold. They whispered to her about the Virgin *Trooditissa* and her shrine in the mountains many of them had visited to offer prayers for a child. Juliana forced herself to smile and to thank them for their advice.

Such innocent excursions did not go unnoticed for long. One afternoon, no sooner had they returned from their latest visit than Niketas arrived at the queen's apartments in full fluster. He threw sharp words at Mistress Morphia who promptly dissolved into tears, and insisted that, considering the lady Juliana's position, henceforth whenever outside the walls of the palace, she must be accompanied not only by servants but by men-at-arms that he personally chose.

"I would be derelict, absolutely derelict in my duty to my lord de Lusignan, your husband, Lady Juliana," Niketas added as if to remind her who her lord was.

Niketas's cheeks so quivered at the gravity of her transgression that Juliana found herself apologizing to him. Niketas accepted her apologies graciously. Morphia showed far less graciousness, and after the assignment of their guards, she only reluctantly agreed to step outside the palace walls. By contrast, having glimpsed sights of the island, Juliana developed a curiosity about the place–if only to discover how to escape from it.

After all, did not Saint Augustine urge one to travel?

Above the market day crowd loomed four riders on camels, the oddest creatures Juliana had ever seen. She had finally persuaded Morphia to visit the market to break what was becoming a routine of her existence. Their new guards accompanied them with a display of professional diligence Juliana suspected to be a pretense for Morphia's benefit.

Camels usually carried hide sacks of copper from the ancient mines in the mountains, salt from the salt lakes at Limassol, and burdens of every kind to and from the sea ports. Bedecked in trappings of red and yellow tassels, these beasts by their majestic gait resembled the roll of a ship in calm seas. With their sheep-like heads, mobile lips, and demure eyelashes, their comical appearance amused Juliana. Surely the Lord had created these creatures for His amusement.

The riders atop of them did not seem the least disparaged by their mounts. They sat proud-backed, cast in black robes from head to foot, a thin cloth drawn up to their glittering eyes, a striking sight even among people from the far corners of the world. Several equally habited riders followed them on finely bred horses, their manes flowing free, polished hooves dancing on the pavement, tassels flying from the breast straps and browbands like the frills of pagan temple dancers.

Awed and intimidated by the sight, Juliana tugged at Morphia's sleeve. "Who are they?"

"Oh!" Morphia, who had grumbled and sighed during the entire excursion, came alive. She tossed Juliana's veil over her face and crossed herself. "Don't let them see you, my lady. They are the *bedu*. They can cast the evil eye. They come from the deserts. They raise horses and sheep, and trap wild animals to trade. They rob pilgrims, too, and sell them to slavery. Heavens protect us from them. The king protects them in the Holy Land because they spy for him on the Musulmans."

The world is a book. . . . Through the silk strands of her veil, Juliana saw the foremost horseman turn his head in their direction. Had he heard Morphia's warning? Fear and excitement went through Juliana when the last of the cavorting riders swept past them. Juliana crossed herself as well. Evil-eyed, indeed. In what strange land and among what strange people had the Lord set her path, and to what purpose?

Despite such occasional excursions, Juliana could not shake bouts of loneliness, the same loneliness that tormented her in Parthenay—and here she could not even speak these people's language. Not that any of the Franks had bothered to learn it. They depended on their bailiffs and dragomen just as she depended on Morphia.

She did not know where Lasalle spent his time, and she did not care. Perhaps he had decided to test the devotion of *the mistress*—traitor and poisoner or not. At least Lasalle's absence lifted Wink's self-imposed responsibility of being her protector from his shoulders. At first worried about Wink, Juliana noted that Djalali's calm, gentle manner with the spotted cats extended to Wink, and the boy sought out the keeper's company at every opportunity.

In Parthenay she had her chatelaine's onerous duties—the laundry and the larder, mending and the morals of her charges, her garden, and Eleanor. Here servants carried out their duties with religious regularity. Yet Juliana could not banish the sensation that behind the quotidian routines, something crept silently along the corridors, something alive and menacing, like a hungry leopard carelessly let loose.

CHAPTER 19

Limassol

Displaying the dignity of a royal dromond, Rhoxsane sailed into the room past the guards who eyed her as if she were a common whore their master usually favored. Her arrival did not sit well with the man who had waited impatiently for her. The unpleasant thought occurred to her that she had been too hasty to hitch her fortunes to this ally. They were alone.

"You are tardy. Do not keep me waiting again." He seated himself in the only chair and flung his cloak over his knee with the gesture of a man who wished to be accorded the respect due a pontiff.

Rhoxsane removed her veil, intended to keep her anonymous during her ride from Kolossi. "I could not evade Darius and his men any sooner, my lord—"

"Here I am known to you as Lord Makheras, remember?"

She curtsied, deeply. "Of course, my lord."

Pleased, if not entirely mollified, Lord Makheras tapped his foot. "What news then, tell me."

Rhoxsane walked to the window overlooking the harbor. A couple of fishermen's boats bobbed next to a small galley, the flag of the House of Ibelín hanging limply from its mast. "Was it wise to land under that banner?"

"Of course it was wise. It was my decision. Or have you sold your loyalty once again?"

If he expected her to protest her current loyalties, Rhoxsane did not intend to oblige him. Unlike a fool, a traitor could always become useful. "I have no news from our ally except for what you already know, my lord. We expected the Lord of Parthenay to be troublesome."

"You mean the lord of your Kolossi," Lord Makheras reminded her with malicious glee, "And his wife?"

Rhoxsane ignored the glee and the correction, but wavered about whether or not she ought to be forthright in the matter. "Much too concerned about returning to Poitou to give us trouble. He has arranged for Morphia to wait on her."

Lord Makheras's foot stopped tapping. That was one bit of news he did not expect. "Did he now? Does he know then?"

"If he doesn't, he will," Rhoxsane said evenly.

"Well then, we may have to take very good care of Mistress Morphia before she decides to share her troubles."

Rhoxsane knew that the target of that threat was herself as much as the maudlin Mistress Morphia. "And how would we do that?"

"The same way you took care of your husbands, my dear." Lord Makheras sneered with the impatience of those who did not concern themselves with ants in their path.

Rhoxsane did not intend to be one of the ants. Of course, Lord Makheras did not know that. Yet. "I fear that it would be too soon after Leontios's...accident. Perhaps a warning would give Morphia a reason to mind her words. After all, your men are still about."

As much as Lord Makheras disliked being contradicted, he had to agree. Perhaps prudence at this ticklish time would be a better approach. Who could have expected the reportedly diffident lady Juliana to arrive at these shores to complicate his plans? Now her husband had decided to use this inopportunity to his advantage. He could hardly blame him. "You do know," he said after a pause, "that if you are wrong and Morphia has already unburdened herself, you will have no choice but to act–"

"Of course, my lord."

"–against both of them." He finished and joined her at the window, hip to thigh, as much as her skirts allowed.

Unless it suited her, Rhoxsane did not allow anyone to educe from her a hint of female weakness. She therefore said, mellifluously, "I almost forgot. Lady Juliana did not travel alone. She came in the company of–"

He shoved his hand into her bodice and twisted her to face him. "Sister Vigilantia. I was wondering when you were going to tell me."

Rhoxsane retained her composure under the greedy groping because she had to. After all, she had entered into this alliance willingly. "I thought that you already knew, my lord. From our friend."

"Did you? Niketas has the same reason to keep things to himself that you do, my dear. Wouldn't you agree?"

She held still while he tugged at her gown, and when the stitches did not give, he tore at the fastenings and ties. She would not assist him because she knew that he wanted to take by force rather than receive by consent.

His voice, as tight as his hand in her hair, singed her ear. "Has he had you?"

She remained upright, her eyes fixed on the door behind him against which she knew his men's ears were pressed. "No."

The man who called himself Makheras laughed. "A pity. I would have enjoyed this so much more."

CHAPTER 20

Kyrenia

The small cavalcade traveled to Kyrenia for the king to inspect the progress in fortifying its castle. They rode abreast, the company behind them. Aimary was in a chatty mood.

"You are so like your father, you know," he said, nearly causing Lasalle's horse to bolt when its rider's spurs pricked it.

"He stole my daughter."

Aimary waved his hand. "Bah. It's not like he wants a ransom for her or intends to keep her as surety for you minding your manners, is it? Tell your wife that. She won't forgive Armand but she will forgive you."

"I thought you wanted me to trade her."

"So I did. But I can see now that you're more wedded to her than she is to you. It happened to your father, too. Ah, here we are."

Built long before the ascension of Isaak Dukas, the island's late, self-styled emperor, the walls had not prevented the castle's defenders from surrendering it to Guy de Lusignan when Richard sent him to reduce Kyrenia. Along with his treasury, Isaak had secreted there his wife and daughter, to no greater avail. Guy had attempted to rebuild the damage inflicted during the brief siege, but he died before the completion. Now masons and carpenters toiled to repair the walls and galleries.

Aimary pointed to the donjon. "A certain trusted waiting woman revealed their hiding place to Guy's men. He sent them to Richard. Richard gave her Kolossi for it. As for the mother and daughter . . . well, you know what happened to one of them. I suppose Eirene has a reason to hate us."

Aimary's expression told Lasalle that he knew well how treachery could reduce even the most impregnable fortress and topple the securest of thrones. Instead of heading toward the drawbridge, Aimary spurred his horse on to the harbor where the crew of a nef hoisted its sail. Halting his men at a distance, Aimary reined in and faced him. "This is where we part. I have to return to Acre. I didn't want to tell you because you'd bury me with your objections."

A flock of gulls flapped overhead, startling Lasalle's courser. He fought to keep it and himself under curb. "From this place? Why? You're as much in danger in Acre as here. Stay or take me with you."

"I knew you'd say that. I wear the crowns of two kingdoms. How do you suppose I divide myself to serve both?"

Lasalle swallowed his answer. Aimary's situation resembled so much his own that he knew a reply would be superfluous. Indeed, Aimary waved his hand. "Don't bother. I didn't expect you to know."

Lasalle settled the courser down but not his anger—and fear. "Why return to Acre now?"

"My vassals there like to slip their halters when left alone too long. That's why I sail from this place. Some of them think of themselves as kings, so I'd like to surprise them with the one they already have. I'll have no repetition of the disloyalty Guy faced. It cost him dearly."

That Lasalle knew. Not only the loss of most of his kingdom to the Musulmans, but with the death of his queen and their two young daughters in that fetid camp before the walls of Acre, it cost Guy his posterity as well. Aside from the dangers of the crossing via Kyrenia, the return to Acre could also cost Aimary de Lusignan his life.

"Besides," Aimary said, "I have to pay for their loyalty. I can't give you the money you'll need here to buy information. But I am told that Niketas squirreled away enough from Isaak's treasure to bribe the *Haute Cour* himself. You'll have to figure out how to get some of it from him. Or all. Don't look so glum. I'll give your fondest regards to your brother."

Aimary saluted him and reined about to trot toward the nef, his men following.

Lasalle's courser strained against the bit to join them. He held it back. *You are so like your father.* But it was Aimary's other words that caught his breath. *You're more wedded to her than she is to you.*

When the nef's sail merged with the clouds, he took his horse through the harbor. Markets and harbors traded in information as much as in goods, and in the previous days he had had no difficulty mingling with their population. No one paid attention to a man dressed like a *serjean* wandering through the crowded stalls. Although his ability to speak Greek had not improved since he landed on Cyprus, his understanding had. What he heard gave him cause to worry. He worried especially about a ship flying the Ibelín flag in the harbor at Limassol. *A traitor will always be a traitor.*

He also knew then that he had to swallow his pride, ride back to Nikosia, and ask Saint Mary's to grant aid after all to a certain young woman who had the misfortune of being married to a Lusignan. In return, Abbess Vigilantia would probably exact some appropriately costly favor from him.

After all, he never had much luck with novices or nuns.

Nikosia

"You must be Lady Juliana," said a soft voice.

With her back to her unannounced visitor and concentrating on tidying the vines, Juliana smiled to herself. She became accustomed to having her name prefaced by 'you-must-be,' and even allowed herself a tiny thrill of pleasure at her temporary status of a novelty. "I am."

"I came to see Hugh. I am Burgundia."

The woman, perhaps in her late twenties, stood there, her hand caressing the rose arbor post. She wore a simple yet formal gown, a golden fillet around her temples kept in place a black veil over her braided hair. From the lines around her lips and her eyes, Juliana sensed a certain careworn air about her and at that moment, unease. She once had her father's striking fair looks, but they had almost faded. Yet her eyes, blue like her father's, regarded Juliana forthrightly. As a younger woman, Burgundia de Lusignan would have been a beauty. And she was still a king's daughter.

Juliana executed a curtsey to the princess, trying to recall what Vigilantia had told her about Aimary de Lusignan's eldest daughter. "My lady. Forgive me for invading your gardens. They are the loveliest I have ever seen."

Burgundia smiled and touched a cluster of roses. "A compliment due to my mother, not to me. My husband says I can make dried flowers wilt. And no formalities, please. We are family by marriage, aren't we?"

"Yes, my lady."

"Burgundia, please." The woman touched Juliana's elbow to raise her up from her curtsey. Her tone became urgent. "Let me speak freely–"

"Bourgogne!"

A man's voice boomed through the garden's greenery. At the sound of it, Burgundia flinched, but her smile tried to mask it. They both turned to the source of the noise.

Feet apart, arms akimbo, the man under the arch of the garden gate wore a surcoat of cloth that indicated wealth with details that barely skirted ostentation. Over his shoulder hung a white cloak in the manner of the Temple brothers, but not their badge. He had light brown hair, carefully cut and longer than knights usually wore. His gray eyes sat just close enough to deprive him of a certain *gravitas* that his clothes intended to convey, and as a result his features gave him the look of a half-grown boy in a man's body. An impatient boy.

"This is Lady Juliana de Charnais, my lord. She's been admiring my mother's gardens. Lady Juliana, may I present my husband, Walter de Montbéliard."

Silently thanking Abbess Vigilantia for her lineage lessons, Juliana curtsied with proper care. "My lord Constable."

Pleased to have his title so readily accorded, the man looked her up and down, his original frown becoming a smile of aggressive *bonhomie*. He bowed to her, his voice no less loud. "We've heard of your arrival, Madame. How devoted of you to follow your husband. We must meet him. Where is he?"

That question could not be easily answered. Moreover, Juliana had the impression that the Constable of Jerusalem's question regarding Lasalle's whereabouts was the true purpose of his appearance. Something else told her that equivocation would be the best answer. "He has a number of duties since the king left for Acre. I am not certain which one he's attending to."

She could tell that her answer at once pleased and disappointed Sir Walter.

"Does he, does he now?" Walter de Montbéliard tapped his riding crop against his boot, examining her and mulling over her words, then turned to his wife with benevolent approval. "Lady Juliana is a woman who doesn't meddle in men's affairs. Is that not a refreshing find in these parts, Bourgogne? We are here to see Hugh and for you to pray at Saint Mary's and to the *Trooditissa*, are we not? Let's not keep Lady Juliana from her gardening." He glanced about the flower beds. "Pretty, very pretty roses," he said, and taking his wife by the elbow, ushered her from the garden before Juliana could curtsey.

Juliana sat on the bench, her heart pounding. Walter de Montbéliard's hold on his wife's arm conveyed not only the right of matrimonial intimacy, but also its authority. Vigilantia said that he was Burgundia's second husband. Her first husband . . . Raymond, Count of Toulouse, that famous lecher, repudiating one wife after another. Younger than his wife, Walter called his wife Bourgogne, although she called herself Burgundia. What had Burgundia wanted to tell her before her husband found them, and why did he remove her before she could? Surely Burgundia had a more compelling reason to seek her out than *bavardage* for the sake of their relationship by marriage.

On this island, many an ancient secret lay buried under the detritus of centuries. Juliana did not wish to know the more recent ones. She had to return to Poitou and reclaim Eleanor. Never mind where Lasalle spent his time.

CHAPTER 21

Contemplating the ironies of her situation, Juliana ended up in the corridor leading to the quarters of young Hugh.

No one had bothered to present her to the boy, although she had seen the corpulent ten-year-old in the company of Father Silbo and in the courtyard with his master-of-arms who was trying to teach the boy the use of a sword and shield, both scaled down to Hugh's size. A few awkward swipes at his opponent rendered the boy breathless and efforts to keep him in the saddle of a trotting pony while holding onto a child-sized lance did not bring better results. Juliana felt sorry for him. Hugh the First of Cyprus would not excel in scholarship or the martial arts, at least not under the present regimen.

This time she heard Hugh's voice, high and happy. Outside his quarters paced a man Juliana did not recognize. She instantly worried about that fact, despite Hugh's joy. She ducked behind a column, her veil snaring on a potted laurel. Afraid to retrieve it, Juliana remained still, ears pricked. Hugh's words reassured her, but only somewhat.

"When did you come? Did you see Father in Acre?"

Juliana peeked out to see the man hand Hugh a fat pouch. "Shhh. Not so loud. No one knows I am here, remember? I didn't see him. I brought you something. Here."

The man spoke French with a shade of an accent, like that of some of the *poulains*. Hugh eagerly seized the pouch. "Oh, *kandiq*. But . . . but . . ." Crestfallen, he sighed. "Father won't let me have any."

The man laughed, a deep, self-confident laugh. "He won't know if you don't tell him."

Juliana leaned out a little more to see Hugh's expression. That solution had obviously occurred to Hugh, but his father's wishes weighed against the temptation. Not for long, however. Hugh looked about, his voice an excited whisper. "Wait. I'll hide it from Father Silbo. And I have something to show you. Wait."

The man laughed and sent Hugh off with a wave of his hand and turned to pace. Too late, Juliana ducked behind the column. *Oh Mary*.

Spurs clinked on the floor stones. "It seems we have a spy. Come out, come out, spy."

To remain hidden would have been pointless, so Juliana stepped into the corridor and waited. He was tall, dark-haired and black-eyed, with an olive-tinged complexion. She did not pay much attention to the rest of him because of the sharp, pointed object in his hand.

"What have you heard, girl?"

"I heard a man encouraging a boy to disobey his father and his tutor, and to lie about it."

The man stopped. He looked her up and down, confused by her answer as much as her lack of a veil and the gown she wore. That one had survived the deck of the *Regina,* and Juliana had insisted on it being washed and mended rather than, as Morphia had begged her, becoming an item of charity. For a couple of heartbeats Juliana enjoyed the surprise on his face until he came nearer to circle her as though she were a trapped ewe.

Accustomed to having her flaws pointed out, Juliana folded her hands and waited. Alas, this man came closer than Sister Domenica ever would have and before Juliana thought to put an end to further incursion, fingertips touched her nape.

The nerve of it took her so utterly by surprise that by the time she belatedly started, the fingertips journeyed, as light as moths, along the curve of her neck to her earlobe, a private, nakedly intimate gesture yet one which by then had caused neither shock nor surprise, only the sensation of being lured to allow more . . .

The man's warm breath brushed her cheek. "No earrings, silver or gold. But what have we here?"

Something cold against her skin replaced the fingertips–a dagger's steel. Juliana froze. The dagger's point slid underneath the chain of her cross and followed it to the neckline of her bodice. Before she realized what was happening, the tip plucked the cross from the sanctum of her bosom. The spell vanished in the remembered terror of having Eleanor pried from her breast.

She jerked away. The wrong way. The steel tip sank into her skin. She gasped, in anger and surprise rather than pain at the same time as the man retreated.

"*Panayia*!"

The dagger disappeared in a jeweled sheath at his belt. Juliana looked down. Droplets of blood welled from a small cut. The sight unnerved the man.

"My deepest apologies, Mistress. I didn't intend to cause your person harm. May I call you a woman? A physician, perhaps? Tell me, Mistress, what can I do to make amends?"

After his brazen bravado, the man sounded so genuinely distressed that Juliana's composure returned to her. With the linen of her shift, she soaked up the blood. "You may consider it is your manners with women that need mending more than my skin, sir."

"Oh Lord." The man drew back from his height to take a better look at her. "You are not a waiting woman. You . . . you must be Lady Juliana."

Angry at herself for having allowed this stranger liberties, Juliana shoved the cross back into her bodice. "So I must. Who must you be?"

Surprise showed on the man's face, and a handsome one, with his long-lashed eyes and fine cheekbones. Juliana noted with disconcertment that he reminded her of Lasalle—perhaps because of his erstwhile self-possession, perhaps the cast of his complexion, perhaps his touch . . . The man hesitated, then gave her a white-toothed smile which no doubt had dazzled many a female out of her wits and wimple. Hand to his heart, he bowed to her. "John of Beirut."

John d'Ibelín, the Lord of Beirut. Sister Vigilantia's efforts to teach her the lineages of *outre-mer* once again became useful. What had Abbess Vigilantia said about this man's father and mother—Balian d'Ibelín and Maria Komnene, the dowager queen of Jerusalem? *He was cruel, fickle and faithless; she was godless, pliable, and fraudulent . . .*

"Then you must be Hugh's uncle," Juliana said very brusquely, wishing to disavow her complicity in all of this.

John d'Ibelín did not seem to notice. "That I am. And I am so sorry, Lady Juliana. How can I make amends, I can hardly express—"

Juliana held up her hand. "Then don't." She would have said something else to give the man a piece of her mind, but Hugh's voice prevented her.

"Uncle?" The boy approached, uncertain of what had taken place. He held in his hand a folded piece of parchment, perhaps Father Silbo's latest lesson in penmanship.

From the end of the corridor appeared the corvine shape of *Sekretikos* Niketas, his head thrust forward as if he spied a sparkling jewel someone had foolishly attempted to hide from him. "My lord d'Ibelín. Allow me to welcome you to Nikosia in His Grace's name."

Juliana saw the piece of parchment in Hugh's hands disappear behind his back. Not wanting to become part of the next act, she curtsied and to her accidental assailant she whispered, "You'd better see to your nephew, sir. No reason to alarm him."

She hurried away in hope that Niketas had not witnessed what had happened. Once in her chamber, she wanted to soak out the blood stain before anyone noticed. Of course Morphia found her and shrieked at the sight of the stained shift which brought the usual flock of maids. They swamped Juliana with offerings of wine and various drafts, poultices for her forehead and unguents for the flesh. She finally regained possession of her person by blaming her own clumsiness around roses, then sent them away so she could think.

During Aimary de Lusignan's absence, she had met three persons who stood close to his throne–his daughter and her husband, and now John d'Ibelín, the Lord of Beirut and Hugh's uncle. Juliana knew that she could not ask Morphia nor anyone else why the Lord of Beirut would feel the need to visit the heir to the throne of Cyprus surreptitiously, and to bring him gifts in contravention of his father's wishes.

She went to the chapel later the very same day to pray for an answer–and in doing so to banish the disturbing sensation of John d'Ibelín's touch on her bare flesh. On the way there, she remembered the veil she left caught on the potted laurel. When she went to retrieve it, it was gone.

Saint Mary's of Tyre, already in some agitation about the imminent investiture of its new abbess, welcomed the daughter of the king of Cyprus and Jerusalem with little surprise. After all, the lady Burgundia's mother had been a generous patroness to the sisters caring for pilgrim women.

Burgundia de Lusignan descended from her litter to be met in the courtyard by the abbess-to-be. Sister Vigilantia stood still, waiting for their visitor, and yet those watching her closely would detect a certain anticipation if not disquietude. Her posture eased when Lady Burgundia offered her a deep courtesy and smiling, gestured to her page and to her woman who rode in a sedan chair, a bundle in silk cloth between them.

"Welcome to Nikosia, Reverend Mother. I offer Our Lady these gifts to remember the occasion of your installation and my fervent prayer that you and your daughters continue your good works in this, my father's kingdom."

Before Vigilantia could reply, the page stepped forward with the bundle in his hands, and the woman, also curtsying, folded back the silk. The gathered sisters exhaled in admiration at the sight of a pair of gloves, a crucifix, and an abbess's staff of office, its crook and the rest of the gifts all glittering gold and silver, pearls and precious gems sewn onto the face of the gloves and set over the staff and cross.

Vigilantia showed no untoward emotion. "Saint Mary's is grateful for your generosity, Lady Burgundia. We shall offer our prayers for you . . . and your father."

"Thank you. Will you allow me to pray to Our Lady for my mother's soul?"

After a brief hesitation, Vigilantia nodded. "You may do so in my private chapel."

With the senior sisters taking charge of the gifts, the rest of the congregation dispersed, leaving their abbess and her guest to proceed through the cloisters.

They walked side by side, Vigilantia's hands under her scapular, but Burgundia could tell that they were tightly gripped.

"You abandoned me." There was anger and bitterness in Vigilantia's voice.

"I did not." Burgundia kept her voice soft. "I secured this position for you just as I secured your refuge at Fécamp. I asked Abbess Mathilde to arrange for your journey here. My father would not have allowed you to return to Cyprus. You know that."

"I did nothing to reveal my presence. Your cousin's wife must have done so. She is so . . . naïve."

"Not as much as you imagine, I think. And none of this is her fault."

For a few moments, Vigilantia did not reply and then she said, all in accusation, "You . . . you married again."

"Yes. When my father forced Raymond to return me to Cyprus, he asked me to marry de Montbéliard. And I agreed."

"How could you after all we've been through in Toulouse?"

Burgundia kept her gaze ahead, just as did her companion. "I don't despise men the way you do and I still wish–pray–for a child. Can you fault me for that?"

Vigilantia stopped abruptly. "You may pray in my chapel for whatever you wish. I will never receive you at Saint Mary's again."

Burgundia faced her companion. "If you so wish. But never is a long time. Just remember, my dear, you are here with my permission and my patronage. I advise you not meddle in Lusignan concerns, especially when it comes to matters of marriage."

CHAPTER 22

The harbor town of Famagusta

Juliana dipped her toes into the wave rushing toward her. It receded, replaced by another in an ageless dance. Since the weather remained mild, she had insisted to Morphia that they visit the seaside. She wanted distance from the thick air of intrigue in Aimary's palace. Now the far-reaching horizon only reminded her of the distance separating her from Eleanor.

She picked up a shell, pink and smooth and warm in her hand, like Eleanor's cheek. She kissed it, tasting the saltiness of the seas and her own tears. No more tears. They would not bring her closer to Eleanor. She wiped her cheeks and looked about her. Lasalle said that pirates had carried Aimary's first wife away, perhaps from this very place. Juliana shook her head to banish such thoughts. Surely the pirates had long gone.

She had asked Morphia to teach her about the island's customs and lore, and words in Greek. This time, she was an apt pupil. Morphia told her that the goddess Aphrodite had come to these shores. A tall tale, of course. Remembering the rest of Morphia's story, Juliana frowned. The goddess had betrayed her husband with Ares, the god of war. Beauty and passion, betrayal, violence, strife. They followed each other, bringing disasters on all caught up in them.

Annoyed, she threw the shell back into the waves. Living with that man was like being one of those shells left stranded on the sand, waiting for a wave to restore them to where they belonged. She did not want to belong to his world of perpetual strife.

Over the waves, her maids' laughter reached her. The three laughed and danced along the edge of the waters, skirts tucked high, daring each other to wade deeper. Morphia rested under a canopy the servants had set up on a rise, stockings rolled down to ease her swollen ankles, calling out periodically to the maids to be careful lest Poseidon snatched them from among the rocks. The men of their guard tied their horses to the shrubs and stationed themselves to ogle the maids more conveniently.

Juliana kept her skirts no higher than her ankles even though her hems became soaked and sand crusted. She walked farther along the water's edge until the sound of the waves dimmed the young women's laughter. Her hand on her cross, she closed her eyes and wished she could fly with the great flocks of birds that crossed the island on their winter flight. *Eleanor, Eleanor, do you even remember me?*

"My lady, my lady!"

The hysteria in Morphia's voice made Juliana look back. Had Poseidon snatched one of the maids?

He had not. The maids shrieked and struggled against the waves to escape from horsemen who appeared as if at Poseidon's command.

They were not the guards, joining in the gambols. They were the *bedu.*

Four of the five black-garbed horsemen swept past the maids to charge at the guards and the terrified servants. The servants dropped whatever they had in hand and fled in all directions. The mules brayed and thrashed in their harness. The guards tumbled and fumbled after their horses that tore loose and bolted in all direction with the *bedu*'s high-pitched cries.

The fifth rider veered toward Morphia, cowering behind her palisade of pillows. She shielded her head in expectation of being decapitated by the curved sword that flashed above her. Instead, the blade sliced the ropes holding up the canopy. The canvas deflated in a heap, burying Morphia under it. Without a pause, the rider sent his fleet-footed mount after one of the guards.

The running man glanced over his shoulder. It was the last thing he saw on this earth. Juliana watched it all as in a dream. The death-dealing rider skidded his horse to a halt past the crumpled corpse and swung around. In her direction.

He remained there, a statute against the sky. The sword dripped with his victim's blood. He let it slip from his fingers. And then he aimed for her.

Eschiva d'Ibelín, the queen of this island was carried away by pirates. Instinct told her to run, and she did, but stopped after a few steps. She could not outrun a horseman, but she had her dagger. She took it with her every time she went outside the confines of the king's residence. She faced her abductor, the dagger pressed into the folds of her skirts. Juliana de Charnais would not be carried off like a market sheep.

She watched the horse's hooves gouge out geysers of sand and water. She saw the funnels of the mare's nostrils flare with each breath. Her fingers cramped around the hilt. She had to let the horseman come closer, so close he could not avoid a collision unless she . . . The reek of hot sweat overtook her; the mare's breath swept her face.

She slashed at the mare's lathered shoulder. The rider hauled his mount up just as she swung at it. The animal's hooves rose above her head. Juliana stumbled out of their way. The rider's cloak landed on her, knocking her to her knees.

Her dagger tangled uselessly in the cloth. Juliana worked frantically to untangle it and had almost succeeded when she was lifted and flung across the withers. The horse gibbed wildly, but the rider brought it under curb and wheeled away from the shore.

She knew they galloped inland because shrubs tore at her skirts. Juliana gulped for air, afraid she would lose consciousness, but through it all, she held onto her dagger for life itself.

The horse came to a halt. She heard men's voices–Greek? No, not Greek. New terror gripped her. *You will be sold from one master to another until you are too worn to turn millstones.*

Dogs barked, winded horses snorted, angry chickens squawked. Chickens? One would think that pirates would prefer a boat to transport her, but no, they had brought her to a farmstead. Surely that was good news. She could ride better than she could swim.

She was hauled from the horse and swung over someone's shoulder. Juliana counted his steps. They led across a courtyard, up a couple of flights of wooden stairs, past a creaky door under whose lintel the man had to duck. One forceful shrug of his shoulder flung her from it, and before she could scream, she landed on something soft and yielding–a mattress.

Juliana curled herself into a ball, clutching the dagger to her. He would have to unwrap her, and then . . .

The footsteps led away. The door creaked, the latch clicked, the footsteps faded. Juliana strained her ears over the sound of her heart and her half-smothered breath. From somewhere below came a woman's voice calling out, then silence.

The cloak smelled of goat hair, horses, and the heavy, musky scent of something carnivorous and wild–the leopards' pen. So much for Lasalle trusting Djalali and his *bedu* friends! Juliana waited for an eternity before unwrapping herself.

They had her in a white-washed room with a clean, comfortable bed and a painted chest in the corner, on top of it stockings and a pair of shoes, the sort servant women wore. In the wall's alcove sat a bowl with a water jar. Sheep skins covered the floors and padded a trunk that served as a window seat. From a sapling pole across two wall corners hung a woman's gown and a headrail of *paroikoi* women. *They intended to disguise her before setting for the seas.* As quietly as she could, Juliana climbed from the bed and helped herself to the shoes. They were a little tight. She sidled to the window.

The house stood on a rocky rise overlooking the sea. Too high to jump. Olive trees grew outside the stone wall enclosing a small garden, a courtyard, and stables. No one was about in the courtyard, not even the dogs. Perhaps the men had ridden out again. Still, there could be a horse left in the stables. She could not be too far from where they took her. If she could reach the stables . . . The room's door would be locked from the outside. Holding her breath, she tried anyway.

The door popped opened, startling her. She waited a few more heartbeats, then crossed herself. Her skirt tucked under her waist belt, her dagger at the ready, she tiptoed as fast as she could down a corridor, down a flight of stairs, past the gigantic *pithoi* and smoke-blackened kitchen. She kept to the shadow of the courtyard wall until she reached the stables. Another heartbeat of hesitation and she slipped inside.

And stopped.

Five men sat on their heels, passing around pieces of bread and a bowl of oil. They talked in low voices, their cloaks thrown back, teeth flashing. The *poulain* knights and *serjeans* squatted like that when eating. *In fact they looked like . . .*

Those facing her looked up. Their dark faces showed no surprise that their catch, a wild woman with a naked dagger in her fist, burst in on them. With a flutter of grins, they stood up one after the other and without a word filed past her. The last man picked up the oil bowl and rose to face her.

"Put the dagger away, Juliana, you aren't frightening my friends. And don't throw it either. You'd miss."

There he was—black robes, black hair, a single silver earring, and that self-confident smirk on his lips.

"You miserable, deceitful—"

"Lusignan?"

She lunged at him with every malice aforethought.

"Oho!" He retreated to keep the oil bowl out of harm's way. "Careful now. No need to waste good olives. Let's talk, shall we?"

She advanced. "About what, my lord? Your deceit or your lies? You killed that man for . . . for nothing!"

"Whatever you think of—"

"And to think I convinced myself that I needed you to save Eleanor from your father's clutches."

"–doing, I wouldn't." He avoided her next sally which nevertheless forced him to retreat before her advance until he backed into the stall post.

She thrust the dagger into the black cloak. "I need you no more than–"

The steel encountered the thickness of the cloth. Still, she had made him flinch and drop the bowl. It shattered on the hard-packed ground. He grabbed her wrists and swung her against the post. Pain opened her fingers.

"But I need you, Juliana."

CHAPTER 23

Juliana sat on the edge of the bed, swinging her feet, watching him discard the layers of his disguise. Indignation at the injustice of it all burned in her veins. A young woman came and dropped an armful of clothes and linen strips on the trunk, and a small jar next to it. She gave Juliana a distrustful look and said something to Lasalle. When he shook his head, the girl left with a twitch of her hips. Arching his eyebrow at Juliana, Lasalle poked his finger through a hole her dagger had left in his cloak.

"I am sorry. I missed," she said to that.

He raised up his shirt. "Not by much."

Below his ribs, next to a not very old scar, a long gash oozed red. Juliana bit her lip and looked away.

With his shirt tail, he wiped the blood, smearing it. "Next time, try it on Armand."

"I did." She wanted to scream.

"Hmm. Try harder." He tossed her a strip of cloth the girl brought. "Put some of that salve on it and tie it, will you?"

"Why?"

"Because I can't very well do it myself."

Juliana dropped to her feet. "I thought I was a hindrance to whatever plans you've hatched here. My lord."

"Don't be petulant, Juliana."

Her fury nearly choked her. Guérin de Lasalle used her Christian name when he wanted her attention, to rebuke her, or when he wanted to wheedle her into . . . "Petulant? You dare to call me petulant? You left us. Eleanor is my first thought when I open my eyes and my last one when I close them. I dream of her. Do you ever think of her? I will go to the ecclesiastical court in Nikosia, I will swear that I was wed to you against my will, and I will ask the court to–"

"I had no choice."

"Why not?"

He smiled and took her fists in his hands. "You still have your wedding ring."

She tried to pull away. He tightened his hold. She did not resist. "You said there are two people on this island you trust."

The way he looked at her told her that she had struck a chord. Instead of answering her, Lasalle let her go and went to the window. Juliana stood there, fists to her sides. Aimary had told her that she ought to forgive him for entrusting her and Eleanor to his men to guard. *It's like yanking a milk tooth, Lady Juliana. Just say what the trouble is.* "You don't trust me. You blame me for Armand taking Eleanor."

He propped his arms on the sill and took a breath full of weariness. "Juliana–"

"I don't want your platitudes. I wanted to spare your men. You consented to our marriage for the same reason. I don't have your certainty, Guérin. I don't know when to cause deaths because they serve my own purpose."

He did not answer her for some time. She waited stubbornly until he did. "Those men are raised to obey. It is our duty to command them. You're the viscountess of Tillières and my wife. You can't escape that responsibility any more than they can."

She was being rebuked and she could find no defense except the truth. "Niketas gave me those men to protect me. Have I been such a hindrance to you that I've caused that man's death?"

He faced her. "No. He caused his own death. Your guards didn't bother to properly tether their horses. They paid more attention to your maids' skirts than saddle girths. Someone suspects that you know something you are not supposed to know."

"Someone? Who? And what could I know? I see Wink when he's not with Djalali. I keep company with Morphia. You're the one who arranged for her to wait on me."

"Yes, and I made a mistake. I put your life in danger because of it."

Guérin de Lasalle did not admit that he was wrong very often. The bloody stain on his shirt spread. Juliana picked up a piece of the cloth the girl brought and motioned him to come closer. He did. She made him pull up the shirt's tail to wipe away the thin streaks of blood. Surely the sight of blood made her hands tremble, not his statement nor the flank grooved by muscle beneath the skin. "I see. And who are those other men?"

"Djalali's friends."

She folded another cloth strip and smeared it with the salve. "Have that girl wash and mend the shirt."

She did not know if he smiled at her advice or the tone with which she delivered it and before she could take umbrage, he said, "Her name is Persephone."

He took off the shirt and waited for her to wrap the last strip around him. Juliana was about to tell him to call Persephone for that, too, but she recognized her own petulance. The procedure required her to come close. The scent of the cloak clung to his skin. At least he did not touch her.

She forced away the thought that ought not to have occurred to her at all. Annoyed that it did, she said, "What a lovely name." And there was the other matter. "What is it I am supposed to have noticed?" She hoped she sounded disinterested in the fact that he had told her that he had put her life in danger.

"The usual. Servants talk. Gossip, rumors, assignations or encounters someone would want to keep secret."

John d'Ibelín. A flush of perspiration sprung up on her nape. "Don't . . . don't fidget. And turn. Again. I don't think Niketas likes me. He must be jealous of you or afraid. Or both. More so now that you've killed his man, I imagine. Keep turning. I met Burgundia and her husband. He was looking for you."

Passing over her sudden verbosity, Lasalle did as told, winding the cloth around him with each turn. He sounded pleased. "You did? What did cousin Burgundia say?"

"We didn't have time to speak. Her husband came. Montbéliard doesn't know a thing about flowers. That's enough. Don't breathe, I have to tie the knot."

When she finished, he inhaled carefully and patted her handiwork. "Did Morphia say anything about her husband?"

Juliana stood back. "She bursts into tears every time I mention him. She says that 'they' murdered him. She swears that Leontios was a saint. So there is nothing I would know to put my life in danger." *John d'Ibelín.* She could not say the name.

"Hmm." Lasalle drew back to give her an incredulous squint on behalf of the entire male species. "Now what wife would swear that her husband is a saint?"

"Obviously a lying one."

"Or a guilty one."

A bolt hurled by Zeus's own hand could not have been louder than the silence in the room. Juliana sat on the trunk by the window.

Lasalle found a clean shirt among the clothes Persephone had brought and pulled it on. He came to her. "Juliana?"

John d'Ibelín. That light, caressing touch. She could not say the name. "What? Oh, nothing. It's nothing. Why would Morphia have a hand in Leontios's death? She truly grieves for him. Back there, she thought that she would be the one killed."

Lasalle nodded. "I know. And that ought to puzzle Niketas. At least until he gets my demand for ransom."

"Ransom? For whom?"

"You."

"What? Me?" Lasalle had gone mad once again. "You want Niketas to ransom me? Why?"

"Because I need the money. Aimary says Niketas has it, and if Niketas is afraid of me, I'd like to know how much. I'd rather get it from my saintly brother, but Geoffrey's not at hand. I don't want to pledge Kolossi to some Venetian and raise Rhoxsane's suspicion. I already sent a man to Niketas to collect it. That ought to take a few days. You'll wait here until then."

That's why he needed her. In his inimitable ways, Lasalle had decided to turn the encumbrance of her presence to his advantage. Perhaps she ought to point out the flaws in his scheme. "Niketas will know that you are the one demanding the ransom. When I return to Nikosia, he'll know me to be complicit and accuse us of robbing him."

"He won't since he scavenged his fortune from Isaak's coffers. And you are not going back to the palace. You're going to Saint Mary's until the spring ships sail to Marseille. I am going to Acre after Aimary until then."

Her heart sank. "I see. So now you trust Vigilantia, too?"

"Juliana–"

She folded her arms. "Do you propose to swim to Acre? You said no captain will risk his boat now."

"Unless he's a fisherman who knows the winds and the waters and someone pays for his boat."

By kidnapping her, Lasalle had gained the means to carry out his scheme. "I see," she said at a loss for how to counter him. For now.

Perhaps glad that she would acquiesce to his plans without further argument, Lasalle reached for the black robes and transformed himself into a sinister stranger, only his eyes visible in the slit of the cloth.

"I'll tell Persephone not to latch the door." He stopped and looked back, the lines at the corner of his eyes cut deep. "I do think of her. Every day."

❧

Anger . . . confusion . . . understanding . . . forgiveness. Christian forgiveness.

Lasalle did not trust her enough to tell her the whole of it. She ought to practice Christian forgiveness. But how could she forgive when she did not understand him, not entirely? She had not told him the truth of John d'Ibelín either. Would he understand? How would she explain what had happened, what she had allowed to happen. She could not understand it herself. The Ibelíns and the Lusignans were rivals, bitter rivals at times. Aimary's throne was teetering. Who'd want to topple him from it but an Ibelín? Lasalle would use her encounter with the Lord of Beirut to . . . to kill him.

Left at the farmstead to ponder her complicity in her predicament, Juliana tried to appear to be of good cheer. The men guarding her were no longer Djalali's friends, but *poulain* men-at-arms who had no idea of the events that preceded her presence. She tried the same good cheer on Persephone who continued to regard her with resentment. Only when Juliana offered to help her in the kitchen did the girl's demeanor warm toward her. Waiting for Lasalle's return, Juliana spent her time minding the fire, carrying water jars from the well to the kitchen, stirring pots of lentils, shelling peas, peeling onions, and smiling through her tears while attempting to converse with the girl who either did or did not understand her.

A few days after Lasalle's departure, Persephone indicated to Juliana that she should come with her. Juliana gladly left the onions and followed the girl to the kitchen yard. Under an awning hung the carcass of a pig strung up by its hocks, Lasalle leaning against it. He wore a shirt and a *serjean's* unbelted gambeson and chatted with a corpulent man whose bloody apron and knife testified to his agency in dispatching the pig. Juliana saw the steaming innards plop from the crimson cavity left in the wake of the man's knife into the waiting bucket. She swallowed. That answered the question of what would be tonight's supper.

Juliana cleared her throat. The butcher wiped his hands, handed Persephone the bucket and lumbered after her back to the kitchen. Hands clasped behind him, Lasalle approached Juliana with a fiendish grin and before she could give him a glower of disapproval, a dagger appeared in his hand. Her dagger. His voice sank into an imitation of villainous intent. "At last I find you unarmed, Lady Juliana."

One never knew when my lord Lasalle would vault from serious to silly. Juliana folded her arms. "Did you get my ransom?"

He presented her the dagger's hilt. "Patience, Sister Eustace. It's a virtue."

"I've already stabbed my kidnapper once, my lord, and I don't see–"

"You will." He pressed the hilt into her hand, maneuvered her in front of the carcass and stood next to it, arms spread in a martyr's surrender, a saintly smile on his lips. "I'll give you another chance. Me or the pig."

Had he shed all of his clothes on the spot, he could not have caught her more off guard. His pose, so perfectly defenseless, became a visceral reminder that Guérin de Lasalle was merely mortal flesh, flesh that someone's steel could render as dead and blood-drained as the pig's carcass.

"I didn't know it would be such a difficult choice. If it helps, I'll close my eyes," he said with a mixture of impatience and daring, and did.

Lasalle had left his senses. She came to hers and shoved the dagger into the chink between the wall stones. "This is not funny. I have to help Persephone."

"Listen." He caught her by the arm to make her look at him. "I can't tell you how to decide if you need to make someone die. But I can teach you how to do it. You will know when it serves your purpose."

Cyprus, the island of Aphrodite. None of the tales she had heard about it mentioned that its effect upon a husband would be to compel him to instruct his wife in how to kill a man. Juliana shrugged him away. "I see."

"Truly?" He imitated her tone.

She heard it and did not try to suppress her irritation, at herself. "Truly."

Of course, what he truly wanted, instead of coaxing Juliana de Charnais to stab a dead pig, was to be in that loft room with her, spread under him or bestride him, not wearing a stitch. Forcefully barring that thought, Lasalle pressed the dagger into her fist, and pointed it and her at the carcass. "Now. As hard as you–"

She stabbed at the still warm flesh. A flash of pain through her wrist made her wince. "There. Happy?"

Lasalle extracted the dagger and replaced it in her hand. "No. It's a dagger, not a ladle. Use the crossguard, like this. Thrust forward and upward, not underhand." Instructing her as if she were a squeamish squire about to be sent into battle, he pointed the blade downward and swept it aside with his free hand. "That way it's easy to stop the blow. Do you understand?"

Compelled by the chillingly precise way he demonstrated it all, Juliana nodded.

"Unless of course you want to stab someone from behind."

"B-behind?"

"Yes, behind, but in your case I wouldn't recommend it. This way," he reversed the dagger's path, "if you lean your weight against the crosspiece you drive it deeper. Do it."

He stepped back, leaving her alone to confront the carcass. Juliana took a deep breath, trying to remember the instructions. This time, the blade sank surprisingly easily into the carcass. Her wrist still smarted, but not as much as before. How odd that such a violent act should make one feel so . . . excited. "Did I . . . did I do it right?"

He pulled the dagger out. "Better. Next time, keep at least one eye open. You'll need to run away. Again."

Juliana ignored the trickle of perspiration sliding down her spine. Why would these instructions seem more intimate than the private acts in which he had the occasion to tutor her? She did not know why the thought came to her. It must have been the influence of this island. "Run away?"

Unsmiling, he nodded. "Unless your aim is very lucky, one blow won't kill a man. But you'll have the advantage of surprise. After that, run."

Juliana shivered. "I see." She hesitated. "Then how would one . . . if one had to–"

He thrust the dagger deep into the pig's side and drew her, stiff-kneed and all, to him. "You'll need to be closer and aim here. Here, where the heart is." He took her hand and held her palm flat where under the cage of his ribs a strong and steady sign of life dwelled within him. "Do you feel it?"

Set me as a seal upon your heart . . . a seal upon your arm, for love is strong as death. She felt it, as keenly as a dagger blow. And when he lowered his head, she closed her eyes and stood again atop Parthenay's keep, and he was about to . . .

She jerked away and fled from him, and this time, from herself as well.

CHAPTER 24

Foolish, utterly foolish. Juliana stared at the ceiling, the bed next to her empty. *Eleanor, Eleanor.*

Since her arrival in Cyprus, she had intended to avoid entanglements in the Lusignans' problems and in Abbess Vigilantia's as well. These now coalesced into one and the same, and that one became hers. Whatever stratagem Guérin de Lasalle planned, she had to forge her own to free him from this place, from his obligations to his family. She had to bring him with her back to Poitou. For Eleanor.

For that, she needed information and the best time to pry information out of my lord Lasalle was when his usually acute attention had been blunted.

He returned to the farmstead just before the purple of the sunset deepened into blackness. Juliana greeted him at the door with a lamp in her hand, her shift askew on her shoulders, and two cups of unwatered wine in her. "Did you get the ransom? Does Niketas know you've kidnapped me? When will I leave?"

He did not move past the lintel. "I did, Niketas knows but has no proof, and you will leave tomorrow. Vigilantia's expecting you."

"Did you have to bribe her?" The question tripped her thickening tongue.

He gave her a skewered smile and tapped the tip of her nose. "I told her you don't cost much to feed, but I ought to have sprung for more wine rations."

He did not tell her of the promise he made to Vigilantia.

"I see." Juliana gestured awkwardly with the lamp, hoping he did not see her blush. "We made supper for the men. There must be something left. I will go and see."

He shook his head and reached for the door latch. "I am not hungry. Sleep well, you'll leave at dawn."

Her stomach lurched and not because of the wine. "Stay."

That was hardly a seductive invitation. To my lord Lasalle, it hardly mattered.

He stayed.

She had once instigated such an encounter, also for her own purposes. That induction into wifehood made her resolved not to repeat it, ever. Her resolve did not last because Guérin de Lasalle did not care for her pledges of perpetual chastity. This time, when he lifted her and pressed her under him into the softness of the bed linen, she knew that she had the advantage of his single-minded purpose, and so she let the wine and the urgency of her mission knock her senses out of their usual well-governed sensibility.

She wanted her heart to remain snared a little while longer, to retain the breathless, searing sensation of one's mortal flesh yielding to another until nothing else mattered, but the haunting sound from below the window gradually invaded her ears and her consciousness. She listened, enthralled by the melody. "It's beautiful," she whispered, suddenly afraid to break the spell of the music and of this temporary sanctuary.

Lying supine, Lasalle did not move or open his eyes. "Uhmm. Pan pipes. The Greeks call them Syrinx. After the water fey. She–"

"–was fleeing from Pan, and asked her sisters to protect her. They changed her into a reed. Pan had nothing left but the reeds to remind him of her. He made them into a flute. Morphia told me."

His mouth relaxed into a smile. "She fled from fear of Pan's lust, Sister Eustace."

"I knew that. I don't want to . . . to flee. Not any more."

"Truly?"

He made the sound of a man either pleased or worried, and her throat ached at the sharpness of tears and laughter. He could do that, he could always do that, but she must not allow herself to be seduced from her true course.

She snuggled herself against him and tightened her arm about his belly. "Yes. Tell me about Vigilantia." When he did not reply, she ran her toe along his shin. "It doesn't matter if you tell me now. I won't be able to speak of it to a soul, will I?"

"Hmm. That's nice. Don't stop. I suppose she's a Greek Aliénor, fully fledged but for the years. She would own everything underfoot if Aimary already didn't. She's not fond of Lusignans."

Juliana raised her head to look at him. His eyes remained closed, but the corner of his mouth twitched as if he knew that she was looking at him. "How fascinating," she said with an ignorant pupil's curiosity. "Tell me more."

He let out a small whine of protest. "Now?"

"Please. I won't be able to sleep anyway."

He shifted to his side, dislodging her. In the moon's light that fell through the open shutters, Juliana saw that his eyes were open, that look in them. He traced her lower lip with his fingertip. "It seems that I have failed as a husband, once again."

Delivered without reproach, the words chilled her despite the heat that remained between them. Juliana fought to keep away the thought of John d'Ibelín. "You did not."

"How gracious you are, Lady Juliana."

She did not want to veer down that path. She had come to Cyprus for only one purpose. "I am not. What does Leontios's death have to do with Aimary's crown?"

Lasalle drew the covers to her chin and looked down at the white oval of his wife's face. In the bare light, her hair spread rust-red on the pillow. She kept it tamed under her veil and wimple or in a single braid when not in company. *You are more wedded to her than she is to you.* "He carried an unimportant message to his master. Someone killed him to take it, no doubt to cause mischief with it."

"If it was unimportant, what mischief could the message cause?"

"A good question."

She had to ask, although her heart pounded in anticipation of the answer. "Do you know who was his master?"

"I know that a ship under the Ibelín banner came to Limassol. Rhoxsane left that day with only her maid and met someone there."

John d'Ibelín. It had to be him. With the name came the sensation of that touch, that feathery touch. Why would it be so? She was a wife and a mother. No, not a wife, not truly. Not in the eyes of the Church. Only a mother. "I see. And Morphia?"

"She could have told someone that Leontios carried it."

Juliana could barely breathe. "Could she have told Niketas? Can't you find out from him?"

"If I could make him carry a red-hot iron or dunk him in the Dardanelles until he confesses, I would. But I can't. Niketas learned the craft of power under Isaak, and since then became craftier."

That day. That day in the corridor. She could not say that she had seen Niketas, perhaps spying, perhaps not, without revealing her encounter with the Lord of Beirut. She had to ask even though she chanced giving him a cause for suspicion. "What does Niketas want?"

"To be the power behind Hugh's throne, but he doesn't know if it would be greater under the Lusignans or the Ibelíns."

She did not dare to ask more but she did not need to because he said, sifting through his own thoughts, "Hugh resents his father, so Hugh may well favor the Ibelíns. I sided with Hugh against Aimary, but I didn't have the time to befriend him. Hugh is too young for all that he could soon face. It frightens Aimary."

Pan's pipes filled in the silence. Juliana could not imagine Aimary de Lusignan being frightened by anything after years of facing Musulmans and rebellious barons. But then she had first encountered Aimary not as a king, imperious and hard-driven, but as an ordinary man with a lifetime's experience, a father who worried about his son on whose shoulders could rest the responsibility for this kingdom before long. An urge to confess to Lasalle all she knew seized her.

"Listen." He propped himself on his elbow, alert as though the intimacy of the past moments had never occurred. "In Acre, I'll make sure that the Temple pays up to you. When spring comes, if

I haven't returned, take the money and the first ship to Marseille. Vigilantia will arrange it. You tell Brissard to hire enough men to take back Eleanor. There will be plenty to hire. Brissard can find my old *routiers*, too, if they are still alive. Armand will release Eleanor if you show no hesitation to use them against him. You must not hesitate, Juliana. Whatever comes, you have to get her back."

Whatever comes . . . She opened her mouth to protest, to object, but his hand came under her hips and he kissed her with purposeful thoroughness. Of themselves, her hands sought out the supple trench of the spine and the solid and unyielding presence of mortal flesh with the desperate intention to hoard in her memory the shape and feel and scent of him. *Set me as a seal upon your heart . . . a seal upon your arm, for love is strong as death.*

CHAPTER 25

Nikosia

"Don't cause the men trouble, Juliana. If you do, I told them to–"

"I know. Tie me to the mule's tail."

Those were the last words they had exchanged. He had not kissed her nor had she offered to be kissed, but he did press the dagger into her hand after he lifted her into the mule litter.

Juliana had no intention of troubling the men because during the entire journey to Nikosia, she absorbed herself in thoughts of last night. They did not dwell on the sort of intimacies a truly pious wife ought to disclose to her confessor, but on what she had gleaned from their conversation in the interludes.

Eleanor. He did think of her. She had wronged him in that. And to correct that wrong, she had to make him leave this island. With her. She could not compel Niketas to tell her what he knew either, but Mistress Morphia certainly knew something. If she could make Morphia tell her . . . To do that, she needed someone who could provide her with the help–and protection–she would need in this world that played by its own rules.

Should you be in need, ask Saint Mary's for aid.

When Nikosia came into view, the men secured the litter's curtains as if they were delivering a concubine to the archbishop, and transported her the rest of the way. The curtain lifted to a sturdy door that opened for her, and she was unceremoniously disgorged into a dark passage. The door shut behind her. The men, under Lasalle's orders, did not chance anything.

Encased in her brown robes and wearing a high headdress from which a black veil flowed, Saint Mary's gate mistress waited until Juliana rallied her resolve and straightened her cloak and gown. Neither took her long. "Would you ask the abbess to receive me, Sister, please? Now."

Without acknowledging Juliana's request, the nun led her across a courtyard to the cloisters. The high-walled, silent seclusion reminded Juliana of Fontevraud. Juliana squared her shoulders. Abbess Mathilde had urged her to undertake this journey. Perhaps the Almighty had already given her a sign without her noticing it.

The gate mistress left her at the end of the cloisters where, next to the rain cistern, Abbess Vigilantia waited. Juliana hurried her steps. The abbess wore a white wimple and a black veil on top of which resided a round cap embroidered with crosses. Her fingers caressed a gold cross, her eyes watching Juliana's approach with a hint of anticipation.

Juliana curtsied. "Thank you for receiving me, Reverend Mother. I know that my husband wants me to remain at Saint Mary's until the sailing season, but–"

"And what is it you want, Lady Juliana?"

"I want him to return to Poitou and reclaim our daughter. The rest, those are not my concerns."

The abbess's eyebrows went up. "But they are your husband's, are they not?"

"Yes. And I want him to resolve them, but to do that I have to return to the king's palace. Abbess Mathilde trusted you to aid me."

Abbess Vigilantia raised her gaze to the square of skies framed by the cloister's roofs. "Trust. Nothing is as bitter as the betrayal of it, is there?"

"No. But I am told that one has to trust to chance."

"Well then, have you heard how Mélusine aided her husband, Lady Juliana?"

Now why would Vigilantia bring up the fable of a pagan serpent-woman? Juliana said quite impatiently, "I am told that *she* had unearthly powers."

"Did she?"

They say that she had cut the hide as thin as a thread to stake out her husband's lands. At Saint Maixent, she had dismissed Mélusine's action as base trickery. "No. She used her wits." She was being tested. "My husband told me who you are. Why you would want to aid me?"

"It would be my gift to you, not to your husband. Do you not trust me?"

"I was told to beware of Greeks bearing gifts."

Vigilantia's lips smiled. "So you did pay attention. You may yet do well."

"Not if I end up the leopards' supper."

The nun laughed, a brief and merry laugh, and then the angles of her face became sharper and her eyes shadowed. "See what an undocile mind you have, Lady Juliana. Here you have a chance to give it rein. Who would reproach a mother for protecting her child? As for that Lusignan you married, I expect that he will revert to his own kind. If you decide to remain wed to him, one day it will cost you and your daughter dearly. Those are not my concerns. I am merely allowing you to play out your destiny."

Words of warning–and prophecy. Juliana's hand went to her own cross and its presence filled her with resolve. After all, had not Abbess Mathilde told her to follow the path the Lord had laid out for her? How then could she step wrong? "How fortuitous that our destiny is so consonant with your aims, Reverend Mother. But I am still curious about the leopards."

Juliana withstood a gaze that appeared to pass judgment on her worthiness. Vigilantia stood up and nodded toward the cloisters. "Then let me satisfy your curiosity."

From the archway approached the novice mistress with two young girls. The girls were pretty, one perhaps twelve years old, the other a couple of years older. Abbess Vigilantia motioned to them and the girls stepped forward and curtsied. Her arms around the girls' shoulders, Vigilantia turned them to face Juliana the way a proud mother would present her daughters. "Children, tell the lady Juliana your names."

The younger girl curtsied. "Ionia." Her older companion did likewise. "Eulogia."

"And what is your mother's name, Ionia?"

"Lady Rhoxsane," Ionia replied quickly. Eulogia corrected her, with emphasis. "You forget, of Kolossi."

Rhoxsane of Kolossi's daughters.

The abbess's fingers curved into the girls' cloaks. "Isn't she indeed." Vigilantia smiled at Eulogia who basked in the approval and then nodded at the novice mistress. The girls curtsied again, and followed the novice mistress, a couple of anxious ducklings.

A squall of wind raced through the cloisters. Juliana shuddered and drew her cloak about her. *During storms you can hear her cry for her husband and her children.* Mélusine aided her husband even though in the end he betrayed her. And Mélusine had reverted to her own kind.

Vigilantia smiled at the skies that had become the color of lead. "Ah, winter is here at last. The girls are delightful, are they not, and so observant. One finds that young boys too often observe more than one would expect. It can become a terrible burden to them, especially when they are afraid of their father and desperate for his approval."

Juliana stood there, her heart pounding with fear and excitement. She crossed herself. *It is difficult to trust to chance. But what is life without it?*

Although she had not been kept in Babylonian captivity, upon her delivery to the royal residence in a litter provided by Saint Mary's, Juliana learned that *Sekretikos* Niketas had already explained away whatever questions there might have been about her absence. He had announced that she had overstayed her visit by a few days, thanks to new-found friends at Famagusta, without consulting her nurse and her guards, one of whom had met with a dreadful accident. The lady Juliana had once again ignored the customs and propriety of the king's court and her position in it.

Those gullible enough had accepted the explanation and others did not dare to dispute it. Mistress Morphia, tearful with joy at Juliana's safe reappearance, had been either persuaded or intimidated by Niketas to adhere to his story. Niketas greeted Juliana personally, feigning concern to mask uncertainty about how to deal with her. He told her that her guards had been dismissed and replaced with more vigilant ones. Niketas assured her that whatever had happened, her life was never in danger, and beseeched her not to speak of it to anyone.

"As you wish, *Sekretikos*," Juliana curtsied. Her ready answer surprised the man.

"How very kind of you, my lady," Niketas bubbled with relief. "It is a most sensible arrangement, don't you agree? Those culprits will be found, rest assured. Do you know where they held you? Mistress Morphia and your maids were too distressed to be of help to us to find you. Did you . . . did you by chance recognize any of the men? A voice, perhaps, a gesture?"

Who would reproach a mother protecting her child? Juliana gave Niketas her best wide-eyed look of innocence. "I can't answer your questions, *Sekretikos*. I promised I would not speak of it to anyone."

CHAPTER 26

Saint Jean d'Acre, kingdom of Jerusalem

Aimary de Lusignan was not happy to learn that his nephew, somewhat removed, had countermanded his orders but neither was he surprised.

Aimary left his two companions and their horse grooms and rode up to Lasalle. They stood on a hillock overlooking the construction of a wall to protect Acre's growing outskirts of Montmusard spreading northward beyond the city's principal land wall and deep moat.

Under the direction of their Greek and Syrian overseers, men and teams hauled rocks and rubble to the sound of the stonecutters' chisels, the dull thumps of masons' mallets, and the rhythmic song of saws and blacksmiths' hammers. A line of hodmen, each bent low under a leather sack filled with dressed stones, snaked from the stonecutters' camp, up the wooden ramps that reached to the top of the wall there for the masons to set. Some of the men hauling the stones were galley-slaves, employed outside the sailing season to construct works such as these. Those who survived the winter of relentless labors would return to the rowing benches in the spring.

The din of the work camp joined with the cries of water carriers, shouts of cooks and their mates, and the shrill voices of laundresses promising clean shirts and bed sheets—the latter not necessarily only for the purposes of sleeping in them. The women's toddlers clung to their mothers' skirts while their older siblings who did not have the duty of minding them foraged the site for anything worth stealing.

In the not so distant years past, Acre had endured sieges and surrenders by Musulmans and Christians alike. The city ultimately had ended up in the hands of the Latins to become the largest in their possession, the capital of their truncated kingdom, its principal port, the new headquarters of the Knights of Saint John, the Order of the Temple, and the religious houses that sought safety in numbers behind the walls.

To secure that toehold in the Holy Land, the Christians had endured nearly two years of besieging the city to recapture it from the Musulmans. Sick, starving, and trapped between the city's walls and Saladín's army that encircled their encampment on the landward side, the Christians threw dead horses and finally their own dead into the moat to fill it so that the siege engines could approach the walls. Fifteen years later, and bones and skulls still sought to escape from the earth.

On the seaward sides no wall protected the city since submerged rocks in the shallow inner harbor prevented the landing of an invading flotilla. This new wall and a deep moat would challenge the next land attack, certain to come.

Aimary dismounted. "What do you think? Will they hold?"

His thumbs hooked on his sword belt, his borrowed horse tethered to a cart's wheel, Lasalle did not take his eyes from the scene before him. "For a time."

"Ha." Aimary looked back at his two companions. "Did you hear that? An honest answer." He came up to Lasalle. "When the harbor clerk came to tell me that a fisherman's boat made it through the storm, I didn't believe him. Then he said the pilot paid with Isaak's own coins, and I knew it had to be you. I suppose you thought I would send you right back. That's why you stayed in the Genoese quarters."

"I thought it would be better to store my stomach for a while than risk the queen's carpets. I am not much of a sailor."

Aimary made a small noise, half in sympathy, half exasperation. "Isabella can buy new ones. She does, anyway. I see that Niketas paid up."

"Fully."

Aimary did not ask how that came about. He pointed his riding crop at the site before him, knowing well why his distant nephew chose to visit it when his sea stomach settled. "Different now, isn't it?"

Yes, different. The stench of the old camp had gone, although the laborers paused to cross themselves when the earth yielded up a tangle of bones and half-rotted cloth once worn by a desperate and determined besieger. Some of the men leaned on their picks and shovels to gawk in their direction at a man they recognized to be their king, a king who wore an ordinary cloak over his gambeson, his horse's livery costlier than its rider's attire.

Aimary pointed to a small rise. "That's where the Musulmans tried to overtop our barricade, remember? My brother held them off with that sword. Geoffrey looked like a windmill. He must have dispatched a dozen of them. We nearly took the city walls that time." The pride faded from his voice. "Nearly."

Who could forget that day, after the Feast of Saint John the Baptist, when the French king's ill-advised attack flung nearly the entire Christian army against the walls in a roar of frenzy? In response, Acre's Musulman defenders raised an infernal noise of their own to alert Saladín to come to their aid. Without the count of Jaffa's heroic and herculean efforts, Saladín's attack would have dismantled the Christians' barricade and crushed the besiegers between his army and Acre's walls.

Aimary was right. They nearly took back Acre that time. Nearly. Even though the barricades held, clouds of missiles from the ballistas on the walls and the even more terrifying barrage of Greek fire raining down on them forced the Christians to abandon their assault. The siege engines and towers that the king of the French brought to the Holy Land in the bellies of his ships became flaming pyres. Those who did not escape burned inside them. King Philip sank into despair; so did the camp.

It was the Lionhearted Richard who had rallied the demoralized men. Two weeks later, Saladín surrendered the city to Richard under a truce whose terms included the release all Christian captives, and a payment of a hefty ransom for Acre's defenders. When Saladín failed to deliver it in time, some two thousand Musulmans paid his debt with their lives.

Knowing that he was not resurrecting a cherished memory, Aimary said, "And where is your lady?"

"Saint Mary's. Vigilantia promised to keep her till spring."

Aimary whistled through his teeth. "Jesus. What did you have to promise her? Not my Cypriot crown, I hope."

"No," Lasalle said. "Just my soul."

Aimary slapped Lasalle's shoulder. "Oh, good. Sooner or later we all pay for what we want." He motioned to the two men who accompanied him to approach. "So, am I to pay sooner or later?"

When Lasalle cast a narrow squint at the two, Aimary laughed. "Renaud Barlais and Fulk d'Yver. Our staunch allies through Guy's troubles. You wouldn't remember them. There are others. I trust them with my life, and you can too."

Lasalle nodded to the men. They gave him a short acknowledgement in return. Aimary pulled from his saddle bag a wineskin and fortified himself before handing it to Lasalle. "Tell me then, what did you find out?"

Lasalle told him what he knew. Aimary took back the wineskin. "An Ibelín ship, eh? I was hoping with John would end our quarrels. Saints save us, neither side can afford them. I suppose I should have offered John another wife, but I heard that he would not part with that Helvis of his. He's like you that way."

Aimary's liegemen listened with impassive attention, their glances sliding away when wives were mentioned. The men's hair showed streaks of gray, like their king's. They had served Guy de Lusignan and now his older brother with fidelity for which they had received fiefs and honors in *outre-mer* and Cyprus.

Aimary handed the wine skin to d'Yver. "We may have to have a chat with Beirut." The men nodded, sharing the king's wine with the ease of soldiers who had shared much. Aimary returned to the subject of family. "And speaking of Brother Geoffrey . . ."

Lasalle smiled to himself. So Aimary knew more about his days in Acre than he let on. No surprise there either.

From the foot of the rise, a dozen dirty children approached with the trained submissiveness of beggars and footpads, their grimy hands outstretched, calling out for alms. Whips in hand, Aimary's grooms moved fore. Aimary held them back. He reached into his waist pouch and threw a handful of coins at the little pack. The juvenile horde fell at the pennies with the yowls of jackals.

"Reginald didn't lie when he said that Geoffrey went to Sidon," Aimary continued when the pack spread out. "You didn't have to threaten him or the Grand Master. De Plessis is our ally. It wouldn't hurt if you humored him."

"I didn't take a vow of poverty or obedience to de Plessis. The Temple owes me money. I want it."

"Ah. So you didn't come to Acre solely for my benefit," Aimary said to lighten the conversation.

"No. If something happens to me, I want my wife to have enough to hire men to get my daughter back."

Aimary reconsidered his next words. Apparently Brother Geoffrey of the Temple had not been entirely forthcoming about how he had managed to persuade his young brother to come to Cyprus. Aimary watched the children scratch out the last of the coins, the larger boys attempting to wrestle them from the smaller ones. With loose rocks and sticks, their older sisters flew at them, little Furies dispensing bloody noses and bruised heads.

Aimary dropped the reins around his horse's neck and shoved his foot into the stirrup. "In that case, you may as well stay in a decent bed. I evicted the dowager from the citadel and had the priest come with the aspergillum. If you intend to stick to me like a tick, you'd better come up with a good story for Isabella."

CHAPTER 27

Nikosia, Cyprus

How does one persuade a ten-year-old boy to divulge a burdensome secret? Perhaps by bringing him into your confidence, by making him feel that he is engaging in a naughty escapade. Young boys liked naughty escapades. Juliana knew of a few otherwise grown boys who could not resist them either.

She therefore walked boldly into the chamber where young

Hugh de Lusignan dutifully submitted to Father Silbo's lesson. The priest paused in his recital when she appeared. Juliana gave him a broad smile. "Oh, Einhard. How fascinating. May I be allowed to listen? Thank you, do continue, Father," she said and took her seat on the bench next to Hugh.

Being so unexpectedly provided with two pupils, at least one of whom promised attention to the subject, Father Silbo resumed his recital of the life of *Carolus Magnus*. Ignoring the surprised Hugh, Juliana nodded at particular passages which encouraged Father Silbo's fervor. At the height of it, Juliana whispered to Hugh, "Do you still have the *kandiq*, my lord?"

The young priest paced about, punctuating the air for emphasis. ". . . and even Nicephorus, Michael and Leon, the emperors of Constantinople, sought his friendship and alliances . . ."

Hugh squirmed and whispered back, "Will you tell father?"

Father Silbo threw a suspicious look in their direction and raised his voice. "Even though they viewed the Franks and all Romans with suspicion of their design, whence the Greek proverb, 'have the Frank for your friend, but not–' " Father Silbo drilled his gaze into Hugh in expectation of the completion of that sentiment.

Hugh tried to save himself. "Not . . . not–"

Juliana hastened to save him. " '–for your neighbor.' We were only discussing the Greeks' penchant for perfidy. My lord Hugh compared them the other day to the Bretons. Do go on, Father."

Father Silbo cleared his throat either in assent to the characterization of the Greeks and Bretons or in doubt of her assertion. Recognizing it best for everyone's feelings to be spared, he turned back to the learned Einhard.

Juliana returned to her scheme without the slightest twinge of guilt. "Not if you bring me some. After the lesson. Bring it to the courtyard with the blue fountain." She stood up and curtsied to the boy and to Father Silbo, and tiptoed out of the room.

She did not have to wait long. Hugh came into the courtyard and not seeing anyone, cautiously circled the fountain. When he passed her hiding place behind an overgrown folly, Juliana reached out and pulled him inside. "Shhh. No one must know we are here."

Hugh gulped, his eyes wide. “I brought the *kandiq.*” From his tabard, he pulled out a small pouch as if handing over his crown.

Juliana shook her head. “I don’t want the *kandiq*. That was only a ruse. Your uncle trusts you to keep his visits secret, doesn’t he? I have a secret, too. Can I trust you to keep mine?”

With visible relief, Hugh shoved the pouch back into his tabard. “I can keep a secret,” he said, a ten-year-old insulted that someone would not believe him.

Juliana smiled. “I knew it. That’s what my lord Lasalle told me.”

Hugh looked up at her. “He did?”

“Yes. He said he wanted to speak to your uncle, but couldn’t without Niketas finding out. You do know that your father’s and your mother’s kin are not on the friendliest of terms.”

Hugh’s lower lip dropped lower. “I know that.”

“Then you are so very fortunate to be part of each, aren’t you? Everyone will know that you will be just to both sides. Like your father tries to be.”

Obviously uncertain how that fact would translate into his fortune, Hugh shrugged. “He . . . he said he’ll take me hunting. But I don’t like . . . I don’t like the leopards.”

That hesitation told Juliana more than Hugh intended on the subject of his father, rather than hunting and leopards, and handed her an unexpected opportunity. “I did not like the leopards either when I first saw them. But I know someone who thinks they are marvelous. Would you like to meet him? His name is Wink.”

Hugh attempted to conceal his lack of enthusiasm for the proposal by resorting to a sniff of superiority. “Wink? What a silly name.”

“I know. Come on, let’s tell him before Niketas finds us.” Juliana ducked out of their hiding spot, hoping that Hugh would follow her. He did. Young boys liked naughty escapades.

They rushed across the courtyards and down the corridors to the leopards’ pen. Surprised, Djalali nevertheless greeted them with his smile, and bowing to Hugh, indicated the barred enclosure. Inside, Wink held the end of a leopard’s long leash in one hand and with a meat lure at the end of a rod in the other, he urged the animal to jump on a thick saddle pad atop a wooden stand. Hugh stood frozen next to Juliana until the cat leapt onto the perch and claimed her reward, all in two gulps.

Noticing Juliana, Wink grinned proudly. "Lady!"

"Good. Very good." Djalali praised Wink and took charge of the beast. He bowed to Hugh. "Salomé ready for your first hunt, my lord. You came to meet her, no?"

Keeping hold on the leopard's collar, Djalali approached them. Juliana held her ground, and so did Hugh, she was glad to see, although she could see him holding his breath as well.

Djalali allowed Salomé to come near enough to stretch her neck and give Juliana a disinterested sniff before giving Hugh a more particular one. Hugh did not make a sound, but Juliana felt a stab of her own fear for Hugh's safety. Bringing the heir to the throne of Cyprus into the company of leopards, even supposedly tamed ones, did not seem like one of her better ideas. Fortunately, the leopard keeper could read people as well as animals, and casually steered the leopard toward her cage. "Salomé like you. You come next time and feed her. She like you more."

Left standing between Hugh and Wink, one boy regarding the other with relief, the other with curiosity, Juliana regained her composure. "That was very well done, Wink. How long did it take you to teach her to do that?"

"Not long. Salomé likes sheep liver."

Wink spoke with confidence which pleased Juliana, but not Hugh. "What a stupid name, Wink," Hugh snorted. "You serve my father's leopards sheep's liver."

Reminded so abruptly of being a servant, Wink looked at Juliana in confusion. Oh dear, boys' rivalries could become nasty very quickly. "He certainly does." Juliana hastened to agree with Hugh. "Just think how pleased and surprised your father the king will be when he finds out you already know what to feed the leopards."

Hugh shrugged with pretended indifference, but Juliana knew that pleasing his father ranked high. She nodded to Wink to go after Djalali, then came closer to Hugh. This was as good a time as any. "And there is something else that your father ought to know, isn't there? About Leontios. But you can't tell him now."

"What? How do you know?" Hugh's surprise became suspicion.

Better bluff than bluster, Juliana decided. "I know many things. So do you, no? We have to keep each other's secrets."

Hugh blinked at her, relief on his face. "I couldn't tell him. I ate too much *kandiq*." He held the pouch closer to him. "I was going to the privy by myself. I saw a lady outside it. She was talking to Leontios. She had a veil over her face. She gave him something and said something and then there was a noise. She left quickly, and Leontios was going too, and he tripped and dropped something and they caught him, and . . . and . . ."

The words rushed out of the boy faster and faster, and Juliana listened with her mind absorbing every one, but only one stood out like a beacon. *A lady*. "I know. They killed him. But they did not see you, did they?"

Hugh shook his head. "Don't think so."

"Good. And you did not tell anyone either, not even Father Silbo?"

"No," Hugh said, pride on his soft, child's face.

She must not alarm the boy, but she could not let him go, not yet. "Did you see what the lady gave Leontios? Was it a message?"

Hugh nodded. "I think so. But they took that one. They looked for the other one, but it was dark. I saw where Leontios dropped it, though. So I waited until they left and . . . and I took it."

Two messages. There were two messages. Lasalle did not know. Juliana could barely hide her excitement. "Oh, well done. What did it say?"

Hugh muttered to his feet, "I don't know. I don't understand it."

Oh, dear. The message must have been written in Greek. "I see. But you hid it, didn't you?"

Hugh wiped his nose on the back of his sleeve. "Yes. I was going to give it to my uncle when he came but then—"

"I came. And Niketas."

Hugh shrugged. "I don't like him. He always tries to be nice to me. I know he doesn't mean it."

Abbess Vigilantia was right. Secrets become terrible burdens to young boys, especially young boys with no friends of their own age to share them. "You are very brave, my lord Hugh. And wise not to trust . . . them."

"I don't," Hugh de Lusignan said proudly with the tone of someone who had been underestimated.

Juliana breathed a sigh of relief. "Do you think you can show me the message so that no one will know that you have it, not even Father Silbo?"

Hugh nodded. "Yes. But how?"

They stood in a leopards' cage stained with blood and urine, crushed sheep bones scattered here and there. "We can meet here. No one would suspect. We can trust Djalali and Wink. My lord Lasalle does. They all think that you are afraid of the leopards. Imagine that."

A pleased, sly grin lit up Hugh's round face. "I am not afraid. I can come. I will give it to Wink."

Oh, clever boy. Juliana wanted to hug the junior Hugh de Lusignan. This apple had not fallen far from the tree after all. Hugh might have been a child in years, but he was not an easily manipulated fool. "What a splendid idea," she said.

The moment the words left her lips, Juliana realized that she had recruited young Hugh de Lusignan for a scheme whose outcome she could neither predict nor control. Was she placing Hugh's life in danger as well? Surely not. Surely Niketas would see to it that Hugh remained unharmed if only to ensure for himself a place behind Hugh's throne.

"Lady, come and see the leopards."

Juliana looked up from her book to see Wink beckoning her. She cast a quick glance at the servants who tended the garden after a storm that had toppled the topiary. Abbess Vigilantia was right. The weather had become cold and the wind dragged rain clouds across the island. On those days, she applied herself to the books Father Silbo lent her if only to hide her own excited ruminations about Hugh's discovery. *A lady and two messages. Who could she be? What was in those messages?* She almost decided that Hugh had changed his mind, but obviously the boy had waited until certain that he could safely send it to her.

With the book under her arm, Juliana followed Wink. "And what have you taught Salomé this time, Wink?" she said loudly enough for the servants to hear. None of them paid attention.

The leopards stretched out in the cage, their tails twitching at the interruption of their sleep. Sweeping up after the cats, Djalali gave her a smile. Juliana returned it, uncertain what Wink had told him, and uncertain where in this place Wink could have hidden a message. The boy unlocked the cage and knelt by one of the cats and reached inside its collar. He drew from it a tightly folded piece of parchment. Djalali handed it to Juliana through the bars. "No search there, Lady, no?"

"No, not without becoming her supper," Juliana agreed and eagerly unfolded the sheet. The ink of some of the words had smudged, but they were written in Latin, not Greek. And no wonder that Hugh did not understand them. The message concerned the terms of the Pisans' contract for collecting anchorage fees in the harbor at Limassol. Juliana inspected both sides of the page. Unless there was some invisible or coded message, this was a copy of a well-known clause.

Juliana tapped her chin while the two watched her. Leontios was not killed because of this message. He died because someone wanted to get hold of the second message, the one that the veiled lady gave him. The one that ended up in the hands of 'them.' Hugh did not know 'them', but Morphia knew. Why else would she be so distraught? As for the veiled lady–that time in the garden, Burgundia wanted to tell her something. Was she the veiled lady or was it Morphia?

"Did I do right, Lady?" Wink asked anxiously.

"You did, Master Wink," Juliana handed the parchment to Wink. "Do you think that Salomé would mind minding this a little longer?"

Wink glowed with pride. "That's Zoë."

"So she is." Juliana curtsied to Wink and Djalali, and forcing herself to walk most decorously, returned to the chamber to plan her next move. Young Hugh de Lusignan had given her a piece of the mosaic. Morphia would have to provide the rest of the pieces.

CHAPTER 28

She was being watched. She was certain of it and never went to the leopards' cage again.

Niketas had replaced not only her guards but also her women except for Morphia who waited on her with tear-swollen eyes, starting and crossing herself every time some clumsy servant dropped a pot or the wind slammed the shutters. Juliana knew that by not confiding to Morphia about what had happened at Famagusta, she added to the woman's distress, but then Morphia had not confided in her either. Yet.

On those occasions when Juliana passed Hugh in the corridors or under a colonnade, she curtsied with a friendly smile and a word or two, and remained in Hugh's company only in the presence of Father Silbo. On the first occasion she deliberately dropped a book she was handing to Hugh and when they both bent to pick it up, she whispered to him, "I burned it."

Hugh appeared relieved, which was more than Juliana could be, given the fact that she lied. *Who would reproach a mother protecting her child?* In her worst moments, she wished that she could make Morphia carry a hot iron or dunk her in the Dardanelles to find out what she knew about her husband's spying. She could, however, take a more simple approach and ask.

When the women brought their supper, Juliana dismissed them as soon as they served it, and shoved the door bolt into place behind them. Startled, Morphia looked up from her cup. "Is something the matter, my lady?"

Her back against the door, Juliana faced her. "We must be careful and lock our door every night. We can't trust the maids or the guards, can we? After all, we don't know who killed Leontios. Or do we?"

Morphia's cup clattered on the floor. She crossed herself, her cheeks gray. "My lady, you must not say such a thing. They . . . they will know."

"Better tell me then who they are so that I will know not to tell them."

Morphia's knees gave in, fortunately in the proximity of the cushions. "Oh, they will know. They knew about Leontios. My poor, poor husband."

Juliana knelt by her and took hold of Morphia's hands. "Leontios died before he could send a message to his master. So that message was never delivered, was it?"

The hedgehog eyes blinked at Juliana. "It wasn't?"

"No." Juliana assured her decisively, having no assurance that either reply could be counted on to favor her.

Surprise overtook Morphia's fear. "Then who has it?"

Morphia did not know about the second message. What only a moment ago seemed so perilous a proposition became the door that sprung open. "I found it and burned it."

The hedgehog eyes became a steady stare of incredulity. "But . . . but wasn't it important?"

"No. No one needed to die because of it. But Leontios did. Who was he sending the message to? Who was his master? Is it Niketas?"

Morphia pressed her fist to her bosom. "Not him. Niketas only let us pass on what we had to those Ibelíns. Leontios said they paid well, and Niketas . . . he took a part. I only did what my husband told me." Tearful moans followed. "Oh, Leontios, such a reward for your loyalty. It's my fault."

The information did not surprise Juliana, except for one thing: why would the Ibelíns kill a useful spy? "Why is it your fault? At Famagusta, you thought that those men would kill you. If Leontios was loyal to the Ibelíns, then he was betrayed. Did you betray your husband, Morphia?"

Morphia crossed herself, panic in her eyes. Juliana touched the woman's quivering cheek. "It was by accident, wasn't it? Surely Leontios has forgiven you. You said it yourself, he was a saint. Who did you tell, Morphia?"

A fountain of tears came with a flood of wails. "I only told her that Leontios was already sending messages to them. Her, I told her. May God strike her dead, the Lusignan whore!"

Juliana sat back. "You told Burgundia."

Confession might be good for the soul, but since Morphia had confided in her, the woman became more and more distraught, more frightened each day even though Juliana spent every moment in her company. Juliana tried to assure Morphia that even if 'they' found out about it, 'they' would now have to dispose of both of them. An unlikely occurrence, given that Niketas would be afraid of Lasalle's swift retribution. After all, Lasalle killed Niketas's man just to drive home that point to the *sekretikos*.

Juliana told Morphia that much, wanting to convince her as much as herself. Morphia would not be convinced.

"You are safe in these walls because of who you are, my lady." Morphia wrung her hands. "I know they are watching me. I wish to join my sister. She's at *Ayios Heracleidios* in Tomassos. I'll find peace only there, I beg of you, give me leave, save me."

No amount of persuasion could sway Morphia, not even the offer to have her seek refuge with the sisters of Saint Mary's rather than to travel to Tomassos. "I can't trust anyone in Nikosia," Morphia sobbed. "I can't have peace anywhere else. I beg of you, my lady, take pity on me."

Juliana took pity on her. The following day, Morphia set out in the company of pilgrims, a figure shrunk by fear in her mule's pannier. A coffer of coins accompanied her, Leontios's gain from his livelihood as a spy for the Ibelíns, now to be offered to the convent as atonement for the sin of disloyalty.

After Morphia's departure, Juliana walked about the gardens, ignoring the world around her. Whoever had killed Leontios did it so that he would not reveal the existence of the second message. A message that ended up in someone's hands, a message worth killing for.

But Burgundia? Juliana could not imagine Aimary's daughter involved in a plot against her father. On the other hand, her mother was an Ibelín. Where would Burgundia's loyalties lie? As for the presence of the Lord of Beirut—little doubt where John d'Ibelín's loyalties lay.

Oh, loyalty. This place reeked of plots and betrayals. She had a part of her answer and only one choice. She had to tell Lasalle so that he could warn the king against his own daughter. After that, Aimary de Lusignan could sort out his own familial problems.

Only one thing prevented her. She was trapped on the island of Aphrodite.

"I came to wait on you, Lady Juliana," the accented, feminine voice repeated.

Juliana forced opened her eyes, trying to shake off sleep heavy with dreams of the previous night. She did not dream about Eleanor, not this night. She dreamt about *him;* bottomless black eyes and the face of a hunting hawk, touch as light as a moth. She swallowed and tried to sit up, her head dulled by the vividness of the dream, her body hollow, hungry. She looked about the chamber. "What?"

Winter light fell onto the mosaics and carpets. Morphia had been gone for days. Juliana had informed Niketas of her departure for Saint Heracleidios without an explanation as to the cause of it. Niketas stroked his beard to hide his surprise or perhaps relief. In an odd way, Juliana felt relief as well. Now she only had to worry about herself, Wink, and Hugh—and the strange woman in her bedchamber. Juliana blinked. No, that was not a dream.

"I said I came to wait on you."

The woman moved about, inspecting the furnishings with studied indifference, the silk of her gown shimmering scales of Poseidon's sea serpents. No waiting woman wore a gown like that. Juliana sat up. The woman faced her and curtsied with a smile on her lips, her plucked brows arched over her *kohl*-painted eyes.

Rhoxsane, the mistress of Kolossi.

CHAPTER 29

The mistress of Kolossi appeared just as Juliana remembered her from that first day on this island–a lady of substance and self-esteem.

"I do not wish my lord de Lusignan to think me remiss during his absence," she said in very good French and with that knowing little smile that mistresses reserve for wives, and resumed her inspection.

Juliana glanced at the door. There were not that many Lusignans in this place, so chances were Rhoxsane did not have in mind Aimary or Hugh. The door bolt remained in place. Being abed and in a bed shift, one could consider oneself at a disadvantage when finding oneself in the presence of a woman in a gown whose train trickled across the tesserae. *She is a traitor and a poisoner.* Where was her dagger? "How did you–"

Rhoxsane ran her finger along the window lattice and frowned at a speck of dust she detected there. "Your servants must do their duties more diligently."

Juliana got herself from under the sheets and quilts. Her dagger's hilt poked out under her folded gown. She wrapped herself in the counterpane, not moving far from the dagger. She noticed that Rhoxsane gave her figure an appraising glance, clearly concluding no competition from that corner. Juliana overcame an overwhelming urge to strike the woman. "I said, how did you–"

Rhoxsane inclined her head toward the wall drapery. "There is a door behind those. Didn't Morphia tell you? I suppose she had other things on her mind. And my lord de Lusignan did not need to use that passage to visit your bedchamber sur-sur–"

"Surreptitiously. And how do you know this?"

"When I was a girl, I used to play here. I see that not much has changed."

Juliana did not think it necessary to pursue the subject of the room's decorations or its former inhabitants. "And what prompted you to visit it this time?"

"Niketas told me that you've lost your woman. Since your husband chose her for you, I thought it only proper that I replace her while he's absent. He went to Acre with the king, did he not?"

Niketas told me. So they were in it together. Juliana reminded herself that she ought to ignore questions she'd rather not answer. "I haven't lost Morphia. I released her from my service at her own request. I'll choose my own waiting woman."

The lady of Kolossi gave a pained sigh. "I am sorry, I thought you knew. It seems that the pilgrims' fare did not agree with Morphia. She died."

The painted face of Rhoxsane of Kolossi remained the only fixed point in a chamber. The rest spun around her and the roar in Juliana's head nearly drowned the sound from a pair of crimson lips. "Lady Juliana . . . do you hear me? Here, take some wine. Drink . . ."

She did. The wine's tang bit into her tongue.

She is a poisoner. Juliana struck out wildly. The goblet flew from Rhoxsane's hand. Juliana collapsed on the floor, choking and retching in painful spasms, trying to expel the last drop of the wine from her throat, knowing well that she had swallowed some of it. Through the rivers of her tears, she saw Rhoxsane back away, the bodice of her exquisite gown indelibly stained. Her face a marble mask, Rhoxsane dabbed the wine splatters from her bosom's glowing skin with the edge of her sleeve. "How odd of Niketas not to tell you. I wonder why. One cannot trust anyone in this place."

She left Juliana to wheeze helplessly on the tesserae and went to refill the goblet with wine from a long-necked ewer. Juliana did not remember having ordered a wine ewer. Her throat burned. Immobilized, she stared at the woman, waiting for the poison to take hold of her, for the pain and the nausea, for the agony and the oblivion. How long would it be for the poison to take her? *Eleanor . . . Eleanor.*

Rhoxsane brought the goblet to her lips and took a careful sip.

She spat it out as quickly as Juliana did. "You are right. The wine has soured. Your servants are unforgivably careless. I will dismiss them and bring my own. They will mind their duties."

The fire in Juliana's throat remained, but the paralyzing terror of her own death, so far from Eleanor, eased a little and her thoughts regained coherence. She could not help Morphia and Morphia was right. Someone had wanted her dead and they killed her, by means of Rhoxsane's poison, perhaps, but on whose orders? As for herself, Niketas's fear of Lasalle would not have saved her either in this instance. She could have easily been smothered, poisoned or stabbed, but Rhoxsane had revealed to her the passage, and had not disposed of her when she could have easily done so and disappeared the same way whence she came.

Now why would Rhoxsane of Kolossi come to Nikosia to tell her of Morphia's death, and to insist on using her own servants? Of course. Rhoxsane had come to Nikosia not for the viscountess of Tillières' sake, but for her own.

"Ionia and Eulogia," Juliana croaked through tortured tonsils.

"What?" Rhoxsane sat the goblet on the table.

Juliana dropped the wine-stained cover and got to her feet although her knees remained shaky. If this woman claimed that she came to be her waiting woman, then one she should be. Keeping her dagger out of sight, Juliana reached for her gown and held it out to Rhoxsane. Her voice remained reedy from the wine vinegar. "Your daughters, are they not?"

Rhoxsane hesitated, but took the gown to help Juliana into it with the efficiency of a maid servant. "Have you seen them?"

The change in Rhoxsane's voice was audible–concern and excited curiosity, and underneath it all lurked fear–a fear for one's daughters. Juliana felt a twinge of compassion replaced by the icy reminder that Abbess Vigilantia wanted her to know that in Saint Mary's custody Rhoxsane's daughters served as sureties for their mother's conduct. After all, their mother was a traitor and a poisoner.

"Yes. They are both well and so very fond of Abbess Vigilantia. I wouldn't be surprised if they chose to make their profession to Saint Mary's. We must visit them sometime."

Rhoxsane's fingers paused on the gown's lacing. "The king will not allow me to see them."

Juliana regained her voice and with it her confidence. "The king is in Acre. He need not know, need he? Surely Abbess Vigilantia will grant her permission. Would you like me to ask her?"

The lady of Kolossi took a step back. "You would do that?"

Juliana faced her unexpected, uninvited, and unwelcome visitor. "Of course. Isn't that why you came? A traitoress cannot make such a plea to the woman she betrayed, can she?"

Rhoxsane managed to remain expressionless. Her fear for her daughters dwarfed her fear for herself, but she could not protect them if she were not alive, and her position secure. Since the visit of Lord Makheras, she could no longer be certain of either. Her hands relaxed. "No. She cannot."

The girl did not react the way Rhoxsane expected to an admission she had so readily conceded. "For that, I wish something in return," Juliana de Charnais said.

Rhoxsane expected that one. "What is it you wish?"

Juliana did not have to think about it. If there are five means of gaining a well-guarded citadel, there also must be the means of escaping from it. "I wish you to tell me about your meeting with John d'Ibelín in Limassol, and after that, I wish you to hire me an excellent pilot with a good boat to take me to Acre."

Rhoxsane curtsied, her relief well hidden. *Oh, you silly girl.* You think you can play in a game that your own so very clever husband is finding to be full of traps? "Of course, Lady Juliana. As you wish."

PART III

The Tower of Flies

He that worketh deceit shall not dwell within my house; he that telleth lies shall not tarry in my sight.

Psalm 101:7

CHAPTER 30

Saint Jean d'Acre, kingdom of Jerusalem

Guided by the belfry of Saint Andrew's, the fishing boat with the grandiose name of *Achilleus* followed the coastline of the *terre-sainte*, ploughing the waters northward along the green ridge of Mount Carmel where Elijah brought down God's wrath upon the priests of Baal.

Acre's mast-clogged outer harbor had welcomed the ships of pilgrims and merchants, galleys of Musulmans and Christians, of kings, bishops, lords, ladies, and soldiers—and now it welcomed the viscountess of Tillières, arriving by less stately means, but ever mindful of God's wrath. On whom His would fall the next time, Juliana dared not contemplate. She did contemplate that the Holy Father had promised four years and forty days of indulgence to those who reached as far as these shores. In view of the last days, she already needed every hour.

The boat's size allowed it to maneuver past two guard towers, one of them rising from the tip of a narrow arm of a breakwater that embraced the harbor. Between the two towers the harbormaster each night raised and lowered a chain to protect Acre's inner harbor and its fortified port. At the tip of the bay's crescent, the Temple Knights had established their new headquarters, siting it as a warning and a challenge to all who approached this Christian outpost.

A few days after Juliana's encounter with Rhoxsane, the mistress of Kolossi had found a fishing boat and a crew to take Juliana to Acre and to serve as her guards and guides. The men came from Kolossi, spoke good enough French, and could be trusted, Rhoxsane assured her.

Juliana briefly wondered how Rhoxsane would explain her absence to the *sekretikos*, but the lady Rhoxsane knew how to spin a suitable tale. Juliana managed to whisper her plan to Hugh. After all, the boy had trusted her. Hugh's silent, wide-eyed acknowledgement told her that he appreciated her confidence in him.

The men of her escort did not strike Juliana as simple fishermen. When she stepped on the planks of the wave-battered boat, it occurred to her that nothing prevented them from throwing her overboard once they left Kyrenia. Nothing, perhaps, except her prayers—and the fact that Abbess Vigilantia held Rhoxsane's daughters as hostages.

The weather favored them and kind wind drove the *Achilleus* to the shores of the Holy Land without as much as a storm cloud. Instead of reassuring her, the sight of the golden-hued city spread along the white-shored bay caused an odd dread to descend on her. When they passed the harbor's guard towers, Juliana knelt on the deck in a thanksgiving prayer. When she crossed herself, the man at the rudder did likewise, pointing to the tower rising from the waters.

"The Tower of Flies. Baal's priests sacrificed animals to him. The flies came there for their blood and flesh. Now the blood of our Redeemer washed the land, no?" The man told her with a smile, relieved by their arrival as much as by Christ's victory.

Juliana did not reciprocate it. She had expected to experience the sweetness of the Savior's presence, but the breeze that suddenly filled the sails carried the smell of blood and the stench of death.

❦

On shore, matters of the crassly mundane kind claimed her attention. They paid for anchorage—a silver mark. Since they brought no wares, Juliana thought the amount exorbitant, but the dues from the port belonged to the king, so she voiced no complaint. At least they passed through the Court of the Chain and through the port's iron gate without further impediment or impertinent questions from the customs clerks.

To the queen of Jerusalem belonged a number of *hôtels* in the city which her steward let to prominent visitors, wealthy pilgrims, and even wealthier merchants for the duration of the *passagium*, the trading season in the *Levante*. Juliana's escort did not conduct her to any of them.

From the Chain Quarter they rode along the wide street to one of the gates to the city, past the Venetian Quarter, past warehouses, bathhouses, courts and inns, hostels and hospitals, past cloisters and churches with their square towers. They passed stables, taverns, and bakers' and butchers' shops along streets that widened into noisy *souks* overflowing with the bounty of foreign and nearer lands where human effort and ingenuity had transformed that bounty into objects of desire, beauty, and usefulness.

They rode by narrow, vaulted passages and down streets shaded by sails and reed mats strung between houses clinging to each other, some four and five stories high. Shops at the base floors opened to the streets, and above them apartments hid behind painted and carved shutters. The men pointed out to her the communes of the Pisans and the Genoese, marked by their banners, adorned by the splendor of their churches, chapels, and merchants' palaces, walled from others for the sake of peace, self-governing according to their charters of privilege granted by kings.

Their hired mules carried them through the usual crowds of mariners, traders, artisans, servants, and slaves with features and dress of all of God's races and creeds. Along bobbed the bulbous headwear of merchants from all over the *Levante* and Christendom, and the flat-topped, black hats of bearded Armenian, Syrian, and Greek priests and clerks. The rest was a riot of street hawkers armed with powerful sets of lungs, fortune-tellers, snake handlers, combcutters, glassmakers, weavers, potters, quilters, sail and rope makers. Tooth pullers and leeches examined their patients surrounded by the curious offering unsolicited advice. Horse, mule, and camel traders extolled the virtues of their animals with shrill shouts and wild gestures. Armorers, coopers, and blacksmiths tapped away next to red-mawed furnaces, turning out objects lethal and lovely, and pilgrims with their clappers, travelers, and visitors contributed their share to the crush and clamor. The ever-present beggars, grotesquely misshaped by feigned, self-inflicted, or God-given maladies accosted the passersby.

With everyone in fantastic and barbaric cloth, clothes, and ornaments, no one could miss the scores of enticingly dressed and painted persons and hardly grown children—and those who resembled them—and thuggish sorts of men everywhere, justifying the presence of men-at-arms hired or employed to guard the more elevated portion of the populace.

Along with the sights came the smells of fresh bread, of mutton, lamb, pork, and pullet and every sea creature imaginable, tenderly tended on hissing grills in lemon and oil; rubbed, basted and marinated in garlic, pepper, cardamom, cinnamon, turmeric, ginger, and cloves. The head-dizzying fragrances from perfumers' stores found counterpoint in the spice markets, and all competed with whiffs of dye works and stables and pigpens, and the crush of humanity.

Beautiful in its location, astonishing in its size, opulent in its wealth and corruption, the Latins' great port and city they called Saint Jean d'Acre enraptured as much as it repelled.

They reached the principal gate to Acre's fortress, built in the north part of the city, next to the sizeable quarters of the Hospitallers. There Juliana was glad to release Rhoxsane's men from their responsibility for her, and had the impression that they shared her sentiments.

Her name, larded with her titles including Lasalle's for good measure, astonished the guards enough to gain her an immediate admittance into the fortress. A new escort led her up the run of broad, steep steps to the king's audience hall behind a door that could well have guarded a royal treasury, but thankfully did not usher her into the king's presence. She wanted to avoid Aimary de Lusignan until she had a chance to deliver her news to Lasalle.

She wanted to avoid the queen as well, but one of the guards returned with a servant Juliana feared was the queen's waiting woman.

Having no choice in the matter, Juliana followed the woman through the halls and hallways, passageways and tunnels, past more guards, to copper-embossed doors. There the woman left her to enter the queen of Jerusalem's private apartments.

Thirty-three years old, Isabella d'Anjou reclined on a couch wearing an expression between boredom and superiority, enveloped in perfume and a gown of white *tafeth* that did justice to a woman who had borne seven children. Instead of a veil over the braids of her black hair, she wore a gold coronet with a *pendilla* of pearls dripping down her temples. In her round, soft face blanched by paste, her dark, round eyes outlined in *kohl* gave her the appearance of an expressionless *eikon.*

A dozen waiting women attended her, one of them playing a *citara*, the others giving Juliana curious glances from their embroidery and from tending to the occupants of several birdcages. The sound of trickling water came from somewhere, the scent of roses permeated the air warmed by braziers. Mosaics and life-like frescoes splashed the walls, colored marble as finely carved as honeycomb dressed the side chapel, spilling onto the columns that segregated a number of alcoves. Juliana detected a heavier scent, like incense, soaking the cushions, bolsters and the soft carpets underfoot. For a dizzying moment, she was in the crypt of Saint Maixent where Mélusine's descendants rested, dead, yet ever present.

The queen reached into a silver bowl brought to her by a woman as black as Djalali and retrieved an egg-sized ball of almond paste coated with sesame seeds. Juliana noticed that under her rings, the queen's plump hands were covered in intricate patterns of henna. "My lord, the king, tells me that you are married to my lord Lasalle." Isabella d'Anjou said before Juliana rose from her curtsey. "We will miss him when you leave."

The statement did not say much or said more than Juliana expected. After all, in this woman the imperial blood on her mother's side had merged with the blood of the recent conquerors of the very same empire. Whether that alloy had created a conflict within her, Juliana could not tell. After four husbands, Isabella had formed her own opinion of men, including Guérin de Lasalle.

Juliana licked her dry lips. The queen's inflection reminded her of Isabella's half brother. She wished it were not so. "It is only concern for the security of our daughter's birthright that calls my husband back to Poitou, Your Grace."

"Is it?" The queen's tone did not indicate the least interest. "An heiress. One to be well guarded. I sent my daughters by Count Henri to Champagne to safeguard their inheritance. Have you provided for your daughter's marriage?"

The question took Juliana aback. "No, Your Grace. She's not yet a year old."

"Even more the reason. The pledge can be later revoked on account of her age. Mine was."

Isabella d'Anjou spoke by rote like she was reading from her psalter, and Juliana realized that it was not an affliction but an affectation. She thought it better to agree until she could determine the direction of this conversation. "Yes, Your Grace."

"Of course God may grant you more children." Isabella was examining the patterns on her hands.

"Yes, Your Grace."

"Your husband went with my lord the king to Arsuf. I wish you to keep me company until they return." Isabella glanced at Juliana's gown. "After you are properly attended." She gestured to a middle-aged waiting woman who stepped forward for Isabella to whisper to her.

To Arsuf. No matter how objectionable to its recipient, a queen's order cannot be easily countermanded. Juliana curtsied to hide her bitter disappointment. "Thank you, Your Grace."

CHAPTER 31

Arsuf indeed!

The queen's woman, Beroniki, appeared to be the same age as Mistress Morphia and equally short of stature. Although years had softened her face, her eyes remained sharp, and unlike Morphia, Beroniki did not allow herself the display of any sentiment. She issued orders to servants in Greek and French with precise pronunciation, her movements, like her speech, economical; her hands, folded over her apron, without a single ring held a ring of keys instead. Juliana instantly concluded that what Beroniki lacked in matronly affections, she made up in matriarchal manners that were not to be questioned let alone challenged.

Instead of being shown to her chamber, Juliana ended up in the Bath of the Women near the king's palace. She joined the company of several women of rank who lounged about, pink and polished, wrapped in fine cotton sheets. Juliana made a polite effort to answer their questions while the bath women rubbed, scrubbed, rinsed, massaged, plucked, plaited, oiled, and perfumed her within a hair's breadth of her life.

Since a queen's order cannot be easily countermanded, Juliana submitted to it all. After Nikosia, she had grudgingly accepted the fact that in this land one could not escape such procedures. She would have traded them all for her sheet-lined tub and privacy in Parthenay, but noted that her companions seemed to have enjoyed the very same procedures, concluded by sweets and wine served on small round trays.

Juliana's only victory consisted of refusing to have her extremities marked by henna paste which the other women had applied to their hands, and some even to their feet and bodies, by a couple of women with that peculiar skill.

Perhaps like honey-pickled dates and sesame paste, it was all a matter of acquired taste, Juliana told herself when, swaddled in a cotton sheaf like a caterpillar, the bath women left her on a chaise in an alcove to recover her dignity. After a while, having been dressed in the queen's gift of a gown with her skin burning in uncomfortable places from the scrapping and pummeling, and with cosmetics trowelled thickly enough to cover every flaw and freckle, she was collected again by Beroniki.

Beroniki brought her back to the royal palace, to a chamber assigned to guests. Juliana rejoiced to find a small chapel there, and next door a bath with a proper tub–an ancient thing in marble. From the carved procession that wound around its exterior, she suspected it to have once been a sarcophagus. The practically-minded *poulains* and the visiting Latins obviously did not mind.

She almost did mind when she discovered that another occupant, temporarily absent, had previously been installed in the chamber–Lasalle. However, since she came in search of him, she could not object to that either.

Despite her misgivings, her gowns and face paint, applied by Beroniki's women, signaled her to be of the queen's household and thus allowed her the freedom of the palace without frightening the servants or summoning the queen's guards. Armed with her new frock and face, Juliana explored the fortress with its high-vaulted corridors, halls of columns the thickness of oak trunks, the rebuilt ramparts anchored by towers once crushed and crumbled under missiles hurled by Christians and Musulmans alike and undermined by their sappers. Standing there on high, the wind from the sea rumbled around the towers and her ears, tearing her veil. Above her head, the wind snapped the banners of the House of Lusignan–silver chevrons on an azure field flashing against the blue of heaven like the scale of a sky serpent. *During storms you can hear her cry for her husband and her children . . .*

Juliana crossed herself. Despite the size and wealth and the many splendors of the city, or because of them, the city was not safe from future attacks. How long it would be before these edifices and these people would face another siege, another breach that would transform the current occupants into prisoners? She wished she could entertain happier thoughts, but her anxiety to reach Lasalle crowded out everything else. That was until Beroniki introduced her to the queen's children—her three by Aimary de Lusignan, and his youngest by Eschiva d'Ibelín.

Isabella's and Aimary's own children, six-year-old Sybilla and five-year-old Melisande, both named after Jerusalem's queens, kept hold on their almost three-year-old brother Almaric who wiggled and wriggled against their restraint, eager to join his older half brothers. Guy and John de Lusignan, dark-haired twins, possessed the energetic curiosity and inclination to mayhem of nine-year-olds. Their older brother Hugh would inherit the crown of Cyprus, but illustrious alliance awaited each of Eschiva's children, intended to tie together the two royal families of *outre-mer* and Cyprus.

Their fifteen-year-old sister Heloise, slender and tall for her age, had the same fair coloring as Burgundia once had, and the same reserved manner. At ten years and of robust figure, Alix de Lusignan resembled her twin brothers.

When Juliana appeared in the chamber, the Lusignan brood drew into a tight little pack. Not trying to hide her smile, Juliana curtsied to them all. "It seems that I am outnumbered by the Lusignan legions."

"You are not." Alix clicked her tongue and took Juliana's hand with a self-confidence that came naturally to her. "You are married to Lord Guérin. You are one of us. Come and see what he brought us."

It appeared that Lasalle had already made the children's acquaintance and left an indelible impression, at least on the younger ones. Heloise kept her distance, but the other children encircled Juliana to take her with them into the walled garden.

The moment they entered, a couple of sturdy mastiff pups threw themselves at the children with furry enthusiasm and excited yips. The younger children responded in kind and soon the lot of them rolled on the ground, shrieking with laughter while the servants ineffectually attempted to curb them. The young Lusignans' liveliness proved so infectious that Juliana wished she could join them.

Behind her, Heloise made a small noise and when Juliana turned to see the cause of it, another young girl stood next to Heloise. "They are such children," she said with disdain.

Heloise gave Juliana a cautious glance. "This is Maria. We call her *La Marquise.* She's twelve."

Of course. Isabella's daughter by Conrad de Montferrat, named after her maternal grandmother, black-haired and round-faced after her mother, her figure displaying the maturity that settled early on Levantine girls, and leaving the unfortunate impression that Maria de Montferrat would not be distinguished by either her looks or her mind.

Maria aimed a haughty smile at her stepsister. "She is lying. I am thirteen. I am going to be the queen."

Heloise kept her restrained manner. "Don't believe her, Lady Juliana. She tells that to everyone."

"Oh, I am too!" With the heavy tassel at her girdle, Maria took an un-queenly swipe at Heloise. "She always does that, Lady Juliana, don't believe her."

Heloise burst out laughing and the two plunged into friendly sparring with giggles until their nurses arrived who put an end to it.

One of the nurses prompted Maria toward Juliana. "Now apologize to Lady Juliana, and welcome her properly. I am sorry, my lady. I am Xene, the principal nurse. This is my sister, Madelena." The woman introduced the other nurse who tried to refasten the ribbon that slipped from Heloise's plaits. The women were Greek and spoke French, both of them in their early twenties, young enough to keep up with their charges and old enough to impose discipline on them.

"You must remember who you are. Modesty and temperance always. Do you want people to talk about you?" Madelena chided Maria who assumed a childish pout at being treated like a child. "After you two apologize to Lady Juliana, go to your prayers."

The girls offered their apologies in a duet of voices that made them giggle again, and hand in hand, they skipped away before their nurses could correct them.

Juliana smiled. Heloise and Maria reminded her so much of herself at their age that she felt a pang of pity for them, and herself. Their lives would soon change, the exuberance of youth tamed by marriage and motherhood.

Under a lone almond tree, Guy and John clashed with their wooden swords in a fierce battle in which Almaric, Melisande, and the mastiff pups took sides. When Xene and Madelena went to remove Almaric and Melisande from harm, the pups attacked the nearest ankle. Almaric screamed and fought like a bear cub, and Melisande dug in her heels and tried to outdo him until the nurses finally separated every one.

"They will sleep well tonight." Xene tussled Almaric's hair. "If there is anything you wish, my lady, you need only ask. Come along you now," she called out to Guy and John, and the boys, with the usual protestations and tarrying, finally followed, dragging the wrecks of their weapons.

Juliana felt a tug at her skirts and when she turned around, Sybilla, who had kept her distance from the others, held out a sadly mangled twig. "It's for you."

Eleanor. With a torn heart, Juliana took the offering and Sybilla threw herself around her waist in a child's hug, a fleeting, shy hug of a child who needed to be hugged, and then she was gone.

These children, but for their parents no different from the sons and daughters of the butcher or baker, had formed their own alliances, friendships, and rivalries. The youngest ones were yet unaware of their place in a chain that bound the handful of families who held on to this part of the world. Juliana stood there battling tears and emotions until Beroniki came to take her to her chamber where an unexpected visitor waited.

CHAPTER 32

The queen of Jerusalem made herself at home, poured two full goblets and offered one to Juliana. The delicate, swirling lines of henna on Isabella's hands protected against the Evil Eye, Morphia had told Juliana. Juliana trusted that a simple crucifix and a fervent prayer to the appropriate saint would be a sufficient protection, but here people obviously insisted on being additionally fortified. Juliana curtsied but hesitated to take the cup. The queen lowered her hand and dismissed Beroniki. "You don't appear to trust me, Lady Juliana," Isabella said, this time free of affectation.

Her thoughts disjointed by her encounter with the children and now the queen's presence, Juliana found herself tongue-tied. "No. Yes. I am sorry, I was just . . . surprised."

"Are you well attended? Is there anything you wish to be done?"

"No, thank you, Your Grace."

"You are cautious. Good. Don't trust anyone. I don't. Not my mother, not my vassals. Never my husbands. Except Aimary. And Beroniki." Isabella took a long sip from the goblet before offering it to Juliana again.

Someone had told her almost the very same thing, and not too long ago. This time Juliana took the cup, wishing that the queen would produce Lasalle instead.

"You doubt me about my husband?"

The sharp tone took Juliana aback. "I–"

"Are you surprised that I am fond of Aimary? He still loves her. Eschiva."

Juliana considered the statement in view of the current circumstances. "Your Grace–"

"I am Isabella. I don't wish to be the queen, not here. You may sit."

Juliana took note and sat down. Very well, she would treat the queen like a demanding acquaintance, and one who had perhaps refilled her cup one too many times, and not only recently.

Isabella lowered her hand to admire the hennaed design, her tone impatient. "Tell me. You are married to one of them. Are they all like that?"

"All?"

"The Lusignans. My sister . . . my half sister wanted Guy, and no one could sway her. He would not give her up either, and not because of her crown. She wanted it. I didn't. Why would anyone want a crown of tesserae?"

"Tesserae?" Juliana said. What a strange way to refer to the Crown of Jerusalem. On the other hand, she wanted to keep the conversation away from the Lusignans.

Isabella touched her brow, currently bearing no crown, gold, pearly, or tesseraed. She gestured to the walls on which in the reflected light a mosaic flock of birds in flight spread their wings. "Aimary told me before we were wed that only if you're close enough can you see that it's all made up of pieces. Pry a few loose, and the rest of it can be destroyed, like this kingdom nearly was. Aimary's the one holding it together. He didn't want to marry me. He did it out of duty. He had his own crown by then."

"You are the anointed queen." Nothing else particularly clever came to Juliana. From what she had heard about the queen of Jerusalem, Isabella d'Anjou was beautiful, meek, and malleable, moved about the chessboard of power in *outre-mer* by her mother. More particularly, Maria Komnene and her allies moved men eager to wear even a crown of tesserae in and out of her daughter's bed, depending on the advantage they all could gain from it. Aimary de Lusignan was clearly not among them.

"How diplomatic." Isabella reached for the goblet, her voice thicker. "You've heard the gossip about how my mother hounded me to annul my first marriage?"

Juliana nodded.

Isabella's mouth puckered. "They don't know, and she doesn't know either, that I would have dissolved our . . . matrimony without her harrying me."

Juliana reached for her own goblet. Sometimes wine quelled more than thirst; sometimes its efficacy lay in its other attributes. This time curiosity got the better of her. "Why?"

"Humphrey wouldn't fight for me, let alone for my crown." Isabella smiled a bitter little smile. "Aimary, he fights for my crown. Not me."

A woman's answer, some would say. In this instance, perhaps a truthful one. *What does a marriage make?* "But you are the crown."

Isabella sighed with hint of impatience. "So they say. I dread what tribulation it will bring to Maria."

"I am sorry."

"Why should you be? Yours would fight for you, wouldn't he? Or did he marry you out of duty?"

Juliana muttered her answer to the cup. "We all have a duty."

The queen waited, silent, expecting Juliana to offer more. When Juliana did not, Isabella did not hide her impatience. "My mother sent a message that she wishes to see you."

The statement dispelled the fog of Juliana's second–or was it third–wine cup, but not enough to prevent her from questioning one's superior. "Why?"

Isabella did not point out Juliana's trespass. "She wants something. That gives you an advantage. Remember it. You promise to tell me afterward?"

That took care of the fog. Here at last the queen revealed the reason for her visit. Isabella of Jerusalem wanted Juliana de Charnais to spy on the dowager queen. Not a terribly original idea and hardly a surprising one in this place of conniving inhabitants. Having lately practiced the art of deception and contrariness, Juliana noticed, to her dismay, that she had enjoyed both. She felt rather bold. Perhaps it was the wine. *Who would reproach a mother for protecting her child?* "Why?"

The queen suffered her questioning. "My mother doesn't confide to me her plots. My brother knows about them, but for him to tell me, I'd have to–"

"Dunk him in the Dardanelles?" Juliana suggested, her tongue and better judgment loosened by the wine.

Isabella laughed with genuine delight. "He said that you had nearly boxed his ears. John deserves it." Her laughter faded. "Sometimes."

The reminder of her encounter with the Lord of Beirut sobered Juliana. She shifted in her seat. How much had he told his sister about it? "I see."

The queen's expression had no trace of her rank. "I know that my husband's life is in peril again. I had nursed him after the last attack. I wish to know who plots against him this time. That's why yours came here, isn't it?"

Juliana kept her composure. "Yes."

"I don't want to lose my husband, Lady Juliana. Can you understand that? You would not want to lose yours, would you?"

So plainly put, the question sank into Juliana's heart. How could she lose a husband when in the eyes of the Church she never had one? How could one tell the queen of Jerusalem that the queen's own half brother, as well as her stepdaughter, could be plotting her husband's death at this very moment?

Isabella stood up, swaying slightly. "You will tell me, won't you."

It was not a question or a request. Holding onto the chair, Juliana stood up as well and curtsied the best she could. "Yes, Your Grace."

And why not? Everyone seemed to be spying on everyone else.

CHAPTER 33

Juliana had heard enough servants' gossip to learn that they disliked Maria Komnene, and that not a few feared her, despite the dowager's public professions of piety and her generous donations to the churches and cloisters. With the return of her son-in-law from Cyprus, Maria Komnene again removed herself to one of her daughter's *hôtels* in the capital. There she continued to receive friends, relatives, and visitors, many displaced by the Latins' seizure of Constantinople, all bringing their tales of woe and violence those conquerors had inflicted on the Christian city.

Juliana wondered if the dowager would resemble the duchess of Aquitaine in appearance as well as in her defiance of public expectations, and prepared herself accordingly. When the dowager's servants came to escort her to their mistress, Juliana climbed into the palanquin with her curiosity keen, wits firmly gathered, and a determination not to accept a single cup.

The porters carried her through the noisy streets to a gate in a high wall. The residence behind it once belonged to a wealthy merchant. She was shown through the courtyard within to a chamber, wooden grilles shuttering its windows. Every table and alcove of the place overflowed with terra cotta jars of all shapes and size, leather and wood caskets, painted bowls and incised pots stocked with powders, roots, and seeds, deflated and desiccated remains of what appeared to be toads and lizards, wafer-thin skins of snakes, claws, feathers, and blanched bones and skulls of birds and their eggs, including ostrich ones, and any number of items that may or may not have belonged at one time to living, breathing creatures. The walls had turned dark from the smoke of oil wicks over which were suspended kettles and pots that simmered and boiled pungent ingredients, all tended by several women advanced in years but no less dedicated.

The heat, smoke, and the smell nearly overwhelmed Juliana. No one took notice of her, but she noticed among the women one who moved among the stations directing, mixing, and sniffing the contents. Suppressing the urge to sneeze into the nearest cauldron, Juliana curtsied in her hostess's direction, folded her hands over her middle, and waited to be acknowledged. After a length of time, the dowager queen pretended to notice her.

"There you are," Maria Komnene said and thereafter ignored her to issue instructions in rapid Greek to the women, after which she simply walked past Juliana, a couple of the women following their mistress.

Not being advised what to do, Juliana fell in line behind them. She ended up in another chamber where the dowager queen and her women disappeared behind a screen depicting a saint Juliana did not recognize. Having nothing else to do, Juliana examined the appointments, selected by someone with a refined and expensive taste. Here light enlivened the mosaics and an assemblage of crosses, reliquaries, caskets and icons that could have been found in the most holy of chapels. Several amulets Morphia had called *enkolpia,* worn as a defense against malevolent spirits, intrigued Juliana. She wished to examine every one, but had no chance.

"Let me see you, girl."

Maria Komnene emerged with half a dozen women in attendance. They had changed her attire—an embroidered *maphorion* that hid her hair, a gown of layers of damask and silk, jewels to spare. In return, the dowager examined every fold on Juliana's gown, the one that Beroniki had recommended. The dismissive little twitch of the dowager's painted lips told Juliana that she knew it.

At one time, Maria Komnene must have been a handsome woman. The shade of her former self remained beneath the layer of paint, the passage of years, and trials of life. Juliana felt a strange tug of sympathy, even admiration for this woman. She wanted to ask how one lived—how one survived in this land—but the dowager's voice crushed those sentiments.

"Most ordinary." Turning to her women, Maria Komnene pronounced her verdict at the end of her inspection with a click of her tongue. "One would expect more of a Lusignan bride. What happened to your nose?"

That was a strike intended to compel an opponent's submission. Good thing that Juliana had promised herself to mind her wits. Her father's fist had landed on her nose a long time ago, leaving a slight deviation. She had not thought about it for some time. In fact, sometimes she even forgot how plain and ordinary she was. *Lasalle made me forget.*

"Why are you smiling, Lady Juliana?" Maria Komnene raised her voice in annoyance.

Juliana did not know that she had, but she did know that blaming the insulted for the insult was a novel approach. At least she knew wherefrom the wind would blow. "You called me to come here, Madame. What about my appearance would then annoy you?"

Whispers of astonishment came from the dowager's attendants. Her eyes on Juliana, Maria Komnene signaled their dismissal, leaving only one waiting woman with her mistress.

"You may sit," Maria Komnene said when the doors closed behind the women. The dowager took to the only chair in the room, her woman on guard by it. Maria Komnene rested her veined hands, each finger ringed and wrists braceleted, on the wide-spaced arms of the backless chair, a posture intended to herald her majesty to most ordinary young women.

Left with the ubiquitous cushions scattered about the floor,

Juliana did not intend to contort herself at the dowager's feet. She therefore piled up three of the sturdiest cushions and sat on top of them, hands on her lap, and waited.

Her improvised seat did not please the dowager either. "It is a custom here to adjust oneself to the world one finds, Lady Juliana. Otherwise, one may be called maladroit."

Juliana went for naïve enthusiasm. "Truly?" She looked about. "Everyone here seems intent on adjusting the world to their own wishes, vial by vial, aren't they? What is it you wish from me, Madame?"

Madame's eyes became steady pinpricks of enmity. "I wish you to persuade that husband of yours to return to Poitou."

That sounded like an order. Maria Komnene intended to get rid of her as fast as possible. It would not do if one were to gain at least some information for the queen. "Why?"

"Because I wish it." The reply came with an undercurrent of disbelief and distaste at having to answer it.

"I see. Is that not too much to expect from this Lusignan's bride?"

Maria Komnene's lips grew thinner. "I was told that you are stupid. You are not, are you. So let me tell you. To remain could be unhealthy. For your husband. And you."

The jolt in the pit of Juliana's stomach told her that she might have been clever in dealing with Niketas and Rhoxsane of Kolossi, but there she had been also lucky. They had more to lose than she did. Against Maria Komnene she might not win by verbal duels and acid wit, but she had to prolong this encounter long enough to gain something from it. "I see. My husband is like Odysseus and not likely to be swayed from his quest."

"Perhaps that is because you are not Penelope. I will make you a philter that will make your husband follow you to Poitou or wherever it is you two belong."

"Thank you. I belong to Normandy. It is difficult to determine where my husband belongs, being a Lusignan. They seem to belong everywhere, don't they? Why not command him?"

Maria Komnene picked up a flywhisk although there appeared to be no insects about. "You are insolent. It is the result of you

Franks lacking manners and therefore excusable. Your husband could meet with brigands, the *bedu,* the Turks, or some accident. You could be returning to Poitou a widow, Lady Juliana."

"Normandy." There. That was clever, but not very useful. And yet . . . why would the dowager call on her for the purposes of warning off Lasalle? A woman of her position had the means to dispose of anyone nosing around, and she did not hide that fact. Yet she had not ordered it done. Did the dowager know something of Burgundia's involvement in Leontios's death? Unless of course Maria Komnene's concern was not for Burgundia, but for her son. *John d'Ibelín.* "What is it you fear from my husband, Madame?"

The dowager queen's stare lost none of its hostility. "Fear? You forget who I am, girl."

This would be a good time to use her wits. "You are not the queen anymore. Or the empress. In any case, look what happened to Constantinople. You and your children are clinging to a sliver of land and you are afraid that it will slip away as well and want to prevent it. It seems that Aimary de Lusignan is the man to do it. Your own daughter thinks so. Why not aid someone who's trying to keep the king safe?"

The dowager queen's glare remained steady through the pause that followed. "Don't think you are clever, girl."

"It is not a question of being clever, surely, but of being right," Juliana countered, caught in the heedless rush of someone in a battle with an opponent who did not turn out as invulnerable as one thought. The trick was to lure Maria Komnene to reveal more. Of course, Madame knew it.

"You know nothing of this land, Lady Juliana. You will do well to heed my warning."

Someone had told her the same thing, not too long ago. "Thank you for your concern, Your Grace. I shall tell it to my husband once he returns with the king from Arsuf."

The dowager queen's smile was reserved for the most naïve of young women. "Do so. You are dismissed, Lady Juliana."

Juliana stood up and curtsied very properly. Once back in the palanquin, she took a full breath. She had left Maria Komnene contemplating whether she had made a mistake in calling on Juliana de Charnais to persuade her husband to cease his enquiries. On the other hand, the dowager left her with a stomach-churning sensation that she truly ought to do so.

CHAPTER 34

Don't drop the pomegranates.

A basket of pomegranates perched on her head, Juliana tried not to breathe or God forbid, sneeze. This was not where she expected to be, in the children's nursery, trying to follow Beroniki's instructions.

Despite her personal preoccupations, she could not escape the season. All around her, the royal household prepared for Christ's Mass and public celebrations at the cathedral of the Holy Cross. Carts loaded with wine tuns creaked into the kitchen yards, and the kitchens swelled with additional help to fill the kettles, ewers, pots, pants, ovens, and tables. In the city, the churches, chapels, houses and their halls dripped with green boughs of pine, cedar, myrtle and garlands of ivy, and everyone's festive apparel, jewels, and ornaments created a feast for the eyes and an opportunity for thieves.

Beroniki told Juliana that since she was, after all, married to the king's kinsman, the queen wished her to attend her with the rest of her women on all public occasions. For those, Juliana was required to learn how to walk, sit, and move about in robes and jewels too splendid to contemplate–hence the reason for the basket of pomegranates and the daily lessons in the company of Heloise de Lusignan and *La Marquise.*

The request–or rather order–surprised Juliana. Once she had duly delivered to Isabella the information she had gleaned from the queen's own mother, Isabella no longer called on her. The information had consisted of nothing more than the queen dowager wishing the wife of my lord Lasalle to persuade him to give up searching for those who would endanger the king's life.

Juliana had not shared the entire conversation or the threat that came with it. Being neither dull-witted nor pliant, the queen already suspected certain members of her own family of the attempts on her husband's life. One thing remained certain. Whatever happened, one must not drop those pomegranates, let alone one's guard.

She quietly blamed Lasalle. Had she been able to tell him what she knew about Leontios's message, she could have avoided the whole episode with Isabella and the dowager. Lasalle's absence had already stretched for what seemed like forever, and each new day ratcheted up her anxiety.

Fortunately, the approaching Christ's Mass meant that the king would return to the capital. Unfortunately, until then she had to subject herself to lessons that, unlike those found in books, did not elevate the mind or teach humility. On the other hand, they did inflict humiliation at one's inability to perform tasks which Heloise de Lusignan and Maria de Montferrat already mastered flawlessly.

The sword side of the royal brood had their own tutors to prepare them for their public appearances, but the boys did not need to master every gesture to the degree expected of their sisters. The public's expectations would be fulfilled if Almaric did not fidget too much and if Guy and John did not poke and jostle each other.

When it came to their sisters, Beroniki proved to be a taskmistress. Her presence also sent the guards and servants into duteous diligence every time she crossed their path. Juliana noted with some amusement that even the great lords of the land who came to the citadel treated Beroniki as if she were their childhood nurse whom they still might disappoint. Juliana shared those sentiments and attended Beroniki's lessons with trepidation.

"One must sit straight, shoulders relaxed, not about the ears, Lady Heloise. Elbows down. We have arms, not chickens' wings. Hands on the seat rests. They are called rests for a reason. We don't tap our fingernails on them no matter how impatient we are, Lady Maria."

Sitting in the wide-seated, backless chairs, Heloise and Maria stifled laughter in order to keep the shallow baskets filled with small pomegranates from toppling from their heads. Xene and Madelena kept their younger sisters in their own corner where the girls eagerly imitated every gesture.

Juliana sat behind them, afraid to blink lest she lose the pomegranates even though her back's every fiber screamed at her. For its legitimate participants, this exercise in the art of shameless self display had a practical purpose. One day, the girls would also wear a crown, and knowing how to carry oneself in those robes would be a requisite skill.

Encased in as many layers as a winter onion, Juliana felt like an imposter. The court dress Beroniki chose for her came with a couple of shifts of fine cotton *bokeman,* a shimmering *khamlet* of wool, two sets of sleeves topped by a silk gown stiff with roundels of embroidery, as beautiful as it was unwieldy. Over it went a samite cloak and over it a veil with more silk and silver embroidery that reached to her heels after falling from a cylindrical, and quite charming, headdress worn by the queen's women. The headdress alone required one to walk absolutely straight which made the women of the queen's retinue tall and stately, but gave Juliana the choice of either pinching her brow mercilessly or allowing it to teeter precariously. At least the instructions to keep one's chin up and spine stiff raised the gown's hem just enough to prevent one's slipper toe from catching it.

Beroniki clapped her hands. "Stand up, slowly, walk to the door, curtsey, return, and sit down again."

This was torture and humiliation wrapped in one. Juliana made it to her feet and to the door.

"Well done, Lady Juliana." Beroniki offered her praise. "But it helps if one doesn't bite one's lip."

Maria and Heloise tittered, hushed by Beroniki. Juliana released her lip, smiled and curtsied at the same time. Her basket slipped. She made a hasty step to catch the cascade; her toe caught and brought her to her knees. Mortified, she stayed there to prevent damage to the gown, waiting for rescue. Her two young companions, valiantly stifling laughter, did not miss a step and returned to their seats without mishap.

The lesson over, Beroniki's women helped Juliana to her feet, uncased her and the others, and brought their daily gowns. The women carried away the robes, cloaks, veils and the jewels to be examined, repaired, and safely stored for the proper occasion. Arm in arm, Maria and Heloise went to their next lessons.

Juliana offered her most earnest apologies to Beroniki.

"You don't need to apologize, Lady Juliana. My girls have been taught since they were toddlers. When they return to Saint Anne's, the sisters will continue to teach them." Beroniki hesitated. "I don't see clumsiness to be the obstacle. Reluctance perhaps, no?"

"But I practice every moment, in my room. I truly do."

Beroniki smiled. "I know. May I be allowed to speak freely?"

"Of course." How could Beroniki think she could speak to her otherwise?

"It seems you can't bring yourself to carry out the duty that comes with your position and place without reservations."

Beroniki's words stung. Duty. Of course she had a duty but not on these shores. "I have a duty to my daughter."

"You are the lady of Parthenay, the viscountess of Tillières, and the wife of Jean Armand de Lusignan. You have his daughter. You have a duty to all of them, is that not so? Just like your husband does."

She was chided by this waiting woman for the very same reason that Lasalle and Aimary de Lusignan had chastised her. Little did they know what she had dared since. "I see," Juliana said. "Thank you."

In this place, one must not ever drop one's pomegranates, at least not in public.

CHAPTER 35

The king returned from Arsuf the following day.

The news spread through the city and before the king's party rode up to the main gate, everyone in the citadel crowded the principal bailey. Juliana waited impatiently among the others, watching Isabella curtsey to her lord and husband with a wife's delighted smile. Aimary bowed to her in return and after a few private words which made the queen laugh, he led her into the great hall for a formal welcoming by the household.

The king's company dispersed and so did the gathering. Juliana searched among those who remained—several knights and a number of men-at-arms, a dozen *turkopoli,* squires, grooms, and servants with horses, pack mules, all bearing signs of their long absence and haste in returning to the capital before the day of celebration.

Lasalle was not among these men. No doubt, he chose to pursue some wild clue when she had information that would end this unbearable affair. Enough of waiting, enough of worrying about what was not her concern. She would return to Marseille by the first ship. Holding her disappointment down and her hem up, Juliana followed the others, her frown clearing the servants from her path if not the muck and horse droppings.

Skillfully avoiding both, someone stepped in front of her.

She saw an onion-shaped helmet with a yellow cloth strip wound around it, its long tail hanging behind; a striped, quilted gambeson they called *jubbah* and a leather-scaled cuirass over it whose lacquering had long rubbed off—a *turcopolier,* a sergeant in charge of the *turkopoli* who had accompanied the king.

Juliana could not bring herself to approve of what she considered cross-bred men, probably of double faith, even though Aimary's kingdom by necessity depended on them. She opened her mouth to scold the man for his lack of manners in the company of decent Christians when he caught her under the arm.

"I ought to have tied you to the mule's tail."

She managed a squeak that did not prevent him from propelling her across the emptying bailey, through the corridors where he steered her, the faces of startled servants flying past her. They came about a corner so fast that the three men who had rounded it jumped back, causing him a split moment of hesitation. She grabbed onto the edge of the wall stones.

The guardsmen of Saint Jean d'Acre saw a Frankish lady, painted and dressed as befitted the queen's women in the ungentle grip of a *turcopolier,* a man not allowed into the citadel's corridors.

They drew their swords.

Lasalle wrenched her back and shoved her behind him with one hand, his own sword in the other. "*Beau Dieu.* Juliana!"

The oath and the language did not disarm the men. They were the king's guards and not given to accepting appearances. After all, captains of turcopoles could curse in French, too, and considering the raw voice, who knew whence the man hailed. Swords leveled at their opponent, the guardsmen advanced.

Keeping her behind him, Lasalle gave way a step at a time. "Call them off or I'll kill at least one of them. Hear me?"

A wild, reckless sensation seized her. The words would not come. *You know you don't have the stomach to have them die for you . . .*

"Juliana. You–"

"What is this? My lord de Lusignan?" A man came up behind the stalking guardsmen. Recognizing that man, the guards' caution dissolved into puzzlement, then rough laughter. They sheathed their swords and backed away, saluting the man who came to rescue everyone from a costly calamity.

Lasalle shoved his sword into the scabbard and went toward the new arrival. He said something to him with a jerk of his head to where Juliana had spackled herself to the wall. The man slowly bowed to her. "Ah. Lady Juliana. I am Renaud Barlais, the king's . . . counselor. What a surprise . . . a pleasure . . . a pleasure to . . ."

The blood-stirring sensation that had strangled her voice prevented her from acknowledging Renaud Barlais, except by bending her knees in a curtsey.

Barlais drummed his fingers on his sword hilt. What a pickle. So this was the lady no one expected to show up in Nikosia, let alone in Acre. If he had his way, she would be locked up with the sisters at Saint Anne's for everyone's good. Unfortunately, that was not his decision. Still, Barlais could not help himself from casting a surely-she-can't-be-worth-the-trouble look at the king's kinsman.

"Sir. My lord the king sent me to tell you that the queen wishes you and your wife to attend Christ's Mass in her party. After that, you are ordered to take your leave until he calls on you. Lady Juliana." Barlais bowed again, this time briskly, and left them to sort it all out. He did not like the look of that girl, not one bit, especially not that righteous glint in her eyes.

Juliana exhaled, struggling to find her usually staggeringly common sense. What could have possessed her to risk those men's lives? At least the task of informing the king of the unpleasantness regarding his own family would not fall to her. And then she would be free of this place, free to return home. To Eleanor.

Nothing was said by either one of them until they reached her chamber—their chamber. Juliana barely opened her mouth to have Lasalle's accusing finger in her face.

"I don't know how you've managed this. I don't want to know. You're going back to Saint Mary's as soon as—"

She held out the superfluous ells of her gown to curtsy the way Beroniki had taught her. "Your mistress sends her regards, my lord."

The finger remained, but the wrath behind it became incredulity. "What?"

Juliana moved herself to a safer distance. "Who. Rhoxsane poisoned Morphia. She would have poisoned me, but Vigilantia holds her daughters hostage. But you already know that. That's why Vigilantia let me leave Saint Mary's. Encouraged me, in fact. Before Morphia died, she told me that she saw Burgundia meet with Leontios, just before he was killed. Right there, by the privy. And Rhoxsane said that she met the Lord of Beirut at Limassol on behalf of Niketas."

She counted on her fingers every point, just as she had memorized them in the days waiting for him. So far he had not interrupted her with the claim that he did not wish to know. "Niketas promised to tell Beirut that you took the money that Niketas safeguarded for the king. Imagine that. I suppose Niketas intends to buy himself the Ibelíns' patronage if his promises of loyalty aren't enough. And there were two messages. I've read the one Leontios carried. Not much to it. Hugh found it and hid it.

Whoever killed Leontios made away with the second one. That one must be important, don't you think, to kill Leontios for it?"

John d'Ibelín. Yet again she could not bring herself to mention her meeting John d'Ibelín. Surely it did not matter. She had implicated him with her words. "You may want to tell the king that his own daughter plots against him or that she knows who does. Oh, and Isabella wants to know who is trying to kill her husband so she sent me to spy on her mother. The dowager wants you out of the way before you find out. That's what I told Isabella. She hasn't called me since."

Her heart loud against her ribs reminded her of what she had left unsaid–that Isabella was married to a Lusignan for whom she professed fondness, but remained solicitous of her half brother and her Ibelín kin. That much Lasalle could figure out himself. "You . . . you need to tell the king. Today."

During her recitation, he had begun to remove his guise and when she finished and looked up, she saw in the wind and dirt-chaffed face weariness and barren bitterness. It struck her with the sharpness of a dagger's steel. "No, not today. Tomorrow."

He wrapped the sword belt around the scabbard and threw it on the bed. Her bed. Their bed. "Tell him what? Tell him before or after Christ's Mass that his daughter plots against him?"

He made it sound like the truth of it was her fault. She lowered her gaze to the carpets and clasped her hands. She wished the sleeves of her gown were wide enough to hide them, but that was not the fashion of the queen's women. "I didn't wish this to happen."

"I know." He sighed and rounded the bed toward her. "Listen. You are not to mention Burgundia in any of this to anyone. Not to Aimary, not to Isabella, no one."

"But how–"

He stabbed his finger at her in anger and frustration. "Did you hear me? I said speak to no one."

She was being talked to like an errant child. "You said you trusted me."

"I also said that I put your life in danger. Do not speak of it to anyone."

She could not resist a tone of spitefulness. "You and Niketas. My lord."

He reached inside his shirt to pull out his cross to dangle it at her eyes' level. "Swear to me."

Startled by the gesture, Juliana balked. "You don't trust me."

"About as much as you trust me, love. Swear it."

The amethysts flashed in the lamp light. Juliana licked her lips. Lasalle waited until she kissed the cross and made her pledge. He looped the cord back about his neck and before he could demand her further submission, Beroniki's woman came, all smiles, announcing that a bath waited for my lord. Lasalle nodded, and just when Juliana thought that they had at least reached an unpleasant impasse, he turned from the threshold. "Why didn't you call off the guards?"

"I . . . Barlais came."

"I see. Then don't worry. About anything."

Of course she worried, but for entirely different reasons than one would expect.

CHAPTER 36

To be caught on the horns of a dilemma did not make for a comfortable spot, and Lasalle's injunction made hers even less comfortable. After his return, they slept under the same roof and occasionally in the same bed with no consort between them besides polite exchanges. This time, she would not make the first gesture to reconcile them. She resented having her concerns subordinated to his. Worse yet, she suspected that she saw more of Aimary de Lusignan than Lasalle did, and yet she had sworn not to tell Aimary what she knew.

Aimary liked to surprise the children by arriving at the nursery unannounced. The younger children always mobbed him with ear-splitting shrieks their nurses and tutors ignored. He always fished Sybilla from the crush and hoisted her on his back, and with Melisande under one arm and Almaric under the other, led the whole procession including hysterical hounds, dueling twins, and cheery servants into the garden.

There Guy and John vied for their father's attention with a display of sword-and-horse play and he would defend himself, left-handed, against both of them with one of their wooden swords until in sheer frustration the boys threw away their swords and threw themselves at him. The king of Jerusalem and Cyprus let himself be overrun to the joy of the boys and pretending to be mortally wounded, let the children pile on top of him.

The children loved that part, but the scene sent shivers down Juliana's spine, even though Aimary gave her a wink whenever he left the nursery. At those times, it took all of her resolve not to drop to her knees and tell Aimary everything, and it became harder the more time she spent with the children. She could not but think that Aimary de Lusignan would have wished to spend more time with them, but his two crowns required his vigilance, and bodily presence, in two kingdoms.

Whenever Isabella came to the nursery, she spoke at length to Maria with a few words to Heloise, no more. The younger children eagerly submitted to Isabella's affectionate inspection. Even Guy and John curbed their exuberance in their stepmother's presence and blushed when Isabella offered them some small praise. Alix pretended she did not need recognition, but Isabella gave it to her anyway, calling for her when Alix thought to make herself absent. Almaric understood the lady in the beautiful gown to be only his mother, nothing more, and saw no reason to give up his naughtiness when a toy or two claimed his attention. One would have to be blind not to see that Almaric was his mother's favorite.

Juliana could easily see who Aimary's favorite was. Aimary always spoke to Heloise first, asking about her lessons and the sisters of Saint Anne, and unlike her public self, Heloise answered with confidence, pleased at the praise her father gave her with a kiss on her forehead and words of encouragement. Sometimes he brought her a book, and Juliana would find Heloise curled up in a secluded alcove, absorbed in the pages. Maria usually teased her stepsister for the obvious reason that Princess Maria and letters did not make for congenial company.

Juliana wondered why at her age Heloise has not been married or even betrothed, especially since Burgundia had not given Aimary a grandchild despite being married for the second time already. Watching father and daughter covertly, Juliana suspected that Aimary did not wish Heloise to be married yet. From the servants' gossip, Juliana knew that Aimary's decision to give Burgundia in marriage to Walter de Montbéliard had not met with approval from some of Aimary's vassals.

It hardly required a stretch of the imagination to surmise that the marriage came without the bride's full approval either–hence Burgundia's likely involvement with those who plotted against her father. Perhaps Aimary wanted to avoid doubling the plots by waiting to find a husband for Heloise who would be more palatable to his vassals and allies–and to her.

When Beroniki told Heloise that Juliana could read, Heloise looked at Juliana with the eagerness of a young pupil. To her shame, Juliana found it flattering. On several occasions, they ended up in a spirited conversation about some matter Heloise read about in her books. They ended up laughing which usually drew *La Marquise* to find out the cause of it. Juliana did not wish to exclude Maria from her budding friendship with Heloise, but she found the serious-minded Heloise a kindred spirit. Juliana was glad for it since, except for Beroniki, the queen's women treated her with polite indifference, the result, she suspected, of the queen's own example. At least she would not be entangled in the sort of a friendship that could lead her to inadvertently divulge what she knew.

To guide her through the days, she drew on the certain presence of the Lord, followed Beroniki's instructions the best she could, and took pleasure in Heloise's company. She soon found out that there were secrets other than her own around her.

Once, when Juliana approached Heloise in her cushioned alcove, she saw Heloise slip something between the book's pages. Juliana did not wish to pry and therefore she curtsied with an apology. With a mischievous smile, Heloise clutched the book to her and gestured to Juliana to join her.

"That," Juliana said to ease the moment, "must be Beroniki's secret recipe for saddle sores."

Heloise laughed. "It isn't." She looked about to see if *La Marquise* lurked about. "It's from . . . from Antioch."

"I see," Juliana tried to remember the circumstances of that principality, currently mired in a war between various family members, the result of one set denying the throne to its legitimate heir, young Prince Rupen.

Not much older than Heloise, Rupen of Antioch came to Acre with his supporters to obtain Aimary's support to reclaim his inheritance. Perhaps aware of the hazard of stepping into a familial quarrel that currently brought no advantage to his kingdom, Aimary de Lusignan offered Antioch's heir apparent advice but no men. The prince and his party left Acre in less of a huff than one would expect. Juliana wondered if that was because he and Heloise had set eyes on each other during the public banquet Aimary pragmatically hosted to keep the doors to Antioch open for future negotiations.

"My father . . . he didn't give Antioch any help." Disapproval of her father's action crept into Heloise's voice. She sucked in her lower lip and looked guiltily at Juliana, yet with a flash of defiance in her eyes at the anticipation of a reprimand.

Juliana did not reprimand her. Heloise had more than a trace of steel in her, which she kept concealed, perhaps even from her own father. Perhaps Burgundia had the same element in her; perhaps she had only lately found it.

"Well then," Juliana embraced Heloise's shoulders and steered her away from the barrage of hand balls that Alix, Melisande, and Sybilla scuffled over, "I'd say that when the time comes, he has in mind another alliance with Antioch."

"Do you think so?" Heloise laid her head on Juliana's shoulder, sounding so wistful that Juliana heard the echo of her own longing to experience life outside Fontevraud's cloisters. She fought off a twinge of fear for what this lovely and intelligent young woman could face if the threat to her father's life became a reality.

"Yes, I do," Juliana assured her, certain that as long as Aimary de Lusignan lived, he would not deliberately inflict unhappiness on Eschiva d'Ibelín's second daughter.

To his stepdaughter, Aimary showed the sort of kind, formal affection for a twelve–or thirteen–year-old heiress to his crown. He also questioned Maria de Montferrat about her lessons but without probing or prodding, and instead of a book, brought her gifts of a ring, a necklace, or hair ribbon, all of which *La Marquise* wore proudly, and telling the girl, against all evidence, that she had grown as pretty as her mother.

Publicly, Maria's mother received from Aimary every gesture of respect and acknowledgement that he wore only the crown matrimonial. When not on formal display, Aimary treated Isabella with an easy, casual affection so that one could mistake them for an ordinary married couple with an experienced, unsentimental husband older by some years than his wife, ceding to her all her rights as the mistress of a household that happened to be a kingdom.

Yet when Juliana caught a sight of the two of them alone on the ramparts or in the corridors with Aimary nodding patiently over some concern or request Isabella brought to him, Juliana could not escape the feeling that his mind was elsewhere, even though her wishes were always addressed. She felt pity for Isabella. The queen of Jerusalem and Cyprus never came to Nikosia, never occupied the queen's chambers there because those belonged to her rival, a rival Isabella d'Anjou could not defeat. Eschiva d'Ibelín was dead.

Fortunately, the requirements of her presence in Isabella's train during the rounds of the court's banquets and celebrations kept Juliana busy. Once she had sufficiently mastered the gowns, headdresses, veils, and cloaks, Beroniki treated her with no special distinction. Still, Juliana took her place with trepidation, afraid she would dunk her sleeves in a stew, have her veil torn off, jewelery snatched, or her gown damaged in the crush at the banquet tables by harried servants, drunken celebrants, or by enthusiastic residents of the city who took to dancing and cavorting with abandon every time the queen's procession left the citadel.

With everyone rejoicing at the birth of the Holy Child, Juliana kept a cheerful face although the Shepherds' play nearly left her in tears, and the sight of the Magi bearing gifts to the manger almost undid her. She counted the days to Candlemas and noted, with determined disapproval, the flagrant sins of touching, movement, and voice committed all around her.

After days in the queen's service, Juliana returned to her chamber exhausted and guilt-consumed. Preferring her own tub anyway, she welcomed Beroniki's permission to be excused from attending the queen on her frequent visits to the *hammam.* At night, with the noise of merrymaking rising to the windows of her bedchamber, thoughts of conspiracies chased about her head, making her toss and turn.

After his own dutiful, and brief, appearance at the Christ's Mass on the queen's orders, Lasalle vanished somewhere about the city, setting into motion his own scheme, woven from the strands of information she had brought him.

She wished with all her might that he would confide in her, just a little. At the same time, she dreaded that he might, for she knew with a stone-cold certainty that Guérin de Lasalle's plot involved a trap for the Lord of Beirut.

CHAPTER 37

After Candlemas, with candles lit and blessed and carried away by the jubilant and exhausted faithful, an escort came for Maria de Montferrat and Heloise de Lusignan to take them back to the sisters at Saint Anne. John and Guy remained with their tutors, their younger sisters under the care of their nurses. Now that the older girls had gone, Beroniki no longer asked Juliana to join the rest of the Lusignan brood. She missed the children.

On a couple of occasions, she asked Beroniki for servants to accompany her to the scribes' market in search of books. Beroniki gave her a maid servant, a palanquin, and guards to take her wherever she wished.

Usually she opted to wander the corridors, pretending to carry out some request or task. She wished to speak to Lasalle, but the king had not recalled him into his presence or if he had, she did not know about it.

She did know by then that in its nooks and crannies the place was rife with flagrant assignations. Several involved the queen's women who in their husbands' absence sought more available diversions. She made no acknowledgement that she recognized either of the parties and said nothing to Beroniki. She did not have to because shortly thereafter the women were no longer in the queen's service. On two occasions she found herself accosted by a man who thought that she wandered about in search of such diversions. On those occasions she very loudly announced herself to be the wife of Jean Armand de Lusignan. After that, she did not even have to reach for her dagger.

"Lady, I said you can't pass. This is the king's chamber."

Torn from her thoughts, Juliana avoided a collision with a guard who confronted her. Out of the way in one of the turrets, the small chamber would have been a perfect place for an amorous encounter. Through the partly opened door, she saw a room with walls painted in lively green and red and blue, lit by oil lamps. Instead of a mistress or a temporary paramour, a couple of clerks scratched away on sheets at high-legged tables. Like a stern schoolmaster, Aimary de Lusignan stood there, a quill between his teeth, his shirt stained with ink, a parchment in each hand, his forehead creased. Amazed and amused by the sight, Juliana curtsied in retreat. "I . . . I am sorry, Your Grace."

Aimary's voice, temporarily hampered by a goose feather, stopped her. "Ah, Lady Juliana. So you found out about my treasure. Come in."

Treasure? Juliana held her skirts to her to avoid knocking the scrolls and stack of volumes that took up the floor and poked from the trunks lined against the walls. The scribes did not acknowledge her presence, but Aimary put down the sheets and stuck the pen in the nearest inkhorn. "You can read, true? And write, no?"

Surprised by that inquiry, Juliana nodded.

"Good, good. I made sure my daughters know how. That way their husbands can't lie to them about the marriage contract, eh?"

Surveying the hodgepodge of documents on the table, Juliana smiled at that pragmatic reasoning and picked up a sheet from a small trunk. The tidy, rounded letters reminded her of her own hand. "A marriage contract?"

Aimary took the document, squinting at it in the light of the flames, his face softening. "Burgundia's letter. She wrote to me when the count of Toulouse cast her away for King Richard's sister." He gave Juliana a self-conscious glance. "You know about it, no?"

Juliana nodded. Nothing escaped public scrutiny, not even such family matters—especially such family matters. Raymond of Toulouse's amorous exploits were not confined to his five—or was it six—marriages thus far.

Aimary's rawboned hand glided over the page. "She looks like her mother. She could have done better than me. And I ought to have done better by her."

Juliana did not know whether Aimary referred the latter remark to Lady Eschiva or to their daughter, and she did not wish to enquire. Her discomfort came from Aimary's confiding to her such sentiment, the sentiment of a father who loved his daughter—a daughter who very likely plotted his downfall. Juliana wished with all her might that she could tell him what she knew, to have that burden lifted from her, but she was not the person to divulge matters which would have dire consequences for two kingdoms.

Sensing her reticence if not the true reason for it, Aimary locked the letter in the trunk. He indicated the rest of the documents, his voice resuming its customary forcefulness. "Ah, but there is other posterity, isn't there. It lives after we are all dust."

Juliana's curiosity got better of her. She picked up one sheet and another, and another. Bold curves of gold capitals graced each new page, the text penned in red. These were not letters. They were judgments of the *Haute Cour*, royal decrees, lists of pleas.

Hands clasped behind his back, Aimary enjoyed her puzzlement. "What do you think?"

"These are the *assisses* of the kingdom."

"Very good. Not all of them. We lost a trunk full when the Musulmans took Jerusalem. A hundred years of laws gone."

"Then who gathered these?"

The answer came with a solid thump of the king's fist against his chest. "I did. I had help to find them, of course, but when I asked my most learned vassals to put them in order, they all claimed they were not up to the task. Liars. But not all was lost."

"Not when one can rewrite them?"

Aimary gave a hoot of hearty laughter. "You are a cynic, Lady Juliana." The laughter died. "The kingdom can't be left to men who won't see beyond their own ambition. If they can make laws or ignore them at their whim, they will again bring us to disaster. And this time, the Musulmans will sweep us into the sea."

A stark truth, plainly told. "But how will you compel them to obey?"

The answer came hardened by bitter experience and tempered by it as well. "Why, by the law, and where it hurts them the most. Loss of fiefs. Loss of life. Or both."

The words leapt at her from the page. *Whenever a liegeman raises arms against his lord . . . whenever a vassal abandons his lord when fighting the Musulmans . . . whenever the vassal refuses to obey the order of his lord which is reasonable . . . whenever a vassal offers advice to the prejudice of the king and the realm . . . whenever a vassal mints his own coin. . . .* Her eyes fell on the reason for the loss of life or fief—*in the case of poisoning of the lord or of members of his family or children. . . .*

"I made sure, too, if the first born is a female, she takes precedence over a brother by a second marriage. What do you think? Will these prop up a teetering crown?" Aimary prodded her.

Reminded so directly of their first meeting, Juliana tucked her chin. Aimary de Lusignan did not engage in polite conversations, but since he asked for her opinion, she gave it. "There may be a crown or two teetering a lot less if these are followed. But the High Court may not see such laws to its advantage."

Aimary laughed. "Well said." He tapped his finger on the next sheet. "See here? I gave them a reason to think otherwise. If a High Court summons a vassal three times and the vassal fails to appear before it, that vassal's fief stands forfeit." He took the pages from her and laid them carefully next to the others. "No one can claim exemption from the law. No one. So here I am, the new Justinian."

Somehow, it did not surprise her that Aimary de Lusignan would take such pride in a task that others would have left to their clerks. "What will you call these?"

"What else can I?" Aimary reached for a parchment the scribes had penned, his hand soft over the letters the way he touched Burgundia's, and handed it to Juliana. *Le Livre au Roi.*

Juliana stood there, wracked by contrary emotions. Aimary de Lusignan not only understood force, he understood power–and his duty to a crown or two that a parcel of ambitious, self-seeking barons could smash to pieces–like Isabella's crown nearly was.

She wished she did not like Aimary de Lusignan; she wished she did not like the king's children; she wished her resentment of the House of Lusignan, wherever located, would not teeter as much as it had since her arrival in this place.

That night those thoughts and ones of Eleanor would not let her sleep and she tossed and turned until the woman who slept in the chamber asked her if she were ill. Juliana wrapped herself in her bed cover and went to the chapel, lit another candle, and prayed to be shown the way, and soon. She had her own duty and she had to leave others to attend to theirs. She wished she could confess her multiplying sins, but did not dare to divulge them, to anyone. With each passing day, she longed to hear only one piece of news–that the sea was open.

Of course when she did, none of it turned out the way she had planned. None of it.

CHAPTER 38

In the dampness and cold of the winter, the sickness first began to stalk the children in the Genoese Quarter. Death descended on the city as silently as the fog. The streets and markets hushed with each tolling of the bells. Prayers to ward off the pestilence and smoke from cedar, cassia, and terebinth fires suffused the air. The people nailed crosses and amulets to the doors and windows, surrounded the beds and cradles of their children with icons. Swinging censors and singing hymns, priests and monks led solemn processions around the quarters of the nationals in clouds of burnt offerings. Beroniki called on all of her women to help nurse the stricken children in the fortress.

In the royal quarters, the first to sicken was little Almaric.

In the absence of his laughter and the mischief-sowing pursuits of his two older half brothers the corridors fell silent. Guy's and John's noisy adventures gave way to subdued prowls around the nursery where Almaric's nurses watched over the boy day and night. A physician, a Greek, was called. He spoke to the nurses and to the queen and the king about drafts and potions, ointments and poultices to be applied to the boy's chest struggling to rise for each wheezing breath. Isabella refused to leave her son's bedside until Aimary bodily removed her by simply picking her up and carrying her to her chamber.

Despite the physician's efforts and the prayers offered in the city's churches, the news grew more grim. Juliana prayed each day with the others, and often remained in the chapel after they had gone. The visible pain of his parents' suffering, and Almaric's own, fueled her own fear and desperation. Her mind conjured up Eleanor, shivering with fever and eyes sunk into blue caves. *What if Eleanor had fallen sick . . . what if she had already died . . . what if?* "Holy Mary, Mother of God . . ."

"Juliana. Almaric has died." At the chapel's door stood Lasalle, alone, his eyes hard. He wore a long tabard, a sword at his hip, fist clenched around it.

The flames of dozens of votives danced on the gold fibers of the Virgin's robes, the Infant on her lap, reaching for His mother. Juliana caught her breath in a sob. *No, it could not be.* She refused to move, to hear, to believe.

He came to her and lifted her to her feet. "Get up. We're needed."

She stood there only a moment and then buried her face in the quilting of his tabard to muffle her sobs. She need not have bothered. The halls and corridors already echoed with weeping. "Eleanor . . . I want to leave now. You promised."

"After Almaric is buried."

She could manage only a half-breath. "You promised."

He took her by the shoulders and held her at arm's length, that look of resolve in his eyes. "Yes. But until then we have a duty. To Isabella and Aimary. Beroniki is looking for you."

She swallowed her grief and nodded. She had a duty.

She sought out Beroniki who sent her to the nursery, to Melisande and Sybilla, bewildered and frightened by their brother's death. Alix, Guy, and John pretended to carry on unaffected, but Juliana saw past that façade.

The dark days of Lent made Almaric's passing even more distressing. The boy died before the Feast of the Purification and was buried in the cathedral of the Holy Cross where only weeks earlier the city had celebrated the birth of the Christ Child.

After the burial, Juliana returned to her chamber where her maid helped her out of her gown. Juliana dismissed the woman and ordered no one to disturb her so that she could curl up and cry for the lively, lovely child she knew for only such a brief time and for the child she could not hold to comfort.

A voice outside the door made her sit up. The door opened against the maid's protestations to Xene's stricken face.

"Beroniki asks for you, Lady Juliana. Guy and John are ill."

They died—along with their sister Alix.

In a matter of days, three of Aimary de Lusignan's children by Eschiva d'Ibelín, as well as their half brother by Isabella of Jerusalem, had died in the plague that struck particularly the young. Despite the unstinting care of their nurses and desperate prayers, death claimed not only the royal children but others in the citadel, and many more in the city.

Libera me, Domine . . . Libera me, Domine . . . The prayers poured from every church and chapel in the city.

For Juliana, time seemed to stand still, composed of vigil at the beds of the sick children, and attempting to console their distraught mothers as one interment followed another. She prayed along with the others, her thoughts on Eleanor. At least news came from behind the walls of Saint Anne's that Heloise de Lusignan and *La Marquise* remained safe. Miraculously, little Melisande and Sybilla recovered after nearly losing their battle with the affliction.

For the suffering faithful, the sole source of comfort came from the knowledge that Easter would bring the assurance of Resurrection, and when the illness in the capital began to wane, an undercurrent of hope began to swirl about the city. Juliana sensed it and with relief came the thought that the sea would soon reopen.

CHAPTER 39

Spring in the year of Our Lord 1205

Winter rains and spring sun, still bashful between the clouds, greened the valleys and the hillsides and sowed them with wildflowers. The lords of the realm opened their stables to drive the horses to fresh pastures, joining the herds of the

Templars, the Hospitallers, and the German Brothers. What a thrill to hear the drum of hooves through the streets and along the paths, to see a stream of the animals released from months of confinement, manes snapping in the wind, eyes rolling, nostrils flared with the excitement of freedom.

In late March, during the last days of Lent, the king of Jerusalem and Cyprus rode out with several of his vassals and the masters of the Orders to take stock of the herds near the orchards of Caiphas at the foot of Mount Carmel.

A couple of fishermen brought to the king a catch of sea bream from the mouth of the Kishon. Delighted with the gift, Aimary de Lusignan ate his fill. After the meal, he felt extremely tired and laid down to sleep. When he woke, he felt worse. Despite the protestations of his men, he got on his horse and rode back to the capital.

If the deaths of the children of Acre shattered the city, Aimary de Lusignan's illness scattered the shards. With the news of the affliction's swift progress came speculations about its cause. A strange new disease? A return of the pestilence that had felled so many? An attempt at assassination by the foul means of poison? By whom? The Musulmans? Al-Adil had nothing to gain from Aimary de Lusignan's death. What of the king's enemies in the kingdom, among his own people? Yes, they had attempted to strike him down before–twice, thrice?–and failed. Aimary de Lusignan would not die by their sword.

The king's illness filled the city with apprehension and the halls of its citadel with lords secular and spiritual. Philip de Plessis, the Grand Master of the Temple, came with the heads of the other Orders. The king's principal vassals arrived, men scarred and weathered by conflicts over the land that Aimary de Lusignan husbanded on behalf of their queen and for their benefit. Notable by his absence was the Lord of Beirut and his adherents, and the king's eldest daughter and her husband, the Constable.

The king's companions who had rushed with their lord back to the city offered little beyond a vague description of the fishermen. Who remembers what fishermen looked like? They were fishermen. Recriminations and accusations threatened to break into violence but cooler heads prevailed, thanks to Renaud Barlais and Fulk d'Yvers and others of the king's party—the Lusignans' party.

The queen, tried by the terrible losses of the past weeks, remained at her husband's bedside until she collapsed into the arms of her women.

In his private bedchamber, as sparse as his field camp, Aimary de Lusignan slipped in and out of consciousness between bouts of violent vomiting, and none of the Greek, Hebrew, and Musulman physicians called to his bedside could ease his trial. At the end of the third day, he regained consciousness and from somewhere his strength to order the physicians and everyone else out of the chamber, calling for three men to remain.

They saw the waxy sheen flow across the bones that rose from under the skin, but Aimary's eyes, already deep in their sockets, blazed still with blue fire. If the three were horrified by their lord's appearance, they did not show it. They had all seen the face of approaching death.

Aimary knew it as well. "Someone couldn't wait. So it's poison. Not a quick one either. Blasted fish. Mixed with the spice, likely. Listen. Bury me in . . . Nikosia. Not . . . here. Nikosia."

Renaud Barlais, Fulk d'Yver, and Guérin de Lasalle nodded. They did not need to look at each other. They knew why in Nikosia. Aimary had taken the crown of Jerusalem and its queen out of duty. Cyprus was the kingdom of his heart and that was where he had buried the queen of both, and his brother.

"The queen . . . Isabella . . . don't press her to marry again if she doesn't wish to. Hear me?"

They knew that would be as difficult a request to fulfill as persuading the queen to have her husband buried in Nikosia.

"Burgundia. Is she here?"

"Not yet, my lord. But we heard she will be here soon," Fulk said, a lie the three had agreed upon.

"Just as well. Tell her . . . tell her I am sorry."

No one asked the reason for it. They knew Aimary would not want them to.

"Look after my girls."

Which ones the king did not name. He did not need to. He did not mention his dead sons. He did not have to either. They all knew that the only ones that mattered now were his living children.

"I want the Court . . ." Aimary tried to raise himself, and they helped him the way they helped a mortally wounded friend, without futile words of comfort women would have offered.

"I want the Court in Nikosia to appoint Isabella Hugh's guardian and you–" with an effort that defied his failing body, Aimary pointed at Lasalle, "–you I want my son's regent."

"My lord–" Lasalle drew back, but the leopard's claw had already struck.

Aimary took a shuddering breath. "Barlais, fetch that cross."

Without a word or quibble, Barlais took down from the wall a cross fashioned of olive wood, a plain, unadorned cross. Aimary thrust it at Lasalle. "Swear before these witnesses you'll accept the regency when the High Court offers it."

The claw struck deeper, and he could not dislodge it. "My lord–"

Aimary's voice broke with the effort. "Swear, I said. Swear you will."

He retreated two steps. "No."

Aimary recoiled as pain stabbed into him. A thin black line snaked from the corner of his mouth. "For the blood of . . . swear."

Barlais took hold of Lasalle's arm, twisting him around. "Christ's mercy, listen." Fierce urgency and grief made him choke. "We don't have time. Agree or the Ibelíns will demand the regency and we'll lose our estates. Cyprus is the key to holding on to what's left of this kingdom. The king is leaving three girls, two are still children. Who'll safeguard them? Isabella? You'll have our support, and the others'. Tell him, Fulk."

Fulk d'Yvers, his arm around the king's shoulders, the lines of his face grooved with anger and sorrow, jerked up his gray chin at Lasalle. "Swear it. Now."

The words lanced through him. He had a duty. He clamped his teeth and laid his hand on the cross. "I swear."

Aimary exhaled a long hiss of relief and sank into the pillow. The cross slipped from his hands. "You tell my son . . . you tell Hugh to remember who he is." His hands searched about blindly. "My sword. I can't find my sword."

Barlais reached for the scabbard leaning against the bed and guided Aimary's hands around the sword's hilt. He grasped it for his last battle, his eyes fixed on the vaulting of the chamber where a sowing of blue and gold tesserae had brought heavens down to earth.

"Now send for the priest."

D'Yver got to his feet and went to the door. The sound of the dying man's breath filled the chamber. The priest, an older corpulent man, pushed past d'Yvers. He took one look at the king, crossed himself and shook an accusing finger at the three men in the chamber. "How dare you delay and deprive a man of *viaticum*."

Barlais and d'Yver glowered back, lost for words and resentful of it. The third man was not at a loss for words. Guérin de Lasalle threw open the door and paused there to look back at them all. "The river of Kishon, thou hast trodden down strength."

The priest puffed up, offended by the allusion as much as surprised by it. "Would you dispute the Lord's doing, sir?"

"I'd say in this case, the Lord will have to decide."

And the Lord decided.

Aimary de Lusignan, Aimary the Second of Jerusalem, the first king of Cyprus, died on the first day of April, a year to the day that the Lord had called to Him the Lusignans' aged adversary, Aliénor, the great duchess of Aquitaine.

CHAPTER 40

With sudden death of Aimary de Lusignan, bitter lamentations returned to Saint Jean d'Acre and the kingdom of Jerusalem.

Whatever their private opinions about their king, his vassals and subjects had to acknowledge that Aimary's reign had brought stability, security, and even prosperity to both of his kingdoms. Many now feared that the personal ambitions of certain barons would revive the bloody years prior to his elevation. Others trusted that the queen would serve as the keystone of the kingdom and prevent conflicts and contentions from again engulfing her lands.

Juliana sat in the cushioned alcove of her chamber, watching the sun sink into the sea, the cross with Eleanor's lock in her hand. Her eyes burned from crying. She wished she had not liked Aimary de Lusignan; she wished she had not liked the king's children. Did God's wrath descend on Aimary and his family for his numerous sins or was his death a punishment on his kingdom? Or both? And yet . . . she felt a twinge of relief, of selfish, shameful relief.

Lasalle's reasons for remaining in *outre-mer* no longer existed. She kept away thoughts of his failure to avert this disaster. The Lord had caused it for His own reason and no human agency could have prevented it. As for her acts of commission and omission, she would confess them to Father Urias and accept whatever penance . . .

"Juliana?"

She looked up. Lasalle stood there, unannounced and unexpected. She had not seen him since the king's illness. Juliana ran her hand over her cheeks and sat upright. "Yes?"

He shut the door behind him. "No, don't get up. Why aren't the lamps lit? Do you want me to call the servants?"

"No, I don't want to see them." She did not wish to see anyone or for anyone to see her, but one could hardly refuse to see one's husband, no matter one's feelings about him. Given what had transpired, she wished she knew what those feelings ought to be.

He knew what his were. She sat there without her veil in a gown of pomegranate silk trimmed by a modest band of pearls at the neckline. Her hair, this time neither plaited nor pinned, fell past her shoulders. The thin line of a gold chain trickled across her collarbones. Her skin shone as pale as the pearls. She had wiped the paint from her face, but had forgotten about the *kohl* and when she looked at him, she was the face of eternal feminine of millennia past and the ever present. The scent of jasmine and spice lingered in the fibers of her gown.

She slipped the cross into her bodice and looked up at him, her eyes even darker in the descending dusk. "Does Beroniki need me?"

He knew the tone of forced politeness. "No. She's with the queen. Aimary . . . he didn't want me to come with him."

He wanted to lay before her the subject she wished to avoid, and she resented it despite a part of her aching to lay before him her own burdened conscience. "I see."

"Christ." He gave a short, bitter laugh, at himself. "He said that he didn't want me to get in a scrape with de Plessis again."

"The Grand Master? Why would you–"

"I . . . I lost my temper with him."

I'll make sure that the Temple pays up to you. He told her the last time they came together, in that farmstead at Famagusta. The confluence of disparate events came to her. She was the reason why Aimary did not want Lasalle with him at the horse pastures of Kishon. "Guérin–"

"I said, I lost my temper."

He had not mentioned the rest of the reasons for his confrontation with the Grand Master, which involved the whereabouts of Brother Geoffrey de Lusignan of the very same Temple, his ever elusive brother; the very same brother who had so creatively coerced him to return to this part of the world. A brother he had yet to find and whom he had spent considerable time pursuing, as yet without success.

"I see. I heard . . . was Aimary truly poisoned?"

"Yes. But there is no proof."

Something compelled her to ask, perhaps her conscience, "Didn't the others have the same fare?"

"No. Someone knew Aimary couldn't resist the offer of that fish and that he would eat them by himself."

Juliana crossed herself. "'I would invite you to share, but I've waited for these, and I intend to have every one.'"

In the fading light, she could see that he smiled and she knew why and she regretted her words since they brought up the subject of an invitation. She had not invited him to anything, but he nevertheless unbuckled his sword belt and laid it on the table and slid himself to sit on the floor of the alcove across from her. "You remember."

Juliana hugged herself. "Yes. The breams. Aimary told me that a fishwife from Kyrenia saved them for him. He said her husband didn't know. I think–"

"–he did. And told someone who had them poisoned."

She considered the most likely candidate for that assignment. "Rhoxsane."

"If she did, it was at someone's orders. You don't go around poisoning kings just because you can."

She opted to disagree. "Maria Komnene could. She can cook up enough poison to wipe out Creation."

"So it's true. Did she offer you any?"

"Just a philtre." Oh Lord. Why was her tongue so careless? She averted her face to hide the flush that crept to her cheeks even though the lack of light made it unlikely for him to see it.

"I see. For someone we know?" he said, imitating her with a pretended prurient interest.

With all the tragedies around them, Lasalle could not resist using his wit on her. Juliana frowned and sat herself properly, the way Beroniki had taught her. "No. What will you do?"

The moment she said it, she regretted it. At least he did not press his prior question, but his answer turned her insides into a nauseous knot.

"Find the fishermen and bring charges against John d'Ibelín before the High Court."

Holy Virgin. So this was the trap Lasalle intended to set for John d'Ibelín. "But . . . but they are not Franks. Even if you find them, they could testify against Rhoxsane but neither she nor they could testify against Beirut."

Lasalle raised his eyebrow at her. "Why, Lady Juliana, what a jurist you are."

Anger at herself, at him, overcame her. "So are you. The High Court is not going to . . ." She stopped. *There are five means of gaining a well-guarded citadel.* And subterfuge was one of them. "I see. Even if the Court is not going to hear the fishermen, the news will raise enough doubt about d'Ibelín, no matter how false the charges might be."

"Now why would you think they might be false, Lady Juliana?"

He delivered the question with a suspicious squint and lawyer's tone of speculation. He knew. No, he could not have known about John d'Ibelín and Nikosia. How could he? Unless someone had told him. She had to think, she had to think like one of *them.*

"Because . . . because you can't find the fishermen, not the real ones. That's what you've been doing, isn't it? I imagine you can produce a couple of fishermen to claim that d'Ibelín put them up to it. You can bribe them with Niketas's money. Of course they will deny any part in poisoning the catch and point to the cooks, a page, or a squire who could have served it all on a platter smeared with something vile, but that would have been too complicated. So the fishermen it is."

He did not interrupt her, and when she finished, he said, in pure innocence, "What a splendid idea. You wouldn't happen to know a couple of fishermen, would you? Preferably from Kolossi?"

Juliana wrestled the volume of her skirts to the side and stood up. Lasalle thought he had a duty to pursue Aimary's assassin no matter what, but she would not allow herself to be drawn any deeper into his ploys and schemes. She would return to Nikosia and ask Abbess Vigilantia to pay for her passage back to Poitou, to Eleanor. "No. You've already found them."

She almost crossed the threshold, and there it struck her. She had not been thinking like one of *them*. She pressed the door shut and faced him. "That's not at all your plan, is it? You're just using the fishermen to force d'Ibelín to defend himself against your accusations. You want him to challenge you."

He remained very still, looking up at her, sorting out what witty evasion to employ this time. "You make it sound like a bad idea."

She advanced, fists tight. "Don't patronize me. It is a bad idea. How could you think to challenge him to a duel?"

"It is believed that in such cases the Lord is the final judge. If d'Ibelín is not guilty, then he will prevail."

"And you'll be dead!"

"Why, Lady Juliana, would you dispute God's judgment? Besides," he said, rising, "you haven't considered that I might win."

"Oh, you!" She flung her full weight at him just as he had taught her, her palms flat against his chest. The impact jarred her wrists, but she ignored the pain because he stumbled backward and went down, and she pounced on him even though her skirts made it a challenge and her hair blinded her. The quilting of his gambeson made it difficult to get a good grip on him, but she did and slammed him against the alcove's buttressing. "How dare you? You've failed to protect Aimary. Failed! You can't undo it, no matter what plots you contrive. You've promised you'll come back and have Eleanor returned to me. And you will!"

She struck his head against the buttressing a couple more times or perhaps in his own perverse way he let her. He put an end to it by rolling over and trapping her under him. Her elbows cracked from his weight. "That hurts!"

He eased back a little, the fierceness now in him, the self-mockery gone. "Yes, I failed. Can you *understand* that? Eleanor is . . . she is safe, whatever you think. If John d'Ibelín isn't behind it then someone is."

He waited for her to say something and when she did not, lifted himself off her and propped himself against the alcove.

Juliana tried to catch her breath. How dare he? How unfair of him to accuse her of not understanding. Her concern was

Eleanor, only Eleanor. *That* he did not understand. But she had not expected his other admission. "You don't have proof that he is behind it, do you?"

Lasalle dropped his head back against the wall and closed his eyes in weariness. "He didn't show up in Acre when Aimary got sick, he still hasn't arrived. Maria Komnene is furious about it. She's already bending Isabella's ear about her next husband. They want to import one from the empire."

Juliana tried to untwist her skirts. "Which empire?"

He grunted out a laugh, perhaps at her question, perhaps at the absurdity of the situation. "Does it matter these days? Maria Komnene is already brewing a philtre for her."

My crown of tesserae. Isabella never wanted the burden of her crown, but others did. "No, I suppose not. It's not as if Isabella has a choice in the matter, with or without a philtre. Her mother thinks . . ." The dowager queen's malicious smile suddenly appeared to her. "You didn't go with Aimary to Arsuf, did you? You went to Beirut to spy on d'Ibelín. That's why his mother wanted me to warn you away from him. That's why you came back to Acre with the *turkopoli*."

"Now what makes you think I'd do that?"

He had not answered her question, she noted, but that did not get him off the hook. This time her curiosity got the better of her resolutions. "Because if you can pretend to be a *bedu*, you can pretend to be a *turcopolier*. The guards didn't recognize you. I didn't either." She frowned at the thought. "At first," she corrected herself.

"Hmm." Lasalle opened his eyes and reached out, his fingertips brushing her lip. "I recognized you. At first."

She jerked her head back. His hand dropped to the neckline of her gown. Her ridiculously impulsive assault on him had shifted her shift, causing her bosom to be almost fully exposed. "Oh, you!" She made a move to strike away his hand, but his fist closed on the fabric.

"You have a scar here. What happened?"

John d'Ibelín. Thankfully, her hair fell over her face, hiding her hot, blazing shame. She quickly tugged at her bodice. He had not noticed the scar before. Why did he have to notice it now?

"What? Oh, nothing. Nothing at all. A thorn. In the garden. Lady Eschiva's garden. In Nikosia."

"What were you–"

John d'Ibelín.

She leaned against him and kissed him. She only intended to blot out that thought, that memory. Perhaps, she told herself, she only wanted to conclude another ghastly day in a span of such, from which one could find no escape, save a temporary one in another's presence.

Lasalle knew that Juliana de Charnais did not come to him withered by the fires of temptation. He knew it, but was glad that she came, whatever her current motivation. He did not wish to know. She had changed in the months since she stood clothed in bedraggled bravery in that hall in Nikosia.

He threaded his fingers in her hair. Her eyes, so stark in her pallid face, looked up at him. Did she see him or someone else?

You are more wedded to her than she is to you.

She did not trust him. For that he did not blame her. She was sometimes afraid of him and for that he blamed himself. He could not rectify either, not without placing her in more danger. She had to leave Acre, she had to return to Poitou, to Eleanor. She had no idea how his failure had tied him to this land, to a family he had cast off at this very place so utterly that he had taken on a new life–by taking the lives of others, for money.

For all of that time he had not cared whether he lived or died. He had a kind of perverse freedom, an invincibility that had served him well to become what he had been. She had changed that. His daughter had changed that. And now he could not divide himself to serve two causes. "A ship will be leaving Acre by way of Limassol and Sicily to Genoa. The *Paradisus.* We'll leave on it. Together."

Her fingertips to his lips silenced him.

What could have been the awkwardness of gowns and gambesons, laces and lacing, shirts and shifts became a matter of systematic collusion until no obstacle remained to impede them.

He savored the warmth of her scented skin in the bend of her neck and shoulder. Her breasts pressed against him when she raised her arms around his neck to kiss him again. She turned her head away and closed her eyes and he took her, soft and acquiescent, in her curtained and spotless bed. He wished she would look at him but knew that she still wanted to deny her complicity in all of this. He wanted to tell her that, but did not want to distract her from her determination to yield to him without surrendering herself.

When they became their separate selves again, lying still and supine, he said, "I love you."

She did not reply. He pretended that she did not hear him but knew that she did. He also knew that she had not said those words to him, not ever.

Outside, the sun had drowned in the sea, and darkness crept toward them. The only thing for him to decide now was whether he would break his word to God or to his wife.

CHAPTER 41

"And I, my lords, wish my husband to be buried next to our son."

The queen of Jerusalem sat enthroned under a baldaquin of deep purple bearing a field of crosses of the Holy City stitched in gold thread. On her brow sat her crown, the royal crown of Jerusalem, eight-sided after the number of its gates, its gold enameled in vivid colors, seeded with pearls and lapis lazuli, with a dozen sapphires, emeralds, rubies and garnets for the Twelve Apostles.

The robes she had worn at her and her husband's coronation gave the queen a majesty no one in the hall would deny. Isabella's *kohl*-painted eyes mirrored the hard gleam of the bejeweled crown. Although she kept her gaze on the man in front of her, she spoke deliberately so that all of those in the great hall could hear her every word.

"It was your husband's wish to be buried in Nikosia, Your

Grace. In his own kingdom." Fulk d'Yvers repeated his words with equal care. He was alone, on one knee, before the queen's dais.

Juliana stood with the queen's women, watching it all, trying to hide herself behind the others. Only Beroniki attended her mistress. The queen had ordered all of her ladies to present themselves in their formal gowns and adornments, a female contingent Isabella d'Anjou intended to counter the male one that filled the hall. Juliana knew the faces of only a few men in the hall. She recognized Renaud Barlais who had had a heated exchange with the man called Fulk d'Yvers outside the hall. She saw Lasalle holding back with the rest of Aimary's supporters. If Lasalle saw her, he did not acknowledge her.

Whispers around the citadel told her of Isabella's private exchange with her late husband's kinsman, the nature of which no one knew. Juliana guessed the nature of it, but since a queen's order could not be easily countermanded, Juliana obeyed Isabella's wishes, her heart filled with guilt and her mind with last night.

I love you. She had heard the words and yet she refused to hear them. She kept her mind on his other words or rather one word–*Paradisus.*

The loud exchange between the queen and Fulk d'Yvers brought Juliana back to the current predicament. The queen's refusal of her husband's request halted what everyone expected to be the formalities of royal succession. The barons shuffled their feet, looking discomforted at each other. Not a few of them missed Aimary de Lusignan already if for no other reason than that he allowed no female tantrums in this hall or anywhere in the kingdom where it mattered.

In the past few days, Juliana heard some of the men voice loudly that the queen ought to grieve for her husband, but for Christ's sake, she had parted from three of them already. Why would this one be any different? They would soon be finding her another one. Juliana then understood Isabella a little more and she pitied her. Isabella knew these men, this land, and what they demanded of her in order for them to keep it.

"Don't think me a fool, my lord. I know why my husband chose Nikosia." Isabella answered, the usual softness of her voice gone, her face under the layer of paste replaced by the mask of Nemesis.

Juliana glanced at Beroniki. From her expression, Beroniki understood why the queen set herself against her barons even though Isabella knew that she could not prevail against them–not like her half sister had. Sybilla had fooled them all and won what her heart desired. Isabella desired Aimary. Someone had taken him away from her. But she would not let him go, not without a fight. He had fought for her crown. She had to fight for him.

It's difficult to trust to chance, isn't it? But what is life without it? Juliana could hear Aimary's voice, firm and kind and dared not blink lest her tears run and ruin her cosmetics.

"My lady," Fulk held his ground against the woman on the dais, "I never broke my word to my lord. Would you wish me to do it now?"

The murmur in the hall died down. The queen drew all eyes.

Isabella did not answer and the silence grew long and deep and longer still. Standing there, Juliana understood the power of a woman's will to fight even though she knew that her battle would be lost. She saw the crowd through the quiver of her unshed tears and knew that the men understood and that some of them understood more than others, and they were ashamed.

She felt a prick of pity for Fulk d'Yvers, too, and for Renaud Barlais who had clearly put d'Yvers up to it, perhaps not having the courage to face the queen himself. Fulk did, and those who faced him could see the sorrow on his creased, sun-ravaged face, and yet a stubborn determination to carry out his last duty to his lord.

Staggering slightly under the weight of her robes, Isabella of Jerusalem stood up. Two of her women made a move to steady her, but Beroniki halted them, not offering aid herself either. It was as if a gale swept over a field of wheat. The barons knelt in a hushed wave, all of them, heads bowed. Steady and suddenly tall, their queen stood there under a sky of gold crosses, her crown as splendid as a reliquary weighing down her brow, the jewel-strewn cloak flowing from her shoulders. She looked over the congregation at her feet, a slow, sweeping glance.

"You have my permission to bury my lord husband in Nikosia."

Church of Saint Michael

Out of the way, in a small parish church by the sea gate of the same name, Burgundia de Lusignan knelt in prayer, veiled and waiting. She did not make a move to acknowledge the man who entered the chapel from the sacristy until he stood close.

"You are taking a chance to be seen here," Brother Geoffrey said before she spoke. "Where is your husband?"

"With some whore. He lets me come here to pray. You have to send your brother a message."

"He wouldn't listen to me. That's why you have to approach his wife again."

The black silk of her veil stirred with her breath. "I can't. You must watch out for him."

"It's not his safety that worries me. He gave my men the slip by dressing like a *turcopolier.*"

Burgundia detected a concern among the evasion. "You didn't think that she would follow him, did you?"

"No," Geoffrey admitted. "I didn't think their marriage would last this long either."

"Are you so knowledgeable of marriages, my lord?"

"Enough to be baffled." Considering the matrimonial matters of his current interrogator, Geoffrey wished that he had not said it. Fortunately, Cousin Burgundia did not pursue that subject. Unfortunately, she pursued the current one.

"And do you know why she would?"

"It seems that our father took the child from her. She came to compel him to return to Poitou and recover it."

"And why did he come here?"

"I . . . I made him."

"Indeed. How?"

Cousin Burgundia wanted to hear it from his own lips. "He's wasting his life guarding woods and weavers in Parthenay when he could be safeguarding a Lusignan crown in *outre-mer.* Your father saw it that way."

Burgundia noted the defensiveness. "And so did your father. Don't waste my time, Geoffrey. I asked you how you made him."

Cousin Burgundia, being half Lusignan and half Ibelín, would not let him off the hook. Unfortunately, she was right. Geoffrey knew that he had brought this on himself, but his was a larger cause. Or so he thought. Geoffrey inhaled and told her of his instructions to Brother Reginald.

Her face raised to the smiling Holy Mother, Burgundia listened without interruption. "And how do you now propose to remedy your egregious meddling in your brother's marriage?" she said when he finished.

He would have disputed her choice of words, but Burgundia was right; they could not waste time. He may as well capitulate now. "What is it you wish me to do?"

"You can be sure that I will not be sending you to eat at the turcopoles' table without a napkin for your penance. I wish you to swear to me in the presence of Our Lady to tell Juliana the truth, and to see to it that they are both on a ship back to Poitou. There is nothing for him to do here now. It is done."

"But what about your–"

Burgundia crossed herself and tugged at her skirts. He took a step to aid her, but she already stood up, her hand pressed to the small of her back. "I said, it is done. Isabella is Hugh's guardian. There's nothing for your brother here anymore. Now swear it."

CHAPTER 42

With the king's last wish granted, a flotilla of ships in Acre's harbor waited to accompany his body, sealed in a casket, to be buried in Nikosia, in the church of Saint Sophia. The four times married and thrice widowed queen of Jerusalem once again became the sole sovereign of her kingdom. To no one's surprise, she called on her half brother to return from Beirut to act in her name.

The barons and the masters of the Orders who had gathered in Acre during Aimary's illness had witnessed the abrupt end of several reigns. The most recent events therefore cast down the Latins of *outre-mer,* but hardly disarmed them. They readily reaffirmed the order of succession to the kingdom, just as Aimary de Lusignan intended.

La Marquise, the queen's daughter by the Marquis de Montferrat, would take precedence over any male child the queen might bear her future husband, her fifth one. After all, Isabella was still a young woman, and a lovely one. With the body of Aimary de Lusignan barely cold, speculations mounted in the capital about his replacement.

No speculation arose about the fact that as the stepmother of young Hugh of Cyprus, the queen would hold his guardianship. The High Court of that kingdom would choose a regent for Cyprus so that no single individual would have custody of the heir's person as well as his throne. And while the barons who held lands on the island began to address the regency for that realm, Isabella of Jerusalem became ill.

She collapsed in the middle of the great hall, in the middle of receiving her vassals' homage. The queen's illness did not take her intimates by surprise. The blows of the past weeks would have undermined the most robust of constitutions, and Juliana had overheard Isabella's women whisper that the queen had not been well for some time. Surely only the worries and sorrows of the last weeks had caused the queen's illness. Surely she would recover in due time. The Lord had His reasons for testing the kingdom.

Lasalle had disappeared once again, perhaps reconciling himself to his failure to protect the king by getting stupendously drunk, Juliana thought uncharitably. She did not wish to think of his threat against John d'Ibelín. It did not matter now. It could not.

With Beroniki's permission, Juliana took a couple of servants and went to the harbor to see if the *Paradisus* had anchored there. She could not believe her eyes. Lasalle had not lied. The ship sat anchored outside the inner harbor with barges around her to refurbish and outfit her for the journey to Genoa to bring back from the Holy Land pilgrims, passengers, and news of the king's death.

Suppressing with great difficulty her excitement at their imminent departure from these shores, Juliana returned to Sybilla's and Melisande's nursery. Publicly, Xene and Madelena had mourned the deaths of the girls' siblings with dignity. Privately, they shared their sorrow with Juliana while showering Sybilla and Melisande with affection and amusements. Xene's and Madelena's selfless devotion to children not their own only reminded her of Pontia's love for Eleanor and of the sacrifice that she had asked Pontia to make for Eleanor's sake.

To distract the children and herself, Juliana brought her basket of pomegranates to the garden. The boys' mastiff pups, almost fully grown, joined them, having transferred their allegiance to their young mistresses.

In the middle of their gambols, Beroniki's woman rushed into the garden and whispered something to Xene. Xene curtsied to Juliana, her voice trembling. "Beroniki wishes to see you, Lady Juliana. You're to veil yourself and hurry."

Her apprehension rising with each step, Juliana followed the servant woman. Beroniki waited for her outside the queen's private chamber, her dignity ever supreme. Before Juliana could utter a word, Beroniki gestured her to keep silent and made her draw her veil to her eyes. Taking Juliana by the hand, Beroniki led her into the chamber.

Since the backs of those who filled it were to them, no one noticed their entry. Juliana saw who they were—three barons, a Greek priest and deacons intoning a prayer, the queen's own women, some of them kneeling, others clinging to the extravagant bed setting into which they poured their tears. A man in a mud-grimed cloak knelt as well by the queen's bedside, his head bowed.

Isabella of Jerusalem lay against the pillows, eyes closed, her face smooth, without expression, her hands folded over a simple wooden cross, the braid of her black hair resting across her breast which breath no longer disturbed.

The sight struck the breath from Juliana's own breast. She regained it at Beroniki's painful grip of her hand and her voice in her ear. "Her hands. Look at her hands. I washed them before the priest came."

Juliana blinked several times. Traces of elaborate patterns remained on the back of the Isabella's hands. Beroniki leaned nearer. "They are on her palms, back and belly, too. A woman came to the *hammam* and offered to draw them for her. She told the queen that those designs would bring her husband's love. The queen wanted another child." Beroniki nudged Juliana back to the door. "She often went to the *hammam* to have them renewed. The woman prepared her own henna and wouldn't let anyone touch it. The queen . . . Isabella told the woman that she wanted her to draw those for you, too, but the woman refused. She said the paste was too precious and meant only for the queen."

The taste of soured wine stung Juliana's throat. "Who was she?"

"No one knows. She was Greek, a Christian, like me. The queen wanted to be sure. She called herself Aphrodite."

Rhoxsane of Kolossi. No, it could not be. And yet, it surely was. The queen's death had been planned for days, weeks, before the king's, carefully planned to take advantage of a woman's love for her husband. "Did she . . . did Isabella get her wish?"

Beroniki crossed herself. "Yes."

The chamber filled with the sound of subdued sobs and loud whispers. Alarmed, Beroniki pushed Juliana out the door. Juliana stole a last glance at the body of Jerusalem's queen–and saw the man who knelt by the bedside look up. At her.

John d'Ibelín, the Lord of Beirut.

CHAPTER 43

The king was dead and the queen died five days later, of grief. Or so they said.

"Lady Juliana!"

Juliana looked up from her trunk. She had spent the last days in a daze. The queen's death turned the tragedy of the king's into a catastrophe. Only one piece of news surpassed those events, and for only one person in the entire kingdom: the *Paradisus* had announced her departure for Genoa the very next day.

She had not heard anyone enter her chamber. The tolling of every church bell in the city bruised her ears and made her head throb and not even a full cup of wine could banish it. The pain did not prevent her thoughts from running wildly from Isabella to Rhoxsane to Burgundia de Lusignan, to Maria Komnene, to—

John d'Ibelín.

He stood in the doorway, his arms against the jamb bracing him upright. In view of the circumstances, he was the last person she expected to see. She expected Lasalle. He had promised that he would send servants to take her trunk to the harbor. The servants had already brought aboard their provisions. She had told Beroniki, Xene, and Madelena that she was returning home. They understood and gave her their blessing. She did not say a word to Melisande and Sybilla to avoid distressing the girls. They still had to face the loss of their mother.

She had few things to pack, a couple of gowns and shifts. The rest of the trunk's weight came from books, secured in a pitch-coated cask, books she had purchased in the scribes' market. She did not wish to take anything else that would remind her of this place. Her only regret was that she had not been able to visit the Holy Sepulcher. She would have to settle for the promised indulgences, and as soon as she reached Parthenay she would confess her sins of omission and commission to Father Urias.

Juliana did not curtsey. "My lord."

John d'Ibelín pushed himself away and snapped his riding crop at the servant women. "Leave, all of you."

Frightened, the women looked at her.

"No, don't." Juliana countered his order without a second thought. She was not going to be alone with a man who could be Aimary's assassin. No, she was not going to be alone with him because of what happened in Nikosia. No, because of what she had allowed to happen.

D'Ibelín took a staggering step toward her. The women exclaimed, their fear replaced by the more immediate concern for the queen's half brother. Having experience of drunken, exhausted, and wounded men, the women propped up the Lord of Beirut to get him into the chair. Juliana's misgivings gave way to common sense. She poured him a cup of wine left over from last night and held it for him while he drank because his hands shook.

"Thank you," John d'Ibelín's gratitude came mixed with embarrassment. He looked up at her, his eyes dull with grief. "She lied. She said she knew who would be the assassin."

The women gasped and crossed themselves. Juliana hoped she kept her expression noncommittal. She had expected him to mention his sister. "Leave us. All of you."

Once she said it, she regretted it, but the women were already leaving in a cascade of whispers, confused about John d'Ibelín's presence. If the women were confused, she was not, not entirely. Another minor and a female at that had inherited the kingdom of Jerusalem. Just as Isabella feared, the crown of tesserae would weigh heavy on Maria's brow. And this time as well the queen's death had tilted the power in *outre-mer* in favor of the Ibelíns. By custom, the High Court would choose the queen's closest male relative to be the regent for her daughter.

The barons wasted no time. A solemn procession had accompanied Maria de Montferrat from Saint Anne's to the royal citadel to be presented to her barons. They had again filled the great hall, this time for the purposes of choosing Maria's one particular male relative, one capable of guiding *terre-sainte* through these trying times. That man now stood—or rather slumped—before

Juliana de Charnais: John d'Ibelín, the lord of the war-ruined barony of Beirut.

He ought to have been in that hall to claim his right to the position. Instead, in the privacy of her chamber and behind closed door, John d'Ibelín was saying words Juliana told herself she no longer wished to hear. "My mother said that I was to be Aimary's assassin. I know your husband suspects me. All the Lusignan allies do. Some others, too. But I swear that I had nothing to do with Aimary's death. Only I can't prove it. And now my sister . . ."

She did not wish to hear anyone's confessions when she had much of her own to confess. There were plenty of priests in the city. Juliana therefore said, very kindly, "I am certain your mother was mistaken."

Taking no hint of her lack of interest, John d'Ibelín shook his head. "She told me the message said so."

Leontios's message. Dear Lord. It had to be. No, she could not care about that now. It did not matter, not any more. The *Paradisus* waited. "I see."

"I didn't read it. I . . . I can't read." He rubbed his eyes. "Not that well. The words look all jumbled to me."

That this man who came from a people who prized learning as much as valor could not read truly surprised her, but more so his confiding to her what must have been his shame of it. Juliana tried to show nothing more than polite acknowledgement of both statements. "I see."

He glanced away. "My mother has her spies."

He said it as if she had asked. Since Isabella had recruited her to spy on their mother, Juliana did not see a need to comment, only a fierce desire to end this conversation. "Then the message lied."

"Or my mother lied," John d'Ibelín said, no doubt to spare her the awkwardness of calling the dowager queen of Jerusalem a liar. "I swear I didn't kill Aimary or have him killed. Good Lord, why would I?"

Of course other evidence pointed to John d'Ibelín's guilt, at least in Aimary's death. Avoiding a direct accusation, Juliana said, "It seems, my lord, that you didn't come to Acre with the others when Aimary became ill. A ship under your flag was seen in Limassol. You went to see Hugh secretly, without his father's permission, and you had promised Niketas and the lady of Kolossi your support and patronage when you became the regent of Cyprus."

"What?" John d'Ibelín leaned forward. For a moment Juliana thought that he would query the source of her information, but he did not. "I know of the woman, but I never met her. And Niketas? I'd never trust that schemer. I don't know why Aimary did. And I always sail to Kyrenia to see Hugh, not Limassol. Aimary doesn't have . . . didn't have much time for Hugh. The boy needed someone . . . I needed him . . . I needed him to know that his mother's family hasn't forgotten him."

She expected excuses and denials of the evidence, not a thorough disavowal. "But a ship under your flag was seen in Limassol. Rhoxsane told me that you had made those promises."

"Then she lied."

Her headache pounded at her. If Rhoxsane were a poisoner, hardly a surprise that she would also be a liar. She should not have asked, she should have left her curiosity be buried with the rest of the coffins. She should have. "You didn't come to Acre when Aimary fell ill."

"I couldn't leave Beirut." He looked up at her, his eyes blurred. "The child died. This one died, too. It was another boy."

Something stabbed her, sharper than a dagger's prick. She felt helpless and stupid. "I am so sorry."

He smiled, a small, grateful smile. "Thank you. Do you have children, Lady Juliana?"

She did not realize that she had her hand on her cross until the points scored her palm. She had to sit down. "A daughter. I had to leave her. I was made to leave her."

He nodded, slowly and solemnly, as if her loss had been a part of his. And at that moment she knew with unbreakable certainty that he understood her, and her loss.

This man understood what it was like to lose a child, if not in death, then by a separation which was, in a terrible way, far worse.

It must have been what she had sensed that day in Nikosia when he had first touched her the way one would touch a child's cheek, with wonder and awe. Yes, that must have been it. How could she explain it otherwise?

Lasalle had never done that. He had not touched Eleanor that way, not ever. Yes, he did pick her up the way one might a helpless puppy, with care but without a sign of love so ferocious that it had to be reserved only for one's child. She felt that love fill her every time she held Eleanor to her. Guérin de Lasalle did not—or could not.

Her headache vanished. Juliana let the ceaseless tolling that reverberated through the halls echoed in her heart. Maybe the path Abbess Mathilde had spoken of was meant to lead her to this truth. *What does a marriage make?*

"Lady Juliana? Are you all right?"

"What? Yes, yes."

"I said that I came to ask a favor of you."

"You did?" This time she could not pretend polite disinterest. What possible favor could she grant to John d'Ibelín?

Her visitor looked up at her with his black, seductive eyes. "Hugh said you can read. Can you read the message for me? I have to know the truth. I don't know anyone else I can trust but you to persuade your husband that I am not the assassin."

Trust no one. Mother Mary, what happened to her wits? The Lord of Beirut was using her. Of course he was. He was as wily as any Lusignan. He also knew that his presence in her chamber had compromised her. Was that what he wanted? God forbid that Lasalle should show up at this very moment. How foolish could she be, letting this man into her chamber. She said, rising, "He does suspect you. But lately not as much."

He did not seem to notice the change in her demeanor. He stood up as well, relief lifting his tired smile. "Then you will do it? I have to be certain. The regent of this kingdom can't rule for long under rumors of regicide."

He thought that she had consented. They both knew what he was asking her. The proof of the guilt or innocence of the *de facto* next ruler of this kingdom had come down to the wife of the man whose family had long contested the Ibelíns' power. *It is difficult to trust to chance. But what is life without it?*

She should have refused. She should have told John d'Ibelín that Lasalle or the servants would appear to take her to the harbor, to board the *Paradisus.*

She should have.

CHAPTER 44

John d'Ibelín left his men at the gate to his mother's *logis.* Juliana dogged his footsteps until they got past the dowager's guards. She remembered the dowager's chamber, now half-shuttered and draped in mourning, the air still thick, this time from the incense and candles surrounding the icons.

Maria Komnene sat among them in the only chair, dressed in the habit of a cloistered nun with a high headpiece from which fell her gold-threaded veil, the usual dazzle of rings on her fingers. Whatever Maria Komnene's grief at the loss of her daughter and grandchildren, the face beneath the paint did not show it. Vials, bowls, and caskets on a table before her provided a bastion against those who would dare to approach. The dowager did not display surprise at their unannounced arrival, merely irritation. "What are you doing here, John? And with this . . . person."

Her son dared to approach. "You've got your wish, mother. Aimary is dead and I'll be the regent, only of Jerusalem, not Cyprus. I want to see that message and for you to tell me who gave it to you."

Maria Komnene took a long sniff from one of her vials. "Why? You can't read."

Her son grabbed the table's edge and heaved it on its side, shattering the table's contents. "Enough! You'll give it to me and tell me who gave it to you."

Juliana flinched at the sudden violence of it, but Maria Komnene only sighed. "Just like your father. There was no reason to destroy such precious gifts. The message is in that ivory coffer. Be careful, it was a wedding gift from your—"

D'Ibelín picked up the container and hurled it against the wall. From the remains of it flew a tightly folded piece of parchment. He picked it up and handed it to Juliana.

The message no longer bore a seal. Her hands now shaking, Juliana unfolded it and went to the window for better light. This had to be the message that Hugh saw the black-veiled lady give to Leontios. It was the message for which Leontios and Morphia died. It was also unsigned and disappointingly brief.

I have proof that John d'Ibelín intends to attack you. Pray have care. With my blessing take whatever steps against him.

Juliana waited for her heart to settle. She had seen that hand before. Where had she seen that hand? *Pray have care. . . . with my blessing. . . .* She looked closer at the slant of the letters. "Someone changed the name."

"What? How can you tell?" John d'Ibelín was standing disconcertingly near.

Maria Komnene sat up in her chair. "You silly girl. What a preposterous idea."

Juliana ignored the dowager's skepticism and her son's proximity to point out the letters to him. "See here? Someone scratched the name and wrote in yours. You can see that the spacing of the new letters is made wider. Whoever scratched out the name didn't wait to prepare the parchment either. Here and here the ink runs a little."

"Nonsense. I can read, girl, and I did not see anything of the kind," Maria Komnene declared from her seat.

Juliana would not let the dowager's contempt dissuade her. True, the evidence before her eyes would exonerate John d'Ibelín—but leave the cause of the message unsolved. *She had seen that hand before.* "Yes, Madame, but your eyes may not see all they read."

John d'Ibelín picked up the parchment by one corner and approached his mother. "Tell me, who brought this to you?"

Maria Komnene's hands gripped the seat's arms. "Why would I? You never asked how your name ended up there, did you? You just never cared enough to protect your family. I have to."

For a moment, John d'Ibelín looked like he was about to do violence if not to his mother, then to the rest of her possessions. "Who else has seen this?"

"No one. Why would I allow that accusation spread around the kingdom?"

John d'Ibelín's voice caught with the same suppressed fury Juliana had heard many times in Lasalle's. "No one? Whoever wrote my name is now free to spread it around the kingdom, isn't he?"

The dowager blinked. "Who would challenge you?"

"A Lusignan, Mother! You said it yourself. For Christ's sake, can't you see that someone is trying to have the Lusignans and the Ibelíns at each other's throats again?"

Maria Komnene's self-assurance wavered. "But who would–"

D'Ibelín handed the parchment back to Juliana. "Is there anything else you can tell?"

"I . . . I don't know."

He tilted up her chin and she let him, and met his eyes, black and bold and resolved to have her answer. "You do know. Tell me. Whatever it is, tell me. You know what the news of this would mean. If they take me down, they will all fight each other for the regency."

Juliana heard his voice and the other one, teary, confessing to her. *I only told her that Leontios was already sending messages to them. Her, I told her.*

"In Nikosia, your mother's spy was a man called Leontios. I think he was killed to get hold of this message in order to alter the name. Hugh wanted to tell you that he witnessed it when you came to Nikosia, but–"

"But Niketas showed up. I remember. Do you?" He made a small, half-embarrassed gesture to where his dagger had left its mark and she stood there this time as well like a trapped ewe. He lowered his hand with a smile. "What else? Tell me."

Maria Komnene had not contradicted her, but Juliana knew that the dowager's shrewd eyes saw more than Juliana wished her to see. She folded the parchment and returned it to him. "I think I know who the writer is. But I don't know who altered the name."

"Who's the writer?"

She may as well throw herself to these two leopards. "Lady Burgundia. I saw one of her letters to her father. It is the same hand. I was wrong about her. The message meant to warn her father, not harm him. Only he never got it."

"Oh! *Psephtis!*" Maria Komnene did not conceal her annoyance. "What nonsense. John, are you going to believe this silly person?"

The dowager's opinion did not matter to Juliana. Her son's did. He moved away from her, considered her for some time, then went to pace about the chamber, the parchment in his grip while his mother poured a flood of Greek words at him, words which he ignored.

Juliana wished she had not agreed to come here, she wished she had not been so keen to discover this message. It pried open the door to rivalries that could engulf the kingdom once again, and this time, destroy it. She could not prevent it anymore than Lasalle could have prevented Aimary's death. A couple of servant women shuffled into the room to light the lamps. Juliana had not noticed that dusk was descending on the rooftops. What if Lasalle were looking for her? For her conscience's sake, she had to tell John of Beirut one more thing, but not in front of his mother. "My lord, I have to return."

He looked at her, suddenly remembering that he was not alone in the room and shoved the parchment inside his gambeson. "Of course. I apologize for having kept you. I'll see to it that my men deliver you without delay. Mother, we are not finished, not by far."

Juliana curtsied to the dowager and left her chamber with the same mixed emotions she had left it with the last time. Once in the courtyard with no servants about, she tugged at d'Ibelín's sleeve. "My lord, wait. I didn't want to say it in front of your mother, but I think the same person or persons had a hand in your sister's death."

John d'Ibelín looked about to be equally certain that no servant overhead them. "It was the henna, wasn't it? Beroniki told me."

"Yes. But why? Isabella's crown always belonged to *La Marquise* and the regency would have been yours anyway. As long as no one knows about that accusation, the barons have no reason to deny it to you."

"Maybe not this one. But think. There is another regency, isn't there?"

She frowned at the prompt. *Think.* Isabella was more than the queen of Jerusalem. She was Hugh's stepmother. "Yes, but it doesn't make sense either, does it? You're Hugh's uncle. You can have that regency, too. Or your brother."

He gave her an odd look, then he quickly smiled. "I am not Aimary. The barons would not agree to have the Ibelíns hold two regencies. The two crowns are separated. I have chosen to guard Jerusalem's. With God's help, one day we will recover the city."

"I see." It occurred to her that in fact she did not see. She only pretended an understanding, wanting desperately to untangle herself from the web of her own making, thanks to her folly in agreeing to read that message for him, thanks to her keeping their association secret, thanks to letting herself be lured by her belief that she could cut this Gordian knot by herself. She knew for certain that neither Maria Komnene nor her son had shared all they knew. "Yes, yes, of course. Jerusalem."

John d'Ibelín assumed an amused, slightly worried expression. "Yes, Jerusalem. As long as your husband doesn't come before the High Court and challenge me to a trial by combat."

She looked up at him. He was tall. "You . . . you know?"

He laughed. "No. But that's what I would do if I were your husband."

Juliana tried to collect her wits. "That would certainly give your enemies a victory."

"I'd say right now someone is counting on us killing each other. That's why you must tell your husband what you saw with your own eyes." He said it without a hint of humor.

"I . . . I wouldn't want him to kill you." Dear Lord. Her wits must have left her entirely and, worse yet, threatened not to come back. She should be kneeling in her little chapel, praying to the Virgin for a safe return journey. She made a move away from him, but he held her hands in both of his, no pretence on his face or in his words.

"And I would not have killed him."

"Oh. You . . . you wouldn't? Why not?"

His answer was a long, thoughtful sigh, and then he kissed her hand, the one with her wedding ring behind her knuckle. "Because you love him."

In the great hall of Saint Jean d'Acre's citadel, the High Court unanimously agreed to offer the regency of the kingdom to John d'Ibelín, the Lord of Beirut, until such time as a husband would be chosen for his niece and the new queen of Jerusalem, thirteen-year-old Maria de Montferrat.

When John d'Ibelín appeared before the Court to accept that responsibility, the first to pledge his unreserved support was Walter de Montbéliard, the husband of Burgundia de Lusignan, John d'Ibelín's cousin and the daughter of Jerusalem's late king. Being mired in such a happy web of marital connection, Walter informed everyone that he and his wife would be departing for Nikosia immediately to ensure that the High Court of that kingdom acknowledged his wife's rights as the guardian of her brother, the almost eleven-year-old king of Cyprus.

Whatever thoughts on that subject John d'Ibelín might have had, they were swept away by the instant torrent of demands of his barons and the needs of the kingdom. The kingdom of Acre, as some began to call it, less with derision than with accuracy. Regardless of the name, for now the security and stability of Maria de Montferrat's sorely tested realm rested on his shoulders. He would not be returning to Helvis, not any time soon, nor did he have the luxury to mourn his own son.

CHAPTER 45

Because you love him.

The words haunted Juliana all the way back to the citadel, merging her worries, misgivings, and confusion. This time she had to tell Lasalle about the message. She had to. But how could she when she had not confided to him her familiarity with John d'Ibelín? No, not familiarity, nothing improper had happened. Nothing. Lasalle had kept plenty of his associations from her. What difference did it make how she came by her information?

She left the Ibelín men at the gate, removed her veil to pass the guards, and hurried through the now familiar corridors. She passed by clusters of servants anxiously sharing the latest rumors. The Lord of Beirut's name floated under the vaulting.

Preoccupied by her dilemma, she belatedly noticed that no guards stood outside the door to the children's nursery. Juliana took a deep breath and let herself inside.

The silence inside pressed on her like the silence of a sepulcher. In the light of a lone lamp, Xene and Madelena were bending over two small figures on the bed, fully dressed and curled in each others' arms. Sybilla and Melisande lying there, motionless.

Juliana flew toward them. "Oh Lord, they are dead!"

Xene took a firm hold of her. "Shh. Only sleeping. We gave them a draft."

Juliana's relief came with a new wave of dread. "Why?"

"To keep them quiet until we get them to the boat. Where in blazes were you?"

Juliana started even though she knew the voice. Lasalle stood at the door, dressed in his *turcopolier* guise, a look on his face that she had seen before, a look that frightened her. "With Beroniki. I was with Beroniki. What are you . . . why–?"

He pressed a sack into her hand. She felt the weight of a flagon and could smell the still warm bread. "Sybilla and Melisande are all that's left of Aimary and Isabella. They have become important."

She struggled with the sack and with this deluge of events. "You forgot about Heloise."

"I haven't. I want these two in the harbor first. She's at Saint Anne. The abbess might need some convincing but I think I can manage it." He nodded to the women. "Let's go."

Not questioning Lasalle's plans or his current appearance, Xene and Madelena wrapped the sleeping girls in their cloaks.

This was madness.

Juliana swung the sack over her shoulder and followed the women through the corridors. They knew them well enough to avoid the guards whom Lasalle had probably also bribed–but not the dogs.

From the end of the passage, the two mastiffs padded toward them, muzzles in the air, nails clicking on the tiles. The dogs paused. The hair along their spine ridge rose. Their low whine became a suspicious growl.

"Oh, Lord," Xene whispered, holding Melisande closer. Juliana stood nailed to the spot. The dogs knew her and the women, but they saw a stranger in strange attire, smelling equally strange to them–and threatening their young mistresses. One mastiff of their size could easily bring a man down. Two of them . . .

Very slowly, Lasalle reached for the clasp on his cloak and let it slide down his arm. With the other, he reached behind his back. "Go on."

Xene and Madelena obeyed without a word. Juliana did too, the flagon heavy against her spine. She glanced back to see the dogs lower their heads and charge.

She saw no more because they turned a corner but she heard the sound of a heavy-bodied scuffle, a muffled yip and thump, a sharp whine and then silence. Xene and Madelena heard it as well. They stopped, looking at each other. They all looked at each other. They heard the tread of fast footsteps and then Lasalle trotted up. He had no cloak and the sleeve of his *juba* had a tear and a wet stain on it. They hurried on without a word.

Once outside the fortress, in the salty spring air, they kept to the shadows until they reached a postern gate. Juliana's heart sank at the sight of the guards who stepped into the light of torches. To her surprise, one of the guardsmen handed Lasalle one of the torches, and the other man opened the gate for them. Lasalle had bribed them, too.

Torch in hand, he took the lead through a maze of narrow streets, the two men, swords drawn, bringing up the rear. They passed several lewd women in the company of equally notorious characters. They would have posed danger to three unescorted women, but with Lasalle and the two other men, they only resorted to shouting what Juliana concluded to be obscenities, in several languages. Ignoring them, Juliana wheezed at Lasalle's back, "A boat? What use is that? The master chains up the harbor each night."

"But not the whole coast."

Head down to watch her step on the broken pavement, Juliana kept up, her heart in her throat. Of course Lasalle would have a plan. He always did. She could not distract him with her questions or her news, not now.

They reached the warehouses and a stretch of stalls pressed up against their walls. Lasalle dismissed the two men and they faded into the darkness. He gave a long, soft whistle, like the sound of a night bird. The door of one of the stalls opened, admitting them.

Juliana caught a glimpse of a veiled woman who held up a lamp to point to the back wall in the warehouse. Passing through another door there, they found themselves on a strip of coastland strewn with stones and rock rubble. The moon's light reflected on the surface of the waters. A short distance from the shore, Juliana saw the outline of a fishing boat. Lasalle waved his torch. From the boat came the reply of a lantern, followed by the splash of a *chaloupe's* oars.

In their nurses' arms, Sybilla and Melisande did not stir. Lasalle motioned to the women to proceed along the shore to meet the rowboat. Exhausted from carrying the girls, Xene and Madelena stepped cautiously among the weed-slick, jagged rocks. Ahead, the *chaloupe* reached land. Without urging, Juliana followed the women, trying to keep her sack from tipping and her feet from tripping on her skirts and the rubble.

"Well now, setting out to fish?"

Out of the shadow of the wall buttress stepped three–no, five men, torches in hand, flames reflecting on the steel of their drawn swords. Xene and Madelena cried out and backed away, shielding their precious burdens.

Instinctively, Juliana took a step back as well–and stumbled over something large and pliable. At that moment, Lasalle flung his torch into the sea. For the span of the torch's flaming arch, she saw at her feet a body, no, two . . . three. The fishing boat's crew, their throats cut, their blood washing away in the lapping waves.

"My lord Lasalle. Kidnapping royal children?"

The voice of the advancing man cut short any shock at that discovery. They were trapped on a narrow stretch of land between the sea and the seawalls of the harbor, several armed men approaching them. In the dark, they could not retreat. Juliana gulped. Lasalle could not save all of them or any of them. They would be killed, their bodies thrown into the sea, never to be found.

From the darkness around them came a whistle. A low, soft whistle like the one with which Lasalle had signaled the stall woman. Had she betrayed them? Only the sound startled the men, too.

"It's an owl, you fools." The man who appeared to be the others' leader advanced with a swagger, swinging a club.

"Get behind, stay in the shadows," Lasalle said calmly, but Juliana had heard that tone before. Tripping over the rocks, Xene and Madelena retreated. "You too, Juli–"

Surprise is your best–

She took three unsteady steps toward the foremost man and let her knees go slack and the sack to slide. The man laughed. Expecting her to faint away next, he switched the club to his other hand to better grab for her. She dropped her sack. The heavy flagon inside landed precisely on the man's toes. He yelped, stumbled, and dropped the club.

And that was when she drove her dagger into the man's thigh.

Blood, hot and thick, spouted over her hands. Howling, the man went down. Behind her, Lasalle made a sound, half a groan of surprise, half laughter, but by then the others charged, torches and swords in hand. Steel countered steel with that keen sound of death and destruction. Their downed comrade and the rocky footing prevented a unified assault and gave Lasalle a temporary advantage. He took it against the first man, caring less for the torch than for the sword, turning the man's rush back into his companions and causing their disarray.

The light of the torches bounced against the walls, glanced off the surface of the waters. Sparks danced in a mad dance of vicious fireflies. On her knees, Juliana groped about furiously, hampered by her wet skirts and half-blinded by the flames. The wounded man howled in short gasps, clutching with both hands his thigh from which blood poured prodigiously, her dagger in it. Given the man's attachment to it, Juliana did not think she ought to retrieve it and Lasalle's advice to run seemed singularly inappropriate. She dislodged a large stone, her impeccably polished nails breaking. She twisted to . . .

In the shadow of the wall buttress, Xene and Madelena cried out. From the blackness more men emerged under the halos of torches. Juliana would have screamed a warning to Lasalle, but he had already faced the new threat.

"Here! Over here. She stabbed me. The stupid bitch stabbed me." The wounded man yelled to the approaching men, sheer panic in his voice.

Those men, however, did not advance farther. Realizing that the arrivals were not their reinforcements, the original attackers bunched up in confusion.

"Tisk, tisk. Five against two? And one a helpless woman at that?" The ironic, clear voice startled Juliana. On the ground, the wounded man groaned. The man who had separated himself from the new arrivals approached him with a confident stride. "Ah, not so helpless, eh?"

He casually folded back his cloak and in the same move his hand came down. For a blink of an eye, Juliana saw the descent of curved steel followed by a gurgling sound that drowned the wounded man's last groan in his own blood. The man in the cloak stepped away lightly to avoid it. Not waiting to witness the last twitch of his victim, he motioned to the others of his command to come closer and when they did, he equally casually replaced his cloak. Juliana blinked. The light from his men's torches revealed a prominent patch sewn to the cloak's white cloth.

A red, cross-shaped patch.

CHAPTER 46

Geoffrey de Lusignan, the former Lord of Parthenay, currently of the Temple, stood there in the unabashed glory of his Order. By his side, hands clasped behind his back, stood Brother Reginald. Considering the blood on her own hands, Juliana thought that Brother Reginald glanced at her with a rather kindly expression. She did not care for Brother Reginald's approval or disapproval. However, one did not have to meet Lasalle's older brother more than once to notice the resemblance he too bore to their ineffable sire. That did not bode well.

A rescuer could not be faulted for expecting a certain degree of gratitude from those he had rescued from certain death. Only in this instance, my lord Lasalle's reaction did not include gratitude. Sword in hand, he struck at Brother Geoffrey with violence uncommon even for him, but before Juliana could be shocked by it, Brother Reginald flung at Lasalle a length of something he was hiding behind his back. It was a piece of fishing net.

Lasalle did not dodge it fast enough. The netting tangled his sword arm and a couple of Geoffrey's men who lingered in close proximity, obviously for that purpose, got a good grip on him and got his sword away from him. Being thus thwarted did not curb his fury. On the contrary.

"You lying, treacherous son of a whore–"

"Don't slander our mother, Guérin. Do you want to air our dirty laundry or do you want to get Sybilla and Melisande and"–Geoffrey paused to give Juliana a courteous bow–"your charming wife out of Acre?"

Geoffrey went to the man Juliana had stabbed and withdrew her dagger from the corpse. He wiped it thoroughly and smiling, handed it to her. "Well done, dearest sister. I am delighted you haven't been spending your entire time in Nikosia with your nose in Silbo's breviary. Ah. You may wish to wash your hands."

Whatever relief and gratitude Juliana might have felt evaporated in that reminder of how alike her husband, his brother, and their sire were when it came to glibness of tongue, purposefulness of plots, and violence of action. Come to think of it, the three had little cause to reproach each other. Juliana dipped her hands in a water-filled crevice, dried them on her gown and returned the dagger to its sheath with a frown of thorough disapproval. "Thank you."

"You are most welcome. One does appreciate appreciation." Geoffrey glossed over her lack of demonstration of it and turned to his brother. "Now, are you going to listen?"

"Listen to you? You owe me, you sanctimonious piece of–"

Geoffrey de Lusignan sighed and clamped his hand over Lasalle's mouth ending, or at least interrupting, that screed. "Killing me is not going to get the women out of Acre any faster, will it?" He leaned closer to his captive audience. "Listen to me, Guérin."

To Juliana, that sounded like a threat. Geoffrey waited for Lasalle to heed it and when it became apparent that he would not, Geoffrey removed his hand and himself. "Let him go."

Reluctantly, the men did and stepped back, maintaining a watchful eye on Lasalle's every move. This time, it consisted of him inoffensively straightening his *juba*.

One would have to be an utter fool not to acknowledge that Geoffrey spoke the truth. Their boat crew was dead and they had no means of escaping from this shore. Geoffrey's men had dragged the dead bodies into the darkness and shoved those who had surrendered after them. Juliana did not wish to think what Geoffrey de Lusignan intended to do with them. Come to think of it, she did not care. Their attackers acted on the order of their master–or mistress.

Geoffrey picked up Lasalle's sword from among the rocks, wiped it clean as well and held it out to him, grip first. Lasalle did not touch it. Geoffrey chose to ignore being ignored and inclined his head to where Xene and Madelena had hidden at the foot of the wall, Sybilla and Melisande asleep on their laps, happily oblivious to the trouble that their very existence had caused.

"What do you intend to do with them? You have no means of protecting them."

"Abbess Vigilantia does."

In Lasalle's reply, Juliana heard a younger brother's seething rage at an older one. Geoffrey's reply was a counterpoint of reasonableness. "Then you'll need my boat crew."

Juliana had not expected the offer and if Lasalle did not either, he took immediate advantage of it. "No. You'll need your boat's crew. You're going to Cyprus with them. You owe me. You owe her."

Her? Burgundia or Heloise? Oh, surely Heloise. "Heloise. What about Heloise?" The words just popped out of her mouth before Juliana realized the implication of it—or that she had handed Lasalle a distraction he waited on.

He snatched up his sword from Geoffrey's hand and had the point of it squarely in the middle of Geoffrey's middle. Geoffrey's men lurched forward in a belated effort to protect their master. Brother Reginald's gesture halted them.

Lasalle pressed the sword tip into the white cloth and for a heart-stopping moment she thought that he would drive it deeper. Geoffrey braced himself with the same expectation.

"My lords," Brother Reginald spoke up, "let us remember that we're not to judge our brothers out of hatred or wrath—"

"—nor should we omit to uphold the justice of the House," Lasalle concluded for him. "Let us remember that I am not beholden to the Temple or to my brother, am I, Brother Geoffrey?"

"No," Brother Geoffrey said after a hesitation and with a hint of something that sounded to Juliana like contrition.

His hands at his belt, Brother Reginald took a cautious step forward. "Then let us remember the children, my lords."

Lasalle's eyes did not leave Geoffrey's. "Indeed. Then you'll all make certain that these children reach Saint Mary's. And you'll see to it that my wife is on the *Paradisus* when it reaches Limassol. I'll meet her there." The sword point sank a little deeper. "And you'll find me another boat, won't you, brother?"

Geoffrey shifted his gaze to Juliana and she saw the twin of his father's eyes. He did not answer, studying her the same odd way that John d'Ibelín did. Lasalle gave him an impatient nudge. "Aren't you, Brother Geoffrey?"

"Yes. Reginald will see to it." Geoffrey nodded, with what private reservations she could not tell.

Lasalle did not lower his sword. "I'll take your horse."

Saint Anne's convent sat a stone's throw from the Temple Knights Quarters, a short ride away from the harbor. Its great, square tower overlooked the convent next to the bell tower of an equally grand church. In the daylight, Lasalle took his bearing by those two landmarks. The ride proved to be more challenging in streets where the occasional interior lamp, a torch, and a splash of moonlight provided light.

He encountered the usual night dwellers, none of them anxious to engage a *turcopolier* who might be followed by others of his kind. His horse's shoes clicked on the striated pavement. Although the occupants of the houses on either side of him were unlikely to enquire about the source of the disturbance, he dismounted to lead the nervous animal.

They waited for him behind the next street bend, just when the horse's sharp snort warned him.

The way they bunched together under their torches, he could tell that like those at the harbor, these men were not trained. They obviously wanted his horse alive, and him dead, so they proceeded with caution. He therefore used the pom of his sword against the horse's ribs to bolt the animal into the men. A couple of them went down, then scrambled after the horse. The others went at him in a disorganized charge so he killed the first attacker simply because the man got in the way of the others.

The others obviously had not considered that whoever had hired them did so because they could be disposed of, after they disposed of him, without anyone asking questions. He thought that his wife would have most likely pointed out that fact to them. He, on the other hand, had no intention of engaging his would-be-murderers in sensible debates. All the same, he backed into a recessed doorway and began to think that unless the rest figured out how to rush him properly, he had a good chance of killing one more to discourage the rest.

That was when the door behind him sprung open.

His first thought, just before someone hit him very hard from behind, was that this ambush had been intended to force him into this very doorway. His second thought was that at least he had smuggled Sybilla and Melisande out of Acre. And Juliana with them. For that, he acknowledged without much gratitude, while plummeting into oblivion, he had his brother to thank.

"Such talents, my dear." Lord Makheras hefted the griddle with which the lady of Kolossi had dispatched the lord of Kolossi. His men were bundling up their catch, tying it up securely. "Handy with pots, pans, and poison. What do you think? Shall we toss him overboard somewhere between here and Famagusta?"

Rhoxsane did not reply. Since Lord Makheras had brought her to Acre, she had carried out his wishes. Poisoning the king turned out to be easy. Poisoning the queen became more challenging until she found out from market gossip of the queen's servant women that Isabella longed for another child, and that she went to the *hammam* almost daily. Women so liked to gossip.

"Aimary told me that in these parts, the way to a crown always seems to pass between a woman's knees. He did not include a regency, but I suppose he couldn't think of everything. And obviously did not." He reached for his dagger. "No matter."

PART IV

Kolossi

For how do you know, O wife, whether you will save your husband? Or how do you know, O husband, whether you will save your wife?

1 Cor. 7:12-16

CHAPTER 47

Geoffrey's men proved to be skilled at oars as well as rescues. Their fishing boat passed by the spit of land where flames in the fire cauldron high in the Tower of Flies marked the approach to the inner harbor. Her heart hammering faster than the first time she had sighted it, Juliana held onto the boat's side until the lighthouse slipped from her view.

None of the plan was unfolding the way she had anticipated it would, none of it. She had expected to leave Saint Jean d'Acre with Lasalle. She had not expected to be leaving it with the daughters of the late king of Jerusalem instead, daughters whom she had, for all intents and purposes, helped Lasalle to kidnap.

Under a lean-to of sails in the stern, Sybilla and Melisande slept soundly on a whorl of nets, tucked in cloaks the men gave them. Next to them in the pre-dawn chill huddled Xene and Madelena. Juliana admired the women's devotion to their charges to risk everything, including their own lives. How did Lasalle manage to persuade them? Perhaps they had not needed much persuading.

"Are you comfortable, Lady Juliana?" Geoffrey de Lusignan came to her, aggravatingly steady on his feet.

Juliana folded back her sleeves stained with the blood of the man she had stabbed. "Yes." She had stabbed a man. *Stabbed him.* She forced away that thought. "No." When dealing with Lasalle's brother, caution ought to be in order, but that had not been her path lately. She wished she could ask Abbess Mathilde what she thought of her journey along His path thus far.

She had hoped that keeping her mind occupied would pacify her stomach. She had therefore parsed and picked over the conversation on the shore, each time with more unease because to her dismay her unease remained unconnected to the short session of carnage to which she had contributed her share.

Events thereafter took place so quickly that she found herself on the fishing boat without a chance to object, protest, or to refuse to be deposited aboard with Xene and Madelena and the children.

Now she perched on the horns of a dilemma once again.

Was she wrong to allow herself to be whisked away before Lasalle returned with Heloise? She should not have insisted that Heloise be taken away from Acre as well, but she could not imagine leaving the girl behind. Perhaps Geoffrey was right. To wait for Lasalle or to arrive with a procession at Saint Anne's would have attracted attention and endangered them all. After all, Brother Reginald had stayed behind to secure another boat for Lasalle and Heloise. They would catch up with the *Paradisus* at Limassol where the ship would anchor for a few days and take on new passengers and provisions for her return journey to Marseille, to Eleanor.

The sun broke through the dawn's haze, warming the air. Juliana looked back at Melisande and Sybilla with the same raw pain that had gripped her when she realized Eleanor would be taken from her. Her mind skipped to the path where Armand de Lusignan had told her, all contempt and triumph . . . what did he tell her? *Guérin escaped your passionate embrace the moment his saintly brother whistled.* Why would those words come to her now? "What did he mean, 'you owe me'?"

Judging by Geoffrey's unguarded look, she caught her fish at the first cast. Could she land it?

She did not expect Geoffrey to sit across from her with his back to the mast, reach into his gambeson and pull out a cross. He cupped it in his palms, his eyes on her. "I sent Reginald to Parthenay to bring Guérin back with him. I told Reginald to tell him that if he refused, the archbishop would learn of your adulterous marriage and your daughter's birth within it. That's why he came to Cyprus."

The sea around her became silent, all at once. She stared into eyes bluer than the *bythos* under the keel, the eyes of a man with the features and form a perfectly chaste woman would have taken for a lover, let alone a husband, in a heart's beat. A man who had pledged himself to another Lady. Above her, a seagull screeched. No, that was not a seagull. That was her.

She leapt at Geoffrey de Lusignan with the fierceness of a leopardess. Her nails aimed for those eyes, wanting to blind, to maim, to kill the author of her anguish. She had the advantage of surprise, but to even attempt to kill Brother Geoffrey of the Temple would have required at least a dagger, and hers was in the sheath at her waist belt.

She did not get another chance because two of Geoffrey's men sprung up and dragged the suddenly deranged Lady Juliana off her brother-in-law. Unfortunately, the two other women aboard came to her aid which resulted in the passengers and crew being flung about the deck among the water casks, cordage and canvas, fishing nets, buoys, and octopus traps in an unscheduled *mêlée.*

The men violated their vows by touching a woman, or rather three, in turn and *ensemble,* and in the process learned that two of the young women came from stout peasant stock and had handled more than one ill-suited suitor. By the time everyone remembered that they were in the middle of the seas, bleeding noses, bruised lips, and severely injured male pride had resulted.

Xene and Madelena could at least fall back on their duty to the princesses to salve their womanly pride. Firmly replaced in her former spot and with a handy fish net dropped over her, Juliana had no such excuse to salve her feelings. With the boat rolling freely under their feet, Geoffrey's men, now laughing, resumed their posts.

Geoffrey found his cross which her attack had knocked out of his hand, kissed it, and looped the cord over his neck.

Juliana could not bear that pointed piety. "Hypocrite!"

Geoffrey rubbed his cheek with the back of his hand and examined the blood there. "Good Lord. Not so helpless indeed. Must we add insults to injuries? You haven't confessed to Guérin keeping company with John d'Ibelín, have you?"

The words she intended to hurl at him did not make it past her teeth.

He squatted by her and reached for the net. "Well, have you?"

She wished she could reach her dagger. "No."

"Good. Guérin would have killed him for that if not for Aimary's death. Imagine the havoc in both kingdoms. None of us need that now, do we?"

She was trapped in the Lusignans' web, like *oktopodi.* Only she had not climbed into this trap willingly. *And neither did Lasalle.* She fought the netting. "How dare you. Your father took my daughter. Because of you. Your brother left us because of you! You dare to look at the face of our Holy Mother? You scorn her suffering just as you scorn mine!"

Geoffrey stood up. He stood there rooted to the deck and then backed away and resumed his seat by the mast. He pinned his peregrine's gaze on her, making no effort to assist her. By the time Juliana freed herself, her fury became searing contempt. "Why confess it now, Brother Geoffrey?"

He ignored the sarcasm. "Because I promised Cousin Burgundia that I would. She is now the one to mind our family's interests here." He winced a little. "Anyway, she wanted to tell you when she saw you in Nikosia so that you could warn Guérin."

Juliana flung away the net, weighing whether or not she ought to ask the next question. Geoffrey knew it and waited until she did. "Tell me what?"

"That the message she gave to Leontios was intercepted. Just as well she did not tell you. As long as you were regarded as a simpleton, you were not a threat. You've read the message that Maria Komnene received instead of Aimary. I don't suppose you recall whose name is now on it, do you?"

That day in the garden Walter de Montbéliard interrupted Burgundia. He said that he was looking for Lasalle. But Geoffrey gave her no reason to trust him. "No. I am a simpleton."

"I said you were regarded as one. My brother, I gather, tried to keep you out of it. Obviously, he failed."

"Obviously." Since Geoffrey had not mentioned his brother's failure to protect Aimary, Juliana did not think it necessary to remind him. The Lusignans' affairs and ambitions in this part of the world did not concern her. She wanted Lasalle. She wanted to tell him that she knew why he left her and Eleanor. It was because of Eleanor. *I had no choice . . . I do think of her. Every day.*

The boat tilted to one side. Shouting to each other, the men worked the sails' ropes. The boat leveled and surged forward. She clamped her hand over her mouth to stifle a sob that threatened to become a wail. *Eleanor. Eleanor.*

"Juliana?" That was Geoffrey's hand on her, a painful, steadying grip. His grip slipped, freeing her.

From the lean-to came the voices of Xene and Madelena. Sybilla and Melisande stirred, growing aware of their surroundings, confused and frightened until their nurses drew them into their embrace with laughter and tears.

Juliana tried to breathe. She must not let her dread conquer her, she must think of the here and now. She held onto the boat's side to reach the lean-to. The girls knew her which only increased their confusion.

"Where are we?" Sybilla looked about, full of suspicion.

Juliana knelt to be at the girls' eye level. Lasalle had left them to her. She had to think, she had to think for their sake. "You are going to stay with the sisters at Saint Mary's. In Nikosia. That's where your brother Hugh lives. Do you remember Hugh?"

Sybilla gave a hesitant nod. Melisande rubbed her eyes. "Where is mamma?"

Xene brushed back the girl's hair. "She is with your father and they are both with the angels. They both want you and your sister to be safe and to learn things you will need. Just like Heloise and Maria did at Saint Anne's."

Melisande's face curdled. "But I want to see them."

Xene kissed her. "You will, my lamb, you will."

Sybilla gave Juliana another distrustful look. The child understood more than Xene's words. In *outre-mer,* even a girl like Sybilla, especially a girl like Sybilla, could not reach her age without having taken in with her nurse's milk the perils outside the nursery. Juliana feared that Sybilla would ask more questions, but the girl shrugged Madelena away and hugged herself, her chin on her knees.

Melisande did not pay her sister mind. She bounced herself on Xene's lap and gave Juliana the brightest of smiles. "I am thirsty. And hungry."

CHAPTER 48

Limassol, Cyprus

They arrived at the very harbor where she had reached this island so many eventful months ago. With Juliana disembarked her dread, regret, and dilemma.

As much as she wanted to see the children safely to Saint Mary's, she knew that she must wait in Limassol for Lasalle and Heloise. In this almost tideless sea that ought to be a matter of hours or a day at most, provided the weather did not intervene. Geoffrey told her that he had to return to Gastria and assured her that his men were more than capable of delivering the girls and their nurses to Saint Mary's. Abbess Vigilantia would not refuse to shelter the sisters of the island's king.

Juliana prayed that he was right.

They took up residence by the harbor in an absent merchant's house within a courtyard behind a gate to protect the owner and his storage bays. Geoffrey left them there with his men and went to hire a mule train. He told her that the house servants but not his men, were at her command. Juliana swallowed a reply to that one.

The rooms on the upper story had comfortable furnishings and came with women servants. Juliana's first command to them called for a tub or two and fresh clothes for them all. After her own bath, dressed in a clean servant's gown, she paced the floor, trying to hitch her raw emotions into the harness of her staggeringly common sense.

She had no other ties on Cyprus except for Wink, and the boy had already found a new life. Hugh de Lusignan would be preoccupied with his future and that future now lay with the High Court. Only one tangible tie to this place remained–Lasalle's Kolossi. He would have no need of it once they left Cyprus.

What should one do with a place at the center of tragedies of years past and the more recent times? Kolossi properly belonged to Eirene Dukas, now Abbess Vigilantia of Saint Mary's. Geoffrey said that she would not refuse to grant refuge to the sisters of the island's king . . . Of course. How simple. Juliana called for a servant and with Xene translating her second command, told him to find her a scribe's writing box. She only needed one sheet, and a steady hand.

When Geoffrey came to inform her that he had hired a litter train and to prepare Sybilla and Melisande to leave for Saint Mary's the next morning, Juliana pushed the parchment across the table at him. "It needs witnesses."

Puzzled, Geoffrey picked it up and after he read it, twice, he lowered the sheet enough to look over its edge at her, his eyebrows knit in the middle. "Why Lady Juliana. You've forged my brother's signature on a charter you forged."

Juliana dipped the reed into the inkhorn and held it out to him. "Three witnesses testified that it is a genuine document. Which one of your men are you going to order to perjure himself for you?"

Geoffrey placed her masterpiece back on the table, took the pen, and in a bold and elegant hand placed his name under hers. Geoffrey's man then came and made his mark without asking questions. Juliana sprinkled sand over the ink and pressed her wedding ring into the seal wax. She handed the forged, duly attested charter to Geoffrey. "Give it to Xene. The rents from Kolossi are for Sybilla and Melisande. Vigilantia has her home restored to her. It is justice. And recompense. At least some of it."

❦

She could not sleep that night and so she prayed. At sunrise, she took her leave of sleepy Sybilla and a tearful Melisande and their nurses. Juliana shed her own tears in the knowledge that she would not see them again in this life. She expected that she would not see Geoffrey de Lusignan again in this life either, or in the Hereafter, but had no tears for him.

Geoffrey left her in the harbor house with four of his men and all of the servants to provide for her security and comfort, he said. Juliana did not care about her comforts. She cared about the arrival of the fishing boats with their striped sails and painted prows and sun-browned men. Their women met them, skirts tucked about their hips, baskets full of Poseidon's treasury balanced on their heads. None of the boats was the one Juliana waited for. When one of the fishing boats arrived with the news that the *Paradisus* had sailed out of Saint Jean d'Acre, Juliana's anxiety became a ravenous beast.

Where was he?

CHAPTER 49

She stood by the window, watching the harbor. She tried to remember what it was like, holding Eleanor to her. She remembered instead what it was like holding *him* to her. Juliana pressed her nails into her palms. Surely she suffered from a disease of the flesh Saint Augustine had warned about. It came to her that she did not care. She may not even confess it to Father Urias.

Where was he?

The boats brought more news; a galley carrying Hugh's sister, Lady Burgundia, and her husband the Constable, landed at Famagusta. From there, with grand pomp, they proceeded to the capital where the High Court was assembling to appoint a guardian for Hugh the First of Cyprus, and a regent for his kingdom. By custom and tradition, the juvenile king's older sister—and her husband—would accept the custody of Hugh's person. The matter to be decided was the regency.

The clatter of dozens of hooves outside the walled courtyard woke Juliana from her thoughts and brought her guards to the gate. The men peered through the wicket before lifting the crossbar. *Let it be news of Lasalle.*

Into the courtyard rode two men followed by servants with loaded pack mules.

A long time ago, men like these rode into a courtyard somewhat like this . . . Good Lord, that was Renaud Barlais and the baron from Acre's hall, the one who had pleaded with Queen Isabella—Fulk d'Yvers.

Juliana tied her veil and reached the courtyard before they sorted out the milling mules. Slashing his way through them with his riding crop, Renaud Barlais forestalled her question with his own. "Still no news of your husband, Lady Juliana?"

The question took her aback with that sickening plunge in her middle. Why would Barlais ask her about Lasalle and why did he sound angry? Fulk d'Yvers gave her a bow, not certain who she was, given her gown and a servant's veil. Juliana did not have the presence of mind to acknowledge him. *Geoffrey must have shared the events in Acre with those two.* Of course he would. They were the Lusignans' allies.

"No-no. But—"

"We bring other news. Dire news, Lady Juliana."

Fulk d'Yvers sounded less angry but no less upset. Juliana clasped her hands to keep them and herself from shaking. "What can be more dire than no news of my husband, sir?"

D'Yvers and Barlais looked at each other. Barlais gave her a dismissive snort. "Why the selection of the regent. In Nikosia. Madame."

Anger revived Juliana's wits. "I know where it is taking place. I fail to see why it would be dire news unless for the fact that you are likely to miss it. Sir."

Renaud Barlais's jaw popped open but the clatter of more hooves saved her from his next blast of ire.

A new group of riders pressed into the crowded courtyard—Brother Geoffrey de Lusignan, his men and servants on horsebacks with a string of pack mules, and in a hurry. A woman dressed in the gown and wimple of a Syrian merchant's wife hung on precariously in one of the mule's pannier, the pack animals braying and bucking about her. *Geoffrey ought to have been halfway to Gastria . . .*

Barlais and d'Yvers accosted Brother Geoffrey the instant he set his boots on the ground. "What? You haven't told her?"

Juliana could have sworn that Geoffrey swore. At least he had the look of a man whose last pigeon had flown the coop. In different circumstances, Juliana would have laughed at him. Not this time. "Told me what?"

The neighing and braying forced Geoffrey to raise his voice. "I didn't see a need to. She'll be on the *Paradisus*."

The nerve of the man. Referring to her like that while she stood in front of them. And then Juliana realized that Geoffrey's tone contained a warning–not to her, but to Barlais and d'Yvers. She would not shout because of the servants and the woman on the mule who observed it all with a busybody's interest. "No, sir. We are both to be on the *Paradisus,* my husband and I."

She expected to be ignored. She did not expect Fulk d'Yvers and Renaud Barlais, barons of Cyprus and Jerusalem, to confront Brother Geoffrey of the Temple as if she had unmasked him to be a Saracen in their midst.

"What?" Barlais saw no need for discretion. "Both? How could your brother renege on his pledge?"

"Pledge? What pledge?" This time Juliana pitched her voice over the mules' complaints.

"Is this true? He's not missing, is he?" Renaud Barlais went after Geoffrey. "He'll come out of hiding when it suits him!"

Fulk d'Yvers would not be left out either. "What? Does he intend to go back to Poitou and leave us here to make our peace with d'Ibelín?"

"My lords–"

Geoffrey managed no more. Barlais struck away a straying mule and stuck his riding crop in Geoffrey's middle. "You, sir, you brought your brother here. Your brother swore on my lord Aimary's own cross that he'll accept Hugh's regency and that is a sacred–"

Barlais swallowed the rest of his words. The whip dropped from his wrist. Not in surprise that Geoffrey de Lusignan had allowed himself to be chastised like a careless groom, but because of the way he shifted his gaze to the girl.

She stood there thunderstruck.

D'Yvers caught on before Barlais did. "She doesn't know?"

No, she did not know. John d'Ibelín had tried to tell her. Of all the words she had encountered on this journey, John d'Ibelín's told her the truth others kept from her. *There is another regency at stake.*

Juliana took a step back, and another. She saw the woman on the mule leave the pannier. Perhaps it was the woman who called her name. Someone did. She saw and heard nothing else until she stood again by the window in her room. The sea shimmered and shone before her in blue and silver scales, a purling banner fashioned from Mélusine's own skin. And on those scales rode a cloud of white sails.

The *Paradisus* arrived at Limassol.

Bells greeted it. The sound struck on the anvil of her heart. And she knew with unswayable certainly that she would not be on that ship and that she would not hold Eleanor in her arms, not in the near days or weeks. She knew as well that she would not hold *him* in her embrace, not in the near days or weeks, and perhaps not ever again and tasted the terror at both prospects.

Juliana did not know how long she stood there and she did not see the servant woman in the room until the woman made a hesitant move toward her. It was then that she heard the laborious huffing, cursing, and scraping emanating from the staircase. From the other side of the door came a tentative tap and Barlais's voice. "Lady Juliana? May we have your audience? Lady Juliana?"

The panic that had descended on her ebbed away. This too was the path on which He had set her. Juliana fixed her wimple, brushed the creases from her skirts, crossed herself, and folded her hands. She nodded to the woman to open the door.

The three men filed into her room with servants behind them, struggling with a coffer. Barlais showed them where to set it and dismissed them. Geoffrey leaned against the wall by the door, leaving Barlais to it. Barlais tapped his knuckles on the coffer's lid, delivering either a peace offering or a sacrifice. "Here. It's yours. We brought this for your . . . your–"

Juliana did not wish peace with any of these men. "Whatever it is, I don't want anything of yours, sir."

Geoffrey did not move from his spot. "It's the money the Temple owes my brother."

"Lots of it," Fulk d'Yvers rushed to vouch for Brother Geoffrey's veracity.

Juliana did not move. *Reginald has orders for the Temple to pay out my contract to you. You must not hesitate, Juliana. Whatever comes, you have to get her back.* "Mine? All of it?"

"All of it." Geoffrey aimed somewhere between conciliation and an order. "The children are safe at Saint Mary's. With this, you can return to Poitou and reclaim Eleanor from our father."

They had decided to get rid of her. Back there, in the courtyard, they had all agreed to get her on the *Paradisus* without Lasalle. *There is another regency at stake.* "I see." This time, she did see and it brought her no satisfaction.

She could tell that Geoffrey had anticipated a hysterical outburst of intemperate emotions, not the mildness of her response. He pushed himself from the wall with a squint of suspicion that reminded her painfully and pointedly of his brother, "Lady Juliana, what are you–"

The sound of door opening interrupted the rest. The woman they left with the servants in the courtyard entered without permission or an invitation, followed by the same servants, this time fighting with a sea trunk. The woman looked younger than one would judge from the old-fashionable cap which held down a veil pinned under her chin by a gold broach and the thick lines of *kohl* around her black eyes. A prominent nose in her long face drew attention to her red-tinted lips which dealt out orders, in Greek, to the servants. She curtsied to Juliana, pointed to the servants to place the trunk next to the coin coffer and gave Brother Geoffrey a look incompetents deserved.

Geoffrey accepted it. "This is Athene. She is a gift. From Beroniki. She'll accompany you back to Poitou. She speaks French."

Juliana was glad that Athene's arrival suspended the momentous implications unfolding before her even though the reckoning could be only postponed, not avoided. *There is another regency at stake.* And that regency would be claimed by a man who had taken great pains to remove two possible rivals.

"I do, my lady, be at ease. If you trusted Beroniki, you can trust me. She sends you her prayers, too."

Juliana took a deep breath to force her mind to the present. The woman spoke with a lispy accent and although she gave Juliana's gown and veil a dismayed appraisal, the offer of alliance heartened her. "And I welcome her prayers. Won't you miss your family, Mistress Athene?"

"My husband left me years ago. I buried our children here. And it's Athene. Like the goddess."

This woman was no Morphia with her frets and fears. "Then I am pleased to have you, Athene."

"And I am pleased to be of service. These are also a gift for you, my lady, from Beroniki. To remember Akko." Ignoring the men who seemed relieved to be ignored, Athene unlocked the trunk. Inside it, packed in a cedar box in folds of felted cloth, nested alabaster jars for cosmetics and glass bottles and beakers for oils and perfumes, sealed with wax and bitumen. Athene moved the box aside.

Underneath it something glittered–bands, stripes, strips, and roundels of green and red and yellow and blue in fine-threaded embroidery; silver and *orfroi* on samite and silk and *khamlet*; flowers and birds and beasts woven in contrasting warp and woof; and here and there puddles of pearls and lapis lazuli and coral as red as ox blood. They belonged to veils, cloaks, and gowns.

Her court gowns.

Behind her, Fulk d'Yvers made the sound of a man who knew the cost of such feminine finery. Looking over his shoulder, Barlais whistled in disapproval at the amount of coin spent on such things. Pleased by the men's reaction, Athene replaced the box and locked the trunk. "There are three more trunks on the mules. Do you wish to have them brought to the ship, my lady?"

Four trunks and the coin coffer. Together, they contained wealth and all the trappings of it–and the power that came with them. *It seems you can't bring yourself to carry out without reservation the duty that comes with your position and place.* Beroniki had tried to teach her more than how not to trample on her tiara. "No. Take this one back to the others and see to the servants."

Athene curtsied to her. She nodded to the servants and ushered them and the trunk from the room. Geoffrey closed the doors firmly behind them and came toward her. "Juliana, it was decided–"

Juliana did not give him a chance to launch into their next plan for her. "Not all the children are safe. Not without Heloise. And my husband is not hiding. There were no storms to delay him in Acre. Something must have happened to him. To both of them. And Brother Reginald. Isn't that true, my lord?"

That question Brother Geoffrey could not avoid. "Reginald returned to Gastria alone. He said that Guérin never made it to Saint Anne."

Barlais lashed his riding crop at the coin coffer and uttered a blasphemy with which Juliana was not familiar. "The king is dead. So is the queen and we haven't found the assassin. The High Court is meeting and we have no candidate. What do we have, my lords?"

"A name."

Barlais and d'Yvers heads snapped in her direction. "What name?"

"John d'Ibelín's name on Lady Burgundia's message warning the king against an assassin," and to Geoffrey she said, "But you know that."

The name may not have surprised Geoffrey, although her volunteering it did. "Ha!" Barlais stuck his balled fist against Geoffrey's shoulder. "My lord Aimary knew it! We have d'Ibelín now."

Juliana wished she could allow Barlais his triumph. "You don't, my lord. Someone changed the original name to the Lord of Beirut's."

Barlais's triumph deflated, replaced by disbelief. "What? That can't be true."

"But it is. My husband couldn't find any proof of John d'Ibelín's hand in the king's death."

Fulk d'Yvers hitched up his sword belt. "We have enough proof. D'Ibelín didn't come to Acre when my lord the king fell ill. No one saw him until the queen became ill. If his own guilt didn't keep him away, what could?"

"He didn't come to Acre because his wife was in childbed. He didn't leave Beirut until she was delivered of another son. Another stillborn son."

D'Yvers stared at her and then he burst out, "How in all saints' names would you know this?"

"He told me. He also told me that he has no wish to take on the regency of Cyprus as well as Jerusalem's. You, my lords, have been chasing after a hare, not a hart."

Barlais saw no need to mince words. "And you, Lady Juliana, you're taken with a man who blinds women to his true aims!"

That stung because of the kernel of truth in it. "I was blinded, true, sir, just as you are." Chin high, she took a step toward Renaud Barlais. "But you seem to be questioning my virtue. Sir."

Barlais and d'Yvers looked at each other, neither believing their ears. That sounded like a challenge and the lady Juliana's confession of infidelity, and yet not a whole one. In the absence of a woman's husband, one deferred to her nearest male relative. Only Brother Geoffrey regarded his brother's wife with a look far removed from censure.

Finding no support from that quarter, Barlais declined to delve further into Lusignan marital matters. "Lady, I am questioning your judgment. In Acre, you almost cost us the regency. You nearly got your husband killed by my guards if I hadn't shown up."

"More likely the opposite."

Barlais intended to pay the girl back for that slight, but d'Yvers pounded the coin coffer. "All we have are your claims to exonerate d'Ibelín, Madame. If you know more, speak now. If d'Ibelín's name was not on the message, whose was? Whoever he is, he'll be charged with murder and condemned. The High Court will see to it."

"No, it won't. He can't be charged and condemned."

Bristling with insulted pride, Barlais approached her. "Don't think you can lead us by the nose, girl. You ought to have stayed at home, wailing, weeping, or weaving, I don't care. You'll tell us how you know this. Now."

Out of the corner of her eye, Juliana saw Geoffrey move toward her and although protecting her person was most likely not the first thing on his mind, she held her ground. "I won't tell you, my lord, because you would doubt me and question me, and I will not reveal what matters only slightly to you, but a great deal to others. Isn't that true, dear brother-in-law?"

Her appeal to Brother Geoffrey halted Barlais's advance and directed his and d'Yvers ire at him.

This time Geoffrey came to her side, hand on his sword hilt. "Not so helpless after all, are you, dearest sister?" He turned to the two men. "She is right. He has to reveal himself to you and to the High Court. The details are not your concern."

Barlais did not back down. "We counted on your brother to claim the regency. Even if he is still alive, he can't be found in time. The Court is deliberating. What do you say to that?"

Geoffrey's measured reply did conceal the edge in it. "I say we are wasting time. We still have someone to remind the Court that a lawful candidate is being denied."

Barlais threw up his hands." And who'd that be? You can't."

"But I can."

There stood the lady Juliana in her servant's gown and wimple, that righteous look in her eyes.

And that was how Fulk d'Yvers, Renaud Barlais, and Brother Geoffrey of the Temple, their banners, pennons and squires, men-at-arms, grooms and servants, their carts, horses, mules, hunting dogs and hawks became Juliana's retinue. Their small army left other travelers, merchants, and pilgrims heading to Nikosia in the mud, and the *paroikoi* by the roadside gawking.

For the first few leagues out of Limassol, Renaud Barlais and Fulk d'Yvers bickered and took turns blaming Brother Geoffrey for sins of commission and omission. Juliana had no intention of defending him and only when the men decided to argue again about her plan, did she halt her mule. She unleashed on them her fury for their selfish desire to preserve their place and power on this island which had left her without her daughter and her husband.

When she finally finished, the men looked so crest-fallen that Juliana reconsidered the fervor of her chastisement. As patronizing and hostile as Renaud Barlais and Fulk d'Yvers had been to her, they had a right to be distressed by what had happened to their lord and lady, and to worry about what would happen to them under the regency that the High Court deliberated, at the present without them. She took measure of these men, old enough to be her grandfathers, men who with their hide-bound ways had grasped and held this island and held onto what was left to them of the Holy Land. "I know that it is difficult to trust to chance. But what is life without it?"

Renaud Barlais choked back what could have been a laugh, ran the back of his sleeve across his eyes, and sat himself taller in the saddle. "What indeed, Lady Juliana."

Fulk d'Yvers snuffled something under his breath that did not appear to contradict Barlais. Geoffrey contemplated her with an inscrutable expression. Juliana returned her mule to the path.

In Poitou, Mélusine had used her wits to secure her husband's possessions. On Cyprus, Juliana de Charnais needed every one of hers to secure her husband's life as well.

CHAPTER 50

Nikosia

This time she did not cross the threshold of the great hall of Nikosia's royal residence unretinued, a drab, weary *peregrina* with only a young pigeon thief for company. Nevertheless, among the barons and knights who made up the *Haute Cour* of the kingdom of Cyprus her unannounced appearance caused the same stir.

The crowd in courtly finery parted before her with a ripple of loud whispers and the murmur of voices. Juliana walked on as if wearing a basket of pomegranates instead of the headdress of the queen's women, the tall one with a veil Athene had chosen for her, a veil stiffened with silver wire. Athena belted a chain of enameled links over a gown of deepest blue *samite*, opened to three layers of shifts, the top most turned by silver and gold threads into a field of fantastic sea creatures. Rings cluttered her fingers and her face paste did not allow for a twitch of her brow.

In her perfumed wake came her current retinue–Brother Geoffrey in his Temple's cloak and behind him in tight-lipped glower Fulk d'Yvers and Renaud Barlais.

Juliana passed by several barons visibly relieved to see Barlais and d'Yvers. They had to belong to the Lusignan faction among the High Court. Barlais and d'Yvers told her the names of some of them, but her attention remained fixed on the baldaquined dais before her.

From there, five pairs of eyes watched her approach. On the ruddy and round face of *Sekretikos* Niketas she saw shock–and fear; on the face of Burgundia de Lusignan delight and relief. Next to his wife, Walter de Montbéliard forced his astonishment into a rigid smile. Between them Hugh the First slumped on his father's throne chair, the heavy cloak of blue silk with silver chevrons making him look like someone trapped under a tent. Hugh pretended sullen indifference to the contentious gathering around him but Juliana sensed that he felt overwhelmed and perhaps frightened.

The fifth face nearly caused Juliana to miss her step.

Heloise de Lusignan, wide-eyed and pale, her hair a gentle yellow fall from under a diadem of pearls stood by her sister's side. Her gown of the greenest of silks transformed her into the image of every man's desire.

Hugh's indifference became a round smile when Juliana curtsied to him. He sat up and his voice squeaked through the hall. "Lady Juliana!"

One must not drop one's pomegranates. Juliana kept herself in a curtsey to let the grandeur of her gown surround her, her voice as steady as her resolve. "My lord and king. Our most Sovereign Lord had seen it fit to end your father's reign, but I pray that He grants you a long and glorious one. Not for your own glory or for the advantage of those who may stand close to you, but for His."

Somewhere in the crowd something dropped to the ground, a sharp sound of metal striking stone.

Juliana crossed herself. Burgundia and Heloise joined her, then in the Greek fashion *Sekretikos* Niketas did, and so did the gathering. Walter de Montbéliard, by right of his wife the custodian of the king's person, did as well. To Juliana, Walter's smile could not mask the malevolence beneath it.

Juliana righted herself without dislodging her veil and took her place with the Lusignan faction. She knew that everyone in the hall watched her and she silently thanked Beroniki and Athene for the paint and gown which had become her cuirasses in this battle.

It did not take long for Walter de Montbéliard to recover. "My lords, now that my lords Barlais and d'Yvers are present, let us continue with the appointment of a regent for my brother's realm."

"Brother-in-law's." Fist to his hip, d'Yvers declared equally loudly and with the same obstinate adherence to propriety he had held to before the High Court in Acre.

Hand to his heart, Walter de Montbéliard bowed to him. "Indeed. Brother-in-law. Let us remember that." Emphasizing each word, he addressed the crowd. "My lords, we welcome your nominations."

The barons looked about, at each other. The buzz in the hall grew, the buzz of wasps about to sting. The guardianship of the boy king belonged to the king's sister, a sister who was also her brother's heir. That thought, Juliana knew, had already lodged in the mind of the High Court. As for the regency . . .

Renaud Barlais did not share their hesitation. "My lord Aimary wished to have the Court chose my lord Jean Armand de Lusignan, Lord of Parthenay and Colos, to become the regent of his son's kingdom. I nominate the Lord of Colos!"

A blast of voices reached to the vaulting. Shouts drowned out each other. On his throne chair, Hugh sat up, his face flushed. Burgundia nodded and smiled at Juliana. Juliana did not acknowledge it. Burgundia's smile died away. She reached for Heloise's arm. Confused, Heloise whispered something to her. Burgundia shook her head. Juliana forced her gaze away.

The noise finally abated. With another bow, Walter de Montbéliard yielded to Barlais. "Very well, sir. Let my lord de Lusignan present himself."

"He's been delayed. I ask, my lords, that we put off this decision until he arrives." Barlais replied with words they had all agreed upon on the ride to Nikosia.

The hall broke into rumbling that grew louder until someone shouted, "It's the king's wish." Others joined in agreement.

"Of course, my lords," Walter spread his arms to mollify the crowd. "If that was King Aimary's wish, we must be bound by it. Who had witnessed it?"

"Myself, my lord d'Yvers, and the Lord of Parthenay."

"Ah." Walter rocked to his toes, hands behind his back. "Of course." He turned to the crowd with the smile of a man who knew he was about to sell a lame camel. "Then the High Court must be bound by it."

Only the dullest of dullards would have missed the exaggerated politeness, the insult, and the insinuation. The murmurs grew silent. The fog of doubt began to ooze through the hall.

And in that moment, Renaud Barlais and Fulk d'Yvers knew the answer to the question Juliana had refused to answer.

Barlais's hand went to his sword hilt. Fulk d'Yvers too made a move toward de Montbéliard only to have Brother Geoffrey hold him fast. Another baron inserted himself between Barlais and de Montbéliard. He whispered something to Barlais. Barlais did not move but his lips did, with silent oaths, hatred and fury burning his eyes.

Perspiration soaked Juliana's shift. *There was another regency at stake.* And a vain, ambitious man who would destroy anyone in his path to it.

"I say, my lords . . ." From the crowd came a loud voice belonging to a man in his early twenties, narrow faced with a certain animal handsomeness and full of belligerent self-confidence. "I say if my lord de Lusignan cared about this kingdom, he'd be here, now, like the rest of us. I call on my lord de Montbéliard to accept the regency!"

And there it was.

Necks craned to see the speaker. Next to Juliana, someone swore. "Odo de Dampierre," the man said through his teeth.

On the dais, Hugh shrank under his tent. Burgundia remained expressionless, her hand crushing Heloise's sleeve. Next to them, Niketas crossed himself and raised his eyes toward the ceiling, whether in prayer of thanksgiving or in supplication for deliverance, Juliana could not tell—yet.

Walter de Montbéliard claimed the middle of the hall. The noise subsided. He gave Fulk d'Yvers an obsequious bow, but addressed the rest of the barons. "My lords, my nephew speaks the truth of our situation. My sole desire is to carry out my late father-in-law's wishes. I therefore ask that his wishes be our guide."

He gestured and a clerk stepped forward, carrying something on what looked like an altar cloth across his outstretched arms. It was a book, newly bound. Juliana could almost smell the freshness of the vellum. The crowd around her pressed forward.

Walter turned to the dais. "My lords, I call upon *Sekretikos* Niketas."

Niketas shuffled down, his staff of office tapping on the floor. He handed the staff to a page and mopped his forehead with his sleeve before unlatching the book's clasps. The spine gave a loud snap. It startled Niketas. He glanced at Walter de Montbéliard who gave him a sharp nod to proceed. Niketas read, his voice as pinched as Hugh's.

". . . whenever a vassal is summoned by the order of the High Court three times and that vassal fails to appear, his property will be forfeit to the Crown—"

Shouts of surprise and chagrin, of support and opposition broke out all around her. Juliana knew those words. *The kingdom can't be left to men who won't see beyond their own ambition.* Aimary de Lusignan's legacy. Only Aimary's determination to save two kingdoms from internecine strife would be used to gain sway over his own crown.

Juliana lost sight of Geoffrey among the agitated crowd. The barons shifted into noisy clusters. Walter de Montbéliard's partisans surrounded him and Odo de Dampierre. A couple of the men looked back–at her. The noise finally receded at the sound of Niketas' staff against the marble.

"My lords, my lords!" Walter de Montbéliard reached out to include all those around him, but singled out Renaud Barlais, stuck in place, his hand on his sword hilt. "As much as it pains some of us, we have heard our late king's wishes. Are we to reject them?"

Barlais knew when he had lost a war. Swallowing his pride and his fury, he shook his head. The buzz in the hall grew louder again, but more subdued.

Odo de Dampierre stepped from his uncle's shadow to take the floor. "It's settled then. We have called on the Lord of Colos three times already. Let's declare him in defiance of this body. Colos is restored to the Crown."

Shouts of agreement drowned out the protesters.

Geoffrey caught Juliana's eye and claimed the empty space before the dais. His cloak with the patch of his Order as much as his presence made the others take note. When he spoke, his voice clear and calm, the shouts died away. "My lords. I remind you that in my brother's unavoidable absence, we have his representative to defend his rights against such a forfeiture."

Odo de Dampierre elbowed his way to Geoffrey. "You, sir, don't represent your brother here. You represent the Temple. We've already settled that."

Geoffrey's fist went to his hip and his left eyebrow went up. "I wasn't referring to myself, my lord Montbéliard."

The insult turned Odo livid, but he was not about to challenge a Brother of the Temple. "Dampierre, my lord de Lusignan. No? Who then? My lord the king? He's subject to the regent we chose and to this Court." He backed away until he reached a safe distance from Geoffrey de Lusignan and there he drew his sword in a move that cleared a circle around him. "Let him show himself and I'll challenge him!"

With gasps and shouts some in the crowd drew back, others surged forward, shoving Juliana forth. She regained her balance and took a deep breath. *It's difficult to trust to chance. But what is life without it?*

"I claim that right."

Odo de Dampierre whirled around. A stream of light from the high windows glanced off the blade aimed at her heart. Juliana gave Odo de Dampierre a curtsey even Beroniki would have applauded.

Laughter rang through the hall. The young man's jaw dropped. The tension broke. Odo de Dampierre blinked and lowered his sword. Walter de Montbéliard's furious whispers yielded up Niketas.

It is difficult to combine officiousness and reluctance, unless one were *Sekretikos* Niketas. "Your husband's absence is regrettable, Lady Juliana, but the law is clear. Your husband failed to present himself when the Court called on all the king's liegemen." Niketas patted his brow. "Since my lord de . . . de Lusignan had not presented himself, his fief stands forfeit and all his rights on this island with it. By the king's order and the High Court's. And the law. Lord Aimary's law. "

Shouts came in support and in opposition. Those in support overwhelmed the others. *No one can claim exemption. No one.* Aimary's own words had dispossessed Lasalle of Kolossi.

Only Kolossi did not belong to Lasalle or to her as his wife–or widow–anymore. *He shall bring every work into judgment, with every secret thing, whether it be good or whether it be evil.* Her forgery and perjury had gained her a degree of victory or at least not a flat defeat.

Ignoring Niketas, Juliana curtsied to Hugh and addressed only him. "My lord, Kolossi cannot be forfeited to the Crown. Kolossi belongs to Saint Mary's."

"What?" That was Walter de Montbéliard's incredulous outburst.

Juliana ignored him as well. "My lord husband granted it to the sisters for their perpetual prayers for the souls of Lady Eschiva and Lord Aimary, your mother and father, my lord."

Walter de Montbéliard took two swift steps to Niketas. "Do something!"

"The king . . . the king . . . ," Niketas stammered under the prompt of Walter de Montbéliard's glare. "The king had not granted permission for such a gift to a spiritual foundation."

The commotion around Juliana mixed dissent and agreement. She kept her eyes on Hugh. Surely this was too much for a young boy to grasp. Confused, Hugh blinked at her. Someone leaned over to him. It was Father Silbo. The young priest bent to his pupil's ear and with each word, Hugh sat himself straighter. "My sisters . . . my sisters and I wish to thank my lord de Lusignan for his gift to Saint Mary's."

Juliana smiled at Hugh, and this time sought out Burgundia, who held her gaze until Juliana backed from the dais, past Odo de Dampierre.

Finding no immediate use for his sword, Odo shoved it back the scabbard and, not certain what to do next, bowed to her with an unconcealed sneer. Juliana spread out her gown in another perfect curtsey. Poor young man. Odo de Dampierre had counted on Kolossi ending up in his hands, after passing through his uncle's.

Walter de Montbéliard did not allow his disappointment to show or to distract him from the greater gain he was about to make. "Well then. Since my lord de Lusignan is not present and holds no fief on this island, let us proceed with the selection of a regent. We have a nomination and a nominee standing before you, my lords."

In the spring of Our Lord 1205, in a decision without precedent, the High Court of the kingdom of Cyprus granted Walter de Montbéliard, the brother-in-law of Hugh the First, the guardianship of the king's person, as well as the regency of the kingdom.

At about the same time news reached *outre-mer* that the amiable Count Baldwin of Flanders, the recently installed Latin Emperor in Constantinople, had been captured by the Bulgars at a place called Adrianople. He had set out to suppress a rebellion by his Greek subjects who were aided by the Kumans and the Bulgarians. In that encounter, the Latins lost almost four hundred knights. The fate of the Emperor of Constantinople was not known.

In Cyprus, the fate of the losing Lusignan faction was better known. Its members retired to the residence of Renaud Barlais where, gossip had it, they proceeded to empty his cellars of their last drop of the island's excellent wine. Gossip had not mentioned that the lady who had caused a stir before the High Court as much by her person's appearance as by her claim, spent that night in the new cathedral of Saint Sophia.

She spent it in prayer, in the company of her waiting woman at the crypt where rested the body of Guy de Lusignan, the Lord of Cyprus and the ill-starred king of Jerusalem. Next to him came to rest the body of his older brother Aimary who had ruled Jerusalem and Cyprus after him as their king. The two brothers had supported each other with unswerving loyalty through their triumphs and their tragedies.

When later that night Brother Geoffrey of the Temple came and prostrated himself before the altar to join her in a penitential vigil, the irony of it did not escape Juliana. She was therefore compelled to confess to her waiting woman the unchristian urge to go over and kick Brother Geoffrey in the ribs, for his own brother's sake.

CHAPTER 51

Whistling happily and followed by his favorite hounds, Walter de Montbéliard found his wife in her bedchamber with her women. They had brushed her hair into a shiny sheet and dressed her in a loose robe over her shift. The color of the fabric's threads reflected in her hair. Burgundia dismissed the women when he arrived.

"You are a Venus, my dear."

She looked at him with her father's eyes. The lamp's light played tricks on him. Walter blinked and smiled. Her belly had rounded out. It was going to be a son, her women assured him.

Walter reached to kiss his wife's hand. She let him and drew the robe to her so that she could sit on a cushioned chair, motioning him to take the other seat, her writing table cluttered with jars and mother-of-pearl coffers between them. Surprising himself, Walter sat. With grunts and snuffles, the dogs curled themselves at his feet. "You've called on me with some urgency, my dear. Nothing amiss with my son, is there?"

Burgundia opened a jar to apply a dab of balm to her hands. The scent of lemons and lavender filled the room. "No. I wish you to tell me what you've done with him."

Walter stretched his legs. "With whom, my love?"

"Don't pretend, Walter," Burgundia said with mild annoyance. "You haven't killed him. You only needed him out of the way while the Court gave you my brother's regency."

After three years of their marriage, Burgundia de Lusignan remained as elusive to him as the day she had consented to marry him. He could never shake the nagging feeling that she had contempt for him. Today, Walter refused to have his mood spoiled. "Gave *us*. Don't forget, my dear, gave *us*. You are the guardian, I am the regent."

"And you remember, my lord husband, that you keep this place only as long as we are wed." Burgundia opened her writing box. "Rumors have it you had my father and Isabella poisoned to get it."

Walter shrugged. "Do they? I will have anyone spreading them hanged. Besides, with or without you, this child grants me rights the Court can't dismiss."

Burgundia brought out an ampul and set it on the desk. Walter sniffed. "Holy oil? Tears of Mary? Perhaps her milk?"

"A lethal poison."

Walter snatched up the ampul. It felt . . . alive in his hand. He held it up against the light. The clear liquid inside shivered. "Now why would you have such a thing about you?"

"Keep it. I have several such, hidden about this place. If you don't tell me where you hold him, I will use one and I will die and your child in me."

He lowered his hand and carefully placed the vial back on the table. He knew his wife enough to choose his words. "They warned me that you come from a serpent's race. I'll have you watched again every moment of every day until you are delivered."

"Here you can't have me watched every moment. You need my presence before the Court, to witness charters, to give consent to your use of Hugh's patrimony. You need me at the banquets you will hold to reward your supporters. Remember my uncle Guy? If I die, the barons will take away from you Hugh's guardianship and the regency. They may allow you to keep your estates, but I doubt it. Kolossi is out of your reach."

Walter drummed his fingers on the tabletop. "You wouldn't condemn your soul and our child's."

"Oh, Walter. God will judge whether I am a martyr or a murderer like you."

Despite himself, chill went down his spine. "I never raised a finger against your father or Isabella. You imagine things, my dear. You wouldn't do it. That is nothing but water."

"Break it then and have your dogs lap it. You're not the only one who knows where to find *toxikon.*"

Her threats did not fit into his plan. Neither did the possibility that his wife might be telling him the truth. Burgundia told the truth on one account. Without her and their child, he had no claim to the highest position on this island or anywhere else. He would remain Hugh's brother-in-law, but certain barons already resented his rise and would oppose his governance. They might even dispute the possession of his estates. He could be like Guy de Lusignan who had lost his crown matrimonial with the death of his wife and children by her. There already were questions and rumors about the more recent demises in the reigning houses of Jerusalem and Cyprus. "If he's . . . restored, what assurance do I have that he won't challenge my position?"

Burgundia did not touch the ampul. "None. I have no sway with him or his brother. You will have to negotiate with his wife. I suggest that you mind her safety."

He laughed, a nervous laugh. "You are willing to risk a war on this island?"

"Are you?"

"Hmph. Spoken like a Lusignan."

"And Ibelín," she reminded him.

One of the dogs under the table commenced a bout of furious

scratching. The liquid inside the glass sparkled. Walter watched it. He had gained much by this marriage and he could lose it all. "It looks like we've reached an impasse. Why don't you call that little cousin-in-law of ours, the nosey, cheeky one. I have a few things to arrange while you two plot against me."

"He's alive. Walter has him. Here, sit down, Juliana."

Burgundia's first words lifted from Juliana a boulder of fear. Her second ones replaced it. Burgundia took her by the hand and led her to the cushions.

Shortly after matins, Burgundia's woman had come to Saint Sophia to find her with Geoffrey at her side. Geoffrey and she had not spoken the entire night, each understanding that only one person would have a way of finding out what had happened to Lasalle in Acre.

"Walter may be the regent now, but he doesn't hold all the advantage. He will give him up. Do you understand? Did you get any sleep?"

"No." Battles are usually fought in the open, with sword and fire. The deadlier ones are fought in the privacy of bedchambers, waged by those already bound by blood and kinship, and made more vicious and wounding because of it. Juliana sat on a pile of cushions in the queen's apartments, now officially occupied by the sister of the king and the daughter of the woman for whom they were created. Burgundia de Lusignan looked beautiful. And happy.

With her own thoughts and emotions churning, Juliana could not imagine the cause of Burgundia's serenity. She did feel ashamed for having suspected Burgundia of plotting against her own father. Burgundia attended to her closely when Juliana told her that Maria Komnene had received the altered note, and how she came to read it, thanks to John d'Ibelín.

"I knew of Walter's ambition," Burgundia said. "I didn't know the extent of it until too late."

"Why did you consent to your marriage?" Juliana knew it to

be an impertinent question, but she wanted to know the path by which she found herself back in Nikosia, and under such circumstances. "Oh, I am sorry, I didn't mean to pry."

"My father did not want Cyprus trapped between the Frankish king and the English one, and he wanted the Emperor's help if the Greeks decided to reclaim this island. That's why he offered himself as a vassal of the Staufen Emperor. Now the Staufens are fighting each other, their barons, and the Holy Father. Walter's family are the Staufens' vassals, and also in a quarrel with them. My father bet my marriage on the Holy Father's favoring anyone who would oppose the Staufens. I had a duty. Cyprus is free of outside meddling. For now."

"I see." Juliana did see. Clever and opportunistic, Aimary wanted to keep the conflicts of Poitou and Aquitaine and Normandy from his kingdom. He had succeeded, at least in that. He did not see the conflict brewing in his own family.

"I used to be the Countess of Toulouse until Raymond repudiated me because I was barren and because . . . oh, never mind. Whomever I had married next would gain only as long as I lived." Burgundia smiled at her middle. "They said that the *Trooditissa* works miracles. I thought I would never have a child. That's why my father chose Hugh to inherit Cyprus. He wanted our line to take root here. Our father thought that he would live long enough to see Hugh reach his majority. I had tried to warn him about Walter. Only his men caught Leontios and took my message from him."

"Yes. The second message. Walter changed his own name to John's. He wanted your father to turn on John, but the message ended up in the dowager's hands. But if Leontios was dead, who brought it to her?"

"I don't know. Someone who knew about Leontios's spying, I suppose. Walter kept me under guard and replaced my women. They all spied on me. I tried to tell you that time in the garden."

Juliana nodded. "Someone made sure that the message reached Maria Komnene and not your father. Do you think it's because they were afraid that he would . . . would—"

"Yes. My father would have had John killed."

Burgundia finished her question but in her own heart Juliana already knew the answer. Aimary de Lusignan would kill his own kin-in-law to protect two kingdoms. He had a duty to posterity. "I hope John burned the message," she said to get away from that fact. "He's right, it could cause trouble for his regency."

"He probably already did. John is no fool."

Juliana's hand touched the place where the tiny scar remained, an almost invisible scar. "No."

Burgundia noticed. "You like him."

It was a statement more than a question and Juliana left it unanswered. "I . . . he said . . . He figured out what Walter had done, but he did not want to disturb peace in either kingdom."

"Yes. John understands his duty. He's like Guérin, isn't he? I knew him a little when he came to *terre-sainte* just before we lost Jerusalem. I was so young. So was he. Many things have changed since."

Juliana wanted to ask about that time, to tell her about Rhoxsane, about Geoffrey's confession, to ask her advice on many other things only the door opened and Walter de Montbéliard entered without other company.

"Don't rise, Lady Juliana. We are all family here, are we not? And so favored by Fortune. I am of course counting my son in my wife's belly there."

Walter took his wife's hand and gave her a worshipful kiss. "Forgive me for keeping you waiting. Regency is so demanding. Fortunately, the High Court grants me all I demand." He took a deep breath of satisfaction. "A lovely day, isn't it? It's time for a celebration after so much gloom. I gave orders to do so."

Despite Walter's protestations, Juliana rose for a curtsey anyway. "My lord Regent."

Walter came to her, animated. "Ah, Lady Juliana. You had me fooled. I confess I took you to be a woman who doesn't meddle in men's affairs."

"And you had almost everyone fooled, my lord."

"Thank you. I am afraid that my wife doesn't appreciate all I have done for her. Us. For our child."

With care dictated by her body, Burgundia lowered herself in a high-backed chair. Clucking with concern, Walter rushed to assist her. His wife brushed him away. "Don't fuss and don't procrastinate, Walter. Tell us where you keep him."

Walter ran his hand over his tabard, a new one with a shining gold chain of his office on top of it, then suddenly turned to Juliana. "Yes, yes, your irritating husband. He ought to be alive. But to get him back in that condition, I will need your help."

She must not show eagerness or anxiety, she must remain composed in the presence of a man who held Lasalle's life in his hands. "How can I be of help to you, my lord?"

"Hmph. Since your husband gave away Kolossi, I owe my nephew a recompense. I decided to give him Heloise."

The words pierced her as sharply as a dagger prick. Out of the corner of her eye she saw Burgundia give her a long look. Juliana had the odd sensation that she understood this man; all ambition and cunning, but not irrational in his aims or actions. "I see."

Her lack of a more emotional reply confused Walter de Montbéliard. To hide it, he went to the window, pretending to enjoy the view. "Do you? Excellent. You can have your husband back if you and my wife publicly support the marriage." He switched his gaze from the *Pentadaktylos* to her. "Of course it is my decision. I only wish to avoid any hint of a sordid family row."

She must not drop her pomegranates, not in front of the regent of Cyprus.

"The girl is clever, too clever," Walter carried on. "A husband like Odo will cure her of that. I wager she won't be a long-barren heifer like you, Bourgogne."

Without acknowledging in the slightest her husband's words, Burgundia gathered her hair over her shoulder, carefully separating the strands. "You have my consent, Walter. Heloise is my sister and my consent is all you need."

"But I want to hear it from the lady Juliana," Walter waved his hand in a vain search for a canonical description of their relationship. "She is representing her husband, isn't she? What do you say, Lady Juliana? Are you going to trade Heloise's maidenhead for your blight of a husband?"

It is one thing to consent to the use of one's body or to have it used without one's consent. It is something entirely different to offer up someone else's. *I can't tell you how to decide if you need to make someone die,* Lasalle told her. *You will know when it serves your purpose.* He had not mentioned these circumstances.

"And one more favor, Lady Juliana. If I do reunite you with your husband, I want you to impress on him that challenging me will not serve well our families or this kingdom."

She had to think, she had to think like one of *them.* Burgundia was right. Walter de Montbéliard did not need her consent to give Heloise to his nephew. Walter only demanded it to humiliate her, to have the fact that she had bought Lasalle's life with the life of an innocent gnaw at her conscience. Except that Walter could not be certain that Lasalle would not challenge him, regardless of her assurances or the consequences. "I see. Would you prefer my consent to Heloise's marriage or having your life and honors, Regent?"

Surprise replaced Walter de Montbéliard's smugness. "Both."

"No."

"What?" Walter threw up his hands in an outburst that made Juliana flinch, but he only sought his wife's support like an ill-tempered child. "See, Madame, see how unreasonable our cousin . . . sister . . . whatever she is to us by marriage? Speak to her. You must convince her. Your child could be fatherless."

Burgundia finished the last twist of her braid. "But not motherless. Choose, Walter."

Burgundia's reply heartened Juliana. "You have my pledge, my lord, that I will try to prevail upon my husband not to cause harm to your person."

"Not sufficient, Lady Juliana."

"But it will have to do, won't it, husband?" Burgundia casually arranged the caskets on her desk. "Truly, how can one pledge to have the full dominion of another?"

Juliana noticed that Walter watched his wife's every move, his teeth worrying his lip. He suddenly shrugged. "It will have to do then. However," he added, heading to the door, "you will have to understand that since I can't be granted an assurance, I can't seem to recall where exactly your husband might be found except that he is on this island. I'll leave you two to tell the good news to Heloise."

On this island. Lasalle was alive, somewhere on this island.

The regent of Cyprus left with his partial triumph and she had hers, equally partial. Something had compelled Walter de Montbéliard to capitulate, at least partly. Juliana let go her outrage, regrets, and guilt. "I don't understand. How did you make him relent?"

Burgundia braced herself on the chair's arms to rise. "There are some matters not to be shared, even with those we love. Especially with those we love. You will find him. I know it. I will speak to Heloise. You can see her afterward if you wish."

Lightheaded from sleeplessness and the events of the last hours, Juliana followed Burgundia to the door, insisting that she could not shirk her part in Heloise's predicament.

Burgundia raised her hand. "Odo is no fool. He will take Heloise away from here and she will be safer under her own roof than mine." She patted her belly and smiled at Juliana. "I know it will be a girl."

CHAPTER 52

Juliana did not know what Burgundia had told Heloise about her hasty betrothal to Odo de Dampierre. She knew enough not to draw Heloise to her bosom in weepy pity. With measured compassion, she told Heloise how she regretted that her marriage was so quickly settled upon her without at least asking for Heloise's consent. Juliana did not intend to mention Lasalle in circumstances related to this marriage, marriages in general, or any other issue.

Her head throbbed steadily from her encounter with Walter de Montbéliard. *He is on this island.* Not a large island, one could ride from tip to tip in several days, but an island of plains, gorges, and mountains, caves, grottos, and half-buried ruins of temples and tombs.

Sitting in the window embrasure, Heloise listened, her eyes downcast, drawing a silver and ivory comb through her hair. Something about Heloise had changed. Of course it had. Antioch's young Prince Rupen must be on Heloise's mind.

"He isn't old. Or ugly."

The comment surprised Juliana. Heloise was not referring to young Prince Rupen. "No. True."

"Burgundia said that if I don't like him I only have to stay married to him until Hugh takes the crown by himself. That's not that long."

"N-no. No it isn't." Four years, some months. Four years and some months in a young girl's life. A young girl who was told by her older sister–herself repudiated by her husband–that she could abandon hers. Burgundia told Heloise to commit a mortal sin and Heloise intended to take the advice without as much as batting an eye.

Heloise removed a few strands of hair from the comb's teeth. "Odo just sent me this as a gift. Do you think it's expensive?"

Juliana tried for perfect equanimity. "Yes, I'd say so. It's beautifully carved, too, I see." It was. It also looked old, its shaft, polished smooth, formed by naked, intertwined figures of a man and a woman.

Heloise did not appear to be interested in Juliana's appraisal of the item of grooming. She ran her fingertips over the carving with fascination. "It's Mars and Venus, isn't it?"

"Yes. It is." For some reason a weight lifted from Juliana. She ought not have felt that relief, considering what she had become privy to in this chamber. "They were called Ares and Aphrodite on Cyprus."

Heloise resumed combing her hair. "I know that." She hesitated. "I am glad that Sybilla and Melisande are at Saint Mary's. Burgundia said that my lord Lasalle sent them there. I am sorry he's not the regent. Hugh likes him."

Juliana could not bring herself to comment on the subject of the regency. As for the other matter . . . "I am sorry that he was not able to reach you too. He wanted to. We both did. I was told that he never came for you to Saint Anne. Did he?"

"No. Walter came with his men. They took me to the harbor to Burgundia. Is he missing then? It's because of Walter, isn't it?"

"Yes." Juliana did not wish to distress Heloise on that account. Still, her own anxiety spoke for her. "Walter said that he's somewhere on the island. Did you see anything aboard? Any sign? Anything odd?"

"No. We were kept in the forecastle until Famagusta. We were both sea sick."

"I see. The last time I saw him he was dressed like a *turcopolier*. He took my cloak and veil for you to disguise you, too." She said it perhaps because of her guilt, perhaps because Heloise faced a situation so much like her own, a time ago.

The comb dropped from Heloise's hand. She reached for Juliana, her eyes wide with excitement. "Oh! I think I saw someone like that. A *turcopolier*. At the harbor." She jumped from the alcove to pace about the room. "I thought he was drunk. We waited for our mules. Walter was very angry because they were too slow arriving. There were so many people about, and those men, with camels. Walter wanted them to be gone. One of the servants said that they were going back to the mountains for more . . . more *kupros*. I thought it odd for someone like that to be going to the mountains with them. But they were gone and I didn't think about it." Heloise laughed, astonished at herself. "I did it. I remembered." Her shoulders dropped. "But not where they went."

Juliana's heart became a shrill bell. *The bedu and their camels.* It had to be. Someone had hired them to bring copper from the mountains to the harbor to trade. And Walter de Montbéliard paid them to take something—someone—back into the mountains with them. One person would know about the *bedu's* comings and goings, one person on this island whom Lasalle trusted—beside herself.

"Lady Juliana? Did I help?"

"Oh, you did. You can't imagine how much." Juliana opened her arms and Heloise came into her embrace and Juliana did not care that her tears ruined Athene's alum paste. "I will pray for you, every day, and think of you no matter where you and I may be."

Heloise's voice shook. "And I will pray that you find him. I . . . I have to go." She tore herself away and the door to the chamber shut in Juliana's face, and she was left there with Ares and Aphrodite, lust and betrayal rendered in ivory and silver.

CHAPTER 53

Apliki

In ancient times, the island belonged to Aphrodite, but Hades and Hephaestus had claimed their part of it.

In time beyond living memory, humans had followed these gods to their lairs deep in the mountains to wrest from them rusty ore and to stoke flames of clay furnaces to release the reddish-brown metal within. When the great empires decayed and the miners abandoned the mountains, the people who came after them had lost much of the knowledge of how to coax fire into transforming the ore into slabs of copper the size of a sheep's pelt. They still knew that the metal would earn them a few coins, although to gain them they had to come under the sway of men who paid the current ruler of the island for the right to work the old mines.

After harvests, men from nearby villages left their stony fields and with their picks and axes entered the mountains' innards. They piled up the ore outside the shafts to let winter and spring rains leach from their new scrapings and the old remnants puddles of sludge. When these dried into verdigris scabs, they scraped them into sacks and carried them on camels' backs to the harbors to sell and receive from the mine masters a welcome pittance.

Like others before him, Aimary de Lusignan had granted mining privileges on the island in exchange for a portion of the profits. Lasalle doubted that Aimary had ever seen one of these places, but he knew that Aimary would find it hilarious to see him laboring in one of them like one of the island's wretched galley slaves.

At first, he could not tell exactly what they sought in the rubble of rock which he and a dozen men pried from the walls and loaded into the baskets, hauled on the backs of others to the surface. He did not know either how long he had lived in the darkness because it was always dark, from the time when they entered the mine to the time when the wicks in their lamps became starved of oil.

He was starved as well—for food, because there was not enough of it, whatever the taste and composition of the barley and lentil gruel with a few olives tossed in—and for air. Being starved of the latter proved to be the true trial. The air became hotter and thicker the deeper they entered into the mountain's side. It made him sick which usually took care of the most recent meal. He was not much use being sick and since the other men grumbled about it, they left him with a couple of others to open a half-collapsed gallery that burrowed deeper into the sweating rock.

Offered a suitable instrument, he could kill most men with reasonable certainty. Here that skill was of no use except for having given him a certain amount of muscle and sinew, the same traits for which a mule or an ox is useful to its master. But he also knew how to use an ax although usually for more lethal purposes than hacking tree trunks into roof shoring. He had also learned enough from master builders of siege engines to know how to fit timbers. For those reasons, the men in the gallery usually deferred to him.

From what the men said and from what he could understand, he knew approximately where he was. Unfortunately, escaping from the mine let alone the mountains turned out to be more difficult than he at first thought. Outside the mine, the pack of guard dogs could easily track him, the mine master did not keep a horse handy, and the mules that dragged in the tree trunks departed with their drivers. Once under the ground, he had no sense of direction and the thought lately occurred to him that he could simply wander into one of the tunnels and disappear into the blackness.

He had not done it, in part because he had not given up on escaping, in part because a man called Martianus kept an eye on him. Martianus came up from Famagusta of his own free will, spoke a mariner's version of French, and became the men's leader because of his skill in prying ore from the rock face with an iron rod and crushing hammer blows.

Only four men in the mine were slaves, also brought up with him from Famagusta, although he was not one himself, not according to Martianus. The man did not say much and his mine mates showed no curiosity about the fact that Lasalle had arrived in the camel caravan, drugged just enough to present no trouble to the beasts or their drivers. They asked no questions because they did not think that he would understand, and because they knew that asking about a Frank dressed like a *turcopolier* in their midst would bring them no good.

It took Lasalle several days of back-breaking labor in the shadows cast by flickering oil lamps in shallow wall niches to conclude that Walter de Montbéliard did not want him dead–yet. No one had bothered to tear off his silver earring or to take his gold and amethyst cross either which further told him that Walter wanted him to remain with his life, limbs, and other attributes intact, whatever the length of term and the conditions of his current confinement in this place.

Physical pain served as a reminder of the Lord's suffering, and he had learned to accept it a long time ago. Injuries to one's pride and person that did not break bones or cleave muscle could be counteracted by a sustained campaign of wit or violence or by resorting to wine or whores and preferably both. He had engaged in the first two options recently, and the latter two had not presented themselves here as a temptation much less an option.

He did understand the purpose of keeping him exhausted. At night, he fell asleep in the middle of contemplating a way to poison the dogs. Rhoxsane would know how. He remembered hearing her voice and smelling her perfume in that doorway in Acre. He remembered as well his pledge to Abbess Vigilantia. He had not carried out his pledge to Aimary, but he intended to carry out his pledge to Vigilantia–if he could figure out how to get out of these mountains. And when–if–he did, he would seek out his brother and kill him as well. This time he would because of one thing he remained certain. By now, his wife would be safe aboard the *Paradisus*, heading to Poitou, to Eleanor.

Nikosia

The capital vibrated with the noise of festivities.

Throngs filled the streets, enjoying the extravagant generosity of the regent who spared no coin in his ward's coffers to celebrate his own rule as well as the other joyous news—the succession to the throne of Cyprus of Hugh the First, and the betrothal of the king's sister, Lady Heloise, to the regent's own nephew.

Hugh's formal coronation would take place when he reached his majority and married. The question of who would be the next queen of Cyprus already caused speculations with wagers placed on the marriages King Aimary had proposed years earlier between his sons and the three daughters of Queen Isabella and her third husband, the count of Champagne. The sisters lived in their father's homeland under the shadow of their parents' uncanonical marriage. Of Aimary's sons, only Hugh remained.

Despite the regent's lavish expenses, not everyone in the city rejoiced.

It took Juliana some effort to persuade Renaud Barlais, Fulk d'Yvers and several others of the Lusignan party—the Lords of Caesaria and Bethsan, along with Reynald de Saisson and Aimary de Rivet—to at least appear to join in the celebrations instead of helping her to search for their missing candidate. She feared that their draconian measures to find Lasalle could endanger his life.

They did not know that she knew someone to help her find her way to him, and she did not want to reveal that person to them for fear for his safety. She only wished she had Aimary de Lusignan to advise her on what particular approach to take.

The Lusignan supporters may have smarted from the loss of the regency, but in the end it provided them with a common cause. After all, only four years and a few months remained before Hugh reached him majority and took the reins of power himself. Juliana left them to plot the downfall of Walter de Montbéliard.

In one of Barlais's chambers which became her home in Nikosia, she had Athene dress her in the same servant's gown and wimple she wore at Limassol's harbor house. She intended to steal away unnoticed, but Geoffrey, suspicious of her already, caught up with her in the courtyard just as she and Athene took to their borrowed mules.

A Knight of the Temple would not usually be so caught by surprise by two women on mules as to find himself overrun by them. Brother Geoffrey was, and once he picked himself up from the courtyard's paving, he did not know whether to be furious at himself or his sister-in law. He knew that Cousin Burgundia would have no trouble telling him.

It took Geoffrey only a few moments to rouse his men, but by then they had to press their horses through the streets plugged by revelers. By the time they caught up with the woman Athene and he bottled up his brother's wife in a blind passage, she had almost reached the palace-fort. Geoffrey ordered his men to block the street's entrance to prevent her making a run for it.

To be sure of, Geoffrey took hold of her mule's bridle. "Juliana, what do you think you are –"

Juliana whipped the mule at Geoffrey's horse. "You let me go. And you take that coin coffer back to Gastria."

"What?" Geoffrey kneed his horse against the mule, exasperation overriding his frayed patience. "I am not at your command. You've played your part well, and now you will–"

She struck his horse with her riding crop, making it shy. Geoffrey dropped her mule's reins to save himself. Juliana pressed her mule against his courser. "Now you will take the coffer to Gastria and keep it there and you will disburse from it as I instruct you. You've lost your right to command me when you threatened my daughter. Your own niece. And now you owe her. You owe her!"

Geoffrey patted the animal's neck to settle it and gave her the same look Lasalle did when he admitted to himself that she had proved him wrong. "Why Gastria?"

"Can you think of a safer place than your Order's keep?"

"No, but–"

"Good. And I want you to send someone to Kolossi. The steward's name there is Darius. Tell him to send here as many men as he can spare with mules and supplies to go into the mountains."

"We gave Kolossi to Vigilantia."

"No, we gave Vigilantia a forgery."

Geoffrey settled down his horse and sat back in the saddle, contemplating her. "Juliana, if you go about unattended, Walter will try to harm you."

She noted that his concern was genuine. "He won't. I promised Walter that when I find Guérin, I would prevail upon him not to kill him. I didn't promise Walter that you wouldn't."

"What the Devil have you–" Geoffrey could not decide whether to be flattered or furious. Finally he shook his head and laughed. "Any other command, Lady Juliana?"

Juliana pulled the mule around him. "Have your men follow me to the palace, if it makes you feel better. You find Niketas and keep him somewhere quiet until I return."

He turned in the saddle after her. "Niketas? What do you intend to do with him?"

"Dunk him in the Dardanelles."

CHAPTER 54

Juliana left Athene and Geoffrey's two men who had followed them at the gate. She gained entrance to the palace easily since a parade of servants streamed in and out of the courtyard. This time she knew her way through the corridors and gardens to the leopards' pen. In her servant's dress, no one challenged her this time either.

Excited by the noise of the celebrations, the cats paced in their enclosure, tails lashing. Djalali recognized her immediately and greeted to her with words she did not understand, but they sounded like a welcome, a worried welcome, and urged her to the door behind the cats' pen.

The leopard keeper kept a neat place with floor swept, walls painted, trunks by the wall, a table by the hearth, one bed half hidden by a curtain in one alcove and another behind a screen in the other. In a chair by the window with its shutters open sat a young man, balancing a book on his knees. He wore a squire's tabard, a belt with silver braiding, and yellow boots. Wink.

"Lady!" Wink dropped the book and rushed toward her, halting to give her a gallant bow.

Juliana could not help but stand there. "Good Lord, Djalali, what have you done to Wink?"

Djalali gave an ear-to-ear smile. "You like, Lady? He eats good. Not you. You too thin. "

"I like. It looks like you pay good, too, for Master Wink to buy such clothes."

Wink brushed his tabard, pleased by his title. "He doesn't. Lord Hugh gave me these."

Juliana could not believe the change in the boy. What a relief that Hugh gave Wink his patronage, despite their original introduction.

Djalali's smile went away. "Prince Hugh now king, no? No more hunt with Lord Aimary."

Wink nodded. "We've heard, haven't we? About my lord de Lasalle . . . de Lusignan."

"Yes." Here were her true allies, a leopard keeper and a boy. "And I need help from both of you to find him. Does Zoë still have her collar?"

"Yes. Always," Wink assured her. "Do you wish to have it back?"

"If Zoë wouldn't mind."

"She won't. You wait." Wink sprung through the doorway and returned with a small square of a parchment. The words on it remained perfectly legible, written in a hand used to such tasks. Juliana refolded the parchment and hid it under her apron.

"It help my lord Lasalle?" Djalali sounded dubious.

"If we find him. But we have to find some camels first. And the *bedu* who own them. You know the *bedu*, don't you, Djalali?"

Djalali sat on a stool and lowered his elbows to his knees. "You know, Lady?"

"Yes. My husband trusted you and he needs your help now. You have *bedu* friends on this island and in the Holy Land. They are sure to know about a copper caravan to Famagusta. Can you send a word to find out where they went from there so that no one knows? But we have to hurry."

Djalali rubbed his chin, his usual cheerfulness giving away to distress. "Yes. Today. But we have to wait to hear. Maybe . . . not long time, no?"

"Not long. Maybe not long." Juliana echoed Djalali's words, knowing that he wanted to warn her of the opposite. She had no choice in the matter, she had to carry out the rest of her plan. "Do you still have your old clothes, Master Wink? I'd like to borrow them."

Saint Mary's Abbey

Abbess Vigilantia left her waiting in the chapter's chamber for some time. Here too Juliana could hear the muffled sound of the crowds outside the walls. Around her, saints brought forth in tesserae and icons shrouded in gold and silver and seeded with gems lent their vibrant presence to the chamber, so at odd with Christ Crucified above the abbess's chair. In the months since her election, the Abbess of Saint Mary's of Tyre had stamped the place with her personal piety in which the stark suffering of her adopted faith found itself among the calm beauty of her childhood one.

"We heard that you have misplaced your husband, Lady Juliana. Do you expect to find him here?" Abbess Vigilantia left the senior sister who accompanied her at the door. The woman quietly closed it behind her.

Juliana curtsied. "In a manner, yes, Reverend Mother."

The abbess's expression said nothing. "As much as we try, we don't seem to be able to purge ourselves of the Lusignans. I pray that you don't intend to join the ladies Melisande and

Sybilla. Mother Mathilde warned me that you cause disquiet in the ranks."

"No, Reverend Mother. I came to ask you for a favor."

Vigilantia settled herself in her chair. "In return for a false offering? Your charter is a forgery."

"But the regent doesn't know that."

The scythes of Abbess Vigilantia's eyebrows became higher. "You do have an undocile mind."

"Who would reproach a mother for protecting her child?"

"And a wife her husband," Vigilantia said with marked distaste. "You've made your choice. What is it then you want?"

"I want to hold Kolossi of Saint Mary's."

Vigilantia did not show surprise either at the confession or her request. She did appear intrigued by it. "And what would Saint Mary's gain in return for our generosity?"

Juliana did not miss the abbess's irony. "My husband's share from lending his mercenaries to the Venetians. There is lots of it, I am told."

Abbess Vigilantia showed less interest in the amount than its source. "His mercenaries? The Venetians? A payment for devastating my own people?"

"For the maintenance of the daughters of the lady Rhoxsane as well as Sybilla and Melisande."

"For Rhoxsane's daughters?"

"Yes. She too seems to be missing."

"Does she? Ah. An accident, incident, or coincidence?"

"I don't know. I do know that the regent has something to do with it, too."

Juliana waited for the abbess to deliver her decision, wondering which set of news would guide her. Vigilantia took her time. "We will have our steward draw up a charter granting you Kolossi and we will have your homage to us for it."

Juliana exhaled, curtsied, and kissed the abbess's ring. "Thank you, Reverend Mother."

"You may not see it as a favor, Lady Juliana."

"I know. Beware of Greeks bearing gifts."

Apliki

The rock fall occurred when they pounded the last of the posts against the galley's roof rafters.

In the light of the oil lamps, he saw the tree trunk buckle and split because of some fault within it he could not see. The failing support tore out the crossbeam. It struck the two men ahead of him and threw them into the lower part of the gallery. Lasalle flung himself sideways to avoid the beam and therefore when he fell on top of them, their bodies cushioned him, but not against the rest of the rubble. Shouts and screams rang in his ears until the roar of the black waterfall swallowed the rest of the timber props and quenched the lamps' flames in a vengeful gulp of the mountain's daemons.

In the sweat of thy face shalt thou eat bread, till thou return unto the ground; for out of it wast thou taken . . . He was laying in the muck of a Parisian wharf. Someone was kicking him. The screams around him receded and perfect silence reigned.

CHAPTER 55

Nikosia

Niketas regretted overindulging in the generosity of his new master. When he thought it wise, he left the groaning tables and the noisy bacchanal in the great hall and sought refuge in the silence of the men's *hammam* to digest lambs' livers seasoned and stacked on skewers, mussels stuffed with pine nuts, mackerel with currants, duck drowned in walnut and pomegranate sauce, peppery meat pies and aged cheeses rubbed with cloves, all of them now besieging his middle. He had tried to soothe them with jellied green almonds and dried apricots ground into a paste and glued with *kandiq,* and to quench it all with wines of sweet and potent taste, to no relief.

He left his guards at the door to the bath, not wanting to be distracted from his thoughts by their grousing for being forced from the guardsmen's feast.

He found the baths empty except for the attendants waiting in vain for clients. He chose a sturdy, bald-headed fellow from Sidon with a girth almost as impressive as his own to undress him and soak and soap him in several phases before he lowered himself on the pallet. He had much to think about.

Anticipating a generous payment, the attendant threw himself at Niketas's hamstrings with such eagerness that Niketas grunted with displeasure. The *tellak* stammered apologies and resumed a more tender treatment. Lulled into semi-consciousness, Niketas ordered the man to continue when the man stopped.

The man did not obey. Annoyed, Niketas raised his head to reprimand him and found himself staring at a man, a Frank, who was not only dressed like a Frank, but who held his dagger's point under the wobbling flesh of the *tellak's* chin. Niketas opened his mouth to shout for help and the Frank made that unmistakable gesture across his own throat, all with a very friendly smile that did not involve the blue eyes under a flight of black brows.

Niketas gulped, attempting to sort out the meaning of it when someone threw a bath sheet over his head. A pair of muscular arms hooked him under his armpits, hoisted him to his feet and slid him, barefooted and all, across the tiles.

His kidnappers shuffled him around several corners and down several corridors to finally drop him on a hard bench. Shivering with fear and the sudden chill about him, Niketas hugged the sheet to him, not daring to move. He could hear sounds from the streets; he heard nothing closer to him. Very cautiously, he undraped the sheet from his head—and nearly tossed it back again.

Only two people were with him in the room, somewhere in the old part of the baths the Romans had first built. One of the two in particular should not have been there at all: Lady Juliana de Charnais, the bane of his existence.

The man with her was the one who had threatened the bath

attendant. Since Niketas did not see a drop of blood on the man's gambeson, Niketas concluded that the *tellak* was still alive. So was he, which gave Niketas certain encouragement. Assassins usually did not dilly dally with their victims.

His relief became provisional once he got a better look at the man. The man crooked up his eyebrow to encourage him. Of course. Niketas did not need to imagine him in the cloak of the Temple Brothers; Geoffrey de Lusignan, the late king's kinsman and the flesh-and-blood brother of the man who had tricked him out of his coin coffers.

"Forgive us for disturbing your bath, *Sekretikos*, but we have an urgent matter to discuss with you," the girl said with the same unfeminine presumption she had displayed before the High Court. She even ignored the fact that he was not properly dressed for the occasion or for her company.

Nevertheless, Niketas's composure returned. "You are forgiven, Lady Juliana. I promise I will not speak of it to anyone."

The girl did not mind having her own words used on her. "So we agree. Especially not to the regent, no?"

Uncomfortable already on the bench, Niketas wriggled. "Of course," and had a mottled piece of parchment shoved under his nose.

"This is a clause from Lord Aimary's contract with the Pisans. It looks to me very much like the same hand that had changed Walter de Montbéliard's name to John d'Ibelín's. I imagine that Walter threatened to kill you if you didn't alter it. But then you made sure that the message reached the dowager, instead of Lord Aimary. Leontios used to pay you a portion of Maria Komnene's bribes for his spying for her, and you were afraid that your own culpability in Leontios's spying would be discovered. You were more afraid that if Lord Aimary killed John d'Ibelín you'd lose the master you hoped to serve one day. Is that not true?"

If they expected him to wither under the volume and weight of those accusations, he would have to disappoint them. Niketas forced himself into a less than abject posture. "Do you think, Lady, that your cares are more precious than anyone else's because they are your own?"

The dagger's blade tapped his shoulder. "Answer the question or I'll remove your tongue."

Niketas did not doubt that Geoffrey de Lusignan would carry out his threat. "I didn't fear Lord Walter killing me. I feared that he would kill my wife and children."

It was Juliana's turn to gape, and she did. She did not know that Niketas had a family. From Geoffrey's reaction, neither did he. Niketas took their surprise for his opportunity. He stood up and wrapped the sheet around him like a patrician before Caesar's court. "I could not let that message reach my lord Aimary. He would have John d'Ibelín killed and then your quarrels would destroy this island like they did Jerusalem and Constantinople. Lusignans, Ibelíns, Montbéliards, Montferrats, Champagne, the Counts of Tripolis, the rest of you. You come and quarrel over this land like a pack of dogs over a bone."

A heavy hand forced him back on the bench. "Then maybe you shouldn't murder your emperors at the drop of a hat," Brother Geoffrey informed him without much sympathy. "*Kapiaste* and don't move until I tell you."

"Is that why your guards tried to kill Morphia?" the girl insisted, ignoring that trend of the conversation.

Niketas did not know why a Knight of the Temple would allow a woman to question him, but there it was. "My guards? They were de Montbéliard's men. They had killed Leontios and would have killed Morphia for fear of her loose tongue if your husband hadn't interfered."

Juliana could not overcome the irritating feeling that Niketas was telling her the truth. Lasalle said that Morphia had expected to be killed, there on the seashore of Famagusta. Instead, she died by poison, by Rhoxsane's hand. "Did you not offer to tell John d'Ibelín that my husband stole the money you had safeguarded for the king from you?"

"No. Why would I let him know that I was deceived?"

"Rhoxsane said that you instructed her to tell him that."

"Did she?" Niketas sounded insulted. "Then she told you that for her own reason."

Juliana wished she could probe further in that direction but she had no time. "Do you deny that you wanted John d'Ibelín to be Hugh's regent?"

Niketas gave her an annoyed sniff. "Of course not. He would need my services. My lord Lasalle would not."

"So you knew that Lord Walter had Rhoxsane poison my lord Aimary and the queen."

That accusation came from the man whose dagger played disconcertingly near Niketas's ear. Niketas tried not to shrink from it. "I did not. Never." He crossed himself. "I swear it on my children's lives. My lord Aimary's life was always in danger. He knew it. Everyone did. But by poison, you say? And Lady Isabella?"

Juliana looked at Geoffrey who gave her a one-shouldered shrug. Unfortunately, it all made sense. "Still, you counted that if Lord Aimary died, by whatever means, the queen would become Hugh's guardian and her brother would become the regent of Cyprus. Only when Rhoxsane poisoned Lady Isabella, Lady Burgundia became Hugh's heir and guardian. And now her husband could claim the regency as well. But first my lord Lasalle had to disappear. All because you've changed a name and diverted a message."

Niketas would not have that one laid solely on his head. "It would have been proper for the High Court to chose my lord d'Ibelín. Only my lord Aimary chose to bring your husband here instead because his own brother offered him up." Niketas cast a blameful look at that brother who returned a baleful one. Nevertheless, Niketas took heart. Perhaps divide-and-conquer ought to be his strategy to get himself out of this muddle. "I knew nothing about Rhoxsane's part, nothing."

"Where is she?" That question came from Geoffrey de Lusignan.

Niketas wondered when they would get to that. "I don't know. I suppose the regent killed her. Or she found refuge somewhere before he could."

Juliana leaned closer. "Let me ease your mind about losing John d'Ibelín as your master. He does not trust you, and he would not have kept you as his *sekretikos*. He also knows that Rhoxsane poisoned his sister and Lord Aimary. That's how we've all ended up with Walter de Montbéliard, isn't it? And now he holds your family hostage and my husband a prisoner somewhere about this island."

Niketas was hard pressed to deny that part. "Am I to be murdered?"

Juliana kept her temper. "One day, most likely. For now you will provide your new master with your loyal services."

"I will?" Niketas tried to hide his relief.

"Yes. And while you do, you'll keep a very close eye on the regent, won't you?"

Niketas looked uncertainly at Geoffrey de Lusignan who had allowed his sister-in-law to conduct this unpleasant interrogation. Brother Geoffrey did not offer any contradiction to her instructions. Instead, he said with a smile Niketas had witnessed Aimary de Lusignan offer to his opponents, "You have your spies, *Sekretikos*. Why don't you have them find Rhoxsane for us. And don't think of it as spying for the Lusignans. Think of it as saving the lives of your wife and children from them."

CHAPTER 56

Great clouds of birds blackened the island's skies and rent the air with their cries and the whirr of their wings. They flew north and west to nest and mate, to bring up their young in the green forests, bays, marshes, and meadows of England, Normandy, and Poitou, and the places between. Not all made the perilous enough journey. All over the island nets, traps, and coated branches caught uncounted numbers of them, puffs of bright feathers left to quiver in pain and terror until their captors came and tore them loose to sell some by the dozen, and to scald and pickle others in jars of vinegar with handfuls of wild herbs.

Juliana felt like one of those trapped ortolans, waiting for Djalali's message to put her out of her misery.

She had Athene wash and mend Wink's clothes, and afterward, over Athene's vigorous protests, Juliana sent her and the trunks, with a genuine charter from Saint Mary's to Kolossi in one of them, to look after the place.

Juliana watched Darius ride into Renaud Barlais's courtyard with a dozen men, mules, and supplies. They were her men. She did not know them the way she knew her guard in Parthenay—young Joscelyn de Cantigny, the cautious and gruff Rannulf de Brissard, Névelon, and the others. Still, they were her men now, men raised to obey. She wore Wink's clothes and in her hand she clutched a wadded piece of parchment a beggar had brought her. On it was scratched a single word, probably in Wink's hand.

Confused by her appearance, Darius bowed to her. "Lady Juliana. We've heard about my lord Lasalle. And about Kolossi belonging to Saint Mary's. Is it true?"

"Yes. And no. I am holding Kolossi of Saint Mary's."

Darius scratched his head and cast about for an explanation from their current host. Barlais stood by the horse trough, watching it all with interest.

After their meeting in the *hammam*, she had sent Geoffrey away. Geoffrey had at first insisted on accompanying her but she reminded him that he had promised to take the coin coffer to Gastria. She stared him down, or rather up, until he ground his teeth and left with his men and her coins, less a few she kept for herself. Considering the entire amount, Saint Mary's would not miss them. Geoffrey's men had given her curious glances as they passed, about as curious now as those from the Kolossi men.

Darius would not give up. "I am my lord's steward, Lady Juliana. Where's my lord Lasalle? And the lady Rhoxsane?"

"We don't know. You are now my steward and I am standing before your eyes. Or is my existence in doubt?" Juliana employed Beroniki's tone whenever a baron strayed into her realm.

"No, my lady, I only—"

"Excellent." Juliana waved for a stable boy and climbed into the saddle of her mule. "The day is still young. We will ride on. We can rest tonight."

Still baffled, Darius got back on his horse, this time without seeking approval from Renaud Barlais. "Where are we . . . where do you wish to go, my lady?"

Juliana guided her mule past Barlais who surprised her with a nod and grin of approval. She acknowledged him and aimed the mule out of the gate, the men from Kolossi following her. Lasalle was right. Those men were raised to obey and it was her duty to command them. "You are familiar with the places about this island, are you not, Master Darius? Can you make out letters?"

Darius caught up to her mule, careful not to surpass it. "Yes, my lady."

Juliana handed Darius the parchment. "I wish you to find this place."

Apliki was not a place as much as an area. They had to travel along mule paths from one small *casale* carved in the wooded hills to the other, becoming lost, retracing their steps, crossing chasm and rocky ravines, reduced to goat paths in a slow and frustrating process. Sometimes they struggled across muddy torrent-beds, sometimes found themselves in meadows where wild roses, spikes of delphinium, and fragile cyclamen danced in glorious abundance amidst poppies, colored by the blood of the shepherd Adonis, the youthful lover of Aphrodite.

At times, the extravagant glory of God's creation astounded Juliana and helped her forget the soreness of her every muscle. She kept herself and her aches under a cloak that covered her from her head to her mule's stirrups.

She did not know whether the men approved or disapproved of her unwomanly attire which allowed her to ride astride instead of in a pannier, or her decision to travel without her woman, and she did not care. A few of them, she noticed, gave her looks that commented more on the content of her garments than the possible reason for her wearing them. She did not care about that either.

She did not care either when monks at the remote, dirt-poor monasteries gave her equally curious glances once they discovered her to be a female in their midst. The brothers kept their curiosity to themselves and offered them lodging, food, and their prayers. Juliana left them with some of her coins and her gratitude.

Concerned that the armed riders would frighten the peasants into lying or concealing what they knew, she told Darius to keep the men away from the stone-and-timber huts, and to open each enquiry with kind words and a few coins with the promise of more. She approached only close enough with one of the men who served as her dragoman.

At one of the villages, a man more bold than the others pointed to the hills beyond. When Darius tossed more coins to him, the man became talkative.

Juliana gripped the reins to prevent herself from riding forward. "What is he saying?"

Her dragoman crossed himself. "He says he heard that rock fell in one of the mines, Lady. Men died."

They found it after a wild dash over ground stubbly with new and decaying tree stumps and old ore mounds that giant moles could have cast up, now covered by shrubs and grass. Mouths of shafts opened here and there in the hillsides, some overgrown and abandoned, others with desultory activity about them. Freed from her orders of caution, the men swept through the encampments. In the mayhem her men caused, Juliana did not know where to point her mule until over her mule's loud complaints, she heard Darius calling her name. She let the mule charge toward the sound of his voice, to a hut with old goat hides tacked to the walls and roof.

Juliana flew from the mule and into the hut. She glimpsed a single occupant on a pile of boughs, a mat of hair stiff with dirt and sweat, a blue-black cheek. Among the remnants of what a *turcopolier* would wear, something shone.

A cross. A gold cross with amethyst stones set at the points.

Her heart sank and sang at the same time. She dropped to her knees and shouted his name, over and over, and her men came running and as many pressed inside as the hut could hold, and she did not care and shouted his name, again and again.

He fought to open his eyes and saw through the film of fever a young boy's freckled face with a slight crook in the bridge of his nose, a striped cloth wound around his head for *turband*, beseeching blackthorn eyes, tears streaming down his cheeks and moistening soft, shapely lips, repeating something with desperate urgency. At first he did not understand because he was used to hearing Greek, and then he did.

"I should've tied you to a mule's tail!"

He started to laugh, and did, and then he remembered that she was not on the ship, but with him, somewhere in the mountains of Cyprus, and the pain became sharper than the one in his ribs, and everything went dark again.

CHAPTER 57

Kolossi

S*et me as a seal upon your heart . . . a seal upon your arm . . .*

He lay so still that at times she thought he did not breathe. "You must not die, you must not die, you must not . . ."

"He won't. But you will fail if you don't eat and sleep, *paithe mou*."

Juliana did not know that she had spoken out loud for Athene to hear her. She was kneeling by the bed in the room at the top of the landing, the one with the beasts on the door, her cross and his gold one between her palms. Lasalle occupied the bed, swaddled from hip to shoulder blades, his arm and shin in splints.

They had travelled to Kolossi over several days, stopping at monastic houses. The brothers, knowledgeable in treating injuries, kept their temporary patient as comfortable as possible and pointed out less bone-jarring routes.

Athene took Juliana by the hand, making her stand up. Dizziness overcame her.

"See. Enough. I will wake you if I need you, but now, you sleep. Here."

Juliana held back to place the intertwined crosses between his bruised fingers and watched them slowly close.

"See, he wants you to let him sleep. You too sleep." Athene guided Juliana to a cot set up by the bed. Juliana went, this time unresisting.

"He was hurt before, no? He will be hurt again. It is because of who he is and what he does. What he has to do." Athene spoke to her not as a servant to her mistress but as a mother to her beleaguered daughter. Athene's words did not offer comfort either. They were a reprimand. Juliana wanted to claim her right to her fear and her own pain. Athene tucked the covers about her and poured a cup from the ewer she kept for their patient. "You have to understand that. You do, I think, almost. "

The wine overcame Juliana's exhaustion and even banished her doleful dreams.

The rest restored her and reminded her of the fact that she was, after all, the lady of Kolossi. Thanks to Athene, however, she found that Kolossi did not require much of her personal attention. Athene had removed, extirpated in fact, all signs of Rhoxsane's presence and applied to Kolossi's household the strictest standards of order and cleanliness. She even gave Darius a piece of her mind when it came to his duties.

Athene excelled at nursing as well as nagging, but they were not left to cope with their patient on their own. A physician arrived from Nikosia, courtesy of *Sekretikos* Niketas. The physician made certain that the fractures had been set properly and he stayed until Lasalle's fever subsided and the bruises began to fade, and his patient could curse him out, in Greek, for his prodding and poking. Juliana noted with relief that Lasalle gave Athene far less trouble for the same offense. When he regained enough awareness of his surroundings, she called him Lazarus.

"They cleared the tunnel because of the value of the copper," he said one day when she sat by him, the penumbra of the declining day around them. “A man there, Martianus, persuaded them it was valuable enough to haul out the bodies. I wish I had a chance to thank him at least.”

She touched his hand. “There was no one by that name. Darius questioned everyone.”

“Did he? Sometimes I think it was all a dream. How did you explain my resurrection?”

“You were hurt in a riding accident. It took some time before the *paroikoi* found you.”

“So now everyone knows I fall off horses?”

“Yes. And now they know why you are not the regent.”

He gave her a slow side glance. “You know.”

“I do now. Geoffrey confessed.” She did not want to reveal the other persons who led her there, least of all one particular person, not yet.

“How did you find me?”

Much to her relief, he did not want to wade into those murky waters either. “Heloise. She remembered seeing a *turcopolier* at Famagusta with the camel caravan. Djalali found out from his friends where the *bedu* went.” Juliana hesitated. She had to bring up Heloise’s fate, as painful to her as it was. “Walter gave her to his nephew. She . . . she intends to leave him as soon as Hugh is of age.” She did not know why she said it. She did not know what she expected him to say.

“She is her father’s daughter. I failed her, too.”

“No one could have done more. Heloise knows it. Burgundia, too.”

He did not answer and Juliana sensed that as much as being tired, he was mulling over what she had said–and had not. His disappearance and injury had delayed their departure from Cyprus, a departure for which she had fervently prayed and which he had promised her. She stood up and straightened the covers. “You need to rest or Athene will have both of our hides.”

She was at the door, closing it behind her when she heard him say, “Juliana–” She did not turn back.

Eleanor. Eleanor. Whenever her mind strayed to Eleanor, Juliana prodded it to the task under her hands. She repeated to herself Athene's words; he had been hurt before, and he will be hurt again. It came with who he was and what he did, what he had to do. She had to accept the inevitability of it. To allow herself to think of Eleanor would invite a conflict within herself she dare not allow, not now.

They received a number of visitors bringing news from Nikosia. Juliana greeted them and fed them and listened to them, weighing whether they came as friends or Walter de Montbéliard's spies, She treated both with equal caution. The visitors brought gossip about the regent's vigorous use of the royal treasury and the proceeds from Hugh's estates.

Saint Mary's had equally vigorously asserted its claim to Kolossi and the archbishop of Nikosia had sided with the nuns. Juliana could imagine Walter de Montbéliard being even more displeased when he learned that she had found his prisoner, alive. She shared each bit of information with Athene who had her own knowledge of the facts and factions in the kingdom.

The news of Lasalle's resurrection had gladdened the hearts of Hugh's supporters. One morning two men arrived, without grooms and servants, none of them wearing the signs of their rank, but she immediately recognized them. Oven peel in hand, she met them in the bailey. Brother Reginald seemed especially anxious to lead away their horses and before Juliana could think of the reason for it, Brother Geoffrey bowed to her. "Lady Juliana. Will I be allowed to see my brother?"

Lasalle was in no condition to do Geoffrey harm, as much as she could find no reason to prevent him. "If he allows it."

Geoffrey looked her over carefully for signs of an impending attack of derangement. "Are you certain you don't want to supervise?"

If Geoffrey de Lusignan had not pledged himself to the Virgin, Juliana would have thought he was trying to flirt with her. "No. You two school boys are old enough."

Geoffrey smiled and gave the bailey and the walls about it an appraisal. "Saint Mary's steward came to Gastria to see about Guérin's coins. You're a veritable camel trader, Lady Juliana."

Geoffrey was trying to be clever, just like his brother, only she had not forgiven Geoffrey and doubted that she ever would. He knew it or sensed it and gave her a bow that could have been a mockery of her, but was not. "Will you then point the way to my brother?"

Lasalle would have committed fratricide if he could, right there and then, but since he could not, he was subjected to Geoffrey's explanations of his failure to deliver Juliana aboard the *Paradisus.* Worse yet, Geoffrey paced about with the same vague look of guilt he habitually wore when they were boys.

"How difficult could it have been, Geoffrey?" he snapped with bludgeoning sarcasm.

"Difficult enough. She's a better schemer than the two of us. She had followed you from Parthenay to Cyprus. And Acre. And back. If she didn't, you'd be dead."

Lasalle ground his teeth. "You didn't come here to ask about my health. You didn't come here to make amends. What do you want?"

Geoffrey stopped his pacing. The look of guilt vanished. "I want you to remember your pledge to Aimary. Especially now, with Montbéliard in the saddle."

One cannot do much with an arm in a sling and a tibia in a splint, but one could reach a half-empty wine flagon and hurl at one's saintly brother. "Get out!"

Geoffrey ducked. The flagon shattered against the wall. Geoffrey kicked the pieces out of his way. "You've always had a case of temper when you knew you are about to lose. Just remember that you aren't the only one to keep secrets in your marriage."

Lasalle had no pottery left to deploy, only curses, which he did.

Thus Brother Geoffrey of the Temple left Kolossi unabsolved of his sins of commission and omission either by the former lord of Kolossi or its current lady. He did leave behind Brother Reginald and a nasty case of disquiet in his own brother's mind.

Juliana came into the room with a tray with Athene's lamb *kibbi,* flat bread, and another flagon of wine since everyone heard the fate of the last one. She sat the tray on the table and picked up the shards from the floor without comment.

Lasalle propped himself up. *You aren't the only one to keep secrets in your marriage.* "Did you invite him here?"

"Geoffrey invites himself. Sometimes he even arrives at the right time," Juliana said, now regretting that she had allowed Geoffrey into Kolossi's bailey, let alone near his brother.

"Not this time. This is not Acre. And I am not hungry."

She tried to make light of the situation. "Yes, you are. You are just angry at him."

"I have a right to be."

She dropped a napkin on him. "I have as much right to be angry at him as you do. More."

That dampened Lasalle's tone and temper. "I know. He told me what you did."

Good Lord, Geoffrey told him about John d'Ibelín! "You...you know?"

He noticed her hesitation, the odd inflection to her question. "In Limassol," he said and saw her flush and force a smile.

"Oh. Yes. Kolossi." She exhaled and sat herself on the edge of the bed. "Good. That way I don't have to confess. I mean I have nothing to confess."

The awkwardness of it hanged over them. She watched him turn over his cross in his good hand. She had her cross where it always was, by her heart which became very heavy.

"Why do you think no one took it?" She tried to sound perfectly calm. Still, now that she thought about it, it puzzled her.

He opened his hand. "Hmm? I don't know. Maybe they thought it would bring them bad luck to steal it. Maybe because they were afraid of Martianus. He struck me as more of a pirate than a miner." He reached out and took hold of her hand. He placed the cross between their palms and interlaced their fingers to hold it there so tight that it hurt. "I am sorry. I meant you to be on the *Paradisus*."

She held her breath because of the tears that welled up in her. "I know. Geoffrey tried. There will be other ships."

"Hmm." He drew her toward him.

She lowered her head to his shoulder. He gave a snuffle of pain. She tried to move away but he would not let her. They lay there without speaking, each with their own burden, listening to the sounds of the bailey below, and the laughter of children beyond the gate.

CHAPTER 58

The tide of days became a flood. She knew Lasalle not to be a patient patient, but flesh heals slower than the spirit, although the former was no longer weak. She had not spoken to Brother Reginald since Geoffrey returned to Gastria, but she concluded that Reginald's avoidance of her went beyond a concern for violating his vows.

At least Brother Reginald's presence provided Lasalle with company other than hers and Athene's. Reginald called on Darius to join them, and the three launched into deep debates about the events in Nikosia and Acre and Constantinople, and all the other places where Latins had triumphed and blundered. They argued about supplies and horses and the training of men; galleys and raids by Musulmans and *corsairs*; and the cost of it all. Sometimes the men forgot that Kolossi was not Lasalle's but hers, or rather Saint Mary's. She let them forget. Ships arrived in Limassol and she did not mention them either.

Neither had she mentioned to him her promise to Walter de Montbéliard since hobbling around on crutches, Lasalle was in no condition to do something rash and violent, except to the crutches. As soon as they and the splints came off, Lasalle insisted that Brother Reginald become his sparring partner. It was a request that, Juliana noticed, Brother Reginald carried out with more caution than Lasalle's physical condition warranted.

She moved about with equal caution, half wishing for Lasalle to regain his strength faster, half wishing he would not drive himself to regain it. Athene shared more of the household duties with her to keep her mind from the passage of days and the passage of ships. With Athene, Juliana went to give thanks to *Ayios Eustathios* for Lasalle's return to her, and to pray for Heloise's and Eleanor's safety. She did not even think of the church as Saint Eustace.

It was a girl.

Burgundia de Lusignan was safely delivered of a daughter. The message reached Kolossi and Lasalle handed it to her when Juliana returned from visiting the village where, as Lady of Kolossi, she had settled a dispute over a dowry.

"A girl." The memory of holding Eleanor returned to her with such force that Juliana nearly dropped the parchment.

"Yes. A girl." He came to her, his teeth set with the effort to walk without crutches. "You don't need to go to Nikosia."

You don't need to go. He wanted to spare her the sight of an infant, a girl, sleeping contentedly in her own mother's arms. Juliana turned away to read the message herself. She felt his eyes on her back. True, the message came from Hugh, announcing the joyous occasion of his niece's birth. It was also an order calling my lord Jean Armand de Lusignan to Nikosia.

Hugh the First had no power to compel obedience to his wishes other than an appeal to the loyalty of his kin, distant though it might have been. Juliana did not recognize the hand and did not know who had shaped the words, perhaps Father Silbo, perhaps someone else. Certainly not the regent. Like the Sirens' song, the message drew them back to Nikosia. She wanted to plug her ears to it. She could not. A king's order cannot be easily countermanded. "We will both go to Nikosia."

"Why?" He limped closer.

"Because I promised Walter I would try to prevail upon you not do something rash and violent to him."

"You promised Walter what?"

"I promised I would try. I didn't guarantee it."

With a half-smile, he reached out to tuck a strand of her hair under her wimple. His hands descended to her shoulders. "From what Geoffrey said, Walter has more to fear from you than me."

She wanted him to kiss her. She wanted to press herself against him and have him hold her until her neck cricked and her legs turned into candle wax. But he did not kiss her and did not hold her.

"Yes, but Walter doesn't know that. We have to find you something to wear."

Beside finding something for him to wear, she had to find out something else, something that had unsettled her since Geoffrey's and Brother Reginald's arrival. It had unsettled Lasalle, too. She sensed it. He would not tell her. He said that he trusted her. At the same time she feared that he would broach the subject of John d'Ibelín.

She cornered Brother Reginald in the stables where he and Darius were arguing about which horses and mules would carry them to Nikosia. The stable boys rushed about, polishing every boss and buckle on the harness.

"Leave. All of you," she ordered them and when Brother Reginald made a move to join Darius and the grooms, Juliana stepped into his path. "Not you, sir. You don't have my leave."

Brother Reginald backed up a step and two more. "Lady Juliana, it is not proper for me to–"

"Of course it is not. It is far more proper for you to deliver messages that threaten to turn innocent children into bastards."

Since he returned from Poitou, Brother Reginald knew that the consequences of his mission, as they had subsequently developed, would come down to him as much as Brother Geoffrey. At times, Reginald wished that the Lord of Parthenay had buried him in that forest. In the present circumstances, he had no choice but to try to exonerate himself as well as his master. "Your husband knows that I only carried out his brother's wishes to aid my lord Aimary. It was my duty to carry out my lord Geoffrey's wishes."

"And so you did. Is that why he left you here? To make amends for the anguish he caused me?"

"Lady Juliana, you have to forgive my lord Geoffrey. He had no intention of hurting you, he told me so himself."

Brother Reginald looked distressed. That was a good sign. "Did he? If I were to forgive him, sir, I would have to hear his message. I don't expect that you would remember it and therefore I cannot forgive him."

She gave Brother Reginald a curtsey and turned her back to him. She did not get very far.

"Lady Juliana, wait." Brother Reginald cleared his throat the way a sinner would before his confession. "I recall the words because he nearly killed me on account of them. Your husband, that is."

She pretended disbelief when she faced Brother Reginald again. "And what words could have caused him to commit such a sinful act?"

Brother Reginald crossed himself. "I was told to say . . . I said . . ." He took a breath of a man diving into the sea. "I told your husband that you are a woman of modesty and more than ordinary virtue . . ." Reginald straightened his shoulders. "And what if a word of your irregular marriage reached the archbishop and he sent someone to make enquiries? Having . . . ," he hesitated and delivered the rest with military efficiency. "Having your daughter declared a bastard would probably not wear on you, but would it not break her mother's heart? Some women love their husbands immoderately, but others have been known to love their children more than their sires. Especially women of virtue and–"

Reginald exhaled. "And that's when your husband attacked me. I was going to say modesty. Your virtue and modesty, Lady Juliana."

Juliana watched Brother Reginald's lips repeat the words that took Lasalle away from her and Eleanor—and now from each other. *Especially women of virtue and modesty.*

Geoffrey had confessed to her only a part of his message. He had not only threatened to have the bishops investigate Eleanor's legitimacy, he had dared to declare that she would one day leave his brother because their marriage could not be made valid—and Juliana de Charnais, a woman of virtue and modesty, would never reconcile herself to anything less than a perfectly canonical one.

I love you. He said it that day in Acre. She did not reply. She never told him. Not ever. The day Brother Reginald came to Parthenay, Lasalle would not, could not, tell her of Geoffrey's threat. He thought that to do so would make it true and that in time she would take Eleanor and leave him, forever. After all, she was a woman of virtue and modesty. Saint Juliana of Tillières.

"Lady Juliana? Will you . . . can you forgive my lord Geoffrey? You are a woman of virtue." There was regret, shame perhaps, in Brother Reginald's question.

She wanted to scream. "Virtue? Virtue? Is that what Geoffrey told you?" She laughed with the irony of it, an irony Brother Reginald would not understand. "I am not a woman of virtue. I have faith and hope and pray daily for fortitude. I am remiss in the other virtues and gladly confess that I can't be charitable toward my brother-in-law. But I do forgive you, sir, for my daughter's sake."

She left Brother Reginald and climbed the stairs to her room, turmoil in her heart and her mind. Virtue! How little they knew of her. She would make her confession to Father Silbo, she would confess to her husband, she would let him know—

"Where have you been? Athene's looking for you." He stood between several opened trunks, their contents tossed about the room, a man who could face a Saracen army with a lance in his hand, but not the assault by silk and *samite* Athene unleashed upon him.

Lasalle held up a familiar item, a black quilted thing. "What about this? Do you think it's proper? Juliana? Are you ill? Maybe we should wait."

What does a marriage make? She could not confess now. She was . . . she was afraid to confess it. She would confess to him after Nikosia. She would tell him about Geoffrey's message, about John d'Ibelín, and about the rest of it after Nikosia, when they stood on the deck of the *Paradisus* or any other ship bound for Marseille.

"What? No. No, it's quite hot today. Let's leave early tomorrow. It is proper. Very proper."

CHAPTER 59

Nikosia

Athene chose a gown for her of fine cloth from Mosul dyed in gray, a waist belt of silver links, and a veil that floated to Juliana's heels, giving her a certain sedate dignity. Juliana wished she could feel inwardly the way she appeared to others outwardly. She entrusted Kolossi to Athene and took only one maid servant with her.

Their small caravan reached Nikosia after frequent rests she insisted on taking for the sake of the animals, but in fact because she worried about jeopardizing Lasalle's recovery. He humored her.

They entered the city unchallenged, and the gate guards at the palace-fort made no move to prevent them from entering. Along the corridors, servants bowed out of their way. As soon as they reached the doors to Hugh's new apartments, the guards let them pass.

It was then that Juliana hesitated.

Lasalle expected it. He took her wife's hand and placed it on his arm and she looked up at him with apprehension and determination, the way she did just before she put her trust in him, a trust he had often betrayed. He wished he could spare her what would come next, and barring that, to make her understand. Since he could not, he smiled at his wife and they entered, together.

Hugh de Lusignan had sprouted in height and his portliness had distributed more pleasingly over it. Fulk d'Yvers and Renaud Barlais, two jowly guard dogs, stood by his side with two others of the Lusignan party–de Saisson and Aimary de Rivet. In his new robes office, *Sekretikos* Niketas did not appear entirely at ease in their company, and that was before he saw Lasalle. Father Silbo smiled at her. De Saisson and de Rivet acknowledged her as an ally whose further usefulness they wished to ascertain.

"My lord de Lusignan," Hugh came forward in checkerboarded tabard of blue and white, his fair hair combined about his ears, his manners attempting to convey awareness of his own position if not power. "We are pleased to see you recovered." Hugh had rehearsed those words, perhaps Father Silbo's. "And we welcome you back, Lady Juliana. My sister wishes to . . . to receive you."

"We are pleased to see you well, my lord, and we grieve the death of your lord father and stepmother," Lasalle gave Hugh a direct and graceful reply without an explanation.

Juliana curtsied.

Hugh's voice trembled. "Yes, my father. And stepmother. And we are pleased to have Saint Mary's offer their prayers for my father's and mother's souls, and to guard my sisters."

"Yes, yes. Well done. But the king needs more than prayers," Barlais interrupted, "Tell him, Fulk."

As usual, Fulk d'Yvers got to it. "My lord Hugh's treasury is empty. He has to borrow from the Pisans and from us. The regent keeps the king's rents and customs dues for his own. He gives charters for a good sum to the Venetians. Niketas there," Fulk stuck out his chin in the direction of the *sekretikos* and then at Lasalle, "Niketas told us you know where Lord Aimary hid some of his treasury for a rainy day. My lord Hugh needs it. Now."

Niketas's stolen loot. The loot that Lasalle had stolen from him by pretending to kidnap her. Niketas thought to turn Hugh's need to his advantage by recruiting these barons to divert attention from himself.

De Saisson picked up a candlestick and poked at the base to examine its composition. He tossed it to de Rivet who handily caught it and hefted it. "The king has no money to pay for his liegemen's maintenance."

And hence the true reason for the call to Nikosia–Hugh's barons wanted to be paid.

"Not all of it at once, my lord." Father Silbo hurried to coat de Saisson's words. "A sum at a time only until my lord Hugh reaches his rightful age and fully reclaims what is his."

Juliana noticed that if any of this came as a surprise to Lasalle, he did not show it. He gave Niketas a kind smile. "And what assurances do we have, *Sekretikos*, that the regent would not seize the coins for himself?"

Looking rather liverish, Niketas clasped his hands over his middle. "The most perfect assurance, my lord. Since you are the one with the knowledge of the coins' whereabouts, you, my lord, will personally see to it that my lord Hugh's debts are paid." He looked at the others, "Only until such time as he reaches his majority, of course."

The skies had opened somewhere.

For Juliana, the marble floors opened under her feet. It opened under Lasalle's, too, but he stayed upright while she dropped to her knees. Men's voices and faces swam about her and she heard herself reassuring them, "It's the heat. It's only the heat . . ."

Someone called her name.

"Juliana?"

Burgundia. Her hair spread loose over her gown tied high under her full breasts, the glow of motherhood about her. Juliana swallowed. She was propped up on pillows in the same chamber where she had spent the first night on this island with Lasalle, the same one where she had gambled for his life with Walter de Montbéliard, the same chamber where she thought that Rhoxsane would poison her.

The chamber seemed fresher and brighter although the furnishings had not changed. Perhaps it was the scent of roses and jasmine from Lady Eschiva's garden, and her daughter's presence that filled the chamber with such light and life. Burgundia sat on the cushion next to Juliana, a cup in hand. "I am sorry about the message. I had Silbo write it. I knew you'd recognize my hand. There was no other way of telling Guérin. Or you. Here, drink this."

The thought of Rhoxsane flashed through Juliana's mind. She took several gulps. "Telling . . . what?"

"That we need Guérin to stay. Here, on Cyprus."

The wine had not soured, but the same sickening jolt went through her. "We?"

"Hugh and I. And Sybilla and Melisande."

Shard-sharp clarity chased away the ringing in Juliana's head. She dropped the cup and tried to rise. "No. You have Barlais and d'Yvers and the others. They will support Hugh and you."

Burgundia held her back, gently and firmly. "They are our vassals, not our family. My father wanted Guérin to look after Hugh until he's of age. Nothing had changed in that."

"You have your cousins. The Ibelíns can look out for Hugh and you."

"They are. They are also casting about for a husband for Maria de Montferrat. The dowager is anxious too for Hugh to marry her granddaughter. Walter thinks that since Alice de Champagne and Maria are half sisters, one day he'll have influence in both kingdoms. He doesn't know that my cousins have an upper hand on him. I want the Lusignans to get an upper hand on him, too. Do you understand?"

She understood. Burgundia had sent that message calling them—calling Lasalle—to Nikosia. The net of family obligations, alliances, and ambitions wrapped the occupants of this enchanting chamber, drawing around them ever tighter.

"Juliana?"

A procession of nurses entered, carrying a bundle in infant clothes. Burgundia took the bundle from them and with the most tender of care entrusted its occupant to Juliana's arms. "I will have her christened Eschiva. For my mother."

The face of a sleeping infant poked from the folds of lawn and linen. Eschiva de Lusignan was the most beautiful child in the world. Juliana could not bear this sweet and cruel sight. "Take her away, please."

Burgundia did not. "Eschiva will need a godmother. And a godfather."

"You cannot do this," Juliana whispered.

"No, but you can. You can make him take up his place with your unreserved support, without the slightest doubt that you accept where his duty lies. And yours."

She wanted to run from this room, from everyone who threatened to keep her from Eleanor, to trap her on this island, forever.

Eyes closed, Eschiva gurgled.

Burgundia stood up and went away and when she returned she motioned to the women to take the infant away. Juliana's heart became as empty as her hands. Burgundia placed something in them; a small packet, tightly bound, and a pair of scissors.

"Two sisters came on the last ship, for Saint Mary's. They came from Fontevraud, I am told. Abbess Vigilantia sent this to me. She said it was for you."

Fontevraud. A place so distant now that she had not thought about it recently. Abbess Mathilde thought about her. She said she would.

With a chastised conscience and shaking hands, Juliana cut the cords and unwrapped the package. A single piece of folded parchment fell out and from it something dropped to her lap.

A braid of hair, no thicker than a dormouse tail and just as soft, curling at the end.

Her heart made a loud thump of joy—and anguish.

Burgundia reached for the parchment and unfolded it. "The lady Eleanor is a great favorite of the sisters. Her nurse Philia . . . no Pontia, is exemplary in her care, but the gifts her grandfather sends for her are beyond the need of a single infant, and set a bad example for the older children. The gifts are therefore distributed according to need, not–" Burgundia laughed, "not according to rank. Good Lord, does it sound like Abbess Mathilde? A rather priggish message for a nun isn't it?"

The anguish and relief nearly overwhelmed Juliana. "Armand . . . he lied to me. He returned them to Fontevraud."

"Of course he did. The sisters make excellent nurses. What would he do with an infant? That's Lusignans for you. Infuriating, aren't they? Just when you think you have them figured out, they surprise you. My mother used to say that of my father. It's a miracle some of us manage to love them at all." Burgundia left the letter on Juliana's lap. "I'll have my women bring you rosewater to refresh yourself and I'll let your husband know that you are feeling much better. My woman will take you to him."

Juliana looked up at Burgundia, searching for a reprieve. Burgundia could hold baby Eschiva in her arms every moment of every day. How could Burgundia ask her for such a sacrifice? "You have your daughter."

Burgundia gave her a sweet and bitter smile. "Yes. And you have your husband."

CHAPTER 60

"My lord, wait!"

Lasalle looked back. Down the corridor, Niketas's rotund form bounced toward him. Lasalle had no patience for the little man who traded his allegiances with the ease of a snake shedding skin. On the other hand, in this part of the world few could blame *Sekretikos* Niketas. He waited.

Wheezing, Niketas reached him and leaned against the wall. "Thank you, my lord, I simply must speak to you before . . . before–"

"Before the regent finds out what you did?"

"Ah. Yes. No. Not entirely. Before you form an ill opinion of me–"

Lasalle continued toward Burgundia's chambers. "Trust me, *Sekretikos.* It's impossible to form an ill-opinion of you."

It took Niketas a moment to take in the insult and resume his pursuit. "My lord, my sole desire is to serve my lord Hugh . . . and if that means serving the regent in the meantime . . . I will do what is in fact most repugnant to me."

"Glad to hear that."

"No need to scorn me, my lord. The sole reason why I wish . . . I wish for you to stay on this island is to serve my lord Hugh by your very presence."

My lord Lasalle stopped so suddenly that Niketas nearly collided with him and before Niketas could take a safe step backward, he found himself facing barely contained rage. "Barlais and d'Yvers knew of my pledge to Aimary. You chose a cruel way to inform my wife of it before I could. For that, one day I'll have Djalali feed you to the leopards. Alive."

Pinned in place by eyes which seemed like those of the spotted cats, Niketas forced himself to search the layers of his official robes. There, he found it. He leaned away to bury his nose in the softness of a silk veil. "Ah, still such an enticing perfume. I pray, my lord, that before you do, you ask your wife how she came to lose such a delicate item. It must have occurred during your absence from Nikosia when she met the Lord of Beirut."

Her husband.

Juliana dismissed Burgundia's woman, and hurried back to Hugh's chambers. She wanted to tell Lasalle that she had not lately qualified in her mind their matrimonial affiliation with canonical proscriptions, she wanted to tell him—

At the very spot where she had encountered John d'Ibelín, Lasalle stepped from behind the pillar, startling her. He gripped her by both of her arms. "Juliana, are you ill?"

"No, no. It was the heat." She lied and Lasalle knew it, but in that instant she also knew that something had happened in the meantime. She could tell from a fleeting look in his eyes. It tore at her heart like nothing else she had ever felt, except the possibility of Eleanor's death. She threw herself into his arms and he held her so tightly that she could not breathe. Her cheek in the quilting of his tabard, she heard the loud drum of his heart racing toward her. "Guérin, I know—"

"Wait." He released her as suddenly as he seized her and stood still, his eyes sharp. From the far end of the corridor came the sound of boots and the click-clack of metal. A man emerged, charging toward them, half a dozen guards behind him.

Despite his sparring with Brother Reginald, Lasalle was no challenge much less a match for these men. Nevertheless, without being told, she took a step backward to move behind him where he would have her whenever armed men came charging toward them. Not this time.

"Stay," he said, perfectly calmly. "It's the regent's embassy."

She stayed. Lasalle did not move either and neither did he place his hand on his sword hilt. The stillness became a silent challenge to the man leading his guards.

Walter de Montbéliard recognized it. Collecting himself, his trot became a stride and after halting his men, an amble the rest of the distance. Hands behind his back, he gave them a bow of some hauteur. "Ah. There you are. Welcome back to Nikosia, Lady Juliana. And with your husband, I see. We've heard much about you, and your restoration, my lord Lasalle. How fortunate you were found so soon after your . . . accident."

Walter de Montbéliard wanted to find out why they came to Nikosia without his knowledge let alone his permission. The guards remained watchful, hands on their sword hilts. Juliana surveyed their faces. *Which one of them had killed Leontios?*

"De Lusignan," Lasalle bowed. "But if the name reminds you of your late father-in-law, Regent, by all means, the former will do."

Lasalle said it without the slightest indication that he intended to do something rash and violent to the regent of Cyprus, at least not in her presence. Still, the way Walter glanced at her, he had not dismissed that possibility. It occurred to Juliana that Walter de Montbéliard had not truly met Jean Armand de Lusignan or

Guérin de Lasalle who, under either name, could wrap a *routier's* menace in the silk of courtly manners.

She decided to give Walter de Montbéliard an impeccable curtsey. "You too are fortunate, my lord Regent, to be blessed with such a beautiful and healthy daughter."

Walter de Montbéliard recovered. "Indeed. Blessed indeed, Lady Juliana. A boy next time, my wife tells me. A boy. A family, nothing more precious, is there? To keep peace in one's family. And one's kingdom."

Lasalle offered his arm to Juliana. "Will you be sharing the news of your good fortune with the lady Rhoxsane? It seems she's missing."

Reassured by his guards' presence, Walter visibly relaxed. "Alas no, my lord. I fear that she too must have met with an accident. Cities are full of violence. Women of rank shouldn't travel about without guards, don't you agree, Lady Juliana?"

"I do. Although it occurs to me that the High Court may not see accidents befalling women of rank as entirely accidental."

Walter de Montbéliard forced a laugh. "Yes, yes. I agree. Suspicious minds are everywhere, aren't they? But accidents do happen, don't they? My wife and I . . . and the king, of course, we are all anxious that no ill befalls you or your husband before you return to Poitou."

Lasalle spared her whatever reply she could have made to that threat.

"Then it will be a comfort to you, Regent, that I've decided to remain on Cyprus until Hugh no longer requires your guidance."

For those who would later ask about the split lip and the splatter of blood on his new robes of office, *Sekretikos* Niketas had a prepared explanation. Only no one had asked, not even the young king, although Barlais and de Rivet burst into laughter upon seeing him trying to staunch the blood.

To his new, presumed master, Niketas made excuses and received from Walter de Montbéliard a few days' release to attend to the many properties granted to him throughout the island over the years. One of them was a copper mine in a place called Apliki. No one knew about it except the regent to whom he was forced to divulge it, along with a list of his other holdings.

Climbing into his litter, Niketas intended to recoup the insult to his person and dignity by telling the brother of the brother who had inflicted it, that he would not be party to the Lusignans' private schemes after all, no matter how much he was paid or threatened. In fact, as soon as he could, he would tell the lady Juliana how, after she left the *hammam*, her own brother-in-law had extracted from him every crumb of information regarding herself and the Lord of Beirut, and how Brother Geoffrey had put him up to carry out this unpleasant task.

All that to keep her husband on this island–and her away from it.

CHAPTER 61

If you decide to remain wed to him, one day it will cost you and your daughter dearly, Abbess Vigilantia had warned her.

They returned to the bedchamber of Renaud Barlais's residence where Juliana had waited to hear from Djalali and from his *bedu* friends. Lasalle did not touch the little braid of hair again after he put it back on the table. He had read the letter with which it came. "You have to go to her."

Every fiber of her wanted to ride to Limassol, to Famagusta, to any harbor and to find there the fastest galley to take her to Marseille, to Eleanor. "She is at Fontevraud with Pontia."

"Yes. I will have you on the next ship."

"You can't. You don't have the money to pay for my passage and Athene's. Vigilantia won't pay it. You've told her not to, remember?" She argued with herself as much as with him, and she did not want either of them to win at the cost to the other. She knew that she wanted the impossible.

"The Temple still owes me."

"It doesn't. Didn't Geoffrey tell you? He talked the Master out of your share. He's holding it at Gastria for Saint Mary's. All of it. The rest of Aimary's money belongs to Hugh. Saint Mary's gave Kolossi to me. You own no lands here, you don't have any rights on this island except through me."

"I'll not have you stay. You forget that I can earn my keep without land or titles. Eleanor–"

The reminder of his former occupation was meant to outflank her and it did, and she struck back with what she had left. "Do you think the slightest harm can come to our daughter without God's will whether you and I are a day distant from her or years?"

He made an unguarded gesture, catching himself at the twinge of pain and frustration. "Don't invoke the Almighty against me, Sister Eustace."

He had not called her that recently. This time it did not imply scorn for her own versions of virtue and righteousness, but of the fact that he had no argument to counter that one. She retreated. "It is not your fault that Armand took Eleanor."

"You can't grant me absolution."

"No. We can't be absolved for being born to our families."

She watched him struggle to find a way out of circumstances neither of them could have foreseen. "You are demanding my surrender, Juliana."

She could see in his eyes a chimera of a hurt recently lodged there. "Surrender is not a defeat."

She thought that he would parry her. He did, but not in the way she expected.

He smiled and touched her brow and her cheek and the corner of her lips and let his hand drop to her bosom where a small scar still remained, and most likely would. A short, stifled breath escaped her when she opened her mouth to confess herself as she had intended many times before, but he replaced her words with his mouth and with his hands on the rest of her.

She reached out, arms around his neck and pressed herself to him. She would tell him tomorrow when they woke up and that shadow would be gone from his eyes, and he would laugh and tell her that he had found a way out of this dilemma.

He was still asleep when she left in the morning with two of her men as guards, and went to Saint Mary's to seek out the nuns who must have seen Eleanor, must have held her. She wanted them to tell her about Eleanor. She wanted to know what it was like, holding her.

The gate mistress returned, denying her request to enter. The abbess wished the lady Juliana to return to Kolossi and to mind that property as her pledge to Saint Mary's promised. Confused, crushed, and despairing, Juliana contemplated sitting covered in ashes before Saint Mary's gate. She went back to Barlais's residence instead.

Renaud Barlais met her in the courtyard, looking like a man who knew he had cheated his way to a grand prize and who did not intend to return it just to salve his conscience. He held the mule for her to dismount. "My lord Lasalle went to fetch the payments for the king's household and for his liegemen. He took some of your men with him." Barlais looked about and lowered his voice. "No one knows where he hid the money. What if something happens to him again? I don't think your husband trusts us."

Juliana handed Barlais the reins. "My husband trusts only two people on this island."

"Ha! And who are they?"

"I can't remember."

Barlais scratched the gray bristle under his chin. "You don't say." He hesitated. "You've done well, Lady Juliana. I regret my words to you. If any of us can be of service to you, just send a word."

"Thank you. And for your hospitality."

"You are most welcome." He reach into his belt pouch. "Your husband left this for you."

In her room, Juliana opened the leather packet. Inside was a parchment. The message on it was written in a familiar hand that struggled to form the letters if not the words.

You followed me to Cyprus to compel me to return to Poitou and reclaim our daughter. The need no longer exists. It cannot therefore serve as the reason why you would ever contemplate being bound to this place any more than the circumstances of our marriage can bind you to me. The decision to stay is mine. I leave you the means to pay for the passage to our daughter for you and Athene should she so wish. For Eleanor's sake I trust in your good sense to use it.

Juliana folded the parchment and saw on the back of it another line. *Without God's will, no harm can come to any of us.*

Tears shook on her eyelashes when she reached into the packet. With a glint, something slipped into her palm. A gold cross set with amethysts. *For Eleanor's sake.*

Her fist throbbed. She did not realize that she had clutched the cross. She opened her palm. Geoffrey had used her doubts about her marriage to his brother to threaten that she would leave him. Only she had witnessed all around her the suppleness of marital bonds and met those who had severed them, ignored them, or made them serve hardly spiritual purposes with, and without, the Church's blessing. *What is more Christian than love, Lady Juliana?*

"Lady Juliana?" Her servant woman came into the room, carrying a market basket. "Lady Juliana? Your husband left this for you. I told him that bread and cheese would travel better but he insisted."

Juliana tucked the cross into her bodice, and wiped her tears. She lifted the greasy kitchen cloth covering the basket. Inside was a ham, salted and cured, with a dagger stuck in it.

The servant woman waited in confusion while Juliana stared at it. She then ordered the woman to pack the trunks and unlocked her scribe's box. While she still could see the page in front of her, she wrote an even briefer message to Burgundia.

CHAPTER 62

Saint Mary's Abbey

The arrival of Lady Burgundia with a court of her servants sent ripples of pardonable excitement through the cloisters. Abbess Vigilantia did not seek to correct it since she knew that she was the reason for the visit as much as the presence of Burgundia's two half sisters, lodged in the safety of the abbey.

Those sisters had to wait while Vigilantia received her royal visitor in private, increasing the rush of rumors and whispers which shifted to the gifts the lady Burgundia brought to Saint Mary's this time—a crown of amber for the Virgin, crystal and silver lamps for the altar, and two carts of grain and cloth for the women pilgrims the nuns sheltered.

"We are honored by your presence after such a long absence, Lady Burgundia. We have been offering prayers for the welfare of Lady Eschiva," Abbess Vigilantia was heard to say with the doors thereafter shut to the curious.

Burgundia examined the glossy faces of female saints veiled in silver and precious stones. "Thank you. No need for formalities. I came to show my gratitude for Melisande and Sybilla. I intend to have you take up Eschiva's education when she is old enough."

Abbess Vigilantia failed to conceal her surprise. "You . . . you are?"

Burgundia turned to her. "Why wouldn't I? You rejected me, but we are after all sister-wives, are we not? The count of Toulouse climbed into your bed from mine, and he cast aside both of us for a more valuable bride. Poor Joanne. A sister to King Richard and he did not deign to spare her Raymond's attentions anymore than Richard spared you his. Whatever injury and injustice you have suffered, I and my family have suffered as well."

Vigilantia leaned into her chair with more than a hint of satisfaction. "Ah. You are asking me to make peace with the Lusignans."

Her visitor gave her a look of pure astonishment. "Good Lord, why would you think that? I am ordering you to make peace with us. You cried with rage in my arms when Raymond sent us both to the *cathari* women. For safekeeping, he said. Do you remember how he laughed? I promised you that I would help you return to Cyprus, and I did. I can imagine your lack of delight when Mathilde told you to take with you another soul wronged by us Lusignans. And then you met Guérin de Lasalle and realized that the poor man loves his wife. I had warned you not to do so, but you thought to sow a little discord between them anyway. Only you have gone too far."

"You would judge me?"

"Yes, I would. Using me to send her daughter's hair to Juliana was a clever trick, I admit. I had Juliana almost convinced to stay by her husband's side with all those assurances you've provided, only he took it into his head that she must leave him because of them. Tisk, tisk, Eirene. With my husband milking Cyprus dry, Hugh's crown is becoming rather shopworn. We can't work at cross purposes."

Rigid with resentment, Vigilantia said, "You abandoned me. You returned to Cyprus without me. You didn't help me, not before I was passed through more men's beds."

Burgundia waved her hand. "Yes, yes. None of us are omnipotent. I could have hardly helped you since I could not then help myself. Now you are here and things have changed for both of us. Let men delude themselves that they got away with their decisions, especially the wrong ones."

"Which particular ones? There are so many to choose from."

Burgundia picked up an icon and held it up to the light. The Virgin, crowned with pearls, gazed at the Infant on her knee with infinite love. Burgundia kissed it and gently placed the icon on Vigilantia's lap. "Let us then pick one and set it right. Now what do you suppose would rouse a pining mother?"

Kolossi

How can one live with one's heart torn in two?

Instead of her husband, Juliana brought back to Kolossi a ham, a dagger, and a gold cross worth enough to pay for her and Athene's passage to Poitou. The first two items told her that Lasalle had hidden a king's treasure somewhere on a farmstead at Famagusta. Chances were that Lasalle had shared that knowledge only with Djalali–and herself. The third item intended to send her away.

My lord Lasalle had chosen to remain and serve the king, she told an anxious Darius and a remorseful-looking Brother Reginald. They did not ask about the details, perhaps because of the manner in which she had delivered the news.

This time, she gave Brother Reginald leave to rejoin his own lord. Brother Reginald departed with a troubled countenance and two of Kolossi's mules to carry the four trunks that Athene had brought from Acre. The gowns the trunks contained rightfully belonged to the princesses of the House of Lusignan in Cyprus. To keep them would be vainglorious. Thus one by one, Juliana severed the threads that tied her to this island.

Only to Athene did she show the little braid of hair and read to her the letter. That night, the gold cross pressed to her heart, she sat with Athene by the open window of her bedchamber. Countless stars poured into the room until dawn chased them and her tears away.

Neither that dawn nor the succeeding ones chased away Juliana's desolation, and neither work nor prayers eased it. Her desolation deepened when Darius came to tell her that the *Paradisus* had returned to Limassol.

The visitors arrived before sunset, under the banner of the Abbess of Saint Mary's, in mule litters, surrounded by servants and men-at-arms.

Darius burst into the kitchen to announce the unexpected guests. Juliana took off her apron and dusted her gown. What could have brought Abbess Vigilantia to Kolossi? Perhaps she wished to make certain that the management of her abbey's fief passed into capable hands. The abbess would expect a proper welcome, she told the flustered servants.

She waited in the bailey with Athene, the servants collected behind them in a pious chorus. They waited for the caravan to enter, for the abbey's servants to dismount and attend to the litters with the crosses of Saint Mary's stitched on the curtains. The servants untied the covering on one of the litters but before they could unfold the steps for the august occupant to make a decorous descend, an imp, red-faced with excitement, dashed out, landed safely on its feet, and charged straight for Juliana.

"We are here, we are here!"

Melisande.

The child's arms attached around Juliana's waist like sea lampreys. Juliana had no time to sort out her shock which doubled when Xene appeared behind Melisande. From the other palanquin emerged Sybilla, holding Madelena's hand. Sybilla approached with far more restraint, and Xene and Madelena did likewise. They curtsied to Juliana and Madelena handed her a sealed message. "The Abbess sent us, Lady Juliana."

"Read it, read it, Juliana!" Melisande clung to her tighter against Xene's efforts to pry the child away.

Juliana broke the seal. *Saint Mary's sends its wards to be brought up in the household of the Abbey's vassal, Lady Juliana of Colos, until such time as their brother, the King of Cyprus, reaches his majority.*

"I–I don't understand–"

Melisande bounced on her tiptoes, rabid with happiness. "I do, I do. We're to stay here. With you!" She stopped, her nose twitching. "I have to pee."

Beware of Greeks bearing gifts.

Especially bearing gifts of young girls, their maid servants, and a dozen mules bearing their personal and household furnishings. Those included four trunks of very expensive gowns that had travelled the length of the island only to be returned to Kolossi.

Pafo, Cyprus

Having risen from servant to a lady with her own manor and servants, Rhoxsane adapted to being a servant once again easily. It was after all a matter of survival. Moreover, since it is often the darkest under the lamp, she did not object to returning to Cyprus after her new master sailed there with his wares of Cairo's bath oils and perfumes.

She left behind in Acre her own identity and well as Lord Makheras's who had finally revealed to the world his true name and his true aims.

It became obvious to her that she had underestimated Walter de Montbéliard. She knew by then that he did not intend to leave any witnesses. Therefore when Walter killed the two men who had ambushed Guérin de Lasalle, she took advantage of Walter's distraction and fled. She knew the markets, she knew the language, and with the appropriate application of her wits she had managed to secure the position of a housekeeper and assistant for an Armenian peddling his wares from one end of the *Levante* to the other. Being a woman, she soon conducted profitable business for him with female customers. Their arrangements had its advantages.

The market at Pafo offered good opportunities and at the end of the day, she decided to follow a small crowd of pilgrims heading for the baths. Along the way, she became distracted by a noisy arrest of Saint Paul with several men dressed like Roman soldiers hauling along the rather vigorously resisting Apostle to the jeering of the onlookers. When she regained attention, she was in a narrow, blind end street. She turned and encountered a man in a pilgrim's cloak blocking her path, hood shading his face.

"Mistress Rhoxsane. Lost again, are we?"

The deep, calm voice sent shivers down her spine, but she showed no fear. "You are mistaken. I am a merchant's wife on a pilgrimage." She tried to pass by the man and he extended his arm, barring her way. Of course. A robber. Rhoxsane quickly stripped the rings from her fingers. "Take these. They're yours. They're all I have."

The man moved toward her, forcing her deeper into the passage. "I will do anything, sir, anything you want. I can do many . . . many things, you will see." She dropped the rings and tugged at the layers of her skirts. She kept a knife in a sheath on her thigh, just for these occasions.

The man did not move any closer. "I know you can. But poisons are your specialty, aren't they? Tell me, do you have any on you?"

The man wanted to hire her. Rhoxsane forced herself to laugh away her nervousness. She dropped the skirts and arranged them into their former neatness. "Yes. Of course. I always keep an ampul. Who do you wish me to . . . to remove for you?"

The man raised his hand. She thought that he would strike her, but he only pushed back his hood and she looked into a handsome face with the bluest eyes, and a smile of terrifying gentleness. "You."

CHAPTER 63

He had buried Niketas's loot under one of the kitchen *pithari* in the farmstead outside of Famagusta.

The place had stood empty since he bought it from the original owners, and since he sent away the girl Persephone and her husband, the pig butcher. Taking no chance, he left his men in one of the town's tavern and taking a couple of mules with him, rode to the farmstead after being certain that he was not followed.

He poured a portion of the coins into a couple of wine sacks and slung them over the mules' pack saddles and covered it all with sheaves of hay. In town, he chose two men to take one of the sacks back to Nikosia. Those coins would pay for Hugh's household for a time. Niketas and Father Silbo would make sure that Walter de Montbéliard would not see a single *besant*.

The rest of the coins went to the money-strapped supporters of Hugh the First of Cyprus. Most of them had left the capital for their estates on the island, retreating into the comforts of rebuilt and fortified settlements. He tracked them down, one by one, and paid them in full the way he would have paid out his own mercenaries.

His coin and news-hungry hosts delayed him for several days to discuss his riding accident, the resulting loss of the regency, and the more recent events in Saint Jean d'Acre and the kingdom of Jerusalem. What was left of it. They missed Aimary as much as he missed him, for all of Aimary de Lusignan's rough handling of some of them and his ruses. If they missed Aimary, they also looked forward to the rule of his son. Hugh de Lusignan would find support among these men. Time would come for Hugh to make his personal acquaintance with his vassals. He could do that for him.

He had no reason to hurry and the days in the saddle allowed him to regain most of his strength. At the end of those weeks, he had the names of several barons who held estates of the Crown of Jerusalem. With the ascension of John d'Ibelín to that regency, they had sailed to Saint Jean d'Acre to secure what they already possessed there–and to add more.

He had to go to Acre. As it happened, being a paymaster to Hugh of Cyprus would not be the sole reason for his return.

He sent the last Kolossi man to Nikosia and rode back to Famagusta. Djalali knew where he had hidden the money and now Juliana knew. If need be, wherever she was, she could tell whoever took over the post of Hugh's paymaster, even if it was Niketas. He regretted hitting the *sekretikos*; not because he had struck an unarmed man, but because he had revealed to Niketas a vulnerability. It was a stupid and dangerous thing and he must not let himself be goaded into it–especially not by John d'Ibelín.

In Famagusta, he picked up another coin sack and rode on to Gastria.

He fully expected to deal there with his brother, the Brother. Instead, the *serjean* left in charge told him that as soon as Brother Reginald returned from Kolossi, the two left for Acre.

How very convenient. Lasalle exchanged the coin sack for a note to pay him the exact amount from the Temple's coffers in Acre. No need to drag all those *besants* across water.

Now he was free to do as he wished just like he had done those years ago, without care or conscience.

The summer came with its searing heat, and long nights in sweat of worry, guilt, and regret in the dark. During the day, Juliana did not allow her true state of mind to reveal itself. Mornings, in the coolness of the exedra, she taught Melisande and Sybilla their letters and listened to them pick out words from the Latin and French books they had brought with them. She taught them how to form letters, to figure ciphers, and to memorize passages and prayers.

She listened to their laughter and giggles and squabbles in the kitchen, in the storehouses, barns, and chicken coops, and in the garden they watered and weeded, and one day Juliana realized that she was happy, for them.

Besides reading, writing, and recitation, other accomplishments for the life Sybilla and Melisande would lead required equally diligent cultivation. For those instructions, Athene spread out Juliana's gowns to teach the girls the names of jewels and embellishments, how to judge cloth and the quality of dye, to pick the perfect pearls, to make stitches and embroidery with needles as fine as hair. She showed them how to spin and weave, to stock their apothecary chests and prepare poultices and potions for toothaches, scrapes, bruises and wounds, how to serve and be served, to walk and sit and sing and dance. Xene and Madelena kept their zealous attention for the girls' welfare even though Kolossi represented a diminution in the quality if not quantity of comforts.

They all rode on mules and donkeys to the seashore, Sybilla and Melisande dressed like *paroikoi* children with their straw hats and bare legs, distinguished from the peasants only by the servants and the men who accompanied them. The sisters made friends, too, among the children of Kolossi's servants and when Juliana allowed them to explore the village a stone's throw from the fortress, they found their own amusements in the fields, gardens, orchards, and pastures. That liberty would soon be denied them.

Despite her bend to mischief and tearful outbursts of temper, Melisande became the servants' favorite. Juliana suspected that Sybilla's aloofness masked caution about the world into which Fate had thrust her and her sister. If Sybilla watched the world about her with caution, so did Juliana.

Thus far Walter de Montbéliard had made no demand to relinquish the girls into his custody. Perhaps other matters occupied him. Perhaps Burgundia prevented him from seizing them. There was, after all, more to Burgundia de Lusignan than met the eye. Much more.

Burgundia. And Heloise. There was a hardiness to Burgundia and Heloise de Lusignan that their younger sisters shared, despite the tragedies of their own lives. With each passing day, that streak asserted itself more although when storms came with downpours and lightning, the girls would burst into her room and snuggle to her like frightened puppies.

Every day, they went to *Ayios Eustathios.* Above them, in the dome of the little church, Christ raised his hand in benediction. He was married. Father Demetrios, that is. Juliana could not get over that thought for some time. And then it did not matter to her anymore. *What is more Christian than love, Lady Juliana?*

CHAPTER 64

Saint Jean d'Acre, kingdom of Jerusalem

Finding one particular woman in a city the size of Saint Jean d'Acre, a cauldron of restive residents and flooded with visitors, proved to be a challenge. Especially when one did not know whether or not that woman was still alive.

Lasalle retraced his steps to the house where Walter de Montbéliard's men had ambushed him, taking care that this time he was not. The house stood empty. He pushed open the door and the stream of light upon the stone floor revealed a black pool. He shut the door behind him and scraped the stain with his boot toe. Blood. Old, dried. From the size of it, someone had bled out his—or her—life here.

The neighbors' tongues loosened a little after he paid them; yes, they remembered something of that day, a stolen horse, no? A lady? A woman? They could not recall.

He rode away, his frustration renewed. Another failure, although not entirely his own this time. True, Walter had no reason to keep Rhoxsane alive. And yet, from the shrugs of the men and the women's averted eyes, he knew that they were not telling him the whole truth of what had happened after Walter's men had hauled him away.

On the other hand, once he had settled what he set out to settle, he had the rest of his life to fulfill his pledge to Abbess Vigilantia to find Rhoxsane of Kolossi. And kill her.

The Temple paid him out the money owed to Hugh's Syrian barons without objections from the Grand Master. They knew each other from their previous encounter and because Lasalle needed the Master's help, this time he kept his temper.

To his surprise, de Plessis, a forty-year-old Angevin with a knack for diplomacy as much as war, also agreed to lend him a couple of brothers and their squires to deliver the payments to Hugh's liegemen. Three resided in the city, the others had gone to their estates since the peace with the Musulmans, which de Plessis had helped Aimary de Lusignan to negotiate, remained in place under the new regent.

"We will assist you, my lord, for the love that we have for King Aimary, may his soul rest in peace. We hold the same love for his son." De Plessis crossed himself.

De Plessis did not mention the Temple's love for the regent of

Cyprus and Lasalle had not mentioned Walter de Montbéliard either, but he did intend to kill two birds with one stone. The problem was finding one of the birds. "In that case, I ask that you allow my brother to be one of the brothers, my lord."

De Plessis sent a I-told-you-this-was-coming look to the two brother-companions who stood by his chair in the Grand Master's quarters. One of them, Brother Mathews, had an answer ready. "Brother Geoffrey is looking after a grain shipment."

"Is he." That excuse did not prevent Lasalle from asking why the Temple had released his blood money to Brother Geoffrey.

The Master heard him out with polite patience. "We thought you were dead."

"You had no proof."

"We agreed, sir, to allow your brother to act on your behalf. He had offered you to my lord Aimary to serve as his son's regent and we had agreed. We don't blame you for what occurred, but in council some brothers wonder about your brother's judgment, considering that your wife joined you here."

"Without my knowledge or permission." A feeble explanation, he had to admit, and an even worse excuse, but it was the truth.

De Plessis cleared his throat. "That speaks as much for you as it does for her, does it not? Brother Geoffrey pleaded most earnestly for your coins so that your wife could return to Poitou. What she has done with them is not our concern. However, now that you are alive, our Almoner will provide for your needs here and Brother Mathew will choose your escort."

The Temple did not wish him to find Geoffrey and Geoffrey did not wish to be found. Lasalle bowed to the Grand Master. "Thank you."

De Plessis raised himself from his chair. "The Order knows of your experience among us, my lord. We would welcome you as a *confrère*. We'll give you charge of the turcopoles."

"I have a duty to Hugh."

De Plessis followed him to the door. "We can wait until you discharge it." The Master paused, his voice low in conciliation. "I have learned that not everything can be solved by the sword."

"No. Sometimes it takes poison."

After her mother's death, Maria de Montferrat returned to the care of the sisters of Saint Anne's to be kept under lock and key until her barons found a suitable husband for her and a king for her kingdom. Until such time, *La Marquise's* uncle took up residence in the royal chambers to govern the remnant of the Latins' former possessions in Maria's name.

The diminution of the realm did not lead to a decline of its importance for those who still occupied it. Messengers, visitors, supplicants, and petitioners crowded the courtyard of Acre's fortress to be funneled into the regent's presence according to consanguinity, affinity, and rank.

Lasalle had returned to Acre less the coins he had delivered, and the Temple brothers returned to their duties. Now he had no choice but to seek out John d'Ibelín, the man held in his wife's confidence and perhaps more.

He did not wait to be formally announced. He took the underground passages and walked to the regent's chamber, surprising the guards who made an effort to shut the doors to him, causing a considerable commotion.

John d'Ibelín looked up from examining a charter. "What an unexpected pleasure, my lord de Colos . . . oh, never mind. Do come in." Without a shade of worry, he turned to the two barons in his presence. "We are certain you haven't come to kill the regent of Jerusalem, aren't we, my lords?"

The men laughed, rather nervously. Three clerks, stationed at their inkhorns and parchments, cast a glance at each other and at the chamber's second door. Lasalle took note of it. The guards watched his every move. They would cut him down the moment he made one. "Would I have a reason?"

The two barons huffed in surprise, their hands at their sword belts. John d'Ibelín laughed and shrugged with pretended resignation and nodded to them to leave. They did, reluctantly, as curious as *souk* wives. He dismissed the clerks as well, whispering something to one of them. When the door closed behind them, John d'Ibelín unbuckled his sword and placed it on one of the scribe's desks. With empty palms raised, he faced his new visitor. "You see I have no weapons, sir."

"Not if you don't count that dagger in your boot top," Lasalle said.

John slowly lowered his hands. Given the fact that Guérin de Lasalle had not offered his own sword in a reciprocal gesture of *chivalerie* told him more than all the information he had about this man. Had his mother had her way, Guérin de Lasalle would have been his rival for Cyprus. After all that had brought them to this moment, John was glad it had not come to that. "Is that where you keep yours?"

His almost-rival looked about the chamber. "Not usually."

"Then you still have me outmatched."

"I doubt it. You're the regent of Jerusalem and the Lord of Beirut. I have to keep in the good graces of the Temple's almoner."

John d'Ibelín took that answer with a suppressed smile. Guérin de Lasalle honed a phrase the way Aimary de Lusignan did. That was either a good or a bad sign. Now that they had their first thrust and parry, he had to address the true reasons why this Lusignan sought him out. "De Plessis is frugal. And yet, my lord, we do have something in common. You asked if you have a reason to kill me. I imagine you could come up with one or two."

"News travels."

"As much as you do. But there is another reason you came here." John decided to chance turning his back on his testy visitor to search among the trunks and coffers stored against the wall. He brought out a small box bound with copper straps. "I've looked for her ever since Walter had you kidnapped. My mother's spies can't find her either. Rhoxsane might be at the bottom of the sea or a cellar, or under Montmusard's foundations."

Lasalle considered that the regent of Jerusalem, like the regent of Cyprus, was telling him the truth. "But you have no proof."

"No."

John d'Ibelín drew a key on a string around his neck, unlocked the little coffer, and extracted a sheet. He unfolded it and held it out to him. "You couldn't find any proof of my guilt in the death of my lord Aimary because I am not guilty. You have no more proof of your wife's affection for me let alone our adultery either except for the suspicion others have cast on her to separate you from each other."

Guérin de Lasalle remained very still. Perhaps disarming himself was not the smartest move and explanations would be now in order, and so John said, "You can read, no? I can't. Not very well. But for our chance encounter in Nikosia, I wouldn't have had in your wife the ally I needed. I couldn't trust anyone, not even my own mother. Fortunately, your wife can tell a forgery better than a legate."

John kept himself from exhaling with relief when Guérin de Lasalle gave the parchment a brief glance. "This accuses you."

"Yes. It was brought to my mother and she kept it, for obvious reasons. Here in Acre your wife recognized Burgundia's hand and that someone had changed the name to mine. I told her there was another regency at stake beside Jerusalem's. I didn't see or speak to your wife again. I kept the message because I wanted you to see it yourself so that you would know the truth."

"But that is not the whole truth, is it?"

"No." John held the sheet to the candle flame until the parchment became a charred scrap. "Walter intended all along for our families to cross swords. Your wife did not want you to kill me. I assured her that I would not want to kill you either."

Lasalle wondered if he ought not run his sword through John d'Ibelín just to prove him wrong, at least on the current subject. "Why not?"

"Because she loves you."

This was a conversation Lasalle did not intend to prolong, if only for the sake of what was left of the kingdom of Jerusalem. "I am flattered. And if you ever–"

The entry door cracked open. A pricking at the back of his neck told him that he had walked into an ambush after all. A guard's face cautiously appeared behind the door leaf. "My lord, we brought–"

"I said wait." John d'Ibelín stopped the man and when the guard ducked back, he said to his annoyed and armed visitor, "You ought to be. There is no reason to avoid Kolossi."

"There is nothing to avoid at Kolossi."

"Except for your wife."

One learns how to avoid being surprised in the middle of surprises. He remembered that the second door led to an exterior staircase. "She is gone to Poitou."

"Not according to Burgundia. She's taken over Lusignan schemes on Cyprus. Here my mother is at full tilt after the Ibelín ones."

Moving himself casually away from the entry door, Guérin de Lasalle did not react the way John hoped he would. "Now why would Cousin Burgundia do that?"

John leaned on the scribe's desk, his hands in the vicinity of his sword. "Because there is no longer a private cause between the Lusignans and the Ibelíns, because we all have a common one. Only you are a difficult man to convince, my lord de Lusignan. Guards!"

Lasalle went first for d'Ibelín's sword, snatching it, belt and all. With the door burst fully open and several men cramming through it, he toppled the scribe's desk into their path.

The obstruction caused a collision as predictable as it was comical, and would have been more so had not the man left at the threshold grasped the fact that my lord Lasalle held under the chin of the regent of Jerusalem the long edge of his own sword.

"My lord, don't!" The man sprung nimbly past the pile, a man with the chest and shoulders of a bullock under a shipmaster's tabard and arms that could pull oars in the wildest seas, and wield a hammer and an iron bar to shatter reddish-brown rock deep within a mountain mine.

Martianus.

CHAPTER 65

Pafo, Cyprus

On a knoll, two leagues from the sea where Aphrodite rose from pillows of white *aphros,* stood the broken remains of her temple. Some columns still reached high, others sank into the ground. Earthquakes had toppled the walls and mingled the fluted column drums and the shattered entablature among the wrecks of walls and buildings that once surrounded the sanctuary.

Not far, half-ruined houses and the cracked walls of small churches provided evidence of the precariousness of the Christians' presence on the island. Further down the coast road, the growing town of Pafo surrounded several churches belonging to Greeks and Latins, guarded by a fortress the Greeks built to defend the harbor against raiding Musulmans. Aimary de Lusignan had almost refurbished the fortress, but the regent of Cyprus did not continue the work for lack of funds, he claimed. The churches marked the place where Paul had received his lashes before converting the island's Roman ruler. The Apostle's pillar became a place of pilgrimage.

These pious pilgrims did not come to the ruins of Aphrodite's temple, and her worshipers had long vanished as well.

Wearing white cloaks with hoods against the dust and the heat, Juliana and Athene had ridden to the abandoned temple without servants, with only four men as their guards. Athene had brought her to this place on their first ride to Pafo, and Juliana thereafter always paused at it. Standing on the knoll in the shimmering haze of late summer, she sometimes thought that she saw the sails of a ship approaching the headland or heading to the open waters to find her way to Messina and Genoa and Marseille, to Eleanor.

She did not bring the children to this outpost of paganism which, for all of its astonishing size and the even more astonishing views out to the seas, seemed haunted to her. And yet, Juliana had to admit to herself, the place also drew her despite–or perhaps because of–the story that Athene told her about it, one which Mistress Morphia had neglected to mention. It was the story of queens, princesses, and common women made equal in their devotion, wearing crowns of myrtle and bringing flowers and fruit and olive oil to anoint Aphrodite's altar, and myrrh and frankincense to burn in her fire cauldrons.

The women came to this place from near and afar once in their lifetime to make their offerings. Here they also waited to offer themselves to some stranger, here in the recesses of the temple and its grounds, perhaps where now fragrant shrubs, cypresses, and stunted myrtle trees grew among patches of soft grass.

This time she did not tamp down her curiosity about what Athene had told her. "Those . . . those women. They went with those strange men, just like that?"

"They were not that strange. They were just men." Athene said and Juliana could hear a hint of laughter in Athene's voice. "They had to bring money to throw at the feet of the woman they chose."

Athene glided between the lengthening shade and retreating light, her veil draped over her headdress, the cloak drifting behind her, an ancient priestess come to life. Juliana shook her head to dispel that image. *Did the women in these parts still . . .* "Hmm. How much?"

In the circles of *kohl,* Athene's eyes seemed far-seeing. "Enough. The women did not come here to become prostitutes."

"What if there were two men vying for the same girl?"

"I don't know. I suppose they tried to outbid each other or drew lots. No blood, human or animal, was allowed in the temple grounds."

"Except the girl's." Juliana regretted that she uttered the thought, and regretted even more when she realized that her hand came to the tiny scar she would bear forever.

"They all came willingly. It was their way. We hurt, accept, and heal."

"Do we? What if we hurt someone else?"

"We heal them too. That's what we do."

They stood alone among the ruins. No one could approach unobserved. The men had tethered the horses well outside the sanctuary and stretched out in the shade of the cypress trees. Two of them claimed a stump of marble for their dice.

It occurred to Juliana that those two remained alert because of Lasalle. He was gone, yet his presence surrounded her in the training of the men protecting her and everyone at Kolossi, in its fortified walls, the stocked storehouses.

"And then they could leave?"

"Yes. Sometimes they had to wait for years, the ugly ones, for some man to take pity on them. It's late. We ought to ride on to Pafo."

Juliana faced toward the seas. The sun's disk descended from deep blue to purple and mauve and blazed in yellow and red. Yes, they would lodge in Pafo for the night.

A blast of wind from the seas tore away her hood and her veil, loosened her hairpins, and on it swirled between the columns. Her eyes stung. She closed them and heard soft, moaning sounds and sobbing ones, of pleasure and pain and sadness, like the voice of Mélusine, caught in time. She did not know whether to condemn or pity the women whose ashes such wind had dispersed a long time ago. She was after all like one of them, waiting. The wind died. It was then that she heard Athene's voice.

"My lady. There is a man by the myrtle trees."

There was, standing next to his horse.

The horse shook his head; the bridle bit clinked. Not a red horse or chestnut or a white one, but a lead-gray turcoman of cleanly muscled lines, like those of its rider. She could not truly see them because a cloak hung from his shoulders with a dusty and scuffed gambeson under it. But she could see those lines in her mind's eye, and she remembered with aching clarity her hands tracing them.

One of the guards rushed up to lead the horse away and she made no more notice of it because she saw nothing else but her husband coming to her.

He stopped and bowed, a slight bow. His cheekbones stood out sharp in a face glazed in a coppery sheen and his teeth flashed white like a row of bleached seashells. *"Epikaloumay te thea se sas."*

Her breath was gone and her mind paralyzed. "W-what?"

"It means I'll pay whatever you want to lay with me even if I have to sell my last goat." He took a step closer. "But I don't have a *denier* on me."

"How do you . . . how did you–?"

"Your men told me to say that. They sneak away to meet the village women here." He looked around him. "I'd say it might have been going on for some years."

"You . . . you came back."

"You never went away."

"I–I couldn't. The children–"

"What children?"

"Yours. Ours. Sybilla and Melisande. Vigilantia sent them to me."

"I . . . see. Is that the only reason?"

Sometimes they waited for years . . . "No."

He led her, carefully and deliberately, as much as she led him, into the darkening emptiness around them, across broken floors where thousands of feet had trod and danced on crushed myrtle flowers.

No flower-strewn, seagrass-filled pad provided their bed where the rubble of walls met, only their cloaks and the ground under them. She braced herself, tensing, anticipating a hard slab of marble, but his arm cushioned her descent.

He would always safeguard her and those who came within his care. She had been conjuring doubts about him, about his true self, about their marriage. She had never truly trusted him the way Mélusine's husband never came to trust her. Abbot Arnold told her that and she did not understand, not then. *He betrayed her when he broke his pledge not to question their marriage. Despite her own ancestry, she gave him her love, trust, and his earthly possessions, yet he doubted her devotion.*

The shedding of cloth felt like the shedding of false skin. When her breasts pressed against him, the sensation awoken in her became so keen it hurt. He did not close his eyes and she suspected that he never did. She looked into them, truly did, and all that stood between them came away. With his weight on her, the tension in her unfolded and flowed out of her body and her mind. She tasted tears and the saltiness of sweat, the alien and the familiar, and she reached for it all and sought it and found it at last.

"Juliana? Juliana. You're crying."

The world crept back to her. She heard the cicadas and night insects and the distant sounds of the sea. She reached out, her fingertips against his cheeks. They were wet, his hair stuck to them. The racing of her heart echoed his. She waited for it to subside though their bodies remained caught in each other and in their cloaks and clothes.

She had kept her secrets from him for no reason that she could now divine and in their hands now rested their safety, and the safety of those entrusted to them by choice or chance. "Guérin, I wanted . . . I so wanted to tell you that–"

"I found Martianus. Turns out he's d'Ibelín's man. John will make a good regent."

She made a move, her elbow inadvertently in his ribs.

"Ah, Christ, woman, don't do that." He gathered her to him and rolled on his back. "That's better." He held her there against the strong and steady beat of his heart. "Of course not as good as I would have been, but good enough."

"Guérin–"

"You're an exhausting woman, Lady Juliana. Now go to sleep."

"But the men . . . they will talk."

"I certainly hope so."

"I . . . I love you."

"Hmm." He kissed the top of her head. "So I've heard."

CHAPTER 66

Juliana looked out the window of her chamber–their chamber. Below, Lasalle and Darius examined horses, recently bought, sleek, noble animals the grooms led around courtyard.

After their return to Kolossi, she walked about in a fog of distraction that everyone noticed. They whispered with sly smiles behind her back. She did not care. The men had welcomed Lasalle with certain degree of apprehension and relief while Melisande ran up to him like a lost puppy. Sybilla held herself aloof to see what the return of their rescuer and protector would bring.

Athene came into the room with an armful of bed quilts. "It will be cold soon. Especially with my lord away, no?"

Juliana stepped away from the window. "He told you he will be leaving?"

"Darius said those horses are a gift for Lord Hugh."

Yes, Athene was right. This day would come, and others like it. "I will so miss him."

"The men too. Herion will have to keep after them, so that when my lord returns, they won't be so green."

Athene was right. It became cooler, especially behind the stone walls. That night, Juliana kept her shift on and, comb in hand, drew the covers to her. She would have the brazier lit, a poor substitute for tucking herself against him, for his arm around her, his breath on her nape.

She glanced at him. He was lying prone, his chin on his wrists. She could tell that his eyes were closed but she kept hers on the line of arm and shoulder, the trench of spine across a plain of muscle. She could tell that he was not asleep. "When will you leave?"

He did not move. "Tomorrow."

Her breath caught. "So soon?"

He grunted and turned on his back. "It's not that soon. Hugh must think I abandoned him."

"What will you do?"

"Annoy Walter. Make certain Hugh knows each baron and knight enough to hold his own against them."

The comb snagged in her hair. "You will teach a king how to best his barons?"

He opened one eye to her. "Are you plumbing for irony, Lady Juliana?"

It occurred to her how easily they could talk even when they talked about the events in Acre, about Rhoxsane, John d'Ibelín, Burgundia, and Heloise. And Geoffrey, a little. Had Heloise found in Odo de Dampierre a husband after all who knew how to lure his wife to him and had she allowed herself to be lured? Juliana yanked at the comb. "Don't tell me you don't see it yourself. A Lusignan teaching a king how to rule unruly barons?"

He drew himself up and took the comb away from her to untangle her hair strand by stand. "Hold still. Only if the king is a Lusignan. Aimary did well, don't you think? Guy would have done well, too, if he didn't believe that when it came down to the safety of Jerusalem, he could trust his barons to put aside their hatred for him."

He had never spoken of his family like that to her, never shared what he had experienced there at Hattín, before the walls of Acre, what had happened afterward. "Why would they hate him so?"

"They wanted to punish Sybilla for thwarting them. For choosing her own husband, for refusing to have their marriage annulled, for sharing her crown with him. She made him promise not to give it up to them, not ever. And he didn't."

"She . . . she must have loved him very much."

He handed her the comb. "And he her. This kingdom is Hugh's. He mustn't allow the barons to rule him any more than Aimary did. Do you understand?"

Yes, this time she did. "Is that why you don't trust . . . anyone?"

"I said I trusted two people on this island. I still do."

"Will you . . . will come back?"

"Always."

He pushed away the quilts and she threw off her shift. She reached for him and leaned back, her eyes open until the ridge of his arm and shoulder obscured the lamp's light.

What does a marriage make?

She never returned to that place near Pafo but fragments of it remained with her every time she watched him ride up to Kolossi's gate. He did return to her like he promised, often after weeks or months. His arrivals and departures came along with the change of the seasons.

Each season too brought changes for Melisande and Sybilla. Their gowns needed to be lengthened and loosened, new pairs of shoes bought, the humiliation of another loose and lost tooth endured and soothed. Juliana thought about Eleanor, growing up under someone else's care and at those times forced herself to keep the days as routine as religious observance. When hosting the occasional messenger or visitor, she would make certain that guards always remained nearby. Then she would let the girls sit and listen, and later explained and encouraged their questions. Athene, Xene and Madelene took on new tasks, teaching the girls about the wider world they would one day enter.

Despite Kolossi's self-imposed segregation from the rest of the island, everyone knew of the events swirling about in the larger world. News confirmed that Baldwin of Flanders, the captured Emperor of Constantinople, was dead. He died at the hand of the Bulgars' own emperor, although the manner of Baldwin's death remained in dispute. Some insisted that the Bulgars' emperor had Baldwin summarily executed, others that he had ordered Baldwin's legs and arms cut off before throwing the rest of him into a pit. Such news gave Melisande and Sybilla nightmares and Juliana spent the nights with the girls hugging her, one at each side, until they fell asleep.

Further afield, the king of England forsook for the time harassing the lords of Poitou, and devoted his attention instead to harrying his powerful barons, even the punctiliously proper, faithful, and chivalrous William Marshal, the earl of Pembroke. Few doubted that in the end, ill would come from it to King John.

Closer to Kolossi, Walter de Montbéliard's determination to increase his power and to fill his private treasury became quite transparent when a call for aid came from the residents of Satalia, a Greek port on Anatolia's coast.

Caught between the Sultan of Iconium who currently besieged them and an Italian *corsair* with some Greek blood in him who held their town, Satalia's residents, in an epic moment of historical amnesia, called on their Christian neighbors for help. The regent of Cyprus let it be known throughout the island and in the kingdom of Jerusalem that he would take up their cause.

Juliana was therefore not surprised when the regent's messenger arrived with a letter for the lady of Kolossi. At least, Juliana told herself, Walter de Montbéliard acknowledged her possession of the place. That recognition, of course, came with a price.

She opened the message at the table set in the middle of Kolossi's hall where Darius brought her the fief's account books. The steward brought them to her to complain that my lord Lasalle's gifts to the junior ruler of Cyprus were becoming expensive. Juliana agreed with him before it occurred to her that Hugh would most likely bestow the very same gifts on certain of his vassals. Lasalle knew that the loyalty of Hugh's barons had its price.

"I saw the messenger. So, what does Walter want?" She did not hear Lasalle come into the hall until his arm wrapped around her shoulders. He had returned a few days earlier, keeping the men busy and her waking up in a pleasant state of lassitude.

"He calls on Kolossi to furnish him with one knight, five men-at-arms, horses and supplies."

"Hmmm. Let me see."

She folded the message. "No. You're the only knight around here. Are you telling me you'd fight for Walter?"

He held her tighter, his breath on her nape. "But Barlais is going and . . ."

Juliana listened to the names of barons anxious to join Walter de Montbéliard for spoils and glory. Unlike the other times, she was not angry. It was Lasalle's way to approach her. "Walter likes to forget that I am neither his nor Hugh's vassal. I am the abbey's. I don't owe de Montbéliard any men, least of all you."

Lasalle turned her to face his fierce scowl. "Your notorious disobedience is ruining your husband's reputation, Lady Juliana."

She tipped up her chin. "I can be obedient."

The corner of his mouth shot up. "I suppose I'll have to settle for it."

She pressed her hand against his heart. "Your death doesn't serve a purpose."

That night when sleep would not come to either of them, he propped himself on his elbow, fist against his cheek. With his free hand he touched her lips. "Juliana, one day it may serve a purpose."

CHAPTER 67

Autumn 1207

With much noise and enthusiasm, certain Cypriot and Jerusalemite barons joined the regent of Cyprus in his expedition to liberate Satalia. Walter de Montbéliard's invasion drove off the Sultan's forces and with that victory under his belt, Walter decided to add Satalia to his expanding catalogue of possessions. The signs that the regent of Cyprus intended to make his presence permanent caused the Satalians to recover from their amnesia. They called on the very same Sultan to liberate them from the Franks. He happily obliged and Walter de Montbéliard's erstwhile victory became an ignominious retreat.

Upon his return to Cyprus, Walter announced that he had all along intended to restore the port to its residents. Some even believed him. Anxious to recover his reputation and augment his losses, he cast about for other potential pickings–the island of Rhodes. For that he had to amass enough wealth and support and he therefore made moves to negotiate the marriage of his ward to Alice de Champagne, which would ensure the Montbéliards' alliance with her powerful family.

In fact, his own wife's Ibelín kin had already made a move in that direction. John d'Ibelín and his brother Philip sent a letter to the Holy Father reminding him about the pledge of Hugh de Lusignan to Alice de Champagne. Walter did not mind the Ibelíns' overtures. He expected that Hugh's and Alice's marriage would extend his own power and influence into the Holy Land. He would follow in the footsteps of his father-in-law, only this time with more vigorous and profitable results. Nothing, and no one, would interfere with Walter de Montbéliard's rise in the *Levante*, a rise as meteoric as that of his Lusignan and Ibelín in-laws.

To distract those who were not entirely distracted from the Satalian debacle by the matrimonial plans, the regent of Cyprus announced a hunt for the island's elusive mountain sheep.

With all the comforts and convenience of civilization on the backs of pack mules, an army of servants and cooks, horse and hound masters, falconers and fletchers, grooms and blacksmiths, men-at-arms, physicians and their assistants, and all those who liked to surround the regent, and those the regent liked to be surrounded by, took several days to assemble and to travel to the gray-blue ridges of the Troodos.

The party included Hugh the First of Cyprus who rode a caparisoned mule, subjected to the regent's attentions which veered from condescension to unctuousness. Walter brought his ward along to preserve the appearance of harmony between them as well as to remind the lords and knights of the island of the legitimacy of his own rule.

Unfortunately, one of the island's knights came along uninvited and his presence spoiled Walter's mood and threatened to spoil his plans to display his ward's awkwardness and timidity. Those included having Hugh ride a mule, for his own safety, the regent loudly insisted, taking as his own mount the newly acquired, high-spirited Barb.

The party set up several camps along the way to graze the horses and mules. To feed the hungry mouths of men and other beasts, the servants bought sheep along the way or simply herded flocks away from their unhappy shepherds.

The more dedicated hunters continued to the region of the red-coated *agrino* who with their great ridged and spiraled horns reigned over mountain crags and valleys. Only when they came to the lower meadows to graze could they be hunted like ordinary deer. Swift, powerful, sure-footed on dizzying ledges, these beasts could not be brought down from them by hunters with dogs. For that reason, the court brought the leopards.

Sitting on the well-padded rumps of docile mules behind their riders, Zoë and Salomé, sank their claws harmlessly into the quilting, feather-tipped hoods over their heads, their black-striped ears twitching to the sounds, leads attached to their collars. Djalali and Wink kept the cats in their own pavilion, away from the dogs, undisturbed by the hunters who gave the Ethiopian and his lanky, soft-spoken assistant respect not accorded to ordinary servants.

In the early afternoon, the trackers reported finding the quarry. Excitement ran through the camp with the regent of Cyprus first to take up the call.

"Bring the leopards. I call for the leopards! My horse, quickly, you fools!" Walter de Montbéliard shoved aside a servant who had tried to fasten his tabard. He vaulted into the saddle of his rearing, snorting Barb. Eyes rolling, nostrils flared, the horse bolted the moment Walter seized a lance from one of his huntsmen.

Not to be outdone, the others sought their horses, lances, and crossbows. They too charged after the regent deeper into the valley, followed by Djalali and Wink with Zoë and Salomé latched to the cushioned mules, and by the hound masters stumbling along with frenzied dogs straining at their leads.

By the time Hugh's servants put on his leggings, fastened his tabard, and found his belt and hunting knife, the rest of the hunters had disappeared in the undergrowth. When the groom trotted up with Hugh's mule, Hugh was swallowing fury and embarrassment in equal doses. He climbed into the saddle without help to slump there with resignation. "We'll miss the sheep," he said to the man who came up to his side.

Lasalle tossed away the remains of a roasted lamb's rib and wiped his hands on his tabard. "The race may not be to the swift nor the battle to the strong, but one can trust that time and chance will favor my lord's favorite leopards."

Hugh's disappointment transformed into curiosity. "It will?"

Instead of a reply, his father's distant cousin winked at him and climbed into the saddle of the long-eared jenny a groom brought to him.

Hugh frowned at first, and then, understanding dawning on him, he laughed. Keeping his mule next to his companion, they rode without hurry after the sound of the hounds.

Left behind, the grooms watched the tails of the two mules disappear in the greenery. "What did he say about the leopards?" said one man to the other.

"I don't know. Something about a battle. I had my hands full of the regent's horse. Something must have frightened him."

"Maybe the leopards, eh? I told the keeper's boy to stay away from the horses. They can smell the cats on him. I wouldn't get near them myself." The young man who minded the king's mule gave his comrade a slap on the side of his head and laughing, sauntered away.

The remaining groom scratched his head. No, there had to be more to it than that.

The rock-strewn valley floor took care of a couple of the hunters overcome by chase fever. Lasalle and Hugh passed them, not offering help to catch their horses or to assist with the riders' likely broken bones. Their grooms would find them. In the next bend of the valley, Lasalle held back his mule.

The surviving hunters had gathered at the base of the mountain, pointing to its heights. A half dozen red sheep threaded a sliver of a path suspended over a sheer rock face, broken here and there by shrubs and trees sprouted in invisible crevices.

From Walter de Montbéliard's gestures, one could tell that he was ordering Djalali to unleash the leopards, orders which, without the king's presence, Djalali was refusing to obey. Hugh stood up in the stirrups, shaking with agitation. "Walter can't use my leopards. They are mine. They are the king's leopards!"

Lasalle scratched his jenny's ear. "There is the chance that chance will favor the king's leopards, my lord. Shall we wait and find out?"

Hugh dropped back in the saddle. "Find out what?'

A burst of shouts from the regent's party prevented Lasalle's answer. Walter de Montbéliard spurred his horse at Wink, his riding crop striking the boy again and again, driving Wink to the ground.

Djalali tore off the leopards' hoods and unhooked their leads from their collars.

Zoë and Salomé bounded up the rock wall, silent, sinuous, and sure-footed. Sighting the spotted flashes hurtling toward them, the sheep took to flight, zigzagging from one barely existing foothold to another, their white legs and underbelly flashing.

Walter de Montbéliard dropped his riding crops and his interest in Wink. "After them, after them!"

By the time Lasalle and Hugh rode up to Djalali and Wink, Djalali had Wink on his feet. Blood streamed from Wink's cheek. At their approach, Djalali dropped to one knee. "I not want to let the leopards, my lord–"

"I know." Hugh reached for his hunting knife and after several attempts slashed away a piece from the bottom of his shirt. He handed the strip to Wink. "Here. You're my keepers. When I am free, he'll never use my leopards, never."

Lasalle tossed to Djalali his wine skin. "I'd say that after today, my lord, your brother-in-law may not ever want to come near your leopards."

Hugh managed to sheath his knife. "Why not?"

From the end of the valley came terrified sounds. Lasalle smiled at Hugh. "I think we will find out."

They came upon a scene which later its witnesses would all describe as chaotic, agreeing only on a few points. The first being that one of the leopards had been distracted and diverted from the sheep which she and her sister had driven to the hunters in the valley's cul-de-sac. There, with her kind's celebrated speed, the leopardess–either Zoë or Salomé–sprung at the regent before he could think to raise his hunting lance let alone reach for his dagger. The attack brought down the regent's terrified Barb with Walter de Montbéliard still in the saddle, although differences of opinion continued about whether the horse was unaccountably unruly before or after the hunt.

All agreed however on the most astonishing part. The young king, having arrived at the scene moments later with the leopards' keepers, had personally and calmly approached the cat crouched over the regent and lured the leopard away from her human prey so that the keepers could hood and leash her and her sister. The regent had thus suffered the indignity of having his royal ward save his life, while his ward returned from the *agrino* hunt without a single ewe or ram, but with accolades and admiration heaped upon him instead in compensation.

In all the excitement, no one had noticed that the former Lord of Colos had prompted the regent's horse to its feet and calmed it enough to strip off its saddle. He made no mention to anyone either that someone had packed the gullet of the regent's saddle with fresh sheep's liver.

CHAPTER 68

Summer 1210

The news of Hugh de Lusignan's bravery surprised those who did not know him, and only confirmed the impressions of those who had come to know him. Hugh the First of Cyprus would not be weak and vacillating king, but his father's son. Being forced to live in the shadow of his overbearing brother-in-law, Hugh had learned to bide his time and to cultivate those who would stand by him.

In Nikosia, many of the barons who first adhered to Walter de Montbéliard began to shift their allegiance to Hugh and he openly favored their company. Time was, after all, on Hugh's side, transforming him into a young man who would never shed his stockiness, but who had his father's bearing if not all of his height, as well as those light blue eyes that could shoot an icy glance, and a head of sun-bright hair. He grew into a quick wit, with an equally quick temper for those whose attitude he found patronizing.

With the two young people who had inherited the crowns of Cyprus and Jerusalem approaching maturity, matrimonial matters in the *Levante* reached their apogee. The barons of *outremer* had sent a delegation to King Philip Augustus of France to select one of his own vassals to be *La Marquise's* husband. King Phillip chose John de Brienne, a man of no particular wealth or renown but of considerable vigor, and the king and the Holy Father remedied de Brienne's shortcomings in the former area by generous gifts.

Since John de Brienne was Walter de Montbéliard's cousin, the choice greatly pleased the regent of Cyprus. With the anticipated papal dispensation, Hugh de Lusignan would finally marry Alice of Champagne as well.

All of that came to Juliana from visitors to Kolossi and from Lasalle's reports, personally and privately delivered. She knew that much of what he told her about Hugh was the product of his own influence, but he did not speak of it.

She thought at those times that Lasalle had been more of a father to Hugh than Aimary could have been, and she now said it.

They had ridden to the shore of the bay at Akrotiri with Sybilla and Melisande, both of them excited by the flocks of long-legged, pink-winged birds gliding into the waters of a briny shore lake they passed. They brought no guards this time only grooms, since Hugh's approaching marriage and majority made a threat from Walter de Montbéliard unlikely. At the sea shore, Sybilla and Melisande ran back and forth trying to chase after gulls, becoming instead distracted by turtles buried in the sand.

The children had grown, now almost eleven and twelve years old. They would be betrothed soon. Hopefully their brother would not give them to husbands they despised. Burgundia's last message said that Heloise had given birth to Odo's son. Had Heloise reconciled herself to her marriage? Such reconciliation was not needed to bear a child. She knew it herself. Juliana shivered and crossed herself. She wanted to protect Sybilla and Melisande and yet she knew that she could not.

Lasalle picked up a couple of shells and threw them into the waves. "You are more of a mother to those two than Isabella could have been."

Juliana let a handful of sand escape between her fingers. "I am not their mother. They know that. I can't give them her presence."

Hugh's approaching marriage and majority would free Lasalle and bring her–bring them–back to Eleanor. And yet, at the thought of leaving Sybilla and Melisande, she felt the same pain that seized her when Eleanor was taken from her. *No. When she had allowed Eleanor to be taken from her.*

She brushed away the sand. Her hands were brown and her fingernails blunt from her garden beds. She had changed. Grown older, wiser in some ways. She thought about Aimary and Abbess Mathilde. They were both right. She had found her way here, on the island of Aphrodite, in more ways than she ever expected. This part of her journey would end. And then . . .

He hooked his arms around her shoulders. "You gave them more than that."

She leaned against him. "What?"

"You gave them of yourself."

"Then we both did. Do you think Eleanor will forgive us?"

"Never."

Juliana wished she could laugh at his dogmatic answer but she did not know whether he meant it in jest or earnest and she did not ask. Surrounded by his embrace and the sounds of the sea, she stood there saying nothing and he did not speak for a long time either.

"John is excommunicated."

Yes, the news of King John's excommunication had reached Cyprus and the Holy Land. The Holy Father had asserted his authority over his earthly vassals. *What does a marriage make?* "Does that mean John will leave Poitou alone?"

"For the time, I imagine. We won't find out until we get…home."

She heard a tentative question in his voice and she answered it. "I imagine that the Holy Father won't be launching enquiries into Lusignan marriages any time soon. You don't have to kill Geoffrey for it anymore."

He held his breath for a moment. "He said that he would–"

"I know. Reginald confessed. It doesn't matter. I think Geoffrey knows that if he tried to work on you on account of our marriage or our daughter, I'd kill him myself. I am quite good with daggers, you know."

His arms tightened around her, his voice low in her ear. "So I noticed. Why, Lady Juliana, you'd commit murder?"

"Vigilantia said, 'who would reproach a mother for protecting her child?'" She did not say the rest of what Vigilantia told her. It did not matter. "Or her husband."

He inhaled. "I promised Vigilantia that I would kill Rhoxsane. Only I can't find her. Walter and . . . and John d'Ibelín might be right. She could be already dead."

If he still expected her to recoil in horror from him, she disappointed him. "I see. God's justice then. I feel sorry for her daughters. She did it for them, I'd like to think. Walter must have promised to return them to her. Odd, isn't it?"

She touched the neckline of her gown, not the place where a tiny scar remained etched in her flesh, but where she had stitched a small pouch with tiny braids of fine black hair, no longer reddish fuzz. Those came by Abbess Vigilantia from nuns who arrived to join Saint Mary's of Tyre in Nikosia. She had four such strands, and she did not intend to stay on Cyprus long enough to receive a fifth one.

"Hmm. We're invited to Hugh's wedding. Ordered, in fact."

He released her and walked toward the girls. Juliana watched him, wondering if he had changed too, not as much in appearance, although she saw a few white hairs by his brows, and a few more fine lines by his eyes. Over his shirt he wore a black Saracen *qaba* that went to his knees with a wide, striped sash and a linked leather belt wound twice about him to hold behind his back the ubiquitous poniard.

He left his sword with the groom who mindfully led along the grey turcoman. Lasalle usually rode it wherever he could, but this time he walked across the shifting sand with long, easy strides, turning his head occasionally to the wind to get his hair out of his eyes, the silver circle of his earring glinting in the sun.

He was a deposed Byzantine prince and a Saracen, all wrapped into one.

Melisande ran up to him, a handful of pink feathers in her fist. She took hold of his hand and dragged him along with excited urging to show him something in a shallow pool. Curious, Sybilla joined them and the three stood, heads bent, around Melisande's discovery.

Juliana imagined them discussing it with some gravity when he suddenly scooped up the thing in the pool to spook Sybilla with it. The usually reserved girl shrieked and ran, bursting into laughter after several paces. Juliana heard Lasalle laugh too and with the long-tentacled thing in his hand pretend to chase after her, egged on by Melisande choking with glee and forgetting all about her feathers. After chasing Sybilla for a short distance, Lasalle stopped and let Melisande, practically levitating with levity, snatch that thing from him and continue along the shore after her sister.

Lasalle turned back to seek her out, his teeth in a flash of pure and utter mischief. Palms up, he gave her shrug, half guilt, half innocence. Juliana stood there and knew with unshakable certainty that as long as she lived, she will not let any earthly power separate her from her husband.

She picked up her skirts and ran to him.

August 1210

John de Brienne arrived in Acre. Still a number of years short of forty, Brienne appeared to the welcoming crowd an acceptable candidate for their king, although his personal purse still had not impressed all of the Jerusalemite barons. Seeing her husband-to-be for the first time, *La Marquise* appeared much more pleased than her barons which they tolerantly ascribed to the romantic notions of their seventeen-year-old queen.

Shortly after John de Brienne landed in Acre, John and Philip d'Ibelín arrived in Cyprus, bringing with them in a grand flotilla Hugh de Lusignan's bride. Although Alice de Champagne was Hugh's stepsister, the Holy Father gave his blessing to the union. Political considerations trumped religious prescriptions which the Holy Father, after all, had the power to waive.

In Limassol, the groom, the High Court, emissaries, ambassadors, lords spiritual and secular waited under canopies that draped the harbor to catch the first glimpse of the bride. Packed shoulder to shoulder, spectators of lesser ranks clung to rooftops, harbor walls, and the newly patched fortifications, garlanded in the blue, gold, and silver colors of the royal couple.

The sight of the principal galley astonished all spectators. As it neared Limassol, a great cheer went up at the sight of its crimson sails with a *croix pattée gules,* the crest of the lords of d'Ibelín. Coming closer, gasps of astonishment from even the most jaded onlookers greeted the ship painted from forecastle to sterncastle in gold and blood-red, rows of shields of the same color hanging from its sides like fish scales. To approach the harbor, three hundred gold oars emerged from the ship's belly to cleave the waters.

The Ibelíns intended to outdo the king of Jerusalem in a display of their wealth and power on Cyprus.

High-prowed barges propelled by oarsmen dressed in the livery of her husband-to-be sped to bring the bride and her immediate company from the ships that settled at anchor outside the harbor.

To the sound of drums and trumpets, the most garlanded barge returned to the quay. A figure in white and gold sat in the stern, surrounded by her principal ladies, her confessor, her stewards, her chamberlain and her clerks. Smaller barges collected the rest of her women who had unpacked their gowns, creased from the sea voyage, like their wearers.

The fifteen-year-old daughter of Henri de Champagne appeared unwrinkled and unsubdued by the journey, the first sight of the land over which she would rule, or by her husband-to-be. Her light brown hair spread on her sleeveless damask robe, sable fur at the garment's openings. Alternating bands of blue and gold, the colors of her father's land, formed the hem of her gown of radiant blue silk, the color of her husband's family.

Without hesitation or being hampered by sea legs, Alice de Champagne walked up the flower-strewn path to her future husband and curtsied to him with a coquettish lowering of her eyes. Forgetting to bow, Hugh de Lusignan stepped toward her and nearly tripped. He reached out and the girl gripped his hand, steadying him.

"Come on, Hugh," said the future queen of Cyprus, "let's not keep the bishop waiting."

Nikosia

The celebrations of the nuptials of Hugh de Lusignan and Alice de Champagne eclipsed the festivities of Walter de Montbéliard's regency. Few knew that Hugh had borrowed heavily to pay for his own wedding.

Burgundia's page found Juliana in the crowd and she gladly extricated herself from the company of Hugh's supporters. They had turned out in force, openly and loudly declaring their loyalty to their liege lord, anticipating Hugh's fifteenth birthday in a few days and the end of his brother-in-law's regency.

Juliana had delivered Melisande and Sybilla to Burgundia's care a few days previously. Brought up in the freedom of Kolossi, she worried about how the two would fare in their brother's court, but Athene's exacting lessons and her own occasional instructions had instilled in the girls composure and comportment surpassed only by their own natural grace. Juliana prayed that Heloise would come from Acre as well, but did not see her or her husband in the cathedral or in the crowd.

In Burgundia's apartments, she found two men. The tall one with the black eyes she recognized immediately. The second, a younger one, she did not know but he bore a resemblance to the Lord of Beirut.

John d'Ibelín came toward her with an outstretched hand, took hers and kissed it before she could curtsey. "Lady Juliana. Thank you for your care and kindness to my nieces. May I present my brother Philip?"

The second son of Maria Komnene's four children gave her an enthusiastic bow. "I have heard much about you, Lady Juliana.

"I am glad that you had a safe journey from Champagne, my lords," Juliana said cautiously. "I don't ever recall such magnificent ships."

"The Countess of Champagne bribed us," Phillip admitted cheerfully. "Blanche wanted us to take Alice away so that she would not press her claim to her father's inheritance. I wouldn't bet on that, but the money was too good to pass up, wasn't it, John?"

John d'Ibelín opted for more discretion than his younger brother. "We're returning to Acre for Maria's wedding. Of course we will keep an eye on the welfare of both of our nieces."

"Of course you will, John. Blanche's bribes will be well spent to remind de Brienne." Burgundia entered, holding by her side a four-year-old girl with cherubim's ringlets of fair hair. Seeing the strangers in the room, the child stuck her thumb in her mouth and buried her face in her mother's skirts.

Burgundia meant her words to tease her cousins, but she also spoke the truth. John d'Ibelín had carried out the duties of his regency with skill and diligence and he had enriched himself and his family without alienating the barons of *outre-mer*.

"Still, you must be relieved to relinquish the regency, my lord," Juliana said.

"I am. Our mother is far less so, but she will have to learn to live with it, like Walter, won't she?" John d'Ibelín turned to Burgundia.

Burgundia held her daughter closer. "Walter is already packing what he can. I can't prevent it."

Something swirled about the corridors of Nikosia besides the noise of drunken celebrants. Juliana gathered that the invitation to Burgundia's chambers had something to do with it. Burgundia took the child's hand and gently urged the girl toward Juliana. "Civa. This is Lady Juliana. She is a very good friend and we will miss her very much. What do you say?"

"Yooliana." Eschiva de Montbéliard gave Juliana a shy smile and after attempting a curtsey buried her face back in her mother's skirts.

Juliana wanted to hug the little girl, so shy and timid and sweet-tempered, so attached to her mother. Eleanor would be older than Eschiva, and surely as lovely and gentle a child.

"Do we have your husband's promise, Lady Juliana? Lady Juliana?"

John d'Ibelín was speaking to her. Juliana had not heard him. Her mind had led her away, far away. "I . . . what promise?"

"That my lord Lasalle won't seize my husband or do him any harm when he relinquishes the regency."

Juliana stared at Burgundia de Lusignan. In this very chamber she had promised that she would prevail upon Lasalle not to do harm to Walter de Montbéliard. Lasalle had kept her promise. Now that Walter's regency was ending, Burgundia would for certain take her own advice to Heloise and repudiate her husband.

"I am asking you not for Walter or myself." Burgundia's voice carried the gentle firmness that Juliana had so many times found admirable. "I don't want my daughter to grow up without her father. Walter loves her. He cannot do more harm. He knows it."

Phillip d'Ibelín shrugged like a man who accepts small inconveniences. "Oh, we'd gladly ... keep after him, wouldn't we, John?" he amended his words.

"Gladly. But Civa likes him." John d'Ibelín picked up the child, hoisting her easily. The girl, losing her shyness, laughed with delight.

Juliana returned to the banquet, her head swimming with confusion. Lasalle was not a man to forgive or forget what Walter de Montbéliard had done.

"Lady Juliana? May I have your audience?"

The voice did not sound familiar and neither did the speaker; slightly stooped, dressed well enough but with certain carelessness to appearance.

"Odo de Dampierre," said the man.

So it was. Walter de Montbéliard's brash young nephew who had conspired with his uncle to seize the regency of Cyprus for the hand of Heloise de Lusignan. The years changed him. The lines of his face had hardened, not from a natural bend of personality, but from a private burden. A fear that something had happened to Heloise gripped Juliana and her glance quickly swept over the rest of the gathering without acknowledging him.

"She is not here," Odo said, and when Juliana came back to stare at him in even greater alarm, he shook his head. "She . . . she left me. Rupen took her. He kidnapped her."

Juliana did not know whether to show relief or sympathy. "I see."

"I . . . I tried to make her happy. She was, I thought."

Heloise de Lusignan had not been kidnapped. She left her husband of her own free will just as her brother was becoming the king of Cyprus in his own right, just as her sister Burgundia had counseled her. Heloise knew that Hugh would stand by her, not appreciating that his own sister, a princess of Cyprus, was handed to the nephew of the man who had squandered his estates' revenues, and who had pinched coins for his household. Odo de Dampierre knew that Heloise left him for the Prince of Antioch of her own free will. Odo could not bring himself to accept it, to live with his own humiliation.

"I see." What did Odo de Dampierre want from her?

"I wrote to the Holy Father to make Rupen return her to me."

"Yes. I see." Juliana could not think of anything else. Heloise would never return to her husband. She had followed her heart and did not care about pledges or vows, before God or despite Him.

"She . . . she often spoke of you. And of the books. I bought her books. I know my uncle had settled it all so quickly. I wish that I had not . . . those were difficult times, Lady Juliana. I wish now that I had more time to tell her that I would try to make her happy. Did she say anything to you then about . . . about our marriage?"

Despite herself, she felt pity for a man in love with a wife who did not love him and did not care that he did. "Yes. I recall . . . I recall quite clearly. She said that she was glad that you were not old. Or ugly. She liked your gift. Very much. A comb, wasn't it?"

The pain in Odo's eyes eased. "Did she? We . . . we used to laugh about it." He looked away, embarrassed.

Juliana tucked her chin. If Odo spoke the truth, Heloise's marriage to him was not an unbearable burden, despite her decision to leave it. That decision she had made a long time before Odo de Dampierre ever set eyes on her.

"Juliana?"

Her name startled her even though she knew that voice. The smile on Lasalle's face went away when he reached her.

Odo de Dampierre's hand went to his sword hilt, but instantly slipped from it. He backed away from her and bowed to Lasalle. "My lord de Lusignan. Forgive me for detaining your wife. It wasn't my intention to . . . to–"

Lasalle held out his hand to Juliana. "You're forgiven, sir. This time."

Juliana accepted the offered hand and with Lasalle steering her into the festive crowd, she reached out with the other to touch Odo de Dampierre's arm. "I am certain the Holy Father will hear your appeal, my lord. Sometimes . . . sometimes it takes time for us to find out where our hearts truly belong."

She kept her eyes ahead, her heart pounding. "You have no idea who that was, do you?"

Lasalle nodded in acknowledgement to those who greeted him. "Walter's nephew. His wife left him for a better lover. What did Burgundia want?"

"For you not to harm her husband."

"I wouldn't dream of it."

CHAPTER 69

September 1210

The month brought eventful changes to the *Levante.*

The truce with the Musulmans that Aimary de Lusignan had negotiated expired and the future relations between the Latins and the Saracens remained uncertain. On September 4, John de Brienne and Maria de Montferrat were married and travelled to Tyre to be crowned there the following month. Hugh the First of Cyprus reached his majority which ended the wardship of his person as well as his brother-in-law's regency of his kingdom.

Juliana spent the dizzying days tidying up all the frayed, lose ends of her years on Cyprus, suddenly torn between the urge to leave it all and take to the nearest ship, and wishing for more time for make her peace with this place. She found Father Silbo and made her confession of her most egregious sins of omission and commission. Distracted by the prospect of his pupil's new duties and responsibilities, Father Silbo gave her a light penance.

At Burgundia's earnest request, Juliana and Athene became part of the new queen's household. Alice de Champagne took to her duties as wife and queen with eagerness and self-confidence. She found her husband to her liking and she did not hesitate to prompt him to assert his–and their–prerogatives. The extent and nature of those prerogatives unfolded behind closed doors of Hugh's private chamber where Lasalle spent the days with the king's leading liegemen, including Barlais, Rivet, and Saissons, but without the presence of Walter de Montbéliard.

The regent's wife and her Ibelín cousins might have been in accord about her husband's future, but his former ward and the High Court were not. Hugh's allies, long chaffing under de Montbéliard's regency, did not intend to forgive him.

In the very same great hall where almost five years ago Juliana had stood in face paint and her stiff and splendid gown to defend the rights of her husband, now gathered the members of the High Court of Cyprus. Just like she did the last time, Juliana found the hall suffocating from the tension in the very air.

She did not see Burgundia among Alice de Champagne's ladies. Neither did she see Sybilla and Melisande. They ought to have been there to witness their brother formally assume the governance of his kingdom. Although Hugh, like his father, would govern with the advice of his council, this time the council consisted entirely of his father's old and Hugh's own new allies. It was an alliance Lasalle had cultivated during the time he spent away from her by judicious bribes, the reputation of his pedigree, and the force of his own character.

This time Hugh of Cyprus sat in his throne wearing a cloak that fit his stature, a cap over his neatly trimmed hair on which a crown would be placed in a few days. He surveyed the crowd with a stern gaze. Next to him sat his wife, a coronet of wrought gold on her brow, her hair now in a single long braid barely hidden by a veil of translucent silk. Alice's gown of dark blue satin came with sleeves with silver chevrons. Her glances in her husband's direction were full of pride and encouraging care.

Only one man stood behind Hugh's chair; the leopard-keeper Djalali outfitted in a green tunic with a wide sash of blue and red, a jeweled color around his neck, the white of his eyes brilliant his dark face. On one of the steps to the dais, wearing the same colors, his apprentice took a casual repose. The young man held the leads attached to collars of two leopards. Zoë and Salomé stretched out at Hugh's feet, their eyes unblinking in their lazy survey of the crowd.

Whatever doubt and regret had weighed on Juliana since her arrival on this land lifted away from her. Hugh de Lusignan and

Alice de Champagne would pass on the blood of the Lusignans and the Ibelíns and of Aliénor of Aquitaine to the future generations in the *Levante.*

Abbess Mathilde was right. The *Pantokrator* meant to bring her to this island, to this moment.

"My lord, I am pleased to return this collar to you and I relinquish the office of your kingdom's regent. I have performed my duties with the advice of your council until this very moment when you have come into your father's inheritance." Keeping a respectful distance from the leopards, Walter de Montbéliard removed from his shoulders the gold links of his chain of office and placed it *Sekretikos* Niketas's hands.

Niketas bowed to Walter to Montbéliard and carried the chain to Hugh as if it were a holy relic, expecting Hugh to accept it back into his hands. Hugh's sharp nod told Niketas to place the thing at his feet, next to the leopards. Niketas hesitated, then gingerly laid the links there and backed away with some haste. A sigh of expectation ran through the gathering.

Juliana stood with the queen's women, counting the faces of the barons arrayed before the dais. There was Lasalle, narrow-eyed, half-listening to a gloating Renaud Barlais mouth something in his ear.

This was not going to be formal relinquishment of Walter de Montbéliard's power. This was going to be his defeat. That was why Burgundia had not presented herself and neither did she allow her sisters to be present. She may have allowed her husband to share her bed, but she would not share his humiliation.

Walter took a breath, perhaps to object to the obvious insult, perhaps to redeem it by praising his own accomplishments. He did not get a chance.

"And I, my lord de Montbéliard, wish you to return to us the rest of my father's inheritance and to recompense myself and the queen . . ." Hugh smiled at his wife, "for the unwarranted expenditures to my household you forced me to make."

The hall went silent. Those were not the words of a child-king, these were the words of a young man who had just become king.

"My . . . my lord king," Walter searched for an ally among the crowd. This time, he met hard, unforgiving faces. This time there was no Odo de Dampierre to come to his aid. Realizing his fall from grace and power, Walter quickly bowed. "Yes, Sire. Of course. May I be allowed a day to prepare a full accounting of your father's treasury?"

King Hugh tapped his foot. "We have a full accounting of my father's treasury. Two hundred thousand white *besants.* I was forced to spend forty thousand more on my household under your regency. You are allowed until tomorrow to return that amount to us."

A wave of excitement shot with laughter spread through the crowd.

"Of course, my lord. Of course. I remain your faithful vassal." Walter de Montbéliard bowed twice more and backed from the dais, the crowd clearing a path for him. He cast a murderous glance at *Sekretikos* Niketas, who gave him a prodigious bow.

And that was the last time anyone saw the former regent of Cyprus on Cyprus.

The following day, instead keeping the appointed hour of reckoning with his king, Walter de Montbéliard packed up his wife and daughter and as much of his household's furnishings and silver and gold as his horses and mules could carry, and fled to Gastria, to the safety of the Temple's fortress. From there, he and his family took a ship to Acre, to be welcomed with open arms by his cousin the king of Jerusalem and his blushing bride.

With the preparations for Hugh's and Alice's coronation at the cathedral of Saint Sophia, the *affaire de Montbéliard* fell temporarily from public attention if not from his former ward's mind, now styling himself *Hugues de Lusignano, rex Cipri.*

Other affairs, however, did claim Hugh's attention.

Ignoring the existence of his sister Heloise's current husband, Hugh the First of Cyprus gave his consent to Heloise's marriage to Prince Rupen of Antioch. At the same time, Hugh arranged the marriage for Sybilla to take place early in the new year to King

Leo of Armenia, the maternal uncle of Heloise's new husband. These two marriages represented an alliance for the current convenience of all parties. Twelve-year-old Sybilla would become queen of Armenia by her marriage to a husband of sixty.

Juliana took in all these news with regret and resignation. She could not influence these decisions or events so she prayed that Sybilla would find her own path in her new home and took some refuge in knowing that Sybilla was after all a Lusignan. And an Ibelín.

These diplomatic maneuvers clogged the harbors of Cyprus and Acre and delayed the departure of ships from their shores. Vessels that had managed to depart were crowded with pilgrims, dignitaries, and officials of all stripes. With the sailing season drawing to a close, fear seized Juliana that their own departure from Cyprus would be delayed until the spring. She could not bear another delay; she'd rather travel overland than be separated from Eleanor another day.

She went to Saint Mary's. Through the barely opened wicket the gate mistress told her, with some self-satisfaction, that the abbess would not admit into her presence either her or my lord Jean Armand de Lusignan. "The Reverend Mother wishes him to know that he's free of his vow to her," were the nun's departing words.

"But sister—" The wicket slammed shut.

"We've been banned by Saint Mary's," she told Lasalle in the privacy of their chamber at Barlais's residence.

Lasalle stood by the window. A storm was gathering over the range of the mountains. Lightning struck the peaks with the roar of thunder. Rain began to pelt the roof. "Why would she release me from my vow? I wanted to tell her that I failed to kill Rhoxsane."

Juliana came to him. "I don't know. Maybe she didn't want Rhoxsane's death on your conscience. She won, I suppose. She has Rhoxsane's daughters. And Kolossi. And her own flock. I wanted to tell her . . . I don't know what. Thank her. Or berate her. Which one do you think would be appropriate?"

He latched the shutters. "Both, don't you think?"

He made her smile despite herself, and then she said, "We have to leave even if Hugh won't give you leave yet. I can't remain here another day. I–I won't."

"What about your own flock, Sister Eustace?"

"Madelena will go with Sybilla when she marries. And Xene with Melisande. They all have been together through so much."

"Hmm. What about Athene?"

"She'd do well at Alice's court, don't you think? Compared to Acre and Nikosia, we at Parthenay are barbarians to her. Can you imagine Beraud yielding to Athene on anything or she to him? We'd have a war on our hands."

"What about Wink?"

"You've seen him. I don't think we can afford to feed the leopards."

He laughed. "You are an eminently practical woman, Lady Juliana."

The storms washed over the island, nearly drowning its capital in a red torrent of the Pedieos that swept away houses, gardens, and markets. When the deluge passed, terrified and soggy residents emerged to rescue the victims of the storm and to clear the debris and the bodies of dead horses, mules, donkeys, dogs, pigs, poultry and the occasional humans.

With the women of the city, Juliana and Athene rushed to the remaining churches filled with the homeless, orphaned, and the injured. Among the groans, cries, and confusion, Athene touched Juliana's hand to draw her attention from bandaging a man's head wound.

"My lady."

Juliana looked up. Lasalle stood at the doorway amidst people streaming in and out of the chapel. He held the reins of the two horses, saddlebags and rolls across the cantles.

Athene said no more and Juliana saw tears in the woman's eyes and knew that there were tears in hers. Athene nodded and that single gesture granted Juliana release not only from her current task, but from all that she had done, and left undone, on this island.

She looked back from the saddle where Lasalle had lifted her and saw Athene moving along the nave, giving directions and comfort and care, an uncrowned queen among women.

They rode through the mud and along ruined pathways, soaked to the skin with nothing more to sustain them than the cloaks and the food Lasalle had packed, and the kindness of the monks' hostels along the way. The sun returned just as they reached Limassol. The town had escaped the floods, but the fierce storms did not spare the harbor.

Not far from the shore, two ships lay on their sides, great gashes in their hulls, the masts broken, torn sails caught on the jumble of rigging. Loaded with loot, barges ferried men back and forth from the wrecks. A throng pillaged the wares and customs houses. There would not be a ship leaving from this harbor for Marseille, not this season.

"Bloody hell." Lasalle dismounted and took hold of her horse's headstall. Juliana forced herself from the saddle. In the still storm-charged air hung fear and violence yet to be unleashed. Juliana imagined that they must have looked like any other refugees, yet their horses, worn as they were, would be a prize to the crowd. Moreover, there were coins in their bedrolls, their passage money. Her knees buckled. One hand on his sword hilt, Lasalle held her up with the other. "I am sorry. We are late."

"You are more than on time, my lord," said a deep, accented voice behind them.

They turned, Lasalle's sword half unsheathed. The man moved back, hands raised. "I come on my lord's orders, sir."

Juliana did not know him; broad-shouldered, thick set, well dressed, his brown hair curling like a sheep's pelt.

"Martianus."

That was the only word Lasalle said. He let his sword slide back in the scabbard, and the man bowed to him and to Juliana, and his calloused hand swept toward the curving line of the coast. A galley drew toward Limassol's wrecked harbor.

It was a galley painted from forecastle to sterncastle in gold and red, shields of the same colors hanging from its sides like fish scales, sails of crimson cloth with a *croix pattée gules* filled by the wind and propelled by three hundred oars, also painted in gold.

Saint Jean d'Acre
The Headquarters of Poor Fellow-Soldiers of Christ

The Grand Master was not pleased to be detained just as he and several of the brother-knights were about to leave for Tyre to witness the coronation of John de Brienne and Maria de Montferrat.

Philip de Plessis left the company to wait in the courtyard and returned to his private chamber. Outside the door, Brother Reginald, looking sheepish, stood guard. In fact, Brother Reginald looked rather sheepish lately. De Plessis almost crossed himself. There was whiff of scandal in the golden air of Acre's autumn.

He shut the door and folded back his cloak to sit on the edge of the only chair in the room. Considering the kneeling supplicant waiting for him, de Plessis thought it better to hear this first before summoning the brothers.

"What is so urgent that you wish to confess now, Brother?"

"I killed a woman."

De Plessis waited, not so much from the shock of the bald confession as from the possible implications of it. "Was she a Christian?"

"She thought she was."

"Was she high-born? Have you broken your vows with this woman?"

"No."

De Plessis took a grain of comfort in that answer. "Was it an accident?"

"No."

The grain of comfort became a speck. "Did anyone witness it?"

"Only God."

Philip de Plessis sighed. "Do you intend to accuse yourself of this crime in the chapters when we return from Tyre, Brother?"

"Yes."

"You know what the brothers' verdict could be. The disgrace this could bring upon us?"

"Yes. That is why I ask to be granted release from my vows."

The proposal did not surprise de Plessis either, considering who had offered it and the circumstances. He therefore made his next words a proposition, not a question. "In exchange for not confessing your sins to us."

"Yes."

Philip de Plessis clasped his hands and leaned his elbows on his knees. A Lusignan sat on the throne of Cyprus. Jerusalem was about to crown a new king, albeit in exile. Walter de Montbéliard had become a refugee under his cousin's roof in Acre. With the Ibelíns keeping an eye on both kingdoms, perhaps now God would look more kindly on the affairs of men on these shores, at least for a time. "Are you not worried for your soul, Brother Geoffrey?"

Brother Geoffrey de Lusignan raised his head, in his troublingly blue eyes pride and purpose. "I never was."

CHAPTER 70

The Fortress of Parthenay, Poitou
Late Autumn 1210

Switch in hand and with the boundless energy of all six-year-olds, the child chased the ducks out of the pond. Her black hair as thick as kitchen broom curled about her face, her stockings drooped, mud and burrs stuck to them and to the hem of her apron which did little to spare her very expensive gown.

Her nurse tried to catch the errant creature, but the child, laughing gleefully, zigzagged among the frightened poultry—and ran straight into a man who stepped from behind the trunk of one of the pond willows.

The child dropped the switch and jumped back, her fright transformed into an angry scowl. She looked about. Her guards stood in attention not far away, making no effort to remove the intruder. Her grandfather said the guards had to go with her everywhere because King John was coming here to take Parthenay away from her. She did not know this king and she did not believe it. "You can't be here," she declared with juvenile majesty. "This is mine."

"Not yet. Don't chase the ducks like that. They don't like it."

Her mouth a horse-shoe of defiance, the child picked up the switch and pointed to the pond created by a crystal clear source issuing from the depths of the rocks. "Lady Mélusine doesn't like them. They foul the water."

There was a look of genuine surprise on the man's face, and then he slowly smiled. "That's why they are called fowl."

The girl's scowl became resentment itself as the suspicion dawned on her that the strange man with black hair and green eyes was making fun of her. The servants did not make fun of her, least of all her guards. She did not know what gave this man the right to do that. She was going to make fun of his voice, a rather odd one, but something told her not to. She would tell Pontia and grandfather, and he would have him dismissed. "I don't like you."

"I can tell."

She looked up at him with eyes as blue as Mary's robe and smeared the mud on her cheek with the back of her hand. Something about that man made her feel very odd. She looked around for Pontia. Pontia stood there as well, her hands over her mouth, her eyes as huge as if she saw the water fairy climb out of the spring. Pontia said that the Lady sat by her bed every night while she slept. Her true mother had sent the Lady to watch over her, and at Lauds the Lady slipped back into the spring. That's why she kept the ducks away. To make the Lady come back. And her true mother.

Now there was another lady standing next to Pontia. She did not look like a servant. Her gown was strange, her headrail did not look like anything from the weavers' looms. The lady was looking at her with eyes as big as Pontia's, like someone who had lost something precious and then found it again. Perhaps that's why she and the man came to Parthenay. They looked like they belonged together. They must have come to see the Lady.

"Eleanor," the strange lady said.

Eleanor of Parthenay started at her name so freely used, with such tenderness and possessiveness that it confused and frightened her. And filled her at the same time with the wildest excitement ever, even bigger than when grandfather brought her and Pontia from the sisters to Parthenay, and told her that this place belonged to her, and Lady Mélusine.

Her steps hesitant, she approached the lady and reached for her hand. "If you want to see the Lady, you have to come with me and be very quiet."

The lady took her hand ever so gently, and looked back at the man. Eleanor sighed with resigned exasperation. Yes, they looked like they belonged together. "Very well. If you want him to, he can come with us."

The lady smiled at her and at the man and held out her free hand to him and he took it. "Yes," she said. "Always."

EPILOGUE

Across the Alps, in the City of the Romans renowned for its holiness and whores, legate Pandulf ordered his servants to pack his bags. The Holy Father charged him with bringing to heel England's king for violating the prerogatives of the Church and ignoring his excommunication. While at it, the Holy Father told Pandulf to send one of his clerks to Poitou, to investigate there a marriage reportedly contracted in a manner not entirely canonical. Unlike the difficulty with King John, Pandulf did not expect much trouble from those parties. Apparently, the young wife unwittingly living in sin had a spotless reputation for piety, modesty, and virtue.

About the Author

Hana Samek Norton grew up in the former Czechoslovakia exploring the ruins of castles and cloisters where she became captivated by history and historical fiction. After immigrating to Canada, and later moving to New Mexico, she earned history degrees from the University of Western Ontario and the University of New Mexico. She currently lives in the Land of Enchantment, is married to an Englishman, works as a consultant, and occasionally teaches. She is a member of the Historical Novel Society which gives her a chance to meet her favorite authors and fans of the genre, enjoys spending time with her husband, travel, gardening, and chasing down obscure references. *The Serpent's Crown* is her second novel.

Acknowledgements

With gratitude to Gabi Anderson, Martha Ellis, Cheryl Foote, Sophie Collaros, and Martha Hoffman. Special thanks to my amazing mother for her relentlessly cheerful support, and to my husband who never fails to nourish my body and soul.

All acts of omission and commission are my own. For additional information, visit www.hanasameknorton.com.

Hana Samek Norton
Albuquerque, NM
October 2015